GULLSTRUCK ISLAND

FRANCES HARDINGE

MACMILLAN

First published 2009 by Macmillan Children's Books

This edition published 2018 by Macmillan Children's Books
an imprint of Pan Macmillan
20 New Wharf Road, London N1 9RR
Associated companies throughout the world
www.panmacmillan.com

ISBN 978-1-5098-6814-8

1 3 5 7 9 8 6 4 2

A CIP catalogue record for this book is available from
the British Library.

Typeset by Nigel Hazle
Printed and bound by CPI Group (UK) Ltd, Croydon CR0 4YY

*To my sister Sophie, a truer traveller than
I shall ever be, who saved lives when others
were seeing sights, and who brought back
tropical diseases and broken bones instead
of photos and souvenir hats*

N

Port
Suddenwind

The Wailing Way

Pericold
Heights

Mother
Tooth

Spearhead

Mistleman's
Blunder

Obsidian Trail

Crackgem

The Hollow Beasts

Sorrow

Jealousy

Sweetweather

King of Fans

Smattermast

PRELUDE

It was a burnished, cloudless day with a tug-of-war wind, a fine day for flying. And so Raglan Skein left his body neatly laid out on his bed, its breath as slow as sea swell, and took to the sky.

He took only his sight and hearing with him. There was no point in bringing those senses that would make him feel the chill of the sapphire-bright upper air or the giddiness of his rapid rise.

Like all Lost, he had been born with his senses loosely tethered to his body, like a hook on a fishing line. He could let them out, then reel them in and remember all the places his mind had visited meanwhile. Most Lost could move their senses independently, like snails' eyes on stalks. Indeed, a gifted Lost might be feeling the grass under their knees, tasting the peach in your hand, overhearing a conversation in the next village and smelling cooking in the next town, all while watching barracudas dapple and brisk around a shipwreck ten miles out to sea.

Raglan Skein, however, was doing nothing so whimsical. He had to take his body on a difficult and possibly perilous journey the next day, and he was spying out the land. It was a relief to see the world plummet away from him so that everything became smaller. More manageable. Less dangerous.

Scattered around the isolated island of Gullstruck dozens of other minds would be adrift. Lost minds, occupied with the business of the island, keeping it functioning. Scrying for bandits in the jungles, tracing missing children on the rises, spotting sharks in the deeps, reading important trade notices and messages long distance. In fact, there might even be other Lost minds floating near him now, indiscernible to him as he was to them.

He veered towards the mountain ridge that ran along the western coast, seeing the individual peaks emerge from the fleece of clouds. One such peak stood a little proud of the rest, its coloration paler. It was Sorrow, the white volcano, sweet, pure and treacherous as snow. Skein gave her a wide berth and instead veered towards her husband, the King of Fans, the tallest middlemost mountain of the ridge, his cratered head forever lost in clouds. For now the King was docile and hazy with the heat, but he too was a volcano and of uncertain temper. The shimmering air above his slopes was flecked with the circling forms of eagles large enough to carry a child off in each claw. Villages on this coast expected to lose a couple of their number to the eagles each year.

But these eagles would have no interest in the little towns that sprawled below. As far as the great birds were concerned, the towns were just more animals, too vast and sluggish for them to bother with, scaled with slate and furred with palm thatch. The muddy roads were the veins, and bronze bells in white towers told out their slow, cold heartbeats.

For a moment Skein wished that he did not know that every town was really a thriving hive of bitter, biting two-legged animals, full of schemes and resentment and hidden treachery. Yet again the fear of betrayal gnawed at his mind.

We will talk to these people, the Lost Council had announced. *We are too powerful for them to ignore us. Everything can be settled peacefully.* Skein did not believe it. Three days more, and he would know if his shadowy suspicions had flesh to them.

There lay the road he would travel over the next few days. He scried it carefully. Even though he had left for the coast quietly and with haste, there was always a chance that news of his arrival had outstripped him, and that enemies lay in wait.

And it was no mean task, spying out ambushes and surprises on this coast of all coasts. Everything about it reeked of trickery and concealment. There were reefs beneath the water of the bay, betrayed only by the foam fringes on the far waves. The cliff-face itself was a labyrinth. Over centuries the creamy limestone had been hollowed and winnowed until it was a maze of tapering spires, peepholes and snub ridges like sleeping lions. So it was all along the west coast of the island, and it was this that had given the Coast of the Lace its name.

The tribe who lived here nowadays was also known as 'the Lace', and they too were full of ins and outs and twists and turns and sleeping lions pretending to be rocks. You never knew where you were with the smilers of the Lace. They were all but outcast, distrusted by everyone, scratching out a living in outskirt shanty towns or dusty little fishing villages.

 3

Villages like the one that now came into view, nestled between a cliff and a beach in a rocky, half-hidden cove.

Here it was, Skein's ultimate destination. The village of the Hollow Beasts.

It was a Lace village. Skein could see it at a glance, even though he was too high to make out the turbans on the grandmothers, the young men's shark-tooth anklets, the bright stones in everyone's teeth. He knew it from the furtive location, the small pearl-fishing canoes cluttering the waterline.

He descended until the freckling of two-legged specks on the beach became foreshortened human figures. His sight alighted on two young girls, one supporting the other.

The taller of the girls was dressed in a white tunic, and he guessed instantly who she must be. Arilou.

Arilou was the only Hollow Beast whose name he knew, and it was the only name he needed to know. She was easily the most important person in the village, and arguably the only excuse for its existence. He contemplated her for a few seconds, before soaring again and preparing to return to his body.

As it happened, the girl supporting Arilou had a name too. It was designed to sound like the settling of dust, a name that was meant to go unnoticed. She was as anonymous as dust, and Skein gave her not the slightest thought.

Neither would you. In fact, you have already met her, or somebody very like her, and you cannot remember her at all.

1
ARILOU

On the beach, a gull-storm erupted as rocks came bouncing down from the clifftop. Half a step behind the rocks scrambled Eiven, her face flushed from running.

No member of the village would take a shortcut straight down the cliff unless there was a matter of some urgency, not even bold, agile Eiven. Several people dropped their ropes or their nets, but not their smiles, never their smiles, for they were Lace.

'An Inspector!' Eiven called to them as she recovered her breath and balance. 'There is a Lost Inspector coming to see Arilou!'

Looks were exchanged, and the news ran off to this hut, that hut. Meanwhile Eiven sprinted across the beach along to the base of the cliff, her feet scooping ruts in the spongy sand. There she scrambled up a rope ladder and pushed through a curtain of woven reeds into the cave behind it.

According to Lace tradition and tale, the caves were sacred places, perilous mouths leading to the world of the dead, and the gods, and the white-hot, slow-pumping hearts of the mountains, mouths that might snap you up suddenly with stalactite teeth if you were judged unworthy. Eiven's family was considered worthy to live in the caves, but only because of Arilou.

Moments later within the cave Eiven was in agitated conversation with her mother. It was a council of war, but you would never have known it from their smiles.

'So what is he planning to do to her?' Mother Govrie's eyes had a fierce and urgent brightness, but her mouth continued to beam, the lopsided swell in her lower lip speaking of stubbornness and warmth. 'How does the Inspector inspect?'

'They say he wants to grade her for their records. See how well she can control her powers.' Eiven had a knife-slash smile. Years of pearl-diving had left white coral scars trekking up her forehead like bird-prints. 'We need to tell the whole village. Everybody will want to know about this.'

Arilou was everybody's business, the village's pride and joy, their Lady Lost.

The Lost were born nowhere but Gullstruck, and even on the island they were far from common. They were scarce among the non-Lace, and much revered. Among the Lace, however, they were all but unknown. During the great purges two hundred years before, most of the 'Lace Lost' had been killed, and their numbers had never recovered. Before the birth of Arilou, none had been born to the people of the Lace for over fifty years.

Young Lost were notorious for becoming entranced with distant places and forgetting their own discarded bodies, or even failing to notice that their bodies existed. As a consequence, nobody ever lamented when a child seemed slow to learn or unaware of its surroundings, for this was often the sign of a newborn Lost that had not yet

6

learned to reel its mind back to its body.

The birth of a baby girl who showed every sign of being an untrained Lost had transformed the village's prospects overnight. Suddenly they were not dependent upon their dwindling harvest of pearls or on peddling shell jewellery. The nearest town grudgingly gave them food in winter, for it was accepted that when the town's own Lady Lost retired, Arilou would have to take her place. Furthermore, the stream of visitors who came to see Arilou paid well for their food and lodging, and for relics to remember their visit to the only Lace Lost. Arilou was a celebrated oddity, like a two-headed calf or a snow-white jaguar. And if any haggard doubts haunted the villagers' pride in Arilou, an outsider would never have known it from the seamless pleasure the Lace seemed to show in discussing her.

But now Arilou needed to be found and made ready for company. Her best clothes had to be prepared. Her hair had to be combed free of burrs and her face would need to be dusted with stone dust and spices. There was no knowing how much time they had.

In the late afternoon two men stepped gingerly into the pulley-chair and let themselves be winched down the cliff by six young Lace men below.

The taller of the two visitors was unmistakably Lost. Whereas many Lost learned to base themselves in their own body, some discovered their physical form so late that they were never entirely comfortable in it. They found the perspective disorientating, disliking the translucent peripheral view of their own nose, and the fact that they could not

 7

see all of their body to guide it. Such Lost often chose a hovering perspective instead, a little behind or to one side of their body, so as to keep themselves in view, monitor and adjust their own body language, and so forth. However, there was always something static about their posture then, and this man was no exception.

He wore his grey hair pushed back into a pigtail, the loose strands across his head pinned in place by his green three-cornered hat. His eyes were hazel, which was not unusual for one of his background. Most islanders were mixed race, for it had been over two centuries since the Cavalcaste settlers arrived on Gullstruck, easily long enough for them to intermingle with the local tribes. However, in the towns there was often more Cavalcaste blood poured into the mix, particularly among the better-heeled, and that was clearly true of this man. What *was* unusual about his eyes was that they were slightly swivelled to the left, and that he did not take the trouble to blink, or adjust the direction of his gaze. This, in short, was obviously the 'Lost Inspector'.

His shorter and younger companion seemed to be 'lost' in an utterly different sense. Compared to the Lost Inspector, he was a-twitch with involuntary movements, clutching at his hat one moment, the handrail the next, shifting his feet or his weight with every swing of the chair. Papers fluttered in the leather wallet he held under one arm. He had a rounded, pouting chin, a touch of Cavalcaste pallor and bright, brown eyes. For the moment these eye were fixed upon the ground reeling treacherously far below him and the mosaic of upturned faces.

He was smartly dressed and obviously a towner. Like many

Gullstruck officials he was both well-heeled and bell-heeled, another result of the Cavalcaste invasion. Centuries before, back on their own homeland plains, respected members of the horse-riding Cavalcaste clans had shown their status through the size of their spurs. But nowadays the powerful were not horseback battle-leaders but law makers and bureaucrats. Instead of spurs, even lowly officials had taken to wearing little bells on the backs of their boots, 'honorary spurs', which jingled in just the same way but did not catch on carpets and ladies' hems.

His name was Minchard Prox, and not for the first time he was wondering if it was possible to find a secretarial post that was less prestigious than being aide to a Lost Inspector but less likely to involve trekking mountain paths in goat-drawn carts, being lowered down cliffs in glorified baskets or coming into contact with the Lace, who set his neck-hairs tingling as if at the touch of a knife.

Down there, three dozen faces, all smiling. *Just because they're smiling, it doesn't mean they like you*, he reminded himself. Smiles a-glitter, for most Lace had their teeth studded with tiny plaques of shell, metal or bright stone. Would those smiles melt away to leave implacable looks as soon as there were no strangers in the village? Perhaps it was even worse to think of the smiles clinging to every face even after they had no purpose, a whole village sitting and walking and sleeping and smiling and smiling and smiling . . .

In the old days before the settlers, the Lace's smiles marked them out as a people to respect. The Lace had acted as peace makers and go-betweens for the other tribes, and had even carried messages to the volcanoes. So it was small wonder that when the Cavalcaste landed the Lace had been the only tribe to approach them with smiles rather than spears.

The helpful Lace had given the settlers lots of advice on how to survive on Gullstruck. Most important of all, they warned them not to build their towns in the Wailing Way, the river valley between the King of Fans and his fellow volcano Spearhead, for the two volcanoes were rivals for the affection of Sorrow, and might some day rush together to continue their fight.

But the land around the river was rich and tempting, so the Cavalcaste had ignored their advice and built a great town in the Wailing Way. Shortly afterwards its citizens started to go missing, one at a time. Only when thirty or so had disappeared without trace did the settlers discover the truth. They were being kidnapped and murdered by the politely smiling Lace themselves.

The Lace had acted as they thought best. After all, the whole township was at risk of being trampled by angry mountains. To the Lace's minds the only way to keep the volcanoes sleepy and happy, and so prevent this disaster destroying the town altogether, was to quietly waylay solitary settlers, spirit them to the Lace mountain shrines and jungle temples . . . and sacrifice them. But when the truth came out the Lace's towns were burned by the enraged settlers, their temples destroyed and all of their seers and priests killed. Even the other tribes disowned them. They were pushed out to the westernmost edge of the island – the Lace coast – and left there to forage for survival as best they could.

As the pulley-chair touched the ground at last, the front of the crowd gave a small, impatient shuffle forward.

'You want stick! You want stick!' There were about a dozen small children holding sharpened stakes twice their own height. 'For walking!'

'Hello, sir!' called one of the girls further back. 'You have lady wife? You have daughter? She likes jewellery! Buy jewellery for her!'

Now the tide was upon them, and Prox felt his face growing red as he sidled through a forest of hands proffering earrings made of shell, bead-studded boxes and pictures painted on palm leaves 'to burn for ancestors'. He was a dapper little man, but the tide of short, slightly built Lace made him feel fat and foolish. Furthermore, behind the jewelled smiles, the singsong calls and the hands slipped into his in greeting, he felt the crackle of desperation like dry weather sparks, and it made him desperate too.

The crowd quickly realized that the strangers were not to be slowed, and simultaneously decided to lead them to the heart of their village instead, to Arilou, their own prized Lost.

'This way! This way!' The human wave that had rushed them and nearly bowled them over backwards was now bearing them along with it.

The visitors were 'guided' by many companionable shoves in the back towards a cave where stalactites hung in pleats like draggled, dripping linen. Prox followed the Inspector up a rickety rope ladder to the cave entrance. A reed curtain twitched aside and strong arms reached down to pull them into a darkness full of voices and – Prox could feel them – smiles.

Outside a girl lowered an arm decorated from wrist to shoulder in shell bracelets and laughed away her disappointment.

'Did you see them, the old thunder faces?!' The laugh shapes hung around the women's mouths as they stared up at the reed curtain with hard, puzzled eyes. Outsiders never seemed to smile.

For a little while the family in the cave moved around so much that Prox could not keep track of them. The mother of the household brought straw mats, strips of dried fish and endless coconut shells full of rum.

'Madam Govrie,' the Inspector said at last in a low, patient tone, 'I very much fear we cannot take further advantage of your hospitality if we are to return to Sweetweather town by nightfall.' As their hostess began to protest that they could stay there overnight, or in one of the houses in the village, Prox felt a restive distrust. Accommodation would turn out to have a fee attached, no doubt. Perhaps they had already arranged to delay their guests and take a cut from whoever ended up providing lodging for the night.

'Please, I must insist.' The Inspector's voice had no real intonation, and there was a rustle in his 's' as if he spoke with a sore tongue, further signs of one not at home in his own body.

'Very well, I'll call her in. Hathin!' Prox was a little bewildered; he had thought the girl's name was Arilou.

A second later he realized that another member of the family must have been called to bring in the child, perhaps her nurse or older sister. And yes, now he could see two children, walking hand in hand from the darkness of a neighbouring cavern. Prox stared stupidly for a moment at the taller of the two girls, noting her face dusted ceremonial white with powdered chalk, her brows tinted gold with pollen and her hair waxed close to her head and studded with brilliant blue hummingbird feathers. This, he realized, was Arilou.

But she must be thirteen at least, thought Prox, looking at Arilou. *They told us to expect an untrained Lost, one not yet in control of her powers* . . .

She would have been a very pretty girl if there were not a certain *softness* in the motions of her face. Her tongue pushed her lower lip forward and glistened between her lips, and her cheeks puckered and bulged without purpose as though she was rolling invisible cherries about in her mouth.

As her smaller sister carefully guided her to sit on a straw mat, her mother ran a fingertip down Arilou's temple alongside one grey, unfocused eye. 'Pirate eyes,' Mother Govrie said proudly. Prox never understood why the Lace seemed to regard a trace of pirate in their ancestry as a reason to boast.

The village's pride in this girl could be seen just by looking at her mouth. Nearly every tooth had been studded with a perfect little round of lazuli into which a spiral had been etched. In contrast the girl next to her had only a few of her front teeth studded in a cloudy quartz that was almost invisible against the enamel.

'Please,' said the Inspector, speaking over Govrie's enthusiasm. 'If you will let us talk to the girl in private.'

At last the Inspector and Prox were left alone with Arilou. Alone, that is, except for the younger child, who seemed to be Arilou's designated attendant. When asked to leave she stared at them unmoving, her smile baffled but intact, and eventually they relented and let her stay.

'Miss Arilou.' The Inspector settled himself to kneel in front of Arilou. A warm and wandering breeze crept into

13

the cave so that the feathers in her hair trembled. She gave no other motion, nor acknowledgement of his presence. 'My name is Raglan Skein. My body is sitting before yours at the moment. Where are you?'

Unbidden, the younger girl took Arilou's long, golden hand in her smaller darker one and whispered into her ear. There was a small pause, and then Arilou's lids drooped a little, darkening her grey eyes like a sudden cloud shadowing the land. She hesitated, as though in contemplation, and then her jaw fell open and she began to speak.

But these were not words! Prox listened dumbstruck to the sounds falling from Arilou's drooping mouth. It was as if some words had been washed out to sea and rounded smooth and meaningless by the waves. And then he was just as startled to hear the stream of noise give way to ordinary speech, clearly spoken in a young girl's voice.

'I am running an errand for the village, Master Skein. At the moment I am storm-spotting many miles further up the coast. It would take me hours to get back.'

It was a moment or two before Prox realized that it was not Arilou who had spoken. It was her little attendant, and now he realized why she had not left the room. However nimble her mind, it seemed that Arilou did not yet have full mastery of her tongue, a not uncommon complaint among the Lost. Her attendant was probably a younger sister, able to understand and translate Arilou's ill-formed sounds through long practice. The words had been spoken with a clear, cold authority, and Prox wondered for a moment if Arilou's true voice was forcing its way out through her meek little interpreter, her personality overwhelming the other like a silver river's torrent rushing down a meagre stream bed.

'Then we will not call you back immediately.' Skein had responded to the confidence in Arilou's voice, and now his tone was that of one addressing an adult rather than a child. 'Do you see a storm? Where are you?'

'I am watching from the Pericold Heights, and I can see storm clouds tangled in Mother Tooth's hair,' came the response. 'I must watch longer to be sure, but I believe that it will reach us tomorrow night.'

Pericold Heights was a promontory some fifty miles up the coast from which one could look out to sea and see a great column of steam, and at its base the outline of Mother Tooth's island like a trodden pie. Mother Tooth was the most belligerent of the volcanoes, and nobody but the birds lived in her reeking, juddering jungles. Storm clouds seemed to form around and above her, as if drawn by her ill temper.

So much for testing the girl quickly and getting out of here, thought Prox despondently. The cliff walks that had brought them to this part of the coast were treacherous enough in the dry. In wet weather the red rock melted like chocolate, and slewed and slithered off the precipices. It was starting to sound like they might find themselves stranded in this backwater.

'You understand that I have come here to test your use of your powers and all that you have learned from the Lost School?' Skein asked. 'I must have you ready tomorrow.'

'I understand. I shall be ready.' A big velvety-black butterfly flickered through the dim cave, and with a perverse impudence settled upon Arilou's powdered cheek. She did not flinch, and it spread its wings below her eye, displaying bars the same lazuli blue as the feathers in her hair. Prox found

15

himself in the grip of an awe he could not express. What could it symbolize, a marble-faced girl with a butterfly cheek? He had seen other Lost of course, but there was something mythic about this child, sitting serene as an oracle in her ocean cave.

It was as though some divine hand had picked the very best out of the village's mess of bloodlines for this one child – just enough strange blood for a Lost, just enough pirate blood for those grey eyes, rich tawny skin, high elegant cheekbones, just enough Lace blood to give her an eerie sense of otherness . . . you might keep her and throw away the rest of the village.

'Then we shall return a little after dawn. May good fortune attend you, and spare you from mist. We shall leave you alone.' Skein stood, and Prox did likewise. While the dust was being brushed from his knees with a long-handled switch, Prox allowed himself one more look at the Lady Lost, still staring out before her as if she held the very sea and sky, rumbling and roiling, within the compass of her gaze.

2
TWISTED TONGUES

'We shall leave you alone.' A courteous promise from Inspector Skein. It was also a lie, albeit not a deliberate one. Arilou was not alone.

The prints of small bare feet formed in the dust of the floor and made their way to the cave entrance. The feet that made them were not invisible, but they might as well have been. So might the face that now peered nervously around the curtain down towards the beach.

No grey eyes, no rich, strange colouring. This was a snub little Lace face of the most commonplace sort, with wide cheekbones, far apart brown eyes and not much to speak of by way of a nose. There was a nervous little ruck near one corner of the smile. In the middle of the forehead was a patch of 'troubled water', a little place the size of a thumbprint where anxiety showed itself in a tension and creasing of the skin.

Her name was Hathin. While Arilou's name was meant to sound like the call of an owl, the fluting of a bird of prophecy, Hathin's name imitated the whisper of settling dust. Dust-like she was indeed, unremarkable, quiet, all but invisible. And right now the fate of everyone she knew rested on her all but invisible shoulders.

The butterfly wandered further up Arilou's cheek, dowsing with its antennae, and wafted its wings against her eyelashes. Arilou's cheek twitched once, twice, and then the Lady Lost made a long moaning sound in her throat, like a newborn calf. Startled from her harassed contemplation, Hathin turned to her sister with a look of quiet desperation, then scampered back to her side to tease the butterfly into taking off.

Was this the great Lady Arilou, her cheek twitching slackly, her tongue-tip licking away the powder at the corner of her mouth to leave a scoop of pink flesh?

'Oh . . . no, don't do that. Here – hold still.' Hathin wiped the powder from Arilou's tongue. 'This is what you want, isn't it?' Hathin fetched a pot of honey and dabbed some on Arilou's lips to quiet her. Arilou's face cleared again, as it often did when she got her way. Hathin drew back with her knees to her chin and watched with wide, bright eyes as Arilou unthinkingly ran her tongue over her lips. *Clear water*, said Arilou's beautiful grey eyes. *Troubled water*, said the thumbprint frown on Hathin's forehead.

Honey-smothered sounds emerged from Arilou's mouth. Hums and mumbles. Where was the prophetess's voice that had almost stirred the visitors to tears?

That cold, clear voice of authority was now choking in Hathin's throat as, for the thousandth time, she listened to Arilou's sounds and tried to force them into words, sentences, some semblance of meaning.

She failed. And the cold, unspeakable truth of it was that she had always failed. Despite all Hathin's efforts, Arilou's language remained a private one. The visitors who had mar-velled at Lady Arilou's wisdom and breeding over the years had never guessed for a moment that her trembling little 'translator' was pulling her high-sounding sentences out of the air.

It was the village's greatest fear and most terrible secret. They never alluded to it by word, gesture or expression. After all, in a land where the Lost wander like winds it is impossible to be sure whether somebody is watching or listening. And yet all the villagers knew that in the thirteen years since her birth Arilou, beautiful Arilou with her sea-coloured seeress's eyes, had shown no more sign of controlling Lost powers than she had of taking to the winds like a gull. The tantalizing glimmer of ability that she had seemed to show as an infant had vanished without trace, like a rock that had borrowed a moment's lustre from a wave and then given itself over to eternal dullness.

Hathin had been born because somebody was needed to guard and guide Arilou day and night. And now, though it was never stated outright, it was clear to Hathin that she had another duty. In a thousand imperceptible ways the villagers seemed to say to her, *And if . . . if Arilou really is nothing but an imbecile, it is your job to make sure that we never need to discuss it . . . and that nobody outside the village ever finds out . . .*

And so from her earliest years Hathin had learned to speak the visitors' language fluently, to eavesdrop on their conversations, to read the hidden signals in their faces. Most visitors came to see Arilou only out of idle curiosity and were easily satisfied by Hathin's performances. Now, for the first time, Hathin could see the enormity and danger of the game that the whole village had been playing for more than a decade. An Inspector had come, and the village's gentle streamlet of deceit was gushing uncontrollably into wider, wilder waters.

The village needed Arilou. Without the money and visitors she brought in, they might well have starved years before. Now it was Hathin, not Arilou, who faced the job of saving the situation.

First things first, however. Hathin had a smaller lie to protect.

She dropped from the cave and approached a couple of women who stood grinding corn in hollows in the rocks.

'Hello, Hathin,' one of them greeted her. 'Where's your lady sister?'

'She's inside, resting. She's out at Pericold Heights, watching for storms.' A question about the whereabouts of a Lost nearly always involved two answers. It was not this, however, that caused both women to stop grinding and peer keenly at Hathin. 'She says there's a storm coming tomorrow evening from Mother Tooth's way,' Hathin said carefully. 'She mentioned it when she was talking to the Inspector.'

The two women exchanged glances and put down their grinding stones.

'Well, something to tell the rest of the village, I think,' said the second woman. 'Be sure to thank your lady sister, Hathin.' And the two of them set off quickly to pass on word, often in a whisper that might have seemed strangely intense for a storm warning. But, as it happened, this was not exactly the message they were spreading.

With the Lace, it was not just a matter of understanding the little that was spoken plainly, it was also a matter of reading the hidden meanings. The Lace had always chosen their words carefully, for it was well known that the volcanoes understood their language and could be woken by a careless phrase. And since their fall from grace the Lace had grown ever more wary of being overheard by a hostile world, and so they had grown used to speaking as if somebody was listening in.

For example, a stranger eavesdropping upon Hathin's little conversation would not have guessed one important thing – that everybody in the village had known about the storm for several hours. There was a streak of tobacco yellow in the sky behind the King of Fans; there was a cold smell on the clifftops; there was the way the herring shoal had changed direction that morning. But after the word had been spread the village would be full of people who would swear blind to the Inspector that they knew of the storm only because the Lady Arilou had warned them.

As Hathin stood alone on the beach, rubbing one sandy foot against the back of her calf and watching her whisper spread through the village, she was summoned by her mother's voice.

'Hathin!' Mother Govrie sat cross-legged with her back to the cliffbase, twisting reed stems into a basket frame. 'You're going to town, aren't you? There's a message for you to carry. They say the Lost Inspector has been travelling with a couple of porters, and right now they're making his lodgings ready in Sweetweather. Porters from Pearlpit.' Pearlpit was another Lace village further up the coast. Mother Govrie gave Hathin only the briefest of keen glances, but she spoke slowly and with meaning. 'Father Rackan has cousins in Pearlpit – you should go and ask the porters if they have any news of them.'

Hathin understood her mother's meaning immediately. The Lost Inspector had Lace porters who might be sympathetic enough to answer questions about the forthcoming test.

Despite herself, Hathin hesitated briefly before departing. For a moment she wanted to throw herself down next to her mother and ask, *What do I do? How can I fool a Lost Inspector? Oh, what do I do?* But she said nothing. There were invisible walls around those things that could not be discussed. Sometimes Hathin could almost see these walls, shaped from clay and tears, bearing the handprints of generations of Lace. She was too young, too tired and too worried even to think of climbing them. Her mother, wrestling the reeds with her strong, calloused hands, was unreachable.

Hurriedly, she gave Arilou a drink of water and left her under Mother Govrie's watchful eye. Then Hathin slipped on a pair of wicker and leather sandals and set off up the route to the cliff path.

By the time she reached the top, the eyes of invisible little Hathin had become bright with more than exercise. On the rare occasions she found herself without Arilou, she felt a guilty, giddy sense of lightness.

Inland from the cliff the land rippled through a series of hills, cave-infested ridges and hidden shafts. Beyond soared the King of Fans.

Usually when the Hollow Beasts travelled south to Sweet-weather they walked the long, zigzag path that followed the cliff edge. However, if rain made this path treacherous, or the villagers were in a particular hurry, they sometimes took a short cut across the headlands. Not the higher foothills nearest to the King of Fans, of course – they had too much respect for the volcano, and for the sharp eyes and talons of the eagles that surrounded him. But they dared sneak across the lush lower slopes, despite the fact that these had all long since become Ashlands, the domain of the dead.

Hathin's father had been carried off by a fever when she was five, and she remembered standing on this very clifftop, watching her mother cast his ashes to the wind so as to free his spirit. *His spirit to pass on to the caves of the dead, and everything else to return to the coral and rock from which the great Gripping Bird shaped him.* But the Lace was the only tribe that still did this.

Almost everybody else on the island now followed the Cavalcaste traditions.

The Cavalcaste had lived in a distant land of grey and yellow plains, where the horizon was a neatly starched fold between land and sky, where nobody ran around without shoes and shirt and where there were no volcanoes to worship. Instead everyone prayed to their ancestors, and kept them happy by dedicating a little plot of land to each of them. Generation by generation the domain of the dead had advanced across the plains of the Cavalcaste's homeland, pushing back the farmlands of the living.

So at last the Cavalcaste had sent out ships, loaded to the waterline with little urns containing the ashes of important ancestors, to claim new lands for their ever growing population of dead. And the tribes of Gullstruck one day had seen a fleet of cream-sailed ships swelling on the horizon like a string of pearls, as the Cavalcaste arrived to take over the island, their heads full of unbuilt cities and their ships full of their dead . . .

Try not to imagine those poor dead, Hathin told herself as

 23

she abandoned the cliff path and set off across the headland, thrashing her way through the watery swaying of the grass. Everywhere man-high staves had been driven into the ground, at the top of which were fixed tiny wooden 'spirit houses', little homes for the cremation urns of the dead. There were even some mossy stones marking where urns had been buried by the first settlers, two centuries before. *Try not to think of all those spirits trapped in little pots, going mad with boredom.*

After an hour's tramp the path became better trodden and the first buildings appeared, most of them slatted wooden houses with stubby stilts and palm roofs. The eager black heads of goats peered at her through fence palings.

In Sweetweather she was invisible, but in a different way than in her own village. The families who seemed content to sit in their raised doorways and stare out into the street all day roasted her in the black sun of their gaze. But they did not see *her*, Hathin, they did not see her face . . . they saw only the traditional Lace salt-and-pepper embroidery of her stiffly woven skirt, the shaven crescent above her forehead to make her face look longer, the little rounded plaques set in her teeth. They saw that she was Lace.

Here as in most places on the island nearly everybody was mestizo, blood-soup, a mix of the old tribes – the Bitter Fruit who had once lived in the northern jungles, the Amber from the south coast, and many more – and the Cavalcaste. Cavalcaste or tribal ancestry showed through here and there in clothes, in tattoos, sometimes in the shape of the features, but over time the differences had diluted and softened. The Lace were an exception, remaining desperately, stubbornly, painfully distinct. In spite of all the distrust and persecution, the Lace hugged their traditional strangeness, their aloneness, for it was all they had left.

The voices of the town settled around her like an odd-smelling smoke. They spoke in Nundestruth, a rolling, pragmatic hybrid tongue very different from the softly musical Lace language.

The town did not so much have a central square as an open space which acted as a playground for everyone's pigs and children. Across this space the town's two finest buildings glared at one another.

The first was the governor's house, three storeys high because it had been built in the days before the Cavalcaste had seen most of their towers toppled by earthquakes and had learned to build squatter dwellings.

The second was a strange, hunched building whose low balconies had pregnant-bellied railings in black iron. This house belonged to Milady Page, the Lady Lost of Sweetweather. Strings of bells hung above the door, a wild, rambling spiceplant had been allowed to run riot over the roof and a set of candlesticks was spiked on to the railings in front of the yard. Milady Page often sent her senses roaming independently of one another, and then brought them back to her body using the bell-chimes, the spice scent and the candlelight to find their way.

The stone steps before the governor's front door were clean of all footprints, while the path to Milady Page's house had been worn into a channel by the stream of people bringing her mangoes, sweetbreads and questions. Everyone respected the governor of course, but his white-painted world had nothing to do with the day-to-day reality of the town, and people had

 25

grown accustomed to turning to Milady Page, who had eyes everywhere.

The poor governor could do nothing without waiting a month for written permission from the capital, faraway Port Suddenwind. Port Suddenwind was a joke. Everybody knew that the government there was a vast, creaking clockwork of laws, laws, laws, most of which even now had everything to do with the snowbound, horse-ridden wastes of the original Cavalcaste plains and nothing to do with sprawling, feverish little Gullstruck. For the Cavalcaste settlers had brought with them a hearty dread of changing or discarding laws, for fear of annoying the ancestors who had invented them. All people could do was carefully pile more laws on top. Port Suddenwind's edicts could cope with thieves who stole sledges or furs, but not those who ran off with jade or coconut rum. They could cope with murderers who tricked victims on to thin ice, but not those who boiled jellyfish pulp to make poisons. There were no rules in place to deal with epidemics of weeping fever, no structures for warning other communities to stay away from the outbreak areas.

In contrast, Milady Page did whatever she wanted when she wanted, and nobody tried to stop her, not even the governor. It was an open secret that he disliked and resented her, but he needed her as much as anyone else did. If Milady Page deferred to anyone, it was to the Lost Council, an organized body comprised of powerful Lost who governed the rest and represented them as a whole to Port Suddenwind.

And here came the Lady Lost herself, Hathin realized, moving through the crowds with a swaying lurch like a small, stocky galleon on a rolling sea. Milady Page had a broad, seamed face like a cracked leather shield. She walked around with her eyes shut, since she could see quite well without them. To stop her eyelashes crusting, however, from time to time she would open her eyes briefly in a 'reverse blink', momentarily dazzling the world with a glassy, hawk-gold stare.

As usual, there was a gaggle of people trotting alongside her, talking to her all at once. In fact there were rather more than usual, because on the evening of the next day the tidings huts would be renewed.

Each district had a 'tidings hut' upon a hill or high promontory. Once a week a new set of writings or pictograms were hung in the hut. These held the news of all the surrounding towns and villages: births, deaths, personal messages, requests for help, advertisements of wares, information about the stirring of the volcanoes, word on the tempests of the sea and so forth. And on that night Lost across the island would send their minds out to visit each tidings hut in turn, before returning with news from all over Gullstruck. On such a sprawling island this system was indispensable, and thus so were the Lost on which it depended.

For now, Milady Page was sailing through a sea of questions and hastily recited messages. She spoke over them all with a rough loudness like a deaf woman.

'Dayla, I know what you want ask – you right, he do that – steal goatbaby. Hey, Pike! Papayas belong-you ready, go make jam this-week-next-week. Master Strontick – go look find hook-scythe by zigzag brook. Ryder, you want merchant-news, ask me two-day-later. Aaaw, you no like wait? Poor Ryder. Ask governor instead.' Milady Page gave a short derisive cackle.

Despite her high status, Milady Page usually spoke

Nundestruth. It was nobody's language, everybody's language, a stew of words taken from the tribes and the Cavalcaste alike. By the time the first settlers' grandchildren were full-grown, they found that however carefully they taught their own children their ancestral tongue, the children caught the hybrid jabber in the streets and brought it home like mud on their boots. 'That gibberish may be good for the fields and the beach but Not Under This Roof!' the parents cried, only succeeding in giving the new language its name. Proper-speak, the old colonial language, earned the nickname 'Doorsy', indoors-speak.

So Doorsy had the parlours, the schools, the university, the doctors' surgeries, the governors' palaces, the offices. And Nundestruth bellowed on the beaches, strutted in the streets and catcalled from the cliffs. It seemed quite happy with the bargain.

'You!'

Hathin flinched to a fraction of her usual size as Milady Page's ringed finger suddenly stabbed out to point at her. The babble of voices stilled, and Hathin found herself pinned to the spot by a dozen hard, wary gazes.

'You think I no know what you about,' said Milady Page. Her lids jerked open for a second, showing her golden irises. 'I know. I know what you Lace about.'

Hathin felt her smile freeze on to her face as her stomach quietly turned itself inside out. For years the Lace had been locked in a guessing game, trying to work out how much Milady Page knew about their secrets, and many suspected that she was playing cat-and-mouse with them.

'Play stake-go-jump, yes?' Page's broad mouth grew

broader, as if an amusing dream was passing behind her closed lids.

With a rush of relief Hathin realized what Page meant. A few sallow summers and hungry winters had driven the townspeople to dare the volcano and cut terraced farms into the sloped lower flanks of the King of Fans. The land was rockier and steeper than the foothills where the Ashlands spread, but there was no other land nearby suitable for farming. The people of Sweetweather, however, were convinced that the Lace were secretly moving around the stakes that they used to mark the edges of these new farms. Of course, they were also convinced that the Lace stole dreams, caused pigs to give birth to rats and could curse you with malaria. But in the case of the claim stakes the townspeople were, in fact, completely right.

The Lace, who understood the volcanoes better than anyone, did everything they could to avoid attracting their attention. They even gave their children names that were imitations of natural sounds, so that when the names were called out the mountains would think that they were hearing bird calls, wind-sighs, water-songs. And they were firmly of the opinion that cutting farms into the King of Fans' kneecaps was just the sort of thing to wake him up in a bad mood. So the Hollow Beasts had been quietly playing a game of claim-stake chess, moving the markers around until nobody knew where anyone's plot started or ended.

This was nothing compared to the Arilou secret, however. Hathin just about had the presence of mind to shake her head instead of nodding.

Milady Page gave a small grunt. 'I be watching you all,'

she said, then gave a half-weary flap of her hand to dismiss Hathin, who obediently fled up the street at a scamper, her heart thudding. What terrified her most about Page's parting words was not the hint of threat but the fact that they had been spoken in Lace – thick, clumsy Lace, but Lace. Occasionally Page would do this, dropping in stray phrases of their language, but not enough for anyone to guess how much of it she truly understood.

Hathin shuddered, as if she could shake off Page's unseen gaze like a shawl. Feeling exposed, she headed for the only inn worthy of guests like Inspector Skein and Minchard Prox.

A six-foot-tall tawny elephant bird with scabbed talons had been tethered to the gate. Ribbons of pale flesh showing through the feathers revealed where leather strips had worn away the plumage. A pack bird then. As she edged past it cautiously, staying out of jabbing range of its long, blunt-tipped beak, the bird bent its elongated neck like a bow and from between wheat-coloured lashes watched her sideways with a fierce stupidity.

'Friendly,' Hathin called out to two men chatting in the doorway. It was a common Nundestruth greeting.

'Sell in street,' one of them said, giving her hardly a glance. 'No sell in here.' He used his fingers to flick at the air, as though hoping the gesture would propel Hathin backwards.

'No sell,' promised Hathin. She extended her unadorned arms. 'See, none shell-sellable.'

'Then why come here no sell? And why come lone?' Lace from the villages seldom dared the paths to Sweetweather without something to sell, and rarely ventured into the town itself without the security of numbers.

'You, miss, come feed mountain, yes?' said one of them. They were smiling for now at least. 'I see you look thisere friend belong-me – you come take him? Yes, she soon time throw you over shoulder, carry you over hill. Better hide, before she catch you.' There was a shout of laughter at the idea of the little Lace girl kidnapping the burly towner and taking him away to sacrifice. It was a joke, but centuries of distrust and fear lay behind it.

Soon somebody would say something that was sharper and harder, but it would still be a joke. And then there would be a remark like a punch in the gut, but made as a joke. And then they would detain her if she tried to leave, and nobody would stop them because it was all only a joke . . .

She stared at one face then the other, her smile tensing and widening defensively. She could never get used to the way that towners' smiles came and went. It made her feel unsafe, as if they might run amok with rage at any moment. Their unornamented teeth looked bare and hungry.

Fortunately, at that moment Hathin saw two more strangers approaching, in shabby Lace garments ruddy with the summer dust. Their shanks were skinny, their feet shoeless, and Hathin wondered how badly Pearlpit and the other Lace villages were faring this season, with no Lady Lost to bring in extra money and food. But they seemed to take in the situation at a glance and hailed Hathin like a little sister. They fell in either side of her reflexively – beleaguered animals always put their young in the middle.

Hathin started by asking after Father Rackan's relatives. She used Nundestruth, knowing that the Lace were never so distrusted as when they were heard speaking in their own

 31

tongue. A little way down the street, however, all three slipped back into the Lace language, like three otters sliding from a riverbank into silver waters.

'So, little miss, it's *your* village where the Lady Lost is a Lace?' was the first question.

'Yes . . . she is my sister. She has not been tested before, and my mother is fearful that the Inspector might send her mind into a volcano, or out over the sea where she might lose her way. Perhaps you might tell me more of the tests? So that my mother can sleep easy?'

The tallest porter gave her a quick glance to see whether she really wanted more information, that she understood they were walking a dangerous line. Hathin faltered a moment – what if Milady Page was listening in from afar? But she briefly half closed her eyes as a sign that, yes, she needed to know.

'There are always five tests, one for each sense. Testing the skills they use in the Beacon School.'

It was almost impossible for parents to teach Lost children, particularly those who had not even found their way back to their own bodies yet. But youthful and untrained Lost instinctively followed bright lights so the Lost Council had arranged for a great beacon to be lit every night on one of the mountains to draw in their wandering minds. And so for a couple of hours after dusk every Lost child on the island would 'attend' the distant school, receiving lessons from teachers who could not see them and did not know their names.

Once upon a time Hathin had struggled to convince herself that she *did* see some difference in Arilou when the beacon was lit, that perhaps Arilou's mind *was* at the school with all the other unseen Lost children. But it had been many years since Hathin had really believed it.

The porter started counting off on his fingers, still talking in an easy, older-brother sort of way.

'Doctor Skein's first test is always smell. He has somebody bury three little jars somewhere nearby, under different coloured stones. The Lost has to send their nose underground and tell the Inspector the whiff of each bottle.

'Then there's finger-feeling. The Inspector has three boxes, all sealed up and dark, and the Lost has to find, without opening them, what's inside each one by "touch" alone.

'Taste. Three corked bottles, two full of yellow wine and one full of honey and water. Your Lady Lost will need to pick out the sweet one.

'Then comes sight. He gives directions for the Lost to mind-drift along for a mile or so. Then they come across something Mr Prox has left there earlier, and they have to describe it.

'Last, there's hearing.' The porter gave her another look, and Hathin blushed. Lace or no, he was from another village, and by now he must be wondering if a test cheat was on the cards. She could only hope that his loyalty to his fellow Lace was stronger than his loyalty to his employer. 'He sends somebody – usually Mr Prox – off where he can't be over-heard, and Mr Prox whispers the same word again and again, and the Lost has to mind-drift to him and hear what he is saying.'

'Not so very terrible then,' Hathin whispered faintly. 'No. Nothing for your mother to worry about.'

'And how many does my sister need to pass?'

'For full grading? All of them. To qualify for a retest – at least three.'

They were back in front of the inn. Hathin bowed her head to her chest, smiling hard to hide the fact that her eyes were filling with tears of panic.

'Wait a minute.' The smaller and slighter of the porters slipped into the inn, and returned a little later with a bundle of cloth. 'It's just odds and throwaways, but maybe you'll find something of use to you in it.'

Hathin scampered back towards her village with the bundle under her arm, her steps winged by worry about Arilou. However free she felt after leaving her sister's presence, after a short while her conscience became unbearable, as if a string that connected them was tug-tug-tugging at her. Everyone else was so busy – would anyone notice if Arilou needed anything?

Hathin scrambled down the cliff slope and was making her way back to her cave-home when she suddenly noticed a familiar figure seated in the middle of the beach, streamers of her hair fondling her face. Arilou stared blindly out to sea, paying no heed to Hathin's approach, or to Eiven, who was dragging her canoe up the beach.

'What's she doing out here?' For once Hathin's voice was almost shrill with outrage.

'Mother's busy, and I've got boats to mend so I brought her out where we could keep an eye on her. She's fine.'

'She's been sitting here in the high sun?' Hathin did not dare say more. She manoeuvred one of Arilou's arms over her shoulder, lifted her gently and supported her into the cave to survey the damage. Sure enough, Arilou had suffered for the touch of fairness in her skin, and there were ruddy bands of sunburn blooming across her forehead and cheeks.

'I'm so sorry I wasn't here, Arilou,' Hathin whispered as she rubbed crushed flowers against the glowing patches. 'Eiven didn't mean any harm, she just . . . doesn't know how to do it.' Even as she spoke, however, Hathin suddenly realized that she was feeling angry not for Arilou, but for herself. Sunburn would mean sleeplessness for both of them. And ultimately it would be Hathin and not Eiven that everybody would blame.

Hathin dusted the sand out of Arilou's clothes, settled her down again, brought more water and then hesitated with the bowl in her hands, still feeling a mixture of annoyance and remorse.

'Arilou –' she leaned forward on an impulse born of desperation – 'there's a bundle in front of me – can you see what's inside it? Tell me, and you can have a drink of water.'

How could you judge or calculate Arilou? How could you say that you knew her? Now and then Hathin seemed to get a sense of her, like knocking heads with someone in the dark. Perhaps it was Hathin's frustration, but it seemed to her sometimes that Arilou was not oblivious to her but stubborn, not helpless but sly.

One thing was certain: if Arilou *was* Lost, she never sent away her sense of touch or taste. Every other moment you could count on Arilou to be thirsty, or hungry, or too hot, or too cold. She was a knot of blind and naked need, like a baby bird.

'What's in the bundle?' Hathin withheld the bowl for a few seconds more.

Arilou had turned her head. Perhaps she had heard the

water slopping in the bowl. Her lower lip looked a little burnt, and trembled slightly. Hathin's resolve crumbled, and she lifted the bowl to let Arilou drink, before opening the bundle herself.

As she undid it, a strange mixture of aromas filled the cavern. A cinnamon stick lay beside a fish-head and some white orchid blooms that seemed to have been crushed.

Doctor Skein's first test is always smell.

Thanks to the kind-hearted porter Hathin could now guess what would be the scents in the three jars. She just needed some miracle to help her work out which would be in which.

A beautiful twilit world was reflected in Arilou's eyes. A single drop of water sat like a pearl in the corner of her mouth. No miracles were forthcoming.

Who else could she ask for a miracle? Only one name came to Hathin's mind. It was the name of a person almost as invisible as herself.

3
FARSIGHT FLESH

Hathin could think of only one sure way of cheating the Lost test, and that was the farsight fish. This fish was found nowhere but deep among the reefs along the Coast of the Lace. Beautifully sleek and iridescent as it was, the farsight fish's true claim to fame was that eating its flesh temporarily let your senses wander, a bit like those of a Lost.

Of course the fish was a very poor substitute for Lost fish-users often spent time throwing up through giddiness, and there was even a story of one fish-addict who had to carry a small rock around in a pouch hung from his neck, because during one fish session his sense of hearing had somehow become inextricably lodged in it.

The farsight fish was notoriously difficult to catch because it was almost impossible to take by surprise. Only the Lace had mastered the art of doing so, and their methods were a closely guarded secret. Many little Lace communities had been saved from starvation by selling the much-prized fish to rich connoisseurs in the inland towns. However, over the last ten years it had become necessary for the Lace to hide another secret – the fact that the farsight fish were becoming increasingly scarce.

Hathin knew of only one man who might have access to farsight-fish flesh, and she had a shrewd suspicion where he hid himself at night. And so, a little after dusk, she went in search of him.

Usually at night Hathin spent an hour busy at the 'doll game'. Parents of Lost babies would often light lots of candles around their child's hammock to gain or keep the Lost child's attention, particularly on moonlit nights, for fear that the little mind would fly up and up towards the moon and never find its way back again. Parents would also perform the 'doll game', holding up a wicker doll from which stretched a string that was tied to some bauble or a bright piece of shell. Again and again the parent would pull on the string, hauling the glittering object back to the doll. It was the oldest and surest way of making a young Lost aware of the idea of its body and persuading it to reel itself back into it.

It was a forlorn little enterprise, but Hathin still performed it religiously. Once upon a time she had had a recurring dream in which she had looked up from the doll game to see Arilou waking into herself, turning a radiant smile upon her. But she had not had that dream for many years.

Tonight, however, she did not go through the doll game's fruitless motions for she had other plans. A mist had descended at nightfall, which meant that no outsider Lost like Milady Page could witness Hathin's stealthy departure from her cave-home.

Such misty nights demanded careful walking, for fear of treading on gulls. Nobody talked about it, but everybody knew that the gull problem was also a result of the disappearance of the farsight fish. Once the sea gulls had eaten the starfish that had eaten the remains of dead farsight fish and had been able to cast their sight ahead of them when visibility was poor. The unfortunate birds still seemed to think that they were able to do this, so whenever a mist settled they had a tendency to fly headfirst into cliffs.

Most of the gulls she chanced upon were recovering from their stun, and groggily bad-tempered. However, one of them had folded over on itself like a fan, in a way that was only possible because its neck was broken. Its head rested on its smooth freckled back as if sleeping. Unfortunately Hathin discovered it by putting her hand on it in the dark, and she recoiled from the terrible softness of its plumage feeling as through red ants were crawling over her hand and arm.

She had never told anyone of her prickling helplessness in the face of death. Eiven didn't have this problem. Like the other girls of the village, she trapped birds with twine and thrust spears through fish as blithely as she would snick a needle through a shirt. But Hathin's attendance upon Arilou had protected her from such duties, and even her own family never guessed at her shameful weakness.

At last Hathin reached the Scorpion's Tail, a fissure in the cliff so named because at the top the narrowing crack curled over like a giant sting. Hathin scrambled through the narrow crevice and found that the darkness was not absolute. Beside a lantern a man sat cross-legged, a tray of tools in his lap and a glass in his eye.

'Uncle Larsh.' He was not really her uncle, but it was a courtesy term for any man older than her father would have been but younger than her grandfather. His name, Larsh, was taken from the sound that withdrawing waves made as they

 39

clutched at weed. She felt a little shy at approaching him, for they had barely ever exchanged words.

'Doctor Hathin.' This was a strange title to use to a girl her age and made Hathin blush a little. Its literal meaning was not quite doctor, rather it was a title occasionally given to unmarried women who nonetheless had a significant role in the tribe, such as doctor, scribe or Lost. 'I rather thought I'd be seeing you.' He took the glass out of his eye and peered across at her. His eyelids always flickered helplessly when he was not staring at something an inch away, as if he only had so much sight left and was trying to ration it. If he always worked in this dim light, Hathin was not surprised that he was going blind. Larsh looked about fifty, but Hathin sometimes wondered if he was younger. His hair was still fiercely thick, but touched with grey. Perhaps if a person went unnoticed for a long time the colour bled out of them, and they sank into greyness. Perhaps she herself would have a shock of grey hair by the time she was twenty.

'Uncle Larsh, I . . . I need to . . . ask for something.'

'I know. You want a piece of the farsight fish. For the test tomorrow.' Larsh smiled a little grimly as Hathin flinched violently. 'Don't worry, nobody will hear us. I always come here to be alone. It seems the decent thing to do. That way everybody else has an excuse not to know what I am doing. You see, like you, Doctor, I have a job that must be done but cannot be seen to be done. You and I are the invisible.'

It was true, she realized. Aside from herself, Larsh was the least remarked individual in the village, despite the fact that he was easily the most gifted craftsman. There was nothing pointed about it, nothing dismissive or unkind. It was just that nobody ever seemed to notice him.

The reason for this was currently lying on the tray before him. Half covered by an oilskin cloth lay what looked a great deal like a farsight fish, one with a few scales missing. In tweezers Larsh held a tiny, delicate oval piece of iridescent shell, which had been polished to a translucent thinness. As she watched, Larsh dabbed one of the bare patches with a brush dipped in resin, and then carefully positioned the tiny iridescent scale which he had been fashioning so that it lay flush with its fellows. The workmanship was exquisite – it had to be if this ordinary fish were to be passed off and sold as a farsight fish.

'It's really safe to talk? What about the Lost? Don't they follow candles?' Hathin pointed at the lantern.

'They're unlikely to see it from outside. And, even if they did, most Lost would not venture in here – it is a place of blood and secrets. Oh, and I would not sit there if I were you, Doctor.'

Hathin glanced down at the stone slab behind her and realized that it was carved. For a moment the angular shapes across it made no sense; then she identified the outline of a foot, a clutching hand, a grimacing face . . .

'A sacrifice,' Larsh remarked as Hathin peered. 'Our ancestors would have tumbled the man down from a clifftop altar so that his limbs broke, and then laid him out upon that stone in the same position as the carving. You see that channel in the centre? That's where the blood ran into the earth so that the mountain could drink.'

Hathin felt the same tingle that the dead gull had given her, but now the red ants were running everywhere,

41

through her clothes and in her hair.

'This . . . This is a temple, Uncle Larsh!'

There was a twist in Hathin's stomach that was only partly fear. The mention of the old Lace sacrifices filled her with the shame of the Lace, but the shame of her people seemed as complex as their smiles. It tugged at the root of her Laceness with a power that was almost pride.

It was a splintered root though, frayed and incomplete. Two hundred years ago all the priests had been murdered in the purge. Centuries of memory had been lost in that one great cull and now even the Lace's own holy places were mysterious and a little alien to them.

'Oh – but we shouldn't be here!'

'I honestly cannot think of a better place for us. Nowadays the village need not shed blood every month to ensure its survival. Now *you* and *I* are the offerings, sacrificed day after day for the good of the village. But I suppose we give ourselves up willingly enough, don't we?'

'What else can we do?'

'Well . . . we could leave.' Larsh gave Hathin an acute look, and for a moment his eyelids ceased to flicker. 'People do, you know. They change their names and their tooth plaques and live where nobody knows they're Lace.'

He sighed. 'It's too late for me. Too many years gone. I thought about it though. Many times.'

Hathin came to sit next to him and watch him work, sensing that Larsh would not mind. 'Uncle Larsh – you have the village's store of dried farsight fish, don't you? You sprinkle it in those.' She gestured towards the fake fish on the tray.

'Doctor Hathin –' Larsh sighed again – 'I really wish I

could help you. It's true, I used to add a tiny salting of dried farsight fish to each of these, but it ran out a year ago. See here?' He indicated the brown flecks with the tip of his chisel. 'Special spices and dried mushroom. Enough to cause a little hallucination – enough to satisfy a towner who knows no better.'

Hathin bit her lip to hold in her disappointment.

He went on. 'I'm sorry. I suppose there's no chance that your sister . . . ?'

Your sister. Not 'your lady sister' or even 'Doctor Arilou'. The villagers were always so careful to give Arilou her due title, as if it might fall off if not held firmly in place. It was the first time Hathin had ever heard someone talk as though Arilou was just a young girl, and she felt as if Larsh had shouted aloud what the whole village had tried not to say for thirteen years. The shock was icy and liberating.

Hathin shook her head, and felt that she had shouted back a confirmation accompanied by trumpets.

'Say it,' muttered Larsh as Hathin stood to leave. 'Just once.'

Hathin hesitated. 'Arilou has never spoken to us,' she said eventually.

'The fish are all dead,' said Larsh.

Hathin turned and padded swiftly from the reaches of the lantern's halo, then squeezed out through the fissure. And so ended the conference of the invisible, in the cavern of blood and secrets, on the night of the mist.

4
TRIAL AND TRICKERY

Ever since leaving his town lodgings at sunrise, Minchard Prox had been suffering from the feeling that he was being watched.

There were the two little Lace boys that tag-teamed alongside him, offering to polish his boots or carry his bags.

As he reached the clifftop path the convoy was joined by an old woman with her head wrapped in the voluminous, turban-like shawl that most Lace grandmothers wore. The slow, mincing gait of the elephant bird, whose leash he held, was already causing Prox to lag behind Skein, and this woman seemed determined to delay him further.

She told him that the pale pink eggs she carried in her basket were almost as cheap as raindrops, and that he should go no further because his ancestors were skulking in the undergrowth, waiting to pelt him with rocks. The conversation made Prox uncomfortable, not least because some of his ancestors really *were* located in these Ashlands.

'Look,' he said, trying to make light of it as sweat trickled into his eye, 'I hardly think my ancestors are going to be crouching in the undergrowth like schoolboys with their pockets full of pebbles.'

'Of course no crouch, little lord,' she said in a soothing mixture of Nundestruth and Doorsy. 'Sit up in grave like gentlefolk in bed, and earth fall from them like blanket . . . and *then* they throw stone at you.'

She kept pace with him, all the while her head a-tilt, watching the underside of his chin with good-humoured cunning. Despite her frailty she started to unnerve him, so keen was she to point out the crags and hollows where she said the unseen dead watched them.

He was so distracted by this that he walked straight into a large mist of tiny flies that shrouded a low bush of rotting berries. The flies sought out his eyes and mouth and pores without hesitation and tickled their way into his collar. For a moment he had a maddened, unreasonable belief that the old witch had led him there on purpose.

While he was flailing, the leash tugged free from his hand and, twitching with fly-bites, the elephant bird discovered a new turn of speed. Panniers bouncing and rocks crackling under its long-taloned toes, it sped away and the boys broke into a sprint to flank it, as if the three of them had run off to join in a game. He lost sight of them almost immediately.

The Lace always made him feel out of control. The current of circumstances was sweeping him helplessly headlong, and suddenly his education and breeding were the flimsiest of paddles in his hands.

He looked desperately ahead for Skein, but the Inspector had not waited for him. Skein's plan had been to make for the pulley-chair and attract the villagers' attention while Prox made his way unnoticed down the zigzag paths with the bird and prepared some locations for the first test.

Prox ran blindly after the faint sounds of trills and whoops. There – was that a clatter of rocks further up that slope?

'Ugly, stupid, hopeless . . .' chanted Prox under his breath as he staggered onward. He hated elephant birds' imbecilic belligerence. At the moment he particularly hated this individual bird, which seemed determined to lead him away from the path and into the Ashlands.

Prox spent the next quarter of an hour slithering up and down the uneven ground, haunted by fleeting glimpses of the bird's bristle-browed head. He lost his bearings almost immediately, for over the centuries the Ashlands had become far larger than Sweetweather, swallowing all the lush land around the town and along the headlands. The sun blinded him, and everywhere weather-bleached spirit houses tilted and clustered.

At least the dead around him were not Lace. Prox found the idea of the Lace scattering the ashes of their dead to the winds horrifying.

That's why the Lace suffer and go hungry, went the whisper among the non-Lace. *That's why they go missing, why they are taken by eagles, and by the volcanoes and the strong sea currents. They let the spirits of their dead be torn apart on the winds so they have no ancestors to protect them or give them good luck. They bring everything on themselves.*

It was said that the Lace did not even mention their dead by name once there was nobody left alive who actually remembered the dead person. They had no tales to tell of their heroic ancestors – just countless legends of the island's weird man–bird god, the Gripping Bird.

Prox tried to imagine his own ancestors invisibly rallying

46

around to protect him, but the old woman's words kept repeating in his head until his mind held only a gallery of abandoned portrait frames, their denizens running wild in this wilderness of black rock and golden grass, their pockets full of pebbles.

At last he found the elephant bird thumping its beak into the undergrowth in search of some small animal. He was reaching for the leash loop that lay on the grass when his eye fell on the leaves of the white hang-head orchids around him. All of them were pockmarked with small circular holes.

The next moment he was stumbling down the slope with all the speed he could muster, his fingers pushed firmly in his ears. Even as a towner, Prox knew what those holes meant: blissing beetles.

Blissing beetles were only near the western mountains, but they were notorious. When the young beetles left their cocoon they ate out such circles spiral-wise. Completed circles with no young bugs in them meant that the beetles had finished fleshing themselves out and that their wings had had time to harden. The plump little insects had only one defence against the dagger-like beaks of hungry birds, but it was a deadly one.

On either side the sunlit world lurched and burned past him. Rocks and hidden briars bit his shins, but he did not stop for them. For all he knew, the air was already humming with tiny agate wings. For all he knew, birds might be thudding out of the air behind him, too entranced by the beetles' hum to remember how they should fly or think or breathe. They said you felt the hum before you heard it, as a throb behind your breastbone. By the time it became a sound in your ear it was too late. Nobody really knew what the blissing song actually sounded like, only that it was beautiful enough to put a smile on the dead face of all who had heard it. Prox was running for his life.

Only when he reached the path did he pause to recover his breath, stooping to clasp his knees. His shoe buckles were knotted with grass. He kicked a stone in frustration.

I could be a Revered Clerk at Port Suddenwind, he thought bitterly as the hammering of his heart started to slow, 'but no. *I have to be* here . . .'

'Why weren't you here?' Mother Govrie snapped as Hathin barrelled into the cave. 'You know she won't let anyone else paint inside her ears. The Inspector will be here any moment, and she has to be ready.'

Hathin could only nod mutely as she struggled to regain her composure.

Mother Govrie regarded her for a few moments. 'Everything *will* be ready, won't it?' she asked after a moment. Hathin nodded, and her mother briefly rasped her rough fingertips across the shaven patch above her daughter's forehead. Hathin sensed the affection and approval the gesture represented, and felt almost sick with the desire to be worthy of it.

Mother Govrie, never cold, never cruel, but calloused by necessity. To her the world was just a great, recalcitrant clod of dough, waiting for her to drive her warm, vigorous knuckles into it until it gave in and became what it had to be.

Arilou consented to have her ears painted the same marble-white as her face, and then Hathin ventured out.

With some trepidation she noticed that the Inspector was in the village and was caught in conversation with Whish and one of her daughters. There was a long-standing rivalry between Whish and Eiven, the two finest pearl-divers in the village. Diving had always been the prerogative of the women – men's lungs were smaller, it was said – and every diver in the village was fiercely territorial about 'their' corner of the reef. For many years Whish had enjoyed the choicest hunting grounds, and the appearance of the younger Eiven as a rival had been a bitter shock. However, the final straw had been a family matter.

Two years before, Whish's youngest daughter had been killed by a visiting landowner. The magistrate had called it an accident, and so the landowner had paid a fine and left town. And nothing more than grief might have come of it, if Eiven had not persuaded Whish's eldest son, Therrot, that something *should* be done. One morning Therrot had marched away from the village with a small pack on his back and a strange, distant, tight look to his face. Only afterwards did his distraught mother learn that he had gone off on a 'revenge quest', giving up his old life to hunt down the murderer of his sister. *He has gone to join the Reckoning*, was the whisper. *The revengers are his family now.* And Hathin knew that they were speaking of the secret confederacy of those Lace who had sworn revenge oaths and who helped bring one another's quests to their bloody conclusions. Therrot had never been seen again and most of Whish's family had never forgotten it. While they played along with the deference owed to Arilou's family, there was a dangerous undercurrent of cold, resentful contempt.

Whish's remaining son, the fourteen-year-old Lohan, sur-prised Hathin by kicking a plume of warm sand across her toes. He grinned when she jumped.

'Are you going to be receiving the Inspector like that?'

Hathin suddenly knew how she must look, peppered with red dust, and with little fly stowaways in her hair. Embarrassment scalded her.

Lohan reached across, pointedly picked something off her clothes and perched it on his thumb-tip to study it with a smile-frown. Then he licked it and, before Hathin could recoil, stuck it on to the end of her nose.

'Get yourself cleaned up,' he said, before sauntering away.

Plucking at the end of her nose, Hathin found herself holding a tiny circle of leaf, and at last she understood Lohan's meaning. The dust, the splashes of golden pollen like fireworks against her dark skirt, these were evidence that she had been up on the cliff that morning. If he saw her that way, Prox might start to suspect that the two boys he had met there had chased his elephant bird into the Ashlands deliberately, and at her request. And if Prox saw little moons of leaf scattered on her clothing, he might realize that the polka-dot holes which had scared him away from his luggage for a critical ten minutes had been picked out not by young blissing beetles but by young, cunning Lace fingernails. In short, it might occur to him that his recent misfortunes had all been part of her plan to rummage through his bags in search of clues to the tests.

She found a place among the rocks to splash her legs with sea water and brush her clothes down. When she emerged she saw a perspiring and harassed-looking Prox urging his recalcitrant elephant bird down the path. Her sting of pity was swept away by a tide of panic.

There was now nothing to stop the tests beginning.

Arilou did not raise her head as Skein walked into her cave, and seated himself before her. He waited there in his own uncanny pool of silence, in no hurry to speak or begin.

Hathin kept her eyes lowered and her hands clasped in her lap to stop them trembling. Her quick search of the elephant bird's panniers had discovered the three boxes and three corked bottles, but the three jars for the smell test had been nowhere to be seen. She could only guess that they must have been tucked in Prox's pockets. Even now he was probably burying them somewhere outside. She could only hope that the village boy she had sent to spy on him would not fail her.

At last the curtain twitched again and Prox entered, his hair bearing the grooves of hurried combing. There was no sign of Hathin's spy. In spite of the morning's hurried activity, she was still unprepared for the first test.

Suddenly there was the racketing sound of somebody raking a stick down the reed curtain at the cave mouth. Neither Skein nor Prox looked up as Hathin rose unsteadily and went to the entrance of the cave.

Her 'spy' was waiting outside. Hathin felt her throat thicken with relief as she scrambled down the rope ladder and drew him away from the cave.

'In front of the Scorpion's Tail,' was all he said. This, then, was where Prox had buried the three scent jars.

There was no time for caution. She pressed her face close to the boy's ear to whisper.

'Did you dig them up and look in them? Which colour stone was each thing buried under?'

'There wasn't time,' he muttered with a shrug.

51

Doused in renewed panic, Hathin clapped her hands to her mouth and then with terrified eyes beamed at him through her fingers. For all she knew, Skein's wandering vision might settle on them – she could not let this interview look like anything more urgent than a furtive boy–girl meeting . . .

'Kick them!' she smiled into his ear after a moment's thought. 'Go back! Kick all the stones around! As if you're looking for shells! Quickly!'

Shakily Hathin returned to the cave, half expecting to find Skein waiting in silence, his countenance and sidelong eyes turned to confront her. But he was talking to Arilou and barely seemed to notice Hathin's reappearance.

'So, Miss Arilou, where are you now?'

Hathin stealthily leaned over to her sister and paddled her finger in Arilou's palm. She could not speak unless she appeared to be translating for Arilou.

'Please, Arilou,' she whispered right into her ear, 'say something, please . . .' As if in response the older girl frowned a little and a soft stream of molten words spilled into the air.

'I am in this room.' Hathin answered in cold, confident Doorsy, as she always did when speaking for Arilou. 'I hope you will pardon me if I do not wear my body. I find it very tiring and would prefer to remain alert.'

'I understand,' Skein said, and there was a smile in his voice if not on his face. 'Are you ready?'

No, thought Hathin, *nonono* . . .

'Yes,' she said.

'The first test will be that of your ability to move your sense of smell. We will allow our minds to flow through the curtain . . .' Skein's voice sank into a calm monotone. No doubt he was drifting his mind out of the cave as he spoke, but there was no change in the unflinching erectness of his seated figure. 'Move to the cliff-face. Now pass your senses along it until you come to a big curved fissure in the rock. Now look for a large slab of blue slate . . .' Skein trailed off. Once, twice Skein's eyes quivered from left to right, and his eyebrows twitched. 'Prox,' he said in a different tone, 'there's a boy there, picking through the stones. Go and ask him to stop, will you?'

'I have found a blue-grey stone,' Hathin allowed a note of doubt to creep into her Arilou voice, 'but it is standing on end, I am not sure it is the right one . . .'

'Miss Arilou, let your senses sink down through the sand, beneath the stone – you are searching for a jar –'

'I sense nothing but sand and rocks . . .' Hathin noticed that Arilou's head was turning as though she really was searching. 'Wait . . . a few feet away I think I have found a jar but . . . but there seems to be more than one . . .'

'Enter the jars one at a time. Tell me what you smell.'

Hathin breathed a small sigh of relief. Thanks to the work of her spy, Skein no longer expected her to know which jar was where, only what was inside them. And, thanks to the Pearlpit porters, she already knew that.

Taking the greatest care not to rush, Hathin described each scent in turn. The fish she let herself guess easily. The cinnamon she hesitated over for a while. She made herself take some time over the last, talking of perfumes, spring-like smells and only eventually recognizing it as hang-head orchid.

'Very good,' Skein said, sounding like he meant it. 'Return to the cave, please.'

Next, as expected, Skein produced three boxes for the

'finger-feeling' test. Hathin had memorized the grain pattern on the wood of each box and had no trouble telling which of them held the conch, the rag of fur and the mouse skull.

When the corked bottles for the taste test were produced, Hathin felt herself turn pale. She had etched a mark into the cork of the bottle of sweet liquid with her fingernail – but where was it? The dent must have healed in the meanwhile, the soft cork rediscovering its original shape. What could she do?

She was on the verge of closing her eyes and trusting to her one in three chance, when she noticed a tiny fly floating in one of the bottles. It must have flown in when she had unstoppered the bottles to taste the contents. It was all she could do not to stab a finger at it and call out, 'That one!' Just in time she remembered to wait for Arilou's murmurs, and then cautiously chose the bottle with the fly.

'Correct.' As Hathin had hoped, the fly had found out the sweetest bottle.

Now Skein asked Arilou to let her senses drift with his up the cliff path. Hathin carefully described features of the area she had known since her birth, and then at the mouth of the natural limestone maze of the Lacery she allowed her voice to falter.

'Strange,' she said, 'there seems to be a w—'

'Prox!' Skein exclaimed sharply. Prox, who had only just stooped his way back into the cave, looked a question. 'Your marker is gone.'

There seems to be a white ribbon tied to a spike of rock, Hathin had been about to say. She had followed Prox and seen him tie it just before she had sprinted down the cliff-face to reach the village before him. She had been tingling to describe the ribbon, terrified that en route Skein would ask her to describe some other fleeting feature that she could not guess, like the shape of the clouds or the colour of a bird. She had almost blurted it out, desperate to end the test . . . and those words would have betrayed her utterly and hopelessly.

'What were you saying?' asked Skein.

'There's a wind,' Hathin stammered. 'A wind rising. A perilous . . . perilous . . .' She felt she had halted on the edge of a precipice, her toes touching air, crumbs of rock falling from her soles into forever.

'No doubt that blew away the marker.' Skein stirred carefully, systematically clicking joints that he had left to stiffen. 'You are tired and will wish to talk to others in the village about the rising storm. Let us meet again this afternoon.'

Hathin's mind fell into numb exhaustion as the two men left the cave. There was still nothing but gaping void at her feet, and she had no idea how to take her next step.

5
CURRENT-CAUGHT

As soon as the Inspectors were out of the room, Hathin's mouth turned to sand. 'Arilou' had passed three tests. That was enough to avoid failing outright . . . but there was still the test of hearing to come, and afterwards they would probably want her to retake the test of sight. If she failed both of them completely, would the Inspectors not become suspicious? Perhaps Prox would think to mention that his luggage had been out of his sight for quarter of an hour? And even if they agreed to give Arilou a complete retest, what then? No, she had to pass all five tests, there was nothing else for it.

Out on the beach she found everybody dragging their boats away from the water, tethering the huts and moving valuables up to the caves in preparation for the coming storm. The sky was still blue, but its colour had deepened and dirtied. As she passed, everybody in turn gave her a quick questioning glance. She gave each a small bitten smile, and saw it reflected in every face. *Things are going well, but not that well.*

Skein sat on the edge of the Lacery with his face towards the sea and his eyes turned to look along the beach. Hathin guessed that he was looking at neither of them.

'He says he has gone to see if a friend has left a note for him.' At the sound of the familiar voice Hathin turned and found Larsh had scuffed his way to stand beside her. Even she, it would seem, had learned not to notice him. She smiled up at his rapid blink and felt a warm rush of fellowship.

'And the other Inspector?' asked Hathin. It had suddenly occurred to her that Prox might be tying up another marker for her to find.

'Over there, arguing with your sister.' Larsh pointed. He looked even older by daylight.

Eiven had her hands on her hips while Prox's face was brick-red with frustration and confusion. Between them lay a boat, its rope in Prox's hand. Beside them stood Mother Govrie, arms folded, biting at her full lower lip.

Hathin guessed what they must be doing. Stalling. Delaying Prox so that she could carry out her next plan. The plan she did not have.

Minchard Prox did not even notice the pad-footed approach of the snub-faced girl with the nervous mouth. He was too busy sweating under the gaze of the two women.

'You will be reunited with your boat.' Feeling outnumbered, he had slipped out of Nundestruth and into Doorsy, hoping to borrow a little stature from the noble cadences as if they were high-heeled boots. 'I must ride the waters in it for the test, that is all. Do you understand? I am to whisper a word for your Lady Lost to hear, and I must be away from all ears.'

Maddeningly, both women smiled and nodded as he spoke, then erupted as one into a flood of contradictions in Nundestruth.

'. . . storm rise, my lord, current yank you to cliff-crush . . .'

'. . . reefteef bite through boat . . .'

'You see this?' Prox waved the rope in his fist a little wildly, flecking the faces of the small group with specks of spray. 'This is a Rope. I Will Tie This End To A Rock. There. That one. Boat stays out there, everything Fine.' He knew he was being rude, but vexation and the oppression of the pre-storm heat had overwhelmed him and he could not apologize.

Now the young woman told him that the sea noise would be too loud, it would be too difficult to hear his whisper . . .

'That's the whole point!' Prox exploded. 'No way that any-body can hear from the shore, you understand? No chance of cheating this test.' The last sentence he pronounced with a certain involuntary venom. Once again, corrosive bubbles of suspicion were swelling in his soul.

Prox had not dared to tell Skein that their luggage had spent a while out of his care. He told himself it wasn't important, that no locals would have dared blissing-beetle-infested areas or been able to capture the hostile elephant bird. But now that he found himself obstructed by Arilou's mother and eldest sister, he was starting to feel like one caught in a game against too many opponents.

'No, thank you!' Slender fingers were trying to manoeuvre the rope from his fingers. He pulled away and stooped to tie a knot hearing two, no, three silver Lace voices mingle like streams. He felt the women's retreat like a loosening of the air, a breath of wind.

He took his time with the rope, knotting it with a certain savagery. He had just finished when a small, soft hand fell lightly on his sleeve. A girl was standing next to him, proffering a large and ornate conch, its ridges flecked with turquoise iridescence.

Do these people never stop trying to sell things?

'No, thank you.' Firm, but kind. He was pleased with himself.

The shell sagged downwards for a moment, and then the girl was stooping by the canoe and placing the shell inside, lodging it in the wedge of the stern.

'Wait! What are you . . . ? No, no, no! I don't want a shell!'

She straightened again, her face uncertain, and he realized how slight she was. Her lips were moving in breathy, almost inaudible Nundestruth. He suddenly imagined her being pushed to the back of the crowd of sellers by taller girls with keener, pealing voices.

'Oh . . . all right,' he sighed, overwhelmed by a sudden flood of pity and resignation. He pulled a coin from his pouch and held it out. 'Will this do?' She shook her head.

She was pointing at the sun. What? What was she saying? Hot? She was pointing out at the cove. At the shell. What was she doing?

'Oh . . . never mind. Here.' He held out two coins, and watched in bafflement and growing frustration as she winced and shook her head again. Prox felt miserably stupid for opening himself up to this ridiculous haggle. 'Oh, for pity's sake, take it back! Just take it!' He reached down and grabbed the shell, but even as he was forcing it roughly back into her hands something cold slopped over his knuckles.

The shell was full of water.

He stared at her, feeling a weirdly intense sense of remorse. She had not been trying to sell him anything at all. While the others had been baiting him like a bear, she had run to fetch him a shell full of water to sustain him while he was in the boat under the heat of the sun.

She had big brown eyes, and a triple crease of worry above them. *Just because they're smiling, it doesn't mean they're happy.* Didn't she look slightly familiar? Only when he saw the little plaques of quartz gleaming like teardrops in her front teeth did he recognize her. It was Lady Arilou's translator. A moment before her face might as well have been a featureless smudge for all the notice he had taken of it. How had it happened? How had this girl become invisible to him?

'Thank you.' He took back the shell. 'Here . . . you should take this.' He held out the coin again, and felt an immense sadness as she shook her head.

Hathin saw Prox's face fall, but she could not bring herself to take the coin. She was, after all, there to distract him.

She glanced up the beach to where one of the old women sat talking companionably to Skein, her head cocked questioningly, her sun-blackened hands rubbing at her skinny ankles. You could not prevent a Lost's eye wandering, but you could snag his attention for a while.

And somewhere, even now, Eiven would be clambering over the rocks, her strong brown toes curling to find purchase amid the nooks and cracks. She would be letting herself gently into the water so as not to make a splash, and then

60

striking out beneath the surface, her lean body undulating like an eel . . .

I failed, I failed. Hathin had not found a way to defeat the fifth test, and now Eiven was having to dare the storm current. While Prox had been busy tying the rope, Hathin had confessed to her mother and sister that she still had no plan for defeating this test. Eiven's agate-coloured eyes had taken in Hathin's helpless misery at a glance, turned cold and then slid off her, as if her younger sister's existence had waned in some indefinable way. When Eiven had raised her head and narrowed her eyes at the sea, Hathin had known in an instant the desperate plan her older sister had in mind.

Silhouetted against the gleaming sea, Prox had looked like nothing but a mountainous obstacle, something to be overcome in order to prevent Eiven being discovered. But then Hathin had seen the reddened sun-weals forming on his neck, and the anguish that puckered his cheeks as he struggled with the rope. And he might be stranded out in the boat under the sweltering heat for an hour as Eiven got into position and the whole village played for time . . . and so Hathin had impulsively run off to fetch him a shell of water.

No, she could not take his coin.

As Prox turned and dragged the canoe to the water, however, Hathin's mind flew back to Eiven. Oh, to be Lost and follow her! But Hathin had only her mind's eye, in which she saw Eiven roll and flow with strong, rollicking pre-storm currents amid clouds of stirred sand that glittered like golden sparks as the twists of sunlight caught them. The sound of waves catching on rocks and tearing like silk would fill Eiven's ears as though they were breaking against her skull.

And the world around her would be leaping and bounding, the rocks rising and falling crazily, the reef rearing up and trying to claw at her belly with knobbed fingers . . .

Prox was now paddling his boat out into the cove. A dusk of clouds was forming in the blue sky, like sediment in an old bottle. *The King of Fans is wearing his mourning colours*, thought Hathin with a tickle of superstitious fear as she saw the volcano blackening in the shadow. The King always remembered things backwards, mourning before death or cataclysm rather than afterwards. *Eiven, where are you?*

Hathin stared out across the water and deliberately let her eyes unfocus slightly. It did no good lodging your gaze on the waves as they slid and fractured. The trick was to see nothing and everything, until you started to notice any tear and break in the rhythms of the water.

Was that a heel surfacing for a moment? Eiven must be close to the surface, making for the rope rather than the boat, trying to make use of the weaker current nearer the shore. There! Right next to the rope the surface was broken by a brown hand spread like a star. The hand snatched towards the rope and . . .

'Miss.' There was no mistaking the soft *s*. Hathin turned to find Skein beside her. 'Be so good as to fetch your lady sister. We must proceed with the test quickly, before the storm descends.'

Hathin dared not look back towards the water, but she suddenly sensed the atmosphere on the beach sharpen, as if every Lace watching the sea had dragged in a silent breath through their teeth. What had they seen?

'Miss?'

'Ye-yes . . . right away.' Hathin turned from the Inspector, swallowing drily, and snuck another quick look out into the cove. No, there was no sign of a hand grasping the rope. Eiven had missed. She would not be able to haul herself to the boat to hear Prox's muttered word, then bring it back.

Everywhere on the beach, the Lace were whisker-tense. A few of the villagers were now nonchalantly jogging towards the down-current end of the beach, only speeding up as they passed out of sight and leaped into the labyrinth of rocks that made up the Lacery. Hathin read the signs clearly enough. Eiven had not only missed the rope, she had been dragged off by the current. The villagers would scramble through the Lacery to the water's edge, looking to pull Eiven from the current's clutches.

Hathin made herself walk steadily back to the cave, her knees weak. As she clambered up the ladder to its entrance her body was abruptly flooded with a warmth that she barely recognized as anger. Why was Arilou not what she should be? Why did the village have to suffer this voiceless emergency? All of this was done for Arilou, done to keep alive the lie that illuminated her like a halo. Hathin suddenly felt that she could not bear to pull aside the curtain and see Arilou waiting there in self-absorbed serenity on the softest mat, stirring her lips in anticipation of the best honey . . .

Hathin swallowed dryness and pulled aside the curtain. The mat was empty. So were the adjoining caverns. Arilou was not there.

No Arilou wandering aimlessly on the beach. No Arilou in her sunspot on the heart-shaped rock. *Oh please no I'm sorry Arilou I'm sorry I'm sorry* . . . Suddenly, from the rocks at the water's edge, Hathin heard a sharp human cry, almost lost amid the steel splinters of the gull cries. She slithered and scrambled towards the sound, terrified of finding either Eiven or Arilou wave-tossed and bloodied among the rocks.

Hathin squeezed through a crinkled crevice and found herself facing a strange tug-of-war. Whish stood on one side, her face terrifying without its smile. Facing her, half stooped as though he expected to have to leap on her, was her son Lohan. Each held one of Arilou's hands. Arilou stood between them, apparently oblivious of the shallow ripples riffling around her feet and the slick slope into the deeper water behind her.

'An accident saves us!' Whish hissed. 'One slip on the rocks, and she will be unable to take the test.'

'Let go of her hand.' Lohan's voice was lower than usual, and very quiet. 'And go back to the beach.' His tone was dangerously gentle. His mother released Arilou, and then stared down at her hand as if surprised at it. Letting the loose trail of her turban fall to hide her face, she stalked away.

'Nobody need know,' Lohan whispered. He turned to look at Hathin, and she was startled to see the question, the entreaty in his face. 'The rest of the village, they need not know what my mother tried to do. The rest of the family . . . why should we suffer?' Hathin flinched from the intensity of the question. 'I found her, I stopped her, that must count for something . . .'

'I can't . . .' Hathin looked skywards, waterwards, anywhere but into Lohan's face. She did not want to see him pleading, frightened; she wanted him to be his usual self-composed, mocking self. 'I can't think. I . . . I must get Arilou back to the beach.'

Arilou gave her somewhere to look, and so Hathin did not have to glance back at Lohan as she led her sister away.

If Lohan had been a little slower . . . again her mind's eye showed her a bloodied figure face down in the shallows, dank feathers in the waxed hair . . . she gripped Arilou's long, golden paw tightly in both of hers. Arilou gave a slight snuffle and Hathin cast a sideways glance at her sister. The corners of Arilou's mouth drooped, and Hathin wondered whether she had sensed her danger . . . or whether this was a pout of protest at being led around by strange hands.

Hathin found Inspector Skein on the beach, apparently unperturbed by the rising wind that flicked at his pigtail and billowed the skirts of his coat.

'Miss Arilou,' he said without preamble, 'we must complete this test quickly. I am sure that you wish to return to your dwelling before the rain comes, and Mr Prox should be brought back before the worst of the storm.' Hathin's eyes burned with wind-whipped sand. As usual she did not experience it as her own pain, but she felt the sting for Arilou, who did not know to blink.

'We should find shelter from the wind,' Hathin declared in her Arilou voice.

'Very well.'

Just within the Lacery, tall fingers of rock enclosed a space like the fingers of a half-closed hand surrounding an upturned palm. Two soap-smooth rocky protuberances offered themselves as seats, and Hathin gently lowered Arilou to sit on one. Skein took the other.

Hathin took Arilou's hand in both of hers and chafed it gently. There was nothing she could do now but hope for her miracle.

'If you will then, Miss Arilou.'

And Arilou raised her head. A faint, trilling bird-like sound escaped her lips, and her hands moved gently as if stroking something soft. Her eyes widened and lightened, seemed to fix upon something. Could it be . . . ? Yes, it really *did* look like she was focusing, her brow furrowing as if in concentration. What did that starry gaze mean?

Please, Arilou, please . . .

Arilou's lips trembled, and parted. Hathin leaned her ear to Arilou's mouth . . . and heard only the usual stream of molten words.

'It is very difficult to hear over the crash of the waves,' Hathin announced in cool Doorsy, while her heart plunged. She had no more plans, there was nothing she could think to do but play for time and pray. 'And your friend has a strange accent . . .' For about ten minutes she continued in this vein, sensing that the ice beneath her was becoming increasingly thin. At last Skein took out his pocket watch.

'We must bring this test to an end soon. Miss Arilou, I shall leave for an interval to see if a letter has been left for me, but when I return you must have an answer ready.'

Hathin waited for him to rise, and only when he settled himself back against the rock did she realize that he was leaving in spirit only. Of course, he had sent his mind to look for a note earlier – presumably he had not found it. A small part of Hathin's mind wondered what message could be so important that he would flit off like this mid-test. But what did it matter? It bought her more time.

When he had remained motionless for about a minute, she dared to scramble to her feet. She had to know whether Eiven had been found. Not knowing was unbearable. But at the same time she knew that she was secretly, guiltily hoping that Eiven, with her barracuda speed, had defied the current and made it to the boat where Prox sat. If she could only find her, there might still be a chance of passing the test.

Hathin took one of the leather laces adorning Arilou's wrist and tied it to a nearby pillar of rock to stop her wandering, then slipped away through the rocky labyrinth.

At the water's edge she found several searchers from the village. She could tell from one look at their faces that nothing had been seen of Eiven.

'We'll keep looking,' Hathin was told. 'Now . . . you go back and do the best you can.'

The shadowed stone was clammy under Hathin's hands and feet as she faced the possibility of a world robbed of Eiven by Hathin's own failure.

She thought of Mother Govrie's eye hardening as Eiven's had done, she imagined standing before the whole village drenched in failure . . . she saw the entire reason for her existence dropping away from her like rain into a dark shaft.

By the time she returned to the place where she had left Arilou and the Inspector, the sky was metal and an orchestra of hollow fluting noises sounded throughout the Lacery as the wind found out needle-holes and crevices.

Skein still sat motionless, his expression serene. Was he 'back'? Had he noticed her absence? He said nothing to remark on her arrival. It seemed that he was still away from his body.

Arilou, on the other hand, seemed restless. She still wore a starry, rapt expression, and had almost tugged her tether free. Occasionally she gave a bird-like twitch of her head, and her hands made soft clutching motions. She was murmuring under her breath, and as Hathin drew closer she realized that for once it was a single word, spoken over and over again.

Could it be? Could the miracle have arrived? Arilou was staring out to sea, roughly towards where Prox's boat would be bobbing on the restless water.

'Kaiethemin . . .' That seemed to be what she was saying. Hathin listened to it a few more times, but she could make no more sense of it than that. Still, what if this really was Prox's whisper, mangled by Arilou's soft mouth? Hathin had no choice but to pray that it was. Her time had run out.

'I believe I know the word.' Hathin marvelled at her own voice, clear and composed.

Skein continued to stare out into some private sky. After a few seconds Hathin could only conclude that she had not been heard, that his mind was still far from his body. She reached out gently and touched his hand.

For a second the world inhaled soundlessly. Then thunder rolled unseen cannonballs across the sky above. There was a downward rush of air, and raindrops struck all around like metal pellets, making the dust jump.

Hathin withdrew her hand from the Inspector's, pinching at her fingers and palm to rid them of their pins and needles.

Invisible red ants were seething up her arm and surging forth to run over every inch of her skin.

The Inspector's hand was cold, and his chest no longer rose and fell. Skein, who had never been comfortable with his body, had left it forever.

6
GOING THROUGH THE GONGS

Hathin untied Arilou, keeping her own manner as calm as possible, and led her back to the beach. Arilou was docile, but her hand kept twitching restlessly in Hathin's grasp, and her gaze still held an eerie brilliance.

Everybody on the beach was bedraggling with the rain, but Hathin could not believe that they felt the chill of it as she did. She recognized Larsh's shambling shuffle and made for him.

'Is the test finished?' Larsh's eye passed over Hathin's rigid, desperate features, over Arilou's rain-streaked powder mask.

Hathin swallowed, and nodded.

'So? What did Inspector Skein say?'

Hathin bit her lips together and met his eye. 'He does not have the name Skein.' She spoke slowly and with all the diamond-cold resonance she could conjure. And she watched Larsh's eyes widen and darken as her meaning hit him in the marrow.

According to the old Lace stories, after you died and went to the Cave of Caves, you had to pay the Old Woman before she would let you pass. In the first cave you had to hand over your name . . .

The dead had no names.

'How . . . ?' Larsh trailed off.

Hathin raised her eyebrows and gave a little shake of her head.

'Where?'

'In the Lacery. In the Gripping Bird's hand.'

Larsh blinked and blinked, his eyebrows twitching as if to shrug off the rain's attentions.

'Get your lady sister inside,' he said at last.

Even when Hathin had manoeuvred Arilou back into their cave-home, her mind and heart were painfully full of Skein and Eiven and the storm. And so she took particular care as she washed Arilou's face clean of powder. She used little shell crescents to scrape the dirt out from under Arilou's nails until the louring of the sky outside made the work too difficult to see, and when Arilou moaned and flinched Hathin realized that she was scratching her.

The reed curtain flip-flapped and spat a figure inwards. Leaden criss-cross light filtered through the weave and patterned a lean, fierce face, a scar like a bird's footprint. It was Eiven. She did not respond to Hathin's incoherent gasp of relief and surprise.

'Leave her with me,' was all Eiven said. 'You're wanted in the Scorpion's Tail.'

The cavern where Hathin had found Larsh alone in the mists the previous night was now full of people. It looked as though everybody in the village but Eiven, Arilou and the youngest children was there.

On a slab of rock lay the Lost Inspector, Skein. Somebody had placed his hands over his stomach as if he had enjoyed a

 71

good meal and settled down to sleep it off. This might have been more convincing if the same person had thought to close his eyes, but Hathin guessed that a superstitious frisson had prevented the Lace from doing so.

. . . and when your dead soul had left your name in the first cave, you passed to a second cave, where you had to hand over your eyes before moving on . . .

With a shock she realized that Skein had been laid on the altar slab that bore the carving of the sacrifice. She wondered if it had been an accident, or whether there had been the unspoken thought: *Well, we need the favour of the divine, and it would be a pity for the body to go to waste . . .*

'We can't talk here.' Mother Govrie, practical as ever. 'Our voices will wander to the entrance if we do. We'll take the Gong Path.'

Skein was draped with Whish's canvas cloak, and then the villagers trooped deeper into the cavern to a place where the water pooled into a black mirror.

There, without a word, everybody took off their outer garments. They all took rapid but measured breaths, stealing as much goodness from the air as they could. Then Whish knelt by the edge of the black pool, drew in one last deep breath and cleaved the water. A few minutes later, her face broke the surface again, with a little whale huff of gasped spray.

'The path is clear,' she said, once she had her breath. The best diver was always sent ahead to check the Path of the Gongs, and in the absence of Eiven this was Whish. A few more deep breaths and Whish plunged again, her back curling above the surface for an instant like that of a dolphin.

Next followed Mother Govrie, and then every other

member of the village, one by one. Hathin was among the last, and as she stepped up to the pool her face was buzzing and tingling with her hastily drawn breaths. She had only swum the Gong Path a few times. She took her last, deepest breath, and then the cold water received her.

It was just a matter of holding herself together through the shock of the cold, and then her eyes were open and suddenly she was her underwater self, slippery and unaccountable as an eel.

Hathin found familiar flint handholds and pulled her way downward to where the underwater tunnel began. She flipped herself face up as she entered the tunnel so that she could push with her hands and feet against the roof. Almost immediately the meagre light abandoned her, and she was reliant on touch and memory.

There were no voices here. But the water was not silent. No, it whispered of every darkened drop that rang into it along the dark stream's seeping, secret length. This strange music had given the Path of the Gongs its name.

And somewhere inside her there was still the land-walking Hathin in her world of worry, clutching herself with fear of fear itself, terrified that she might panic and have nowhere to flee for air. But the underwater Hathin, the mermaid-minded Hathin, knew a strange peace in the blackness, despite the risks.

Anyone swimming blind would have followed the tunnel to its finish and found themselves at a dead end, but Hathin had been taught where to find the lowside passage and twisted her way sideways and down to pass through it. Then she let herself rise, bubbles beading their way out of her mouth as her lungs expanded. She broke the surface, and gasped the world and its worries back into herself. Ready hands pulled her out of the pool to clear the way for the next swimmer.

This cavern was one of the many secrets of the village. Every child was taught to swim the Path of the Gongs so that if the village was attacked everybody could flee into the Scorpion's Tail and through the tunnel without fear of pursuit. This cave was linked by a series of tunnels to the great sinkhole near Sweetweather and beyond but here the only light was provided by a galaxy of glow-worms. Then flint clicked, a wick hissed, a tiny flame tugged timorously in unfelt draughts, and Hathin could see that she was standing in a cavern full of teeth.

. . . and in the third cave of the dead you had to hand over your mouth . . .

Row upon row of ghostly teeth, many the height of a man, jutting from the floor, tapering from the ceiling. Stalagmites, stalactites. The cave was agape with them, and beyond their bite was nothing but dark throat.

Around her, the villagers that peopled Hathin's world were almost unrecognizable. The turbans of the old women, the embroidered aprons of the young wives, the young men's belts of tools and tricks, everything that let you know them at a glance had been left behind. In the near darkness, their eyes were yellow stars in hollows, their faces swathed in wet hair.

And yet Hathin knew each of them, even in the darkness. She knew them by their teeth.

Nearly every Lace with their adult teeth had them ornamented in traditional ways, with tiny plaques of turquoise, mother-of-pearl, greenstone, agate or pink quartz. Now the

lantern's light played over each wide, hard, frightened smile
and winked in the little gems.

'Is Hathin here?' asked a row of lazuli crescents. It was one
of the village's many powerful grandmothers, and the kindness of her voice blunted the edge of Hathin's fear. 'Tell us
what happened, child.'

Hesitantly Hathin told the assembled teeth about Skein's
tests, about the disappearance of Arilou . . . she faltered, and
then told them only of finding Arilou at the water's edge, with
no mention of Whish's presence. As she did so, she felt fingers
brush gently against her hand, a warm living contact that felt
strange in this place of darkness and the dead. She found her
voice again, and recounted everything that had occurred
until she discovered Skein's body.

'What are we going to tell the other Inspector?' asked
Hathin finally.

There was a brief and unpromising silence. 'She does not
know,' came Larsh's voice. 'Hathin, the other Inspector is
gone. Somebody cut the rope.'

'We don't know when.' Lohan's voice, close beside her. He
must have been the one to touch her hand. 'By the time we
noticed, he and the boat were long gone. There was nothing
we could do.' Hathin understood. Even if Prox's boat was not
smashed to pieces by the storm, the current would sweep him
helplessly out to sea, to cook to death beneath the sun.

'So . . .' asked Mother Govrie's mother-of-pearl-studded
smile, 'who was it?' There was a silence, as everybody adjusted
to the brute simplicity of the question. 'Somebody got scared.
They thought our Lady Lost was failing her test, or that the
Inspector suspected something. They panicked, they found

his empty body, they killed him. We haven't found a mark on the body yet, but if there's an urchin-spine puncture or scorpionfish-poison swelling, we *will* find it. Then they cut the rope so that the other towner could not come back and start asking questions. I understand *why* it was done, and whether we like it or not it *is* done, and our only choice is to weather the storm as a village, but *who was it*?'

Another pause.

'You can hardly expect her to own up to it.' Whish's tone was acrid. 'After all, she's not here.'

For a mad moment, Hathin thought Whish was casting aspersions on Arilou. It gave words and a shape to a faint, smoky idea that had lurked in Hathin's mind ever since she had discovered Arilou sitting across from the dead Inspector beneath a purple sky and whirligig of gulls . . . but the next instant she understood Whish's true meaning.

'I wonder,' Mother Govrie remarked coldly, 'if you would be throwing accusations around so freely if Eiven *was* here.'

'She was in the water,' Whish pointed out. 'And nobody knows where she was for about an hour.'

'She was swept away by the current!' Hathin's outrage jolted her out of reticence. 'We all saw!'

'For all we know, she managed to swim to the rocks and come ashore through the Lacery,' answered Whish. 'Then she could have swum back through the shallows and cut the rope.'

Hathin took a deep breath, but the unseen hand was back on her wrist with an urgent, restraining pressure.

'Any of us could have done that,' said Lohan quietly. 'Dozens of us were in the Lacery looking for Eiven. *I* was there. *You* were there.' The silence bristled and Whish did not answer.

'If only it was one dead Inspector,' Mother Govrie remarked bluntly, 'we could do a bit of business with a rock and say he fell. But two . . .' There was no doubt in anyone's mind that Prox was dead, or as good as dead. 'We need to decide whether they left us or never reached us. Their porters are Lace – anybody know their families? Can they be made kindly?'

'Pearlpit Lace,' murmured one of the old women. 'I would trust Pearlpitters to help us spin a yarn nine days in ten, but this is a tenth day if ever there was one.'

'So we do not pull them into our story. Now, the porters will know when the Inspectors set off, and that they had plenty of time to get here before the storm struck – they will not believe that the pair of them were caught in the rain and lost in a mudslide. So both the lord Inspectors got into the boat for the sake of the test, and the current carried them out to sea.'

'What about Milady Page?' asked one of the young men. There was a murmur, for the Lost matriarch of Sweetweather was held in respect and some awe.

'Yes . . . she . . .' Hathin's mind flinched at the thought of Page's quiet threat and appraising golden glare. 'She said she'd be keeping an eye on us.'

'If her thoughts were on us, then she saw all,' Mother Govrie said simply. 'If they were not, she saw nothing. Either way, there is no point in worrying about it.'

And so Mother Govrie went on, hard and shrewd as a general deploying troops. And even though they all knew that a crack in their account would probably mean hangings, their terror waned because the story was in Mother Govrie's firm brown hands, and everybody knew what to say. Next to the wall Father Rackan listened with a slow rhythmic nod. He was the priest the village officially did not have, and nobody expected him to say anything.

'So . . .' one of Lohan's friends finally asked, 'what do we do with the nameless Inspector in the cave?'

Mother Govrie looked over at Father Rackan, and after a hesitation everybody else did the same. That was all the answer that was given. Father Rackan would take care of it.

The black pool accepted them again, one by one. They swam back down the Path of the Gongs. They climbed out, picked up their carefully folded selves and put them on. Nobody gave the swathed body of Skein as much as a glance as they trooped to the cave entrance and peered out at the pelting sky. Most could be seen smoothing their hair back and readying their expressions as if preparing to step out on to a stage, with the sky and rocks as audience.

They emerged, in twos and threes, and the performance began. They talked about how the storm was starting to ease, and that soon it would be safe to venture over and repair the ravages to the huts. A couple of the children were sent to the caves to make sure that the Inspectors had found somewhere dry to shelter, and ran back to report that they had found nobody but Eiven and the youngest children. Then one of the divers 'noticed' that Eiven's boat was still missing, and the whole village expressed consternation as it was suggested that perhaps the Inspectors had been washed away.

'There is nothing we can do about that now,' said Mother

Govrie at last. 'Not until the storm weakens and the paths can be trusted. Then we'll send messages to Sweetweather.'

The King of Fans remembered everything backwards. Now that a death had occurred he could no longer remember why he was wearing his mourning colours. By the next morning the louring cloud had melted away entirely. The thunder of the rain had ceased, leaving only the sound of two dozen pearly-pink waterfalls trickling down the crevices in the cliff-face.

And little was said, for the whole village was playing a prickly waiting game. They must undoubtedly send word to Milady Page, asking her to spy out for a small boat which had been washed clear of the shore. But how long could they leave it, pleading the treacherousness of the slippery clifftop roads? *We must give the Lady Lost a chance to find the Inspector's boat*, they said, and nobody admitted even to themself that each second's delay was spent in the hope that rescue would be impossible, and that Minchard Prox would never get the chance to contradict their story. Most of the villagers were kindly enough, and this truth was too bitter tasting for them to dwell on it.

At last Mother Govrie gave the nod, and two young men were sent with a message for Milady Page. And the whole village returned uneasily to repairing the huts that the storm had ravaged, because when the messengers returned everyone would find out how much Milady Page had seen.

They did not come back until well after noon. When at last they did, there was an uncertain light in their eyes, as if they were deciding whether to run from something or hit it with a rock.

'Milady Page is dead.'

Milady Page, the Lost matriarch who for forty years had sailed about Sweetweather like a portly galleon, had been found face down in her own yard, her goat nibbling at her shawl. No trace of a mark or bruise, just a serene and knowing smile on her face. Never slow to speak her mind throughout her life, she had gone to the land of mysteries without explanation.

7
TEETHING TROUBLE

The village of the Hollow Beasts reared back from the brink of this news. Not knowing which of them had killed Skein had been a fearful mystery to face, but it was homely and comprehensible compared to this. What could it mean?

Sweetweather was in a state of shock and unsure where to turn. How could they call for reinforcements? Milady Page was their message system, their main link to the rest of the island. They might as well have been told that their chunk of coast had been sawn off and pushed out to sea. How could they find the culprit? Milady Page was their scout, their brigand-finder, their roaming eye. Who could take charge and tell everyone what to do? Milady Page was their wise woman, their crisis-handler.

Last night all over the island the tidings had been renewed. The town had gone to bed expecting that next morning Milady Page would deliver them news of the whole of Gullstruck. But now Milady Page was no longer a news-bringer, she was herself a piece of news in insufficient detail.

'The towners kept asking, where is Milord Skein? We need him to read the tidings for us, we need him to tell us if there are murderers running away from the town . . . So we had to tell them what we'd already told Milady Page's household – that Skein and his man were gone in the boat.'

Everyone in the village felt the pang of the lost opportunity. If they had only known of Milady Page's fate, perhaps they could have spoken honestly of the manner of Skein's death. Milady Page had left her body only hours after Skein, and in the same peaceable manner. Perhaps his death had been part of the same strange calamity, or could have been made to look as if it was. But it was too late. They had chosen their story and now they would have to stick to it. Besides that would still have left Prox's disappearance unexplained.

'Then they said, we must put out word and get one of the cities to send us a new Lost, we must tell them that we will give them a house, and a goat from every village in the district. And *we* said, we already have a Lady Lost, remember? You can give her your house and goats if you have a mind. And then . . . they all looked at us as if we'd walked up out of the sea with shells for eyes.'

Hathin walked around with her head full of the image of Arilou in a Doorsy house in Sweetweather, her yard musical with goats. A long queue of people snaked from her door. They wanted her to find missing children and runaway husbands and tell her the price of pearls in Smattermast. Hathin's eye misted and she could not swallow.

The post-storm coolness lasted barely a morning, and then the coast settled into blithe, shimmering heat. It was bright and beautiful and broken and nothing was right. Sweetweather glared like a great summer-maddened dog looking for someone to bite, and everything was hanging, waiting for its teeth to close.

82

The news of Milady Page's death and the disappearance of Skein and Prox were duly placed in the tidings hut, but nobody expected a quick response. Nearly all Lost sent their mind to check the tidings at the very start of the week when they were renewed, and did not visit them again until the following week.

And yet a few days later news did come through the mountain passes from the town of Knotted Tail. It came in the form of Jimboly.

Since the storm, the village of the Hollow Beasts had drawn into itself defensively. So it was that the first they knew of Jimboly's return to the coast was a loud long whistle and a swishing rain-on-a-bonfire noise. And a few minutes later there she was up on the clifftop, still swinging her dry pig's bladder full of peas above her head and whistling between her fingers.

She bounced her way down the rubble-face like a local and stood there gasping and grinning, her lanky limbs and loose clothes painted with the fresh red mud left over from the storm, her pet flickerbird fluttering about her head at the furthest extent of its leash.

'Jimboly!' Mother Govrie tried to sound disapproving. 'One of these days the volcano'll hear you whistling and he'll wake up and snatch you away to nursemaid his children . . .'

'And a very fine nursemaid I'll make. Anyway, I was at a party with the mountain last night and he filled his crater with rum – he won't be awake for days.' Jimboly grinned, and because she was one of the few outsiders who knew how to smile, nobody could be angry at the little blasphemy.

Jimboly's long face was admired by the Lace women, who

 83

always shaved their foreheads to make their own look longer. The angularity of her jaw somehow made her look more mischievous, and black hair with blue lights escaped from under her dark red bandanna. You seldom saw her without a smile. And when she smiled it was almost impossible not to like her.

Her smile was her shop window. Set amid the strong white teeth were teeth of tortoiseshell, coral, turquoise, jade, pearl and even gold. One jade tooth even had a peacock engraved into its surface. Jewel-toothed, but not Lace – you could see that at a glance. Lace placed delicate studs in their teeth, but did not replace the teeth entirely. However, non-Lace were interested in whole teeth to replace those lost through age or accident. Usually Jimboly sold them fixed-up pulled ones, but the richest non-Lace would sometimes buy replacements made of metal or gems. All the teeth in Jimboly's mouth were of this last sort.

Jimboly herself was not Lace, nor did she quite seem to know *what* she was. 'A spoonful of a dozen bloods, most of them curdled,' was the way she usually described herself. Her roaming had given her a knack for languages, and she was the only non-Lace Hathin had ever met who could make a decent stab at speaking Lace, though without the subtleties.

She pulled teeth for free, taking only the tooth as payment, and she drilled Lace teeth and inlaid plaques so swiftly and surely that many Lace preferred her work to their own. Jimboly was everybody's favourite tooth fairy.

She was always valued as a source of news and gossip too, her tales more whimsical and amusing than the dry facts surrendered by the Lost's tidings huts. This time, however, her news was neither.

In the last week, she had travelled from Knotted Tail, through Leaping Water and past the little outposts of High-leap, Lame Cape, Seagrin, Eel's Play, Jumping Rock . . . and everywhere the Lost were dead. They had all drifted away silently in the night, apparently at the same hour as Milady Page, leaving their bodies like snakeskins.

'People are saying it's a plague,' Jimboly informed them. 'Some people are hoping that maybe their minds have all been swept out to sea in the storm and they'll come back. Some people are still propping their lordships and ladyships up on pillows and trying to feed them soup. But they'll stop that when they start to smell in the heat, I guess.' She grinned around her at the villagers' gasps and murmurs.

Jimboly was the first person to visit the village since the ill-fated Inspectors, and so the villagers crowded around her, eager to have word from a friendly source. There was something queer in the air of Sweetweather now, and the Lace were becoming even warier about visiting it.

'And no marks on them?' asked Mother Govrie, her voice as brisk and practical as if she was asking for a recipe. 'No sign of a bite or scratch? No trace of poison?'

'Ooh, you have such a grisly mind, Mother. If I was a child of yours and heard your bedtime stories, I'd be like this all the time.' Jimboly bugged her eyes and pulled her hair straight up as though terrified, then laughed. 'No, apparently, not a scratch. And no sign of strife either; nearly all of them settled down comfortably. They fancy that even Milady Page was only face down in the mud because she fell out of her hammock. She had her brocade shawl under her, you see – the one she always used to flop across her face when she was resting, to keep off the mosquitoes.'

'How *do* you find out all these things, Doctor Jimboly?' asked one young woman.

'Ritterbit brings me the best titbits.' Jimboly answered the question as she always did, and paused to stroke the head of her little pet. 'Don't you, Ritterbit?'

Ritterbit had been riding on her shoulder for the better part of a year, as far as anybody could tell. He was a beautiful black flickerbird, with a splash of gold on his tail that was only visible when it flared. The tiny red leather collar around his neck was linked to Jimboly's coral necklace by a slender chain of bronze links and tiny bells.

'I caught him pecking at my shadow,' Jimboly explained to a little boy who stood watching Ritterbit with fascination. 'He looked pleased with himself, so I knew he already had a thread of my soul inside his little gullet. I caught him in a wicker trap, but then what was I to do with him? Could have wrung his neck, I suppose, but he's such a little beauty, isn't he? I suppose I fell in love. Well, I couldn't let him fly off and unravel me, so the only thing for it was to keep him close so he couldn't start pulling my threads loose.' Hathin thought that this was probably one of Jimboly's jokes, since Ritterbit seemed suspiciously tame, as if petted from the egg, but you never could tell with Jimboly.

'They say that someone who dies from a flickerbird dies unmarked,' remarked Larsh, who had joined the group without anyone noticing. 'Perhaps the Lost—'

'No, no, if a flickerbird unravels you, it takes weeks, even months,' Jimboly cut in. For some reason she was always sharper with Larsh than with anybody else. Perhaps she guessed that if he wished he could carve tooth plaques even finer than hers. 'Months of waning and weakening and weeping. To die in a single night like that, you'd need seventy of Ritterbit's cousins to swoop down and carry off your shadow like a piece of whole cloth. Anyway, the governor doesn't think it's flickerbirds, or the storm, or plague. Minds of men are behind this – that's his thought.'

Jimboly busied herself cleaning her round-headed bow-drill, aware of the attentive ears that ringed her.

'Has he said as much?' asked Eiven.

'Yes, and he's not the only one that thinks so. There's an Ashwalker prowling around. Hoping he'll be called in for a manhunt, from what I hear. Well, the governor has to do something, doesn't he, since one of them's dropped dead in his district? Wouldn't surprise me if he did call in the Ashwalker.'

The Ashwalkers were all descended from the tribe of the Dancing Steam, who hailed from the inland hills around the volcano Crackgem, amid the orchid lakes with their choking smells and eerie colours. Even these days many of the Dancing Steam still wore a token blue-black sash or garment as a sign of their lineage, dyed using the wild indigo that grew in the hills, and fermented with wood ash not from bonfires but from cremation pyres. It was said that every dead spirit thus bound into the Ashwalkers' clothing served them by giving them magical powers.

Needless to say, the Ashwalkers had been delighted when the colonists had originally turned up, bringing entire shiploads of dead people's ashes, all in convenient little pots. The colonists had been considerably less delighted to find blue people raiding their settlements and packeting their ancestors. However, since that time a truce had been struck and the Ashwalkers had earned a grudging respectability as last-resort bounty hunters. If given a licence to chase down a particular felon, the Ashwalker was then allowed to claim the ash from their pyre. This was more than execution. This could mean spending eternity dyed into a bandanna or a sock.

Everybody knew that there was an Ashwalker living alone in one of the wild local valleys, but he was hardly ever seen and most people were thankful for that.

Jimboly quietly ground a workmanlike hole in the front of a ten-year-old's incisor, slipped in a snug little plaque of pink coral and then looked around her.

'Why so silent? All this might be bad news for the Lost . . . the *other* Lost, I mean . . . but it's festival time for you lot, isn't it? You have the only Lost within a day of Sweetweather, probably the only Lost this side of Sorrow . . . maybe *the only Lost on Gullstruck Island*.' Jimboly glittered a grin and took her measure of them. 'So the next time folks in town get fangy at you, you can just look them right in the eye and say, oh, I don't think our Lady Lost will be so keen to find *your* goat when it goes wandering or, hmm, didn't you want to know if a storm front was coming, and don't you need our Lady Lost for that?'

Hathin could see in every face the effect of Jimboly's words. Until now the Hollow Beasts had been caught up in trying to guess which of them had cut Prox loose, and whether Skein's death was linked to that of the other Lost. They had not properly considered how all their lives might change with Arilou as Chief Lost. But now they gingerly let their minds sneak a peek into a foreign world, a Doorsy world. Good food and a house and goats and a front door and people

88

willing to knock on it. Wealth and respect.

As people were starting to chatter in a cautiously hopeful way, Hathin listened, overcome by cold horror. All the Lost had died. Arilou had not died with them. Soon the world would ask why. Hathin could think of only one answer. Underneath she had clung to a shred of hope that somehow, miraculously, Arilou would turn out to be Lost after all. Now that last hope had died, and she was left staring at the village's threadbare myth of their Lady Lost, seeing how easily it could be torn apart by a few good questions.

Even worse, right now Arilou was barely fit for company, let alone fit to take over as Chief Lost. For a few days after the death of Skein, Arilou had kept up the same twitching, restless intentness of manner, until Hathin started to wonder if she was tick-infested. That morning, however, Arilou's face had been crumpled with petulant exhaustion, as if she had spent a sleepless night. For once she deigned to pay some attention to her surroundings, but only to show her annoyance with it. She had spent the morning lunging for fruit, kicking out at bowls of water, striking away helpful hands. How could they let her be seen like that?

Watching from a distance, Hathin saw Jimboly stroll off to barter with Larsh. Their negotiation, never cordial, today seemed almost hostile. As well as her dentistry tools, Jimboly always carried with her assorted oddments for sale, and these sometimes included small birds and animals. Whenever she visited the Hollow Beasts there seemed to be a scrawny pale-necked pigeon, poking its beak disconsolately through the wicker of its cage. People wondered why Larsh bought them, since there could be little eating on them. They always had a skinny look. Hathin, however, had once seen Larsh releasing one on the beach and could only guess that he felt some pity for their imprisonment. She told nobody, for she did not think anybody else would understand.

Jimboly seemed to guess the truth, of course, but that just made her grin and come back with more pigeons.

Ah, and now Jimboly was off to play with the younger children as usual. How did she always manage to become an instant insider?

By the looks of things, Jimboly was leading the children in a throwing game. There was a high rock on the edge of the Lacery with a beautiful smooth hole running right through it, like the eye of a fat needle. The children were standing behind a line Jimboly had drawn in the sand and trying to throw small rocks through the hole. All the while chattering away . . . What was she asking them? Hathin ventured closer in the hope of overhearing, but it was not their words which caused her to break into a run.

She suddenly glimpsed two figures on the far side of the 'needle'. Hathin's own mother was stooping to splash the slopping sea water against Arilou's dusty legs. Both had their back to the needle. As Hathin neared the Lacery she saw a sharp-looking stone flit at last through the hole, on a course for the nape of Arilou's neck. Hathin tugged air into her lungs for a scream . . . and Arilou suddenly threw up her arms, lolled her head forward and sank clumsily to one knee.

She had been hit. No, she had not been hit. The strange motion had dropped her beneath the path of the stone.

And when Mother Govrie rounded the corner to confront the culprits there was shouting, and children scattering, and

Jimboly standing aghast amid dropped pebbles with her hands clapped to her mouth.

It had an odd beauty to it, Hathin decided, both devious and direct. If you want to know if somebody is a Lost, why bother with buried bottles and white ribbons when you can throw a rock at them from behind? Perhaps they don't duck, and that leaves you none the wiser, but if they *do* duck . . . well, you are probably looking at a Lost. Hathin could no longer hope that Arilou really was a Lost, and yet through some freakish chance, she *had* managed to duck.

Hathin ran to her sister's side. Arilou's beautiful mouth was pulled into a rubbery, pained gape. Her knee was grazed and glossy with sea water.

'I won't let her do that again,' whispered Hathin in Arilou's ear. 'I won't let her do anything you don't like, ever again.' The promise was made in a rush of protective anger, but there was also a sting of guilt. Back when she was much younger, something had happened that meant Hathin could never, ever tell anyone how she disliked and distrusted Jimboly, whom everybody else loved.

When Jimboly had first visited the village Hathin had been six years old, and for a time it had seemed that her arrival was the most wonderful thing that had ever happened. Jimboly had played at being a gull-witch, chasing the children among the rocks. Hathin had watched sadly from the sand, her hand curled around the unresponsive hand of Arilou.

Jimboly had shrieked her way up to the pair of them, waving her arms wildly, her hair falling across her face, then had halted panting when Hathin and Arilou failed to flee.

 91

'I'm really sorry . . . we can't play.' Hathin had felt miserably embarrassed. 'It's . . . It's Arilou.'

Jimboly had glanced up and down the beach, and then her mouth had spread in a mischievous multicoloured smile. Before Hathin could react, she had stooped down, wrapped her strong arms around Arilou's waist and lifted her.

'I have your Lady Lost!' she had screeched in her witch voice. 'Come and rescue her if you can!' And off she had run with Arilou draped over one shoulder, closely pursued by Hathin, who had been bewildered, then frightened, then exhilarated as she found herself chasing alongside other wild-eyed, sand-cheeked heroes of her own age. For once, just for once, *she had been in the game* . . .

Afterwards Jimboly had taken all of the children back to her little goat-hide tent. She had shown them ritual wooden dolls with real teeth, and fearsome rows of human and animal fangs along arcs of wire, for those who had lost their own teeth.

'What about you lot?' Jimboly had asked through her grin. 'Anyone here got wobbly teeth?'

There had been several, of course, and Jimboly had rated them like cocks for a fight, while the competitors strove to show her how far they could twist them. It had turned out that her pockets were full of spiced fruits and wooden toys, and before long she had made bargains for all the teeth, if they 'happened' to come loose by morning.

'What about you, Hathin?' Jimboly had asked. 'Anything loose behind your smile? No? Well, what about Arilou?' To Hathin's dismay, Jimboly had prised Arilou's mouth open. Arilou apparently had a wobbly tooth.

'I don't think she cares about her tooth much, so she won't miss it – how would you like a reward for bringing the Lady to me?' In Jimboly's hand there had been a little slab of black rock painted to look like a squatting toad. It would have fit snugly in Hathin's palm, but Hathin had shaken her head.

It was only as the children were leaving that Hathin's attention had been drawn by a large maraca-like object made of stitched leather patches, with a beaded handle. It had been tucked away in a pocket of Jimboly's travelling pack. As the other children scampered off, Hathin had lingered to look at it.

'Sharp eyes.' Jimboly's voice behind her. 'You've spotted my little rattle.'

'What . . . what is it?' Hathin had asked, startled by her own boldness. Jimboly had watched her for a few seconds, eyes a-glitter. Then, apparently reaching a decision, she squatted down and brought her grin close to Hathin's ear.

'In it,' Jimboly had whispered, 'are twenty-nine white teeth, polished inside and out so they're as bright as a governor's china. The owners of the teeth are all dead – they have to be, or the rattle doesn't work.'

'What's it for?' Hathin had felt a burning need to know. 'Well . . . you take it by the handle, and you think hard about somebody . . . and you shake it. And that's all I'll say. Goodbye, little sharp-eyes.'

That night Hathin had not been able to sleep for thinking about the strange rattle. It frightened her, but her mind wouldn't leave it alone, any more than her friends could leave off fiddling with their loose teeth. In the early hours she had decided that she would promise to collect any teeth Arilou lost for Jimboly's next visit – and in exchange ask for the secrets of the rattle.

Hathin had ventured through mists to Jimboly's little tent, eager to find her alone. To her surprise, the door flap had not been tied shut and nobody was resting on the bedding mat. Instead, her eyes had been drawn to the mysterious rattle. No longer tucked away in a pocket, it had lain in full view, nestled up against the wooden pillow.

Hathin had entered. Her mind had seemed full of heat haze as she had stooped and picked up the rattle. She had raised it gingerly and shaken it once. It had given an angry rattle, a bony chitter.

Something had instantly swooped from the door of the tent, and the rattle had been knocked from Hathin's hand.

'Do you know what you've done?' Hathin had found herself staring up at Jimboly, who suddenly seemed to be nine feet tall. 'That's a Death Rattle. Whoever you thought of when you shook the rattle will be making that noise in their throat within the week. They're going to die, do you understand that?'

Hathin tried to speak, but could only manage a little yelp of terror.

'I can try to stop it,' snapped Jimboly, 'but I need a living tooth. One of yours, or one from your sister. Quickly! Go get your sister!'

Hathin had obeyed and sprinted back to her home, even though she suspected that Jimboly had seen her coming and hidden away, deliberately leaving the rattle in sight to lure her in, for the sake of gaining one extra tooth – a Lost tooth, perhaps. Hathin had stifled her sobs so that she wouldn't wake anybody, furtively readied Arilou and brought her back to Jimboly's tent.

Jimboly had looked vexed but craftsmanlike as she had levered open Arilou's mouth, and slipped her tongs inside. A quick tweak, and then Arilou had been making small watery-sounding wails and pushing her tongue into her cheek. Hathin had burst into helpless tears.

'It's all right.' Examining the little tooth in the early light, Jimboly had recovered all her good humour at once, and her smile had opened like a treasure chest. 'Everything's going to be all right now, Hathin. I'll make sure nobody dies.'

Everything was not all right. Hathin had been crying because as her hands tightened around the rattle she had known in her stomach what it was, what it had to be. And in the instant the teeth had rattled within it, her mind had flown unbidden to Arilou.

8
HEAT HAZE

Nothing was real, and he had no arms or legs any more. He floated through a land of fairy-tale gold, where the air was a golden comb, too fine to see, but he could feel it rake through him as he moved. He was cupped in a golden nutshell, and he could not guide where it flew.

No, he was a barren land, and he pitied the little explorers that trekked across his skin, even while he hated them for the way their feet stung him. His throat was a roaring volcano crater a mile deep, and lava boiled just beneath his skin. His eyes were blind with ash.

No. He still had limbs, sprawled over the belly of a boat. He had ears, and became aware that the deep roar of the sea had faded to a hiss. He had eyes, swollen almost to closing, and could make out the dark, blurred shapes of men standing over him.

'Sir? Sir? What happened to you, sir?'

The water from their bottle struck through his innards like a spear made of sky. It choked him and burned him and unglued his tongue.

'Cast adrift,' he managed to say, at last. 'My name . . . My name is Minchard Prox.'

Within twenty-four hours of Jimboly's arrival the village had started to receive a mixed parade of visitors. However, these were not locals coming to pay their respects to Arilou as the new Chief Lost for the district.

The first set of visitors were the Lace porters from Pearl-pit who had arrived with Skein and Prox. They turned up in the early afternoon and seemed eager to be gone again, perhaps unwilling to have it known that they had visited. They looked about them with a bitter, hard curiosity, but asked no questions, did not even leave openings for hints to be dropped. They wanted to take their elephant bird and leave.

The bird had been tethered in one of the smaller caves. Eiven followed Hathin to the cave, and looped a leather cord over the bird's head.

'You'd better check that everything there is as it should be, so we get no complaints,' Eiven told Hathin sharply, nodding towards the pack on the bird's back. Her meaning was clear. *Make sure there's nothing in there to incriminate us.*

Much of the contents were as Hathin had found them when she searched the pack previously. However, this time she noticed a pocket on the side of the pack and drew out a leather-bound book with a brass clasp. When she flipped the clasp and opened it, she found that half the pages were crowded with dense, immaculate handwriting. The rest were blank.

Hathin and Eiven held each other's gaze in mute conference. It was some kind of diary or notebook, but they could tell nothing more. Although they understood the older pictograms, and some of the hybrid signs that had emerged from a mingling of these with colonial letters, this Doorsy script might as well have been written in cloud patterns as far as they were concerned.

'Did Skein enjoy his hospitality here?' asked Eiven at last. 'Did he seem . . . troubled by anything?' *Did he suspect anything?*

'No,' Hathin said slowly, and then remembered his curious determination to float away and look for messages, right in the middle of the test. 'Well, nothing he found here.'

Eiven took the book from Hathin and narrowed her eyes. She flicked back two pages, to where there was one that finished with a banner of unwritten space, as if an entry or account had ended. Then she tore out the two written pages that followed it.

'Well, now we've definitely put his mind at rest,' she said, her smile grim. She pushed the torn pages into Hathin's hands and set about carefully picking away the frayed edges until one could not tell that anything had been ripped out.

Hathin watched with her heart in her mouth, marvelling at the way in which Eiven could make a swift decision and commit herself to it. Hathin herself would have tried to hide the whole thing, or more likely stood with the book in her hands in a paralysis of terrified indecision, and probably been discovered with it. Eiven was right as usual. If the book always rode in the pack pocket, it would be missed if it was not there.

The elephant bird's talons scored the sand testily as they

led it back to the porters, the torn pages tucked away in the swathes of Hathin's belt.

The porter who had given her hints about the tests seemed to recognize her.

'Thank you, little sister.' His smile became pensive. He glanced away from Hathin down to where a gaggle of the younger boys were splashing and diving for pebbles, their heads dark beads afloat on the rolling water.

'You have a lot of children here,' he said at last very quietly, and Hathin sensed that he was no longer talking to her even before he looked up at Mother Govrie.

'It's a good place to rear them,' Mother Govrie responded, with a slight questioning edge to her voice. She had picked up on something in his tone. 'Plenty of reefs in the shallows where they can learn to dive, and the coral wall around the cove to keep the sharks out.'

'There's beaches just as good further up the coast. It's not healthy here for children. Did you know that a little girl died in Sweetweather, the same night as Milady Page? She was wander-witted and her parents thought she was Lost.' He gave Mother Govrie a long, steady look, then stretched his legs and stood. 'You're living in the lap of a volcano, Mother. We can taste it in the air. So we're getting out, back to Pearl-pit, before the air gets too difficult to breathe.'

And get out they did, without further ado.

The next caller dropped in and then out again in the predawn, before even the first of the divers had left their huts. On the beach they found the only evidence of his visit – the imprint of a man's bare foot, stained with blue around the heel. The advancing waves soon licked away this print as they had its fellows, but not before half the village had seen it.

Until she saw the indigo-tinted footprint Hathin had not quite believed that the Ashwalker was on the prowl. Now the early daylight turned chill against her skin.

Hathin had only seen the local Ashwalker once, long ago. She had got lost and had found herself in a dimple of a valley matted with briars high as her eyebrows and hazy with the thrum of bees. Her nose had filled with a strange reek, and at last she had glimpsed ahead a lean-to shack with small, dead running birds hanging along the fringe of its palm roof. Beyond it were four great barrels, streaked with sky-coloured dribbles, and standing in one of them a blue man. He had been stamping and churning, foam flecking his bare chest, the whites of his eyes startling against the dark streaks that painted his face. And she had run and run and torn her arms and blouse to pieces against thorns, for fear that the Ashwalker would chase after her, leaping the creepers on his long blue legs.

Ashwalkers were called in to hunt only the most fearsome murderers, for punishment at their hands condemned a criminal in the next life as well as this. This Ashwalker could not hunt criminals without a licence and, whatever Jimboly said, the governor was hardly likely to have given him one. It made no sense to call in an Ashwalker to discover the truth. Such men were hunters, not detectives.

And yet, despite all this, it seemed that the Ashwalker really had left his pungent shack, and for some reason his steps had led him to the cove of the Hollow Beasts.

*

100

The third visit to the Hollow Beasts occurred a couple of days later. It was an official envoy from Sweetweather. He made it known that the Lady Arilou was invited to attend upon the governor that afternoon, to discuss the matter of instating her as Milady Page's replacement.

Many villagers leaped and shrilled with excited laughter, then stood and stared at the prospect, appalled, then giggled helplessly again. It was awful. It was wonderful. They had no choice but to accept. The slightest hesitation, and rumours might start to spread that Arilou had not perished with the other Lost because she was *not* Lost. They would say that the villagers had killed Skein because Arilou had failed the test. And . . . ah, then there was the house to think of, the goats . . .

There was one source of relief, anyway. The governor might think that all the Lost had been murdered, but if he wanted Arilou to become Sweetweather's Lady Lost, surely he did not suspect *them* of anything.

The young men retrieved green and supple trees from the uplands and lashed their slim trunks together with bark strips to make Arilou a litter in which to sit. They spread it with embroidered cloths and crushed herbs against the raw wood to scent it. Arilou remained fractious and uncooperative. She still seemed hazily awake to her surroundings, as she had been the preceding days, but her motions were if anything clumsier and more fretful than usual. She lurched and struggled as a long white ceremonial tunic embroidered in yellow was pulled over her head, and her long hands batted at the necklaces of pink and pale gold coral as they were trailed around her neck.

There was no doubt or discussion about who would form Arilou's delegation. Mother Govrie shaved anew the scalp above her daughters' foreheads, and they all beat the dust out of their stiff skirts and embroidered blouses. Whish could be seen scraping her children's teeth clean with a little split stick, so their plaques would be gleaming for the visit, her own lips grimacing and wincing in sympathy.

Arilou was hauled up the cliff in the pulley-chair, Hathin clinging to her all the while to stop her lolling out of her seat. At the top Arilou was arranged carefully in her litter, and they set off down the cliff path to Sweetweather, keeping their voices low out of respect for the volcano.

The only thing that saved Hathin from all-consuming terror was the scale of the situation. When she had been faced with the task of fooling a single Inspector she had felt panic, but now that she had to speak in Arilou's voice in front of the governor and his entire town, all she felt was a blank sense of falling. *Take as many deep breaths as you can*, she told herself. *It's like diving. It'll be fine once you're in.*

It was as they were entering Sweetweather that Hathin decided the Pearlpit porters were right; there was a taste of volcano in the air.

She noticed it when they encountered the sentries at the town's edge. These were young men who always made a point of singling out Eiven when she came to sell pearls or shells, asking her about her business in town in a way that was half challenge and half overbearing flirtation. Eiven, never easily overborne, gave as good as she got, and Hathin had always suspected that she rather enjoyed the sparring.

But today they showed no sign of recognizing her. Instead they were formally polite in a way that ran cold water down Hathin's spine.

The streets of Sweetweather seemed uncommonly quiet. None of the town's children were playing on the street.

'I haven't seen those for a while,' Mother Govrie said under her breath.

Following her mother's gaze Hathin realized that over many of the doorways were hanging squares of cloth, each daubed or dyed yellow. 'They look a bit like the green cloths people hang to ward against demons,' she murmured in her mother's ear.

'They're wards against demons of a sort,' Mother Govrie muttered, jutting her swollen lower lip and narrowing her eyes, and Hathin knew from her tone that these cloths were meant as protection against the Lace. 'It happens from time to time. It does little harm and it always passes. Remember why our village has the name "Hollow Beasts".'

According to local Lace folklore, the village had once found itself in danger of attack while all its menfolk were absent. The Gripping Bird himself had decided to defend the village, but since he had no gift in arms, instead had woven dozens of jaguars and other fearsome beasts from grass and placed them on the headlands. Daunted by the alarming silhouettes, the soldiers had hung back for a week, giving the women, children and old people left in the village long enough to dig their way into the caves using eggshell spades that the Gripping Bird had given them. One of these tunnels was said to have become the Path of the Gongs. The enemy had eventually discovered the empty cove, and left in perplexity.

'The towners have always kept their friendship on a string,' Mother Govrie continued quietly, 'dropping it into the hands of the Lace just so that they can tug it out again. So let them have their silly fears – it's the better for us. It's all grass jaguars, Hathin – that's the only thing that keeps us safe from them.'

In the heart of the town the governor's contingent was waiting, a delegation of twenty or so with many of the town's stronger young men at the back. Their faces were smileless, and to Hathin they looked like battle masks. Then, giddy under the heat, there was a swimming moment when she felt she knew how she and her fellow Lace must look. *The towners wear their thunderfaces like their black scarves as a sign of mourning*, she thought, *and then we walk in smiling . . .*

And yet even as she thought it she could feel her own smile spreading and tightening with the tension.

The Lace came to a halt, barely five yards from their hosts. A white-haired man with a wobble to his chin walked forward and Hathin realized that it was the governor.

'Lady Lost,' he said.

And the panic that had shackled Hathin suddenly broke away. She reached out and slid her hand under one of Arilou's long hands, palm to palm, and gently raised it. Another supporting hand under Arilou's elbow . . . and Arilou was flowing upwards to stand in the litter. As if compelled by a single thought, the two young men who flanked the litter stooped and placed hands ready for Arilou's hesitant steps.

And the Lace's Lady Lost stepped forward on to air that became hands, and like a thing of foam drifted down to earth, the train of her robe slithering and tumbling from the lip of the litter to pool behind her.

Arilou's free arm floated up, and she extended it towards the governor and produced a rough, undulating squawk from the depths of her throat.

Hathin heard her own voice speaking even before she had quite decided what to say.

'We greet you, governor of Sweetweather,' she declared in her clear, cold Arilou voice. Part of her mind was almost calm. Another part was terrified that Arilou would do something else peculiar that she would have to work into the conversation.

'Lady Lost.' The governor spoke again. 'I am obliged to you for accepting our invitation.' So that was how Doorsy should sound, polished like a conch's innards. 'Our town has been robbed of its Lost, and this is an intolerable situation. After conferring with my advisors I decided that the best – the only – solution was to invite you here.'

The governor reached into his pocket and pulled out a folded square of paper. For a moment it looked so like the pages Eiven had torn out of the notebook that Hathin almost reached guiltily for her own belt pocket where they were hidden. The governor's paper, however, unfolded into a single sheet.

'This was found in Inspector Skein's locked room at the inn. It was pinned to the headboard of his bed.'

The governor perched an amber-lens monocle in one eye socket and started to read:

105

Sightlord Fain,

I will be in the village of the Hollow Beasts for another day, testing the child Arilou, and if the storm breaks and the paths become impassable I may be forced to sojourn there longer.

I have seen enough while travelling down the Coast of the Lace to convince me that our worst fears are justified – indeed, the problem is far more severe than we guessed. Sooner or later I shall have to reveal my findings to D. If we do not act quickly, yet more deaths and disappearances will occur. I must continue my investigations, for the sake of Gullstruck.

If you are right, then we are both in considerable peril – after your meeting we will better understand the hazards we face. As soon as it is over, leave a message for me in the Smattermast tidings hut. I shall look for word from you every two hours.

Raglan Skein

The name of Fain meant nothing to Hathin, but she had heard the title 'Sightlord' before. The Sightlords were the leaders of the Council of the Lost, and all of them were themselves powerful Lost.

'Evidently,' the governor went on, 'Inspector Skein and this Sightlord Fain had arranged to leave each other notes at particular locations so that they could communicate long distance. Inspector Skein was expecting urgent news from the Sightlord, news of an island-wide threat. Lady Lost, you must see how important it is that we try to learn at the first opportunity what Fain discovered at this meeting.'

He paused, and Hathin sensed that an answer was

expected. But Arilou had fallen into a serene silence, giving Hathin nothing to 'translate'.

'Our Lady Lost must return to the village,' Mother Govrie said after an awkward pause, 'to think on what you have said.' She then had understood at least some of the conversation. Hathin was painfully aware that the other Lace were having trouble following the smooth, swift syllables of the governor's Doorsy.

'I have expressed myself with imperfect clarity,' the governor cut in quietly but firmly. 'We hope and intend that your Lady Lost should take over the duties of Milady Page immediately and read the tidings huts tonight. She will want to refresh herself, of course, and so the residence of Milady Page has been made ready for her to take possession of it. Our gathering here is the Lady's official inauguration.'

A bead of sweat trailed down the back of Hathin's neck, burning like quicksilver. Her eyes darted from face to face. One young couple were dressed in deep mourning, the woman's hair, temple and chin bound in the bandage-like Cavalcaste mourning headdress. The Pearlpit porters had said that a little girl in the town had died. Could these be her parents, staring at Arilou with acrid, black hostility? And there were the shopkeepers, arms locked across their chests like dropped door-bars. And Jimboly was here too, her face set and smileless, eyes fiercely inquisitive, Ritterbit flitting from one person's shoulder to another.

Something is in danger of happening. And, if I say no, it will happen here, now. If I say yes, then there's a few hours for us to think of something . . .

Arilou stepped forward unsteadily and put out a hand to close on the governor's middle knuckle. Perhaps she had been attracted by his ring.

'I thank you for the honour you do me,' Hathin whispered, but it was hardly necessary. On some incalculable whim Arilou already seemed to have accepted.

Only Hathin was permitted to stay in town with Arilou, perhaps because her presence was so negligible. Milady Page's house smelt of the spices that had been used to sweeten the air and the resin burned to clear the premises of the taint of death.

Lemon and cane-sugar juice in a slim glass decanter. Peaches. Stone flags with pictures on them. A clock with a hollow, pacing tick.

Outside, the hanging heat, the black stares of the waiting townspeople. Hathin sensed their hostility and suspicion, but she did not fully understand it. Arilou's mysterious survival must have set them all muttering. And yet they had invited her to Sweetweather.

For that matter, what did Hathin herself suspect? She no longer knew. Skein's letter had thrown her mind into confusion again.

It was obvious the governor was convinced that the Lost had been murdered, and she could see why. *I must continue my investigations, for the sake of Gullstruck*, Skein had written. *Deaths . . . disappearances . . . we are both in considerable peril.* Skein had been investigating something on the Coast of the Lace and had stumbled upon a dangerous secret, one that he had not dared commit to paper even in a locked room. Could it be that he had discovered the threat that

108

was about to wipe out the Lost?

And if he had been killed by this great menace he described as threatening the whole island – then surely it had nothing to do with Arilou or the Hollow Beasts? But that made no sense. If none of the Hollow Beasts had killed him, then who had? Not to mention that the mooring rope of Prox's boat was unlikely to have cut itself. But if one of the Hollow Beasts *had* killed Skein and loosed Prox's moorings, then surely it could only have been to protect Arilou's secret, with no connection to this greater mystery.

If a Hollow Beast was responsible, who had it been? Hathin had a horrible feeling that Whish was right. The other villagers might have hesitated, but Hathin really *could* picture Eiven jabbing the Inspector with an urchin spine and then cutting the rope as deftly and dauntlessly as she had plucked the frayed paper pieces from Skein's journal.

Nobody can prove anything, she told herself. *Whatever people here might suspect, there's nobody to give evidence against any of us* . . . Hathin halted mid-thought, sick at the realization that like the rest of the village she had been drawing comfort from the belief that Minchard Prox would never talk to anyone.

'I'm sorry, Mr Prox,' whispered Hathin into her hands as she imagined Prox's boat overturned by the storm and his drowned body rolling along the sea floor, without the cremation that would give his soul peace. 'I'm sorry, I'm sorry . . .'

*

Even while Hathin entertained these unquiet thoughts, in a little room leagues away words were spilling from the sunburnt mouth of a half-delirious man. Not far from his bedside, a quill scratched swiftly and neatly across the page, catching each and every word.

9
NO MORE NAMES

While the little clock gnawed away the hours, Hathin knotted kindling from the fire into a crude doll and with trembling fingers played the doll game over and over, just to give herself something to do.

At least the Doorsy house did seem to have cured Arilou's bad mood. From time to time her hand swung across to bat at the decanter, her way of asking for more lemon juice. After she had drunk, she would slump back droop-lidded and contented, with her tongue-tip peeping out between her lips.

When at last there was a rap at the door, Hathin's heart seemed to leap up and punch her in the throat. She fumbled the door open and found Lohan standing there.

'I told them that the Lady Lost needed a spare attendant so that she could send for things,' he explained as he sidled into the room. Hathin felt almost sick with gratitude. 'So . . . ?' He spread his hands in a tiny shrug. *Is there a plan?*

'Perhaps . . .' Hathin said in a small voice, 'perhaps I will have to explain that Lady Arilou, being so new to this . . . isn't able to find her way to the other tidings huts to read any of the news. But if I have to tell the towners that, they . . . they won't be happy.'

'It'll do,' answered Lohan. 'Just until things calm down. And Lady Arilou –' he gave a token nod in her direction – 'would do well to remember that she is now the Lady Lost for the district, and if they don't like what she says, they can go skin fish. If she scares them a bit, maybe they'll back off.'

And then Lohan would not let Hathin talk about the tidings huts any more. Instead he told fishing stories, many of them very funny, while the row of peach stones between them grew in length.

The new Lady Lost's escort arrived at the door just as the first stars were freckling the sky. There was no more time, and the three Lace stepped out and walked the route up towards the tidings hut, flanked by a small crowd of towners.

At the clifftop was a stone hut with a domed palm thatch. Usually it presented a solitary silhouette against the sky, but tonight it was surrounded by a seethe of people. An unusually large number of people, even for a news night.

Over the years Hathin had seen a little of the dance-speech of bees. This night it seemed as if the hanging lanterns around the shelter had done the same; as they swung agitated by the wind, 'Honey this way,' some of them seemed to say, but most were dancing 'Trouble, trouble, time to swarm . . .' The same bee fear was in the crowd's movement, the waves of whisper.

At last Arilou's white flax gown attracted attention and the crowd moved forward. Hathin noticed the way they touched at her sleeve, reverent yet distasteful, eager but wary, their old dependence on the Lost warring with their distrust of the Lace.

'Lady Arilou, find us the murderers of Milady Page, search the hills for brigands . . .'

112

'Lady Arilou, tell us if eagles carried away the Lost Inspectors . . .'

'Lady Arilou, you must see if any other Lost are alive . . .'

'Who is it?' A call from inside the shelter.

'A young Lady Lost from one of the villages, Milady Lampwarden,' came a cry from the crowd.

Each hut was inhabited by a warden who was responsible for renewing the posters and keeping lanterns alight in the hut so that any wandering Lost could always read the messages. The lampwarden would also read aloud all of the messages in a cycle, for there were few Lost who read both Doorsy script and all the different styles of pictogram.

'There's a new young Lost? Why in the name of all that's sweet did nobody tell me? Well then, let her come through!'

The crowd parted, and Hathin led the unresisting Arilou up the steps into the shelter, past the hunched figure of the elderly lampwarden who stood in the doorway. The old warden remained motionless, staring moodily out into the darkness. She seemed to be listening for something. All around her hung wooden tablets, deerskin squares carved with crude messages, pieces of painted bark. Amid the Doorsy messages there were some carved in the old, swollen pictograms, dream-like in their strangeness – birds with bunches of grapes for heads, serpents twisting around broken moons.

Here was all the latest news of the town and surrounding villages and, most important of all, the news of the death of Milady Page and the disappearance of the Lost Inspectors. And in a moment everybody would expect Arilou to cast her mind out to all the other tidings huts and return with news from Smattermast and the rest of Gullstruck . . .

113

'Our Lady Lost is very tired . . .' Hathin was in no hurry to return to the crowds.

'Then let her rest lest she sicken,' whispered the old woman. 'I think a plague has stricken the Lost, just as they say. This is the night when the mind of every Lost on the island should be passing through this hut. But none of them have visited.'

'Doctor Warden . . . how can you tell?'

'I can tell,' the old woman said simply. 'Everyone speaks of feeling a gaze on the back of the neck. Why should it matter if the gazing eyes are many miles away? I have taught myself to feel their gaze upon me. None of them have been here tonight.'

Hathin stared at her. She had never heard of anyone who could sense the Lost's presence and wondered if perhaps the old woman's life alone on the clifftop had taken its toll on her wits. And yet . . . perhaps this woman could be an unexpected ally. Perhaps together they could convince everyone that Arilou was ill, needed more rest, more time . . .

'A pair of eyes are now closed,' whispered the old woman, returning to her seat. 'Eyes like ice . . . silver, and star-staring.' She ran her fingertips over her arms gently, as if chasing a sensation across her skin. 'I looked into them once,' she murmured, and Hathin realized that there were tears in the woman's own pale eyes. 'Once, when I was very young. He was a Lost, and although he did not seem to look at me, I felt his gaze shiver over me like an eel. And for the rest of the day I felt him watching me.'

Hathin tried to imagine the old woman lithe and young, but it was too late to see the truth behind the jowls and pot belly.

114

'I had to travel back to our village in the mist, and he must have lost track of me on the way. For months, every time I stood in a chill wind or breasted a wave I felt the cold of it and thought of him, and believed for a moment that he had found me again. But he had not.'

'Did he . . . did he ever find you again?' Hathin was fascinated, despite her own worry.

'Yes – I made sure that he did, in the only way I could. I spurned all suitors and came to work as warden. On the first day, as I stood with my taper lighting one of my lanterns, I felt it again, like being stroked by feathers of cold. Gently stroked. I learned to feel other glances, but they were always quick, like a pat on the cheek. His was the only one that lingered.'

You gave your life for a look, thought Hathin, unable to comprehend.

'This is the first time he has missed his appointment,' the warden said, chafing her hands together, the way Hathin had seen old women do at funerals. 'He would not if his eyes could still open. They are closed, they are closed forever.'

There was a sudden breeze from the doorway. One of the lanterns went out, releasing a wisp of smoke. As Hathin watched, the old woman walked from lantern to lantern, holding a hand up to each one in turn until she reached the dead one. Only as she watched her fumbling with her taper did Hathin understand the meaning of the warden's slow, feeling motions. She was blind.

Hathin hurried to help, guiding the taper. The warden smiled, and then her fingertips took a friendly hold of Hathin's hand. The wrinkled fingers felt over Hathin's twisted grass rings, then the shell jewellery on her wrists. The shadow crevasses in the woman's face shifted and started to tremble. Abruptly she thrust away Hathin's hand.

'Get away from me! Filthy little Lace!' Her blind eyes were like marble.

'Hathin . . .' Lohan was in the doorway, his face pinched with urgency. Still shattered by the old woman's sea change, Hathin became aware that there was now a seethe of disquiet sounding from the crowd outside. 'You have to talk to them. Leaving it any longer won't make things better.'

Shakily, Hathin led Arilou out of the hut. The noise of the crowd swiftly died, so that everyone could hear Arilou's faint, molten incantations.

'People of Sweetweather,' declared Hathin, hearing a crack in her voice, 'I have sent my mind abroad, and I am troubled. My spirit is weary and I could not see the lanterns of the tidings huts. Perhaps they are not yet lit . . .'

A score or so of muted conversations began, alarmed, indignant, distrustful.

'Why did you let a Lace in here?' The old lampwarden's voice suddenly seared through the night. 'Why did you not tell me that a shell-fanged Lace was in my hut? Putting her filthy hands on my lanterns.'

Buzz, buzz. Bee suspicion, bee rage.

'What were you doing to the lanterns?' somebody called out.

'What did you people do to the lanterns in the other huts?' came another cry.

'Why don't you want us to know what's happening on the rest of the island?'

'Oh, come *on*, children! It's *obvious* why they don't want us to know.' Hathin would have recognized the raucous, humorous tone anywhere, even with the new bite to it. Somewhere amid the feverish crowd Jimboly was standing with her grin a-glitter, her bird dancing about her like an unquiet thought. 'Think! Every hut dark except this one? Every Lost dead except the Lost of the Lace? What do you *think* they've been doing? What do you *think* Inspector Skein's letter meant? You heard it! He *knew* he was going to die, *that the Lace were going to kill him.* Him and every other Lost on the island! He must have writ it down – *that's why they tore those pages out of his journal*!'

Jimboly knew. How could she know?

'Here!' Jimboly's angular figure was just visible beyond the crowd, waving a piece of parchment over her head. 'Here's all the proof you need! Letter from the bedside of Mr Minchard Prox, washed ashore up the coast at Sapphire Hale! He says he was set adrift in that boat on purpose, his rope cut! And he says Skein wasn't ever in that boat! So they lied! What other lies have they been telling?'

Could it be true? Could Minchard Prox really be alive? But if he was, how had his letter found its way into Jimboly's hand, instead of the pocket of the governor?

Buzz, buzz, roar. Hathin felt the hatred like a blast of heat.

'I am your Lady Lost!' she shouted out against the tidal wave that seemed to be arcing over her. 'I am your Lady Lost, and I demand . . .'

Arilou suddenly wailed and lurched backwards. Hathin turned to look at her, saw her licking at a cut lip and realized that somebody had thrown something at her. Arilou's voice rose from a groan to a harsh, full-lunged scream and she began to flail out with her arms, jarring the blade of her hand into the face of a man who had stepped forward to grab her robe.

'My eye!' He promptly doubled up and crouched on the floor. 'She's cursed my eye!'

Desperately Hathin tried to drag clutching hands away from Arilou. The young woman in the mourning headdress lunged out of the darkness and seized Arilou by the shoulders.

'Give me back my little girl's soul!' she screamed. 'You took it and drank it down for its power – I can see her staring out of your eyes!'

These were no longer people. A new expression knobbed and buckled the crowd's features until their faces looked like fists. The tide of hands dragged Hathin and Arilou this way, that way.

'Leave me alone!' Hathin screamed as she felt somebody take a fistful of her hair. 'I am your Lady Lost! You do not know what I can do – if you do not unhand us, I will . . .'

And as if in answer to a cue, there were a couple of screams and the crowd parted to show a glare of gold. Flames were licking around the doorposts of the tidings hut.

More screams, and people rushing forward to kick dirt against the flames or slap at them with aprons or hands. Hathin felt the painful grip on her released as the crowd surged towards the hut, and she seized Arilou's spasming arm. In a moment or two the crowd would remember the Lady Lost and notice her attendant dragging her desperately away along the dark path . . .

Suddenly Lohan was at her side, commandeering Arilou's other arm and pulling the older girl into a faster pace. His eternal smile still hung about his face, but his eyes had frightened sparks in them.

'Let's take the Ashlands,' whispered Hathin. He nodded mutely, and they left the path and slipped across the undulating cemetery.

'Lohan,' Hathin whispered after they had been walking in silence for some time, 'was it you who set fire to the hut?'

'I had to distract them. They looked set to tear you to pieces. Any injuries?'

'Somebody threw something that hit her in the mouth. She was bleeding, but not badly. I don't think she's lost any teeth.'

'I was asking about you, actually.'

Hathin shook her head numbly. 'I can't go back,' she said in a tiny voice.

'Nobody's asking you to go back. The towners attacked their Lady Lost, so they don't get a Lady Lost, and let's see how they like it.'

'No . . . I mean, I can't go back to the village. I've . . . I've failed.'

'You didn't fail,' Lohan muttered grimly. 'Somebody else succeeded, that's all. I got the chance to run around town listening to people before I came to find you. I had a good idea that someone was playing some kind of rumour game. Oh, the towners always look to us when they need someone to blame, but it's *her* putting a point on their spear, it's *her* giving them direction.

'You know why the Ashwalker's been roaming around? Because someone went and told him that the Lost deaths were murders and that all the townspeople wanted to see him given a licence. And then, because he'd been seen around, the towners got it into their heads that the Lost *were* murdered, and they've been turning up daily at the governor's door to ask why the Ashwalker hasn't yet been hired. Then the way Inspector Skein's letter has been repeated and misquoted . . . and somehow she got hold of his journal . . . but for the life of me I still can't work out *why* she's been stirring things up.'

'It doesn't really matter,' Hathin said limply, barely caring what he was talking about. Her beaten, battered brain could hardly make sense of the wildfire accusations back at the tidings hut. But she understood one thing: Arilou had been stoned out of Sweetweather. The townspeople had rejected her. The long game had been lost, and nothing now stood between the Hollow Beasts and destitution. 'It's over. All I had to do was one thing, and I couldn't do it, and now I can't see how it can be mended. There's no reason for me any more, and I've let the whole village down.'

They had reached the top of the cliff above the village, where once the Gripping Bird had stationed his jaguars of grass.

Lohan halted, biting his lip. 'Those old women won't give you any trouble,' he said at last. 'They'd better not. You've got more guts than all of them put together. You've done more than any of them would dare to protect the village – I *know* what you've done, Hathin. When Skein was found I worked out why you happened to be down by the water's edge, near those rocks where my mother took Arilou. It's the best place on the beach for urchin quills.'

'What?' Hathin could not manage more than a single quavering note.

'I haven't told anyone,' Lohan said gently, 'and I won't.

I've been helping to keep your secret from the start. When you were herded off home with Arilou and couldn't act for yourself, who do you think it was that cut the rope on the other Inspector's boat?'

'You . . .' Hathin stared at him. 'You loosed the . . . You think I killed Inspector Skein?'

Now it was Lohan's turn to stare, and Hathin saw his face start to mirror her look of horror. Above them the King of Fans trailed fans of mourning black, at their feet the orchids rocked with silent laughter and beside them gaped a hissing gulf of darkness. There was no comfort for either of them.

'We have to go down to the village,' Lohan said at last, his voice strained and rapid.

'I can't,' whispered Hathin numbly. 'I just . . . can't.' 'All right – you stay here with your lady sister.' Lohan gave a long sigh, but Hathin was staring at his feet and could not judge why. 'I'll go down and tell everybody what happened, and then I'll come back and tell you what they say. Will you be all right up here?'

Hathin nodded but could not look at him.

Lohan said nothing more. He clambered to the cliff-scramble path and dropped himself over the edge. At the very last moment he glanced over his shoulder and Hathin was struck by the hurt, aghast look that had etched itself on to his face. Stung by sympathy she gave a wider smile and a little wave, but by then he had dropped below the lip of the cliff and he did not see it.

Hathin sank to her knees beside the seated, trance-like Arilou and peered down at the beach, towards the village that no longer felt like hers. Her future seemed utterly unfaceable.

121

If the townspeople had decided that Arilou was part of the conspiracy that had killed the Lost, how could the Hollow Beasts take her back? Surely they must drive her away for the safety of the village? And as for Hathin . . . perhaps Lohan was not the only person who thought she had killed Inspector Skein. Perhaps everyone thought that.

Lohan was taking an eternity. Of course, the village must have told him not to go back up the cliff. Hathin was no longer useful and neither was Arilou. They would be left there on the clifftop until they starved or took the hint and vanished into the darkness.

But no – there he was, down on the beach! Even if the village hated Hathin now, they did not want her to starve waiting for a message; they would at least let Lohan return to talk to her.

Lohan was carrying a lantern, perhaps so that he could guide Arilou's steps back down to the village. The lantern was half cloaked and only a sliver of light emerged. He was running along the beach at a stoop, as though fighting a strong wind. Then he straightened, and Hathin realized that the figure was too tall and strongly built to be Lohan. The next moment the man swung back his arm and flung the lantern which smashed against the side of the nearest hut.

Hathin could only stare like a dreamer as the flames flung loving, golden arms around the summer-roasted palm thatch. From the rocks all around other lanterns rose like fireflies and hurled themselves against the stilted huts. And in the new flood of light, the black rock-line grew heads and arms and legs and suddenly there were dozens of people on the beach, hacking holes in the sides of the

122

burning huts with hoes and scythes.

An animal-sounding cry, and somebody burst out through one of the holes. White hair spiralled upwards from its head like smoke, and the frail shoulders were winged with fire. A hoe swung and the apparition fell. The crowd closed, and all Hathin could see was a forest of hoes and sticks being raised and swung down, sparks of red light occasionally gleaming on the metal.

'Father Rackan,' croaked Hathin. She could barely hear her own voice. 'Father Rackan.' She balled her hands into her eyes, trying to push out the image, but the darkness of her closed lids was full of it. *Oh no, oh no . . . Father Rackan . . .*

The crowd was staring down now, wavering. They were slowly lowering their weapons, realizing what they had done. In a moment they would run for it, try to escape their crime . . .

An eerie, high-pitched whistle echoed through the cove. There was a figure standing apart from the crowd, the fire-light throwing her shadow into monstrous proportions across the sand, her flickerbird flitting about her head like a familiar. She shouted some words that Hathin could not hear, took out a bottle, swigged from it and then hurled it at the nearest hut. Instantly the flagging flames found new life, and with thin, childish screams short figures jumped down from the door of the hut and fled.

Jimboly flung back her head and laughed her inimitable laugh, which rose up into a screech as she chased after the fleeing children with a dozen men at her heels. It was her gull-witch-game screech, but now her erstwhile playmates were screaming and running in earnest.

123

Hathin could only watch, and watch, and press her fists against her open mouth until it hurt.

More Lace had realized what was happening now, and were charging from their huts, some flinging nets over their waiting adversaries in the hope of slowing their attack, some parents bursting forth with skinning knives to cover their children's flight.

Oh no, oh no, oh please no . . . Paralysed, horrified, Hathin saw little knots of Lace scatter as they were caught in lantern-light, heard the rattle as others tried vainly to scuffle their way up the cliff scramble-path. *The caves, the caves, oh please run to the caves* . . .

A couple of the Lace women ran naked down the beach and dived so cleanly into the water that it hardly offered protest. Barely a moment later there was a red-tinged flash from the nearby rocks, and a loud bang echoed around the cove. The black skin of the water spat white as something struck it. There were men, Hathin realized, standing up on high rocks aiming long-barrelled guns down towards the water.

One of the women had looked a lot like Eiven.

'Eiven!' Hathin was on her feet, but her cry was lost as the ragged echo of a second gunshot rebounded through the cove. As the bullet kicked another flash of foam, Hathin suddenly guessed that the two women had been deliberately leading attention away from the cave of the Scorpion's Tale, and the fugitives who would be crowding through it even now.

. . . *please reach the caves, please, holy ancestors, let the rest all reach the caves* . . .

And Hathin wanted to scream it aloud, even if it meant she was shot by the long-barrelled guns and fell into the fire-stricken madness below, for she almost felt that by doing so she could force the others to run faster, to *get to the caves*. But before she could do so she realized that she could hear someone calling out in Nundestruth.

'Caves!' It was Jimboly, raven-voiced and exultant. 'I know where runoff! Caves behind crack like fishhook!'

And as the beach blackened with a seethe of forms running cliffward Hathin could hear another voice screaming in Lace over and over again.

'Run!' came the scream. 'Run! Run!' It was Lohan's voice, and as silence scythed suddenly through his words, Hathin knew that they were meant for her.

Hardly able to see or think, she grabbed Arilou's hand and ran.

10
AMID THE ASHES

Arilou stumbled again and again, but Hathin dragged her to her feet mercilessly, ignoring her faint pained mewls and keeping an arm tight around her waist to support her weight.

As Hathin thrashed through brambles and cobweb hammocks she was painting over the images she had seen on the beach, trying to imagine escapes, feints. Father Rackan had simply fallen, stunned by the blows. The musket on the heights had missed Eiven. The children had lost Jimboly amid the rocks and had been herded back to the caves by Mother Govrie, Mother Govrie who thought of everything. Lohan had stopped screaming because he had been spotted, nothing more. And there was no way Jimboly could know about the Path of the Gongs . . .

Right now the whole village would be escaping down the water tunnel, leaving their pursuers to stare perplexed at the unspeaking blackness of the pool. Soon the villagers would haul themselves dripping into the cavern of the teeth, and wait there to rendezvous with stragglers and those who had fled by other routes. If Hathin could only drag Arilou all the way to the Sweetweather shaft, she could enter the caves that way, and there she would find them . . .

It was at the edge of the Ashlands that Hathin's life was saved by a tussock that hooked her foot and sent her sprawling, so that she brought Arilou down with her. Winded, Hathin could only lie and gasp while all around green fireflies spiralled and winked and cruised as if they were dizziness sparks spinning from her own eyes. She was just recovering her breath when her attention snagged on a pair of distant fireflies nestling in the grass. They were red instead of green, and as she watched one of them pulsed four times, gradually increasing in brightness.

'I not sit in thisere grass.' A male voice speaking Nundestruth. 'Lace train snake. I want sit where can lookout snake come.'

'All right. You lookout snake, I lookout Lace.' There were two men crouched in the grass, smoking their pipes and watching the path. Hathin had been running so blindly, she would have stampeded right into their line of view if she had not fallen.

So the Lace trained snakes to attack their enemies, did they? Another fable traded as truth in the town. Very like a snake, Hathin slid through the undergrowth on her stomach, pulling on Arilou's sleeve to guide her after her.

A faint thudding behind her, and Hathin froze. From the direction of the pipe-smokers came a faint *click-et* of a gun being readied, followed by an exchange of softly called hails.

'Bywater how fare?'

'Deed done but Lace Lost runoff. Think she walk on water, runoff downcoast.'

'No. Bullet wait above water, man wait by all path. Lace Lost must runoff in cave already.'

Slowly the meaning of these words sank into Hathin's

shellshocked mind. The mob had not simply seethed to the beach on an irresistible tide of anger. No. There was planning behind this. Somebody had got hold of muskets, and posted sentries to make sure nobody could escape the village – and had known even before the attack about the retreat into the caves.

She remembered Lohan's words during the flight from the tidings hut. Yes, this was somebody's handiwork. Somebody with a long face, and a warm, hoarse laugh, and a flickerbird on a string.

If only Hathin had been crawling alone! But she was with Arilou, who wanted to slump dull-eyed on the grass, who needed to be guided every inch, who tangled in everything. Tears of desperation trickled down Hathin's cheeks as she nudged her sister's recalcitrant knees and elbows forward.

Only when they were over the next ridge did Hathin dare pull Arilou to her feet again. Here her nose stung with the smells of the foothills: orchid-dust, damp ash and the volcano's breath like old egg.

There were more men on the paths nearer to Sweetweather, exchanging whispers and beating at the bushes with restless savagery as though hoping to startle Lace into flight like partridges. The Lace who had killed Milady Page and Inspector Skein and all the other Lost so that only their own Lady Lost would survive. The Lace who used their eerie powers to poison crops and move boundary stones and put ague-juice in the springs. The Lace who spoke to volcanoes and trained snakes to kill and cut children to pieces with obsidian knives. Hathin could feel the grass jaguars' growls through the soles of her feet like a tremor in the rock.

As she led Arilou past them at a stoop Hathin counted her

own heartbeats and felt the time slipping away from her. How long would the rest of the village wait for them in the cavern of the teeth? Would they wait for them at all?

Jimboly's smile had melted off her face, leaving her mouth with the crinkled cruelty of a clam-lip. Her eyes darkened as she scratched out letters on the vellum with a jade nib. She was happier with pictograms, but the person to whom she was writing was particular about receiving his letters in Doorsy script.

She felt that having to write this message might yet ruin her evening. Until now her delight in the events of the day had been that of an artiste watching a few finely introduced sparks result in a peacock fan of explosions across the sky. But she was writing to a man who was interested only in the charred aftermath, the cold, blackened facts. A man, furthermore, that even Jimboly regarded with a shrinking of her spirit.

The facts were that despite all precautions the Lady Lost Arilou had escaped, along with one of her sisters. Arilou was of course a drooling imbecile, whether or not she was Lost, and Jimboly had little respect for her. It was quite possible that Arilou had seen nothing to make her dangerous, and even if she had there was little likelihood that she had managed to communicate it to anybody. However, Jimboly's instructions had been very specific.

'If we cannot say whether a flagstone is dirty,' the last message had read, 'it is as well to give it a good mopping just in case.'

Jimboly had given the cove of the Hollow Beasts a mopping unlike any the coast had seen in centuries. Now she was wondering, with some trepidation, how to tell her employer that she had somehow missed a couple of important specks.

While she was pondering this, Ritterbit hopped through the ink and across the page to leave his own message.

'Foot,' the message ran. 'Foot foot foot foot foot.'

Jimboly laughed a long laugh, her good spirits entirely recovered.

The governor's hand trembled as he reached to pull the curtains back from his window. They were good thick curtains made for the chill, honest, snowbound climate of the Cavalcaste plains. But here on the Coast of the Lace their main use was as a shield against blame. If the governor did not see something past the curtains, he could not be blamed for it.

How hard it was to protect a tiny haven of order here! He looked sadly around at his carefully aligned paintings of distant hunts through pine forests, which he maintained with the fastidious reverence of one who had never ridden a horse or seen a pine forest.

Dealing with the village face to face had been the job of Milady Page, and he had hated her for it, for making him feel absurd and useless in *his* town. But now he had to step forward and try to fill the ragged hole she had left. He sighed and opened the door, letting in the world in a flood of flies, smells and voices. As soon as he did so he tasted volcanobreath on the breeze and knew that the town was no longer *his* town.

The governor held himself erect throughout the conversation with the crowd, but all the while he could feel the red earth of his world crumbling under his feet. There was nothing for it but to yield ground to their demands one step at a time, trying to dissemble his retreat from the approaching abyss.

He had done everything he could to avoid bloodshed. He had summoned the Lace's Lady Lost to town hoping to test her, investigate her, perhaps arrest her, safely away from her village so that none of the other Lace could get involved. And his people had seemed happy with that. What had changed?

Confronted with the crowd and their bloody hoes, he told himself he had only one option. What had been done was brutal, horrible, but there was no undoing it. What was he to do – arrest the whole town as bloodthirsty murderers? If they turned on him too, farewell to all order! Better to side with them, ride the dragon and try to get a bit between its teeth.

And so he guided the townspeople's halting, surly account of the doings in the cove. *When you say that you went to teach them a lesson*, he suggested, *I assume you mean that you followed the Lady Lost after she fled suspiciously, and tried to arrest her. But there was resistance, causing a regrettable fight?* A hesitation among the crowd, looks of suspicion and then slow nods.

But their rage had not burned itself out. It had found more fuel. A journal was placed in his hand, and eager, soot-grimed fingers turned the leaves to show him where two pages had been torn away. It had been done skilfully, the ripped fragments picked out, but the two corresponding pages were now loose and could be pulled out to show the frayed edge.

There was also a letter which came from a port further up the coast. As the governor read it his eyebrows rose and his cravat damped and started to chafe. Such a letter should have been sent straight to him, and he could not guess how it had fallen into the grasp of this hungry horde.

He turned the letter to and fro in his hands to buy time

 131

while the crowd hung like thunder. At last he made the decision they had forced on him, and tried to make it sound like his own.

When he shut out the world again, he sat down feeling older than his years. So Minchard Prox had survived. And his testimony showed the lie in many things the Hollow Beasts village had claimed.

Whatever dark fate had claimed Skein on the night of the storm, the Hollow Beasts had lied about it. Skein had feared for his life, and had said so in a letter to Sightlord Fain. Perhaps there really had been a conspiracy to kill all the Lost and raise the Lace once more to their long-lost position of power. Perhaps Skein had suspected something and come to the coast to investigate. That would make sense. He must have jotted his fears and discoveries down in his journal . . . forcing the Lace to tear out the incriminating pages after they had killed him.

And who had been the Lace's ringleader in all this? The governor could not imagine a community without a single leader, and who better to run the great Lace conspiracy than their one Lady Lost?

Most of the dead Lost were not the governor's problem, but two of them had died within his personal jurisdiction. He had to be seen to do something, and his people had told him what they wanted. *Law and order must be protected*, he told himself, glancing about his tidy, candlelit parlour for reassurance, *sometimes at the expense of law and order*. He had sent a message to Port Suddenwind asking for instructions, of course – and perhaps decades hence one of his successors would actually receive the reply to his letter. And when it did arrive it would probably quote some ancient Cavalcaste law, maybe decreeing

132

that the guilty parties should have their yak herds confiscated, or that the whole town should wear beaver fur hats out of respect for the newly dead.

So he reached for a pen to write out a licence for the Ashwalker known as Brendril, granting him the right to pursue the Lady Lost known as Arilou and any companions assisting her on a charge of Conspiracy to Murder Milady Page and the Lost Inspector Raglan Skein.

Brendril was not sleeping when the message came. There was a bright moon, so he was half reclined in the hammock behind his shack, grinding a murderous smuggler's knuckle bones into a fine creamy powder with a pestle and mortar.

Laid out carefully on the ground near the hammock was a folded pile of the smuggler's clothes. Brendril had spent the day washing the bloodstains out of them and darning the knife slashes, for he was nothing if not conscientious. In a leather bag on top lay the dead man's earring, his water-skin and the shining blob of one metal tooth that had melted in the pyre. All of these he intended to take to the governor the next day. Brendril's payment was the ash, and he was determined that he would take nothing more of value, or even allow it to be lost by his negligence.

It was a hazy, smoky, sultry night and his mind was at peace, the rhythmic grinding of the pestle sounding like a cricket in his ear, a little smoke still seeping from the pyre. He no longer smelt the acrid stench from the yellow, foamy broth in the dyeing vats and the crumbs of indigo mulch drying on the palm-frond mats, or the sickening stink of molten fat. He no longer felt the bite of the ticks beneath the clothes he never removed. His eyes were almost closed, little crescent moons in a face of midnight blue.

They widened in an instant as a loud clatter wakened the jungle beyond the clearing. In several directions he heard scuffled retreats through the undergrowth. Most were almost certainly wild turkeys frightened from their grit-picking. The loudest, however, was probably a human animal whose courage had lasted long enough for them to ring the wooden summons bell, but no longer.

Sliding barefoot from his hammock, the Ashwalker slipped into the jungle. He noticed no chafe of his clothing, for in his mind he wore only spirits sewn one to another piecemeal – each garment's dye containing the cremation ash of a dead criminal. He seemed to feel the way the bandanna around his head blessed his sight, the dribbles of indigo that streaked his forehead and eyelids teaching his eyes to see in the dark. He did not even notice the briars, since a set of patterns in the clouds had once told him that his kerchief would numb the pain of all thorns and stings.

The wooden bell hung from a tree, nothing but half a barrel with a shinbone for a clapper. Beside it the other half of the barrel waited for messages, pleas, gifts. Today a small scroll in a leather case awaited him. He read it carefully, gripping the very corners so as not to stain them with the indigo that painted every inch of his skin.

He had been waiting for this. A licence to hunt down those responsible for the deaths of Inspector Skein and Milady Page. The killers were thought to have fled into the cave network. At the bottom of the paper he read the name of his quarry, and experienced a shimmer of what in another

134

person might have been called excitement.

A Lost. Who could guess what powers a Lost would give him if persuaded into indigo?

Brendril slipped back to his hut and dressed quickly for the hunt. According to the papers he had been sent, the Hollow Beasts on the beach had tried to lose their pursuers in the network of caves that riddled the hillside. This Lace Lost would try to do the same. But there were several entrances to the cave labyrinth, and the largest was close by.

Soon Brendril was picking his surefooted way through the nocturnal thicket, in the direction of the Sweetweather shaft.

As Hathin and Arilou neared the Sweetweather shaft the ground started to dip and the trees grew in height as if determined to disguise the treacherous drop. The main shaft was a great, steep, funnel-shaped descent some thirty feet deep. However, Hathin avoided this and hunted out a much smaller cave entrance behind a splay of giant ferns, known only to the Lace, and pulled Arilou into the earthy-smelling darkness after her. A barely controlled slither down a steep tunnel, a squeeze through a narrow crevice, and they were in the cavern of the teeth.

In the first instant Hathin saw that none of the village was there waiting for them. In the second instant she saw why, and her blood ran cold.

Everywhere about her, the great hanging teeth of the cavern had been smashed from their roots and shattered, and the pieces piled up with diabolical care to form a heap in the black pool which led to the Path of the Gongs. The entrance to the underwater tunnel was completely blocked.

'No!'

Stealth forgotten, Hathin staggered to the pool and waded in, losing her footing and scraping herself on the shards of rock. Her shaking, icy fingers grappled one jagged stone piece after another and flung them out of the pool. Even though she knew that the villagers would always send someone to check that the Path was safe, she could not help imagining her family and the other villagers trapped in the musical darkness of the underwater passage . . .

'Arilou! Please! You've got to help me, you've got to . . . please, just this once!' Many of the rocks were too big for Hathin to lift alone, even with the strength of desperation. There had clearly been several people busy there, making sure that this end of the Path was blocked before the attack on the beach. 'Arilou! I can't do this by myself!' She ducked her head beneath the water, and tried to shift a great, molar-shaped rock away from the hidden opening. As she tucked her arms around it, she felt something brush against her wrist.

She released the rock and grabbed towards the trailing touch. With a shock she found that she was gripping an icy hand. For a moment she thought it had deliberately slid into her grasp, but the hand was too cold and the wrist had no pulse. Hathin jerked convulsively away from the contact, and her fingers caught in the bracelet which was floating in a soft ring around the other's wrist. Hathin's eyes and nose and mouth filled with water and she burst to the surface, choking and streaming and staring at the shark's tooth bracelet that her sudden motion had torn from the cold wrist.

There had been no time for the villagers to send a scout ahead up the Path of the Gongs. The attacking towners had

136

known about the cave of the Scorpion's Tail, and with the sound of pursuit behind them, the Lace had had no choice but to slip into icy darkness and trust to the mercy of the mountain. And so the foremost had drowned, grappling desperately with the rocky barrier, the others behind her unwittingly blocking her retreat, knowing only that she did not advance, and unable to retreat themselves as the air died in their lungs . . .

The bracelet belonged to Whish. The best diver was always sent first along the Path, and Whish was the second best. Eiven had not even reached the caves.

Hathin staggered out of the water, feeling new cuts and scrapes chilling on contact with the air. Arilou leaned back against the wall with the serenity of a blind seer, her head a little tipped back so that stray droplets from the roof could fall into her slack, beautiful mouth. And this, more than anything, was beyond bearing.

'I should have let the Death Rattle take you!' The caves' many voices joined Hathin in a chorus. 'I should have let Whish push you into the sea! Then none of this would have happened! All of this, *all* of this, happened because of *you*!'

There was a sharp, palm-sized shard of pure white stone in Hathin's hand, and something savage seemed to have control of all her muscles. Arilou stirred her head a little, as if she had felt rather than seen a shadow fall upon her, and then her throat moved clumsily, and she continued her parched and pathetic attempts to catch in her mouth the meagre drips from the roof.

Hathin hurled away the shard of rock, and saw it shock apart against the opposite wall. Once the stone was out of her hand the rage abandoned her and left her shaking. Unsteadily she knelt, cupped water from the pool and brought it over to Arilou. She could not help it.

Arilou had barely taken a gulp when Hathin jerked into alertness, her ears catching a distant sound from back down the tunnel. A spit and spack, the crack and tumble of tiny rocks. Somebody was descending the spiral path down the main Sweetweather shaft.

Could it be another fugitive from the Hollow Beasts? No. Any Lace would have used the small, secret tunnel. Whoever was coming, it was not a friend.

Hathin hurriedly heaved her sister to her feet. If any of the village had survived, they would have taken the route further into the mountain. So Hathin turned toward the darkness of the deeper caverns with the weight of her sister on her shoulder. Hope refused to die, and beat in Hathin's chest like a fist.

11
DREAD OF DYEING

Brendril had hoped to start the hunt alone. When he was halfway down the Sweetweather shaft, however, he looked up and noticed a number of the townsmen staring down at him from the brink. They had taken one look at his raven-wing blue figure and known him for what he was. They had smelt a kill in the offing, and because the angry blood was still banging in their veins they had decided they wanted a part in it. And so they had followed him, their faces filled with uncertain hostility as though he had already told them to go away. He thought of flies on a fallen fruit and said nothing. Brush them away, and they would come back, perhaps even sting.

The trick to descending the great shaft was to find the edge before it found you, and then descend it in a very gradual spiral, like flotsam drawn down the funnel of a whirlpool in slow motion. Otherwise, you were likely to find yourself treading air and darkness for a second and an eternity. While Brendril was gently manoeuvring his way from invisible ledge to imperceptible handhold, it became clear that a couple of his new followers were a little unclear on this trick. However, there seemed no point in letting the resultant screams distract him, so he continued without looking up or down.

At the bottom, while the towners were fashioning makeshift stretchers for their injured and filling the caves with noise and the smell of their rushlights, Brendril examined the caverns, looking for traces of his quarries and some clue to which of the many passages they had chosen for their retreat. Beside a black pool littered with rock shards he found what he was looking for – and yet, it was not what he had been expecting.

On the pale rock floor were prints from two very different sets of feet. One solitary print was pinkish with dust and showed the outline of a narrow foot with long toes and a tendency to roll. A second set of feet had left wet prints leading from the pool into one of the nearby tunnels. These feet were smaller, shorter and more squarely placed.

What surprised Brendril was the size of the prints. He had not thought to ask the age of the Lady Lost and her retainer. For the first time he realized that he was on the trail of children. It did not so much stir an emotion in him as make him aware of the place where it should have been, like a tongue-tip finding out a narrow hole and remembering the missing tooth.

Wet footprints dry quickly. The young fugitives could not be far ahead of him. Brendril set off in pursuit.

At this moment, the owner of the wet prints was stumbling through the darkening tunnels, lips moving as if in prayer. But Hathin was not praying.

She had never walked these caverns, but nonetheless she knew them. Some of the stories taught to Lace children were nothing but old legends, but others had meanings encoded in them. The version of the Legend of the Rivals that was taught in the village of the Hollow Beasts was also a means of remembering a list of directions. As she took each shivering step, Hathin was allowing Mother Govrie's soft, storytelling voice to speak in her mind.

For centuries the King of Fans thought of nothing but dancing with the great plumed fans of cloud he used to shield his head. One day when he paused weary, the fans drooped in his hands and for the first time he glimpsed Sorrow. A silver river of tears formed in his eyes as he beheld her beauty. He took her to wife, and was so in love that it was some time before he noticed how strangely and coldly his wife received his tender caresses . . .

So far, the story had guided her between two rocky out-crops shaped like fans, through a narrow wedge-shaped tunnel where water ran over the walls like tears, then through a hole as round as a wedding ring.

Where now? What came next?

There was a whisper from the walls around her, as if the shadow was trying to answer. The tunnel was widening to either side, and the darkness before and above her was alive with winged movement. Hathin realized she stood at the edge of a vast cavern, in which the shadow spun, slung and snatched fragments of itself. It was flickering and whirling with bats.

. . . One day as he approached her chamber the King of Fans heard voices and knew that his wife was with his own brother, Spearhead. His heart, which had overflowed with love, became filled with dark rage, and winged imps of jealousy . . .

The cavern was the largest she had ever seen, an

 141

enormous ghost ballroom with stalactite chandeliers. Bats blackened the high ceiling, flitting crazily or clustering suspended, each a neat little dangling triangular package, heads a-twitch. Hundreds, thousands of bats. Their dung was piled waist-high on the floor like dull oatmeal, so that you could barely see where the funnel-shaped floor descended to a great pool in the centre, fed by drips from the ravaged ceiling.

It was important *not* to enter this cave, Hathin suddenly remembered, *not* to walk into the King's anger. She faltered, again trying to remember the next part of the story, all too aware of the growing sounds of pursuit from the tunnels behind them. Arilou slithered and lurched, nearly losing her footing, and Hathin flinched as the rattle of her shell bracelets was taken up by the echo.

She snatched off her own bracelets and those of Arilou, and stared down at them with a sudden pang. They were treasures, painstakingly built up a shell at a time over years . . . but survival depended on silence.

Hathin covered her face and darted into the cavern. She dropped the fistful of bracelets on to the nearest vast, soft mound of bat dung, kicked droppings over to hide it and withdrew before the fumes of the mounds could start to poison her lungs. She did not need legends to warn her of the dangers of grottoes such as these.

Brendril continued through narrow veins linking little antechambers, all the while painfully aware of the glow of the towners' torches close behind him. After some time he started to notice the bats, first in ones and twos. And then there were more, a dozen, then dozens, then tens of dozens.

He reached the edge of the great bat domain, and his attention was caught by one of the heaps of dung. There was a slight dint and disturbance, as if it had been stirred by a recent step.

Brendril was about to cross the threshold when by pure chance he saw a pattern of bulges on the opposite wall, and recognized among them a macaw-like beak and beneath it the shape of a cruel human mouth. The old paint was long-faded, but this cave was an ancient Lace temple, guarded by a demon shaped like the Gripping Bird. Brendril felt suddenly breathless.

Another step forward, and he would have placed himself in a sacred domain. His control over the captive spirits in his clothing would no doubt have been broken instantly. Ash-walkers were not priests, and they avoided temples.

He turned and edged back along the tunnel, into confrontation with his now perplexed and angry followers. For once he did allow himself to speak with them, since they clearly needed some reason for the whole queue of them to retreat and let him past. His explanation was passed along the line.

'He says he can't cross the cavern,' he could faintly hear one of the furthermost explaining in weary disgust, 'or his trousers will stop working.'

They pulled back to let him through, and murmured as he scouted around, staring intensely at the walls. However, when they found him determined to travel up a rocky mousehole tunnel too small for anything but wriggling on one's belly, murmurs became challenges. The general feeling

143

among those whose trousers had nothing to fear from macaw demons was that they would rather cross the bat ballroom that the fugitives apparently *had* passed through than wedge themselves like corks in a pipe that they almost certainly *hadn't*.

And so as Brendril wriggled slowly up the 'mousehole', taking care not to rip his tunic and feeling little breezes lick at his face from a hidden opening somewhere ahead, he heard the rest of the search party slithering and splashing through the ballroom, calling to each other as they looked for the next cavern, their voices getting fainter as they ventured into further reaches of the bat palace.

Brendril continued up the tunnel even when the tone of the cries from the great cavern changed, became hoarser, wheezier, desperate. He ignored his erstwhile companions crying that they could not clamber from the sloping pool, could not get breath, could not find their strength . . .

He had nearly been outwitted. He had nearly allowed himself to start thinking of the Lady Lost as simply a child. If she could lead a whole village – perhaps even a whole tribe – in a secret and murderous crusade, then whatever her years she was no mere girl. He was certain now that she had simply entered a few paces into the ballroom of the bats to make it look as if she had gone that way, counting on the strange magic of the temple to destroy all pursuers, and then had escaped the same way the bats did, up through this strange little tilted mousehole of a passage.

Brendril continued his crawl upwards, careful but relentless.

*

. . . And so at the end of the mighty battle between the brother volcanoes, Spearhead fled roaring, his sides charred and a great piece missing from his rim, rucking and raddling the earth behind him . . .

Gasping, Hathin gave one last heave, and pushed Arilou out of the tilted tunnel into the pale daylight, then scrambled after her. Arilou had been worse than dead weight, continually waving her arms like weed and making small murmurs of distress.

Hathin flopped exhausted on the earth and became aware that her limbs were shaking uncontrollably. They were on a hillside of thorned pink shrubs and lolling grass over which flickerbirds bobbed and dipped and flexed their tails. They were far nearer to the summit of the King of Fans than she had expected, and his cloud-fans seemed close overhead.

. . . And the King of Fans returned to his wife whom he still loved, and thought for a moment that she had shed a single tear in grief for what had happened. But when he drew close he found it was only a gleaming white stone, for Sorrow is named for what she gives, not what she feels.

Beyond a series of rolling ridges, Hathin glimpsed a vast, mist-wreathed white cone. That was Sorrow. Drawing an imaginary line between herself and the white volcano, she made out a large pale rock at the crest of one of the ridges. Sorrow's 'tear'.

'We have to get up now,' she whispered. Her voice seemed to make no impression on Arilou, but Hathin was speaking to herself as much as to her sister. 'Come on, we have to. When we find the others they'll carry you, I promise.'

The white stone ahead was the last marker in the legend,

the destination point. It was somewhere under which people might shelter and wait for stragglers, or at least leave a scratch on the rock to show where they had gone. This was the hardest part of the journey, every ripple of the land fooling Hathin into thinking that they were closer than they were, every upward slope dragging at their muscles. But Hathin knew that if they paused for too long their exhaustion would catch up with them.

At last the marker stone reared on a ridge above them. Limbs aching in anticipation of rest, Hathin staggered up the slope with both arms around Arilou, and the two collapsed beside the white rock. When Hathin could muster the strength to move, she scrambled to her feet and made a circuit of the great stone, leaning one hand against it to steady herself. There was an overhang large enough for three people to shelter beneath, but nothing had gathered there except living flies and a dead lizard. She made another circuit, another, the tears pushing up her throat, and finally climbed up on to the rock in case some mark had been left by one far taller than herself.

The moss had drawn maps, the birds had made offerings, the beetles had left rust-coloured sigils, but there was no scratch of a Lace shell. *We are the first here*, said the cruel, remorseless voice of hope. *We are the last here*, said the gentler voice of despair. *There is only us. We are alone.*

They were not alone. Staring across the rippled ridges, Hathin became aware that she could see a single dark figure against the pink and golden slope. The stab of hope lasted for only the barest instant, for this was a figure of midnight blue.

*

146

Sooner or later fugitives always fled to the slopes of the volcano, hoping that others would be afraid to follow them. But Brendril had the spirit of an old Lace priest bound into one of the patches of his shirt, to make him invisible to the volcano. The cord he used as a belt held the soul of a woman who had burned someone to death, to prevent him being scalded or singed by the temperamental landscape. Even when he had to cross one of the King of Fans' charred scars, he anointed his feet with ceremonial oil and walked swiftly across, hearing his footsoles hiss painlessly against the smoking black rock.

The distant specks he pursued had become human figures. As their route started to weave he knew that they had seen his ink-blot shape against the pale hill.

Clambering to the crest of yet another ridge, he had his first good look at the pair of them. As he had suspected, neither of them could be more than thirteen. The shorter girl wore the same stiff skirt and embroidered blouse he had seen on a hundred Lace girls. The other wore a long pale tunic embroidered in yellow thread, and he guessed that she must be the Lost.

He had thought to find her leading the way, since navigation would be best left to one who could command an eagle-eye view at will. However, it was the shorter girl who gripped the passively dangling wrist of the Lady Lost and led her, almost dragged her, up the side of the hill. This could only mean one thing. The Lady Lost had left her body to the care of her attendant because she had sent out her mind to keep an eye on him.

The Lady Lost turned her head blindly in his direction,

147

and then her legs folded oddly and seemed to give beneath her.

'Oh, not now, Arilou, please, not now!'

Hathin threw herself on her knees and gripped Arilou by the shoulders. Arilou's face was quivering with an expression Hathin had not seen in her before. She had seen shock, dismay, rage, disquiet, but never this look of deep, soul-shaking panic. Again Arilou was moving her hands about, feelingly, searchingly, grasping at stones, at grass, her head turning with a twitch as though hoping to catch some elusive glimpse.

Hathin felt a chill pass over her. It was one thing for Arilou to be doing that in the tunnel, bewildered by the dark, but now they were in the light. Arilou's senses had often seemed confused, perhaps short-sighted, and a lot of the time she seemed to care little what was around her, but she had never seemed so . . . *blind*. Right now she looked as if she was trying to see something, expected to see something and couldn't.

'Please, I'm here, we've got to, we've got to . . .' Hathin tried to hoist Arilou's weight, but their legs gave under them and Arilou continued twitching and drawing in audible gasps of fear. 'I'm here, I'm here . . .'

But, she suddenly realized, it wasn't that Arilou didn't know where Hathin was. It was that Arilou didn't know where Arilou was. Hypnotized, Hathin watched Arilou's look of fevered concentration as her fingers fluttered over the surface of the earth as though trying to read it. And then Arilou reached upwards with trembling hands, snatching fistfuls of nothing and dragging it to her, clumsily hauling in an invisible rope hand over hand in a motion that was all too familiar . . .

'Oh, don't you dare!' shouted Hathin. 'Don't you dare tell me you're trying to reel yourself in! Don't you dare tell me you're trying to play the doll game! That's it, isn't it? You left your body in that nice Doorsy house in Sweetweather, and then you went back and you couldn't find it, is that it? Don't you dare tell me after everything that's happened that *you've been a Lost all the time*! You had your chances to be Lost, and now it's too late, you're only allowed to be an idiot! Don't you dare tell me that all along you've been Lost and could have saved everyone, because you didn't, and now they're dead, they're dead, they're all dead . . .'

Hathin tightened both arms around Arilou and heaved at her dead weight. 'You're not going to get me killed as well! Get up! Get up!'

The younger girl was crouched beside the Lady Lost, trying to lift her, calling something in a high, faint voice that Brendril could hardly hear. The girls flattened themselves as the wind rose, and Brendril was tensing to begin the run down the valley when he became aware of a papery pattering further up the slope. Other clouds had come to join the King's fans, he suddenly realized, and the distant ones were dropping faint misty streamers that meant rain. And suddenly the grass around him was jumping and shocking beetles into dozy, beleaguered flight and there were cold finger-taps on his skull and shoulders and neck.

The only available shelter was a big black rock with an

 149

overhang further along the ridge, and Brendril sprinted for it. Panic made his footsteps slither uncertainly, and he lost his footing three times before reaching the rock. Crawling under it, and tucking his feet up to keep them dry, he fumbled in his pack until his fingers curled around a wooden handle. A moment later the Ashwalker was crouched under a large black parasol, smudgy with the wax he had used to waterproof it.

The Lady Lost had collapsed in exhaustion; he saw that now. The younger girl had given up trying to lift her and watched him round-eyed across the dip, as incapable of proceeding as he was. They were barely twenty yards from him, and unreachable, and for once no signs appeared to Brendril to dilute his frustration.

They were exhausted. He was still full of energy.

They were slow. He was fast.

The indigo dye, however, was not.

Hathin stared in incomprehension across the narrow gorge-like valley that divided them from the Ashwalker. She could make out his features quite clearly now. She could see the way indigo dye had run out of the bandanna that swathed his head, trailing dark fingers down his face and neck. She could see the white scars of briar scratches on his blue calves, the fraying garments that he wore in layer upon layer, the new over the old. And he looked back at her with white-ringed, waiting eyes.

But Hathin was not ready to talk with Death just yet, so she tightened her grip around Arilou once more and, with an effort of more than muscle, lifted both of them to their feet.

And the King of Fans said, I have been betrayed, but I shall not be betrayed again. From this moment my memory shall run back to front. My past is full of happiness and pain I cannot bear to recall, so I shall not. I shall instead gaze into the book of the future and remember only that, so that I may behold treachery before it happens. From this moment I look only forward.

12
SORROW IN SILENCE

We have run off the edge of our world, thought Hathin as she stared up through a grey faceful of rain. *There are no stories to tell us where to go now. We have passed the point where the stories end.*

She wiped her wet face with a wet hand, tasting the salt of sweat and tears, and stared about her. If they kept running up and down the ridges she knew they would wear themselves out, and the Ashwalker would catch them. Their only hope was to scramble uphill while it was still raining and lose him in the King's fans.

Oh, in the cloud they might be invisible to the Ashwalker, but what of the King himself? Would he not notice them immediately?

So what? thought Hathin suddenly. *So what if he steals us away as nursemaids for his children? Even if he chooses to burn us into cinder patterns, so what? At least then we'd go straight to the caves of the dead, instead of spending our ever-after as an Ashwalker's handkerchief. What have we to lose?*

The grass thinned to clumps as they struggled up the slope, then yielded to a shifting shale made up of blackened pebbles that slithered away under their feet. The wind became stronger as they mounted higher, snatching their breath away. Arilou's weight in Hathin's arms was agonizing. Every step was impossible and got them nowhere and yet, somehow, they reached the clouds at last. Instantly the wind became vindictive, bullying and buffeting. Occasionally fragments of pale blue sky skimmed high above their heads. It was cold up here, and Hathin's sodden clothes chilled her.

Then, just at the point where the wind was at its cruellest, where they could not stand and could not breathe and could not see for the tiny pebbles that stung their faces and eyes, suddenly there was no more up to climb. And Hathin knew that they had reached the top of the long looping saddle-ridge that linked the King of Fans to his ice-white wife, allowing the two mountains to hold hands.

The wind lessened, the air grew colder still and the clouds shifted. Jagged rocky pedestals loomed with eerie suddenness so that it seemed they had drawn in to surround the two girls, and Hathin halted, feeling like a captured intruder. But then the vapour thinned some more, and a great blackened slab became visible, resting on two smaller boulders. It was as though a long table had suddenly been made ready for the sisters, lichen tracings like embroidery across its length. Two stump-like rocks awaited them like stools.

You could not run from a volcano. And you never, never turned down a volcano's invitation.

Her legs almost giving under her, Hathin guided the still-whimpering Arilou to one of the 'seats', then shakily lowered herself on to the other, fearing all the while that she would see the Ashwalker leap out of the mist. But they had stepped into a dream, and dreams have their own rules.

 153

The King has decided not to destroy us for now – what does he want with us?

The very centre of the table was split, and a single flower grew from the crack, a slim and perfect white bloom with a long, downy orange tongue. Notoriously, the King of Fans liked to have young girls and women around him, the fairer the better. Could it be . . . was it even possible that in giving this flower the King of Fans was *flirting* with them? If so, then the flower could only be meant for Arilou.

The King of Fans remembered events that had not yet happened. What if he already remembered kidnapping Hathin and Arilou, forcing them to serve him as nursemaids into old age, until each of them gnarled into one of the tiny, twisted trees that dotted his sides? If he remembered it, didn't that mean it was bound to happen? Hathin tried to twist her exhausted brain back to front.

A flower . . . a *snow-white* flower. Perhaps it was not meant for Arilou at all. Suddenly Hathin thought of a future that might have created this present, and away to bring that future about.

Gingerly, quietly, Hathin slumped off her chair on to her knees and started scrabbling on the ground for a sharpened stone.

Brendril trod very carefully amid the cloud fans of the King. His magical protection might render him invisible to the volcano, but that was worth nothing if he drew attention to his presence by setting off rockslides or startling birds into the air. The rain shower had been just long enough for the girls to get out of sight, but their steps had left a slight furrow

154

in the shale, and he followed it closely, hoping that his own footprints would be lost in it.

At last he reached the top of the ridge and discovered a great stone slab was borne on the backs of two low, turtle-like stones. An altar, clearly. The two girls had unquestionably passed that way, for a plant growing from the slab's crevice had been snapped off close to the base. Whatever ritual they had come here to perform, however, they must have completed it. The Lady Lost and her companion were nowhere to be seen.

But stark lines and shapes had been scratched into the overgrown and charred mass covering a rock nearby. It was, he realized, a picture.

Two figures in the old Lace pictogram style. One had a picture of an eye floating above her head to show that she was a Lost. They were holding hands, and clasped between their combined fingers sprouted something . . . a flower. The pair of figures was drawn again, again, again, to show a progression. They were walking, first on the level and then up the side of a cone with a blunt tip – clearly a volcano. Down the side of the volcano ran a single teardrop.

Brendril straightened and stared out towards the volcano called Sorrow.

The hastily scratched picture seemed to have done its work. It had, of course, been a message for the King of Fans, telling him that the two sisters would take a gift from him to Sorrow, a single flower. Words would have done no good at all, for a second after they were spoken they would have belonged to the past, and the King could not remember the past. But a picture would endure into the future. This way, as they left his lands, the King would still have the picture before him, so that he might just keep in mind who they were and why they should be allowed to leave.

But thinking like this made Hathin's brain ache, and she had enough to worry about. She was approaching the domain of Sorrow.

The ridge that joined the King and Sorrow was really a long, thin plateau, like a hanging bridge half a mile wide. The edges of the plateau were hidden in cloud, and it was easy to imagine one was trapped on some strange and interminable plain. As Hathin passed on to this weird, raised plateau, the petulant wind abruptly abandoned them, giving way to an eerily soft breath of breeze that rose and fell as gently as a sigh without passion.

The black shale yielded to grey, and everything was coated with a ghostly, ever-shifting white powder. On either side the plain was dotted with lone rocks, shallow tracks on the windlee side of them as if they had been trying to roll from this wide, white waste but had surrendered to despair.

House-high wraiths of mist and cloud chased across the plain like ladies-in-waiting on an urgent errand. Here there were no birds, no trees, no grass. Legends spoke of those few heroes who had dared to speak with the King of Fans and survived. There were no stories of anyone approaching Sorrow.

The ground started to decline, and then Hathin became aware of a glimmer of colour amid the deathly landscape. Jewelled hues, startling in their brilliance. The veils of mist yielded and yielded, until Hathin halted and found herself looking into the eyes of Sorrow.

They were mismatched, the larger lake tear-shaped and peacock green, the smaller peacock blue and oval. The water was motionless and lucid, concentric ripples of sediment staining the bottom with hummingbird hues. Lidless, lashless, pitiless. Beyond the lakes the ground ascended sharply, rising towards the invisible crater.

'Lady Sorrow . . .' Here Lace and not Doorsy was the language of solemnity and ritual. 'I bring a gift from your royal husband.' Hathin spoke as loudly as she dared, but the soft air caught her voice like a moth between gloved hands and crushed the life out of it.

A sound – a sweet, sibilant rattling – somewhere above. Perhaps a threat. Perhaps an invitation.

Gripping the flower in one hand and Arilou's hand in the other, Hathin advanced, hearing the white rocks crackle under her feet. She halted at a cleft stone, in which she placed the flower, its flaming tongue the only warm colour in the scene, for even Hathin and Arilou were now covered in white dust.

How would the white mountain react? Everyone knew that she was beloved of both the King of Fans and Spearhead, but nobody knew which of them she preferred. Would she take the bringing of a gift from her husband as a favour or a slight? For the King's flower was a sign of her power over him, but also of her allegiance to him . . .

'Lady Sorrow . . .' Hathin spoke on impulse, but this time kept her voice at a whisper out of respect. 'You deserve more gifts as bright as this. Lord Spearhead would burn a hole in the very sky if he knew that you were wearing such a token from your husband. He has been robbed of the sight of you, good lady – the only comfort he can be offered is the chance to send you a present fairer than this. Let me go to him, my lady – what message shall I take him from you?'

A faint hissing again, and a thin veil of white gravel and dust bounced and smoked down the slope to Hathin's feet. Hathin stooped to fill her shaking hands with it and tied it carefully in a knotted cloth, for she was loath to spill a gift from Lady Sorrow to Lord Spearhead, particularly with Lady Sorrow watching.

It had looked like a trap. However desperate their situation, Brendril could not at first believe that the Lady Lost had really chosen to flee into the domain of Sorrow. The picture had to be a false trail to lure him to his destruction, and a clumsy one at that. But it was *too* clumsy, he realized. He was meant to see it, of course, but the longer he looked at it, the more certain he became that it could only be meant as a challenge. The Lady Lost had invited him to follow her if he dared.

Well, he would accept the challenge and follow his commission, even into the court of Sorrow.

And so he walked the plains of quiet, where great wraiths of mist hurried silently by without seeing him, until he came to the twin lakes, and between them a flower with a flame-coloured tongue. What kind of ward had the Lady Lost set up against him?

It is not in the nature of an Ashwalker to walk away from power. He knew that the volcano could not see him so, taking care to make no sound, he padded his way to the flower and gently stooped to pluck it from its cleft. Only as he did so did he notice that his hands were not their usual blue, but a deathly white. Too late he realized that he was covered in the white dust. The volcano could not see *him*, but she could see the ash. Right now a ghostly man-shape outlined in the fine ash would be clearly visible to her . . .

He started backwards, and his hasty heels kicked rocks to the left and right, filling the dead air with the gunshot crack of their collisions.

Above him there was a hiss, a rattle, a rumble, a growing roar. No time to dart from the path of Sorrow's anger. The Ashwalker vanished beneath a torrent of rocks that ricocheted and crashed down the slope for a little age and then gradually stilled once more. For a long time dust sighed itself back to earth. The midnight blue figure was no more to be seen, and all was quiet again in the court of Sorrow.

For hours Hathin struggled down the slopes of Sorrow. The cloud hid everything, and Hathin had to listen all the while for the telltale hiss of rockslides. When the strain of supporting Arilou became too much for Hathin's arms, and when her leg muscles were aching with each treacherous downwards step, Hathin let the pair of them tumble to the turf. There had been no trace of the Ashwalker for several miles.

After she had recovered a little, Hathin found shelter for them in a cave which was the cold remains of a great lava bubble, half collapsed. She was heaping leaves and dead furze around them to warm them when Arilou gave a physical jolt

 159

as if somebody had punched her. Her eyes seemed to fix on a location over Hathin's shoulder. So wild was her look of horror that Hathin involuntarily glanced behind her. There was nothing, nothing but spiralling mist.

Arilou's mouth dropped open, and a horrible, low, harsh sound came out, as though someone had squeezed her like a bellows and forced the noise out of her. A pause, then her jaw fell again and she started to scream – long, ragged, ugly, moaning screams, all the while staring rigidly at the mists.

Again Hathin found herself imagining an Arilou wandering invisible in search of her carelessly discarded body. She imagined this spectral Arilou moving among the houses of Sweetweather, then floating back to her village to find the huts gone, and only blackened marks where they had stood on the beach. And then following sandy tracks into the caves, perhaps even into the Path of the Gongs . . .

Arilou's screams were white-hot lava. She started to move her arms wildly and stiffly from the elbow, beating at her own face.

'Here! It's me!' Hathin grabbed Arilou's hands and pressed them against her own face, hair, shoulders, so that Arilou might know and recognize them, even if she could not hear her voice. 'I'm here! I'm with you. I've got you, I've still got you.'

She put her arms tightly around Arilou and rocked her until the screams became croaks, then gentle sobbed breaths. Hathin kept her arms around Arilou even when the two lay down to sleep.

It was only as exhaustion clouded her mind and she was

slipping into sleep that Hathin wondered why the Ashwalker had not come running at the sound of Arilou's screams. But no padding steps came, and it seemed the mists had swallowed him whole.

13
A SLIPPERY SLOPE

'Mr Prox?'

He felt an attentive hand on his shoulder, and with a sickening effort opened his eyes. Outside the window of the sedan chair, waving palms polished the sky to a burnished blue, and a white-faced house burned his mind.

'We're here, Mr Prox.'

His head seemed to be made of brass, and it took all his effort to raise it.

'Here.' A silver stopper was tweaked from a leather-bound bottle and the bottle was lifted briefly to Prox's lips, allowing him a short swallow. He tried to take hold of the bottle, but it withdrew. 'Forgive me – your stomach is still too weak to stand more than a sip at a time.'

The sedan door opened, and Prox almost fell out into a glaring hell of pitiless colours and sounds. How long had he been travelling? Days? He thought it was midday, but could not be sure. As the sedan carriers unburdened the elephant birds, setting down loaded packs, leather water bottles and cages thrumming with pigeons, Prox stared at them without knowing what he saw. His left elbow was gently but firmly commandeered, and he gratefully leaned into the support.

'I'm afraid they'll want to greet you, but we can make it all quick and painless, I think,' came the murmur in his ear as he was helped up the path towards the gleaming house.

'Greet?' Prox's voice came out sounding rusty. 'What? Who?'

But before there could be any answer, the whats and the whos came out of the house to meet him, all solicitous respect and ceremonial chains winking in the sun.

'The governor here in New Warkbridge,' murmured the helpful voice in his ear. 'Deaf as a post. You only need to bow and smile at him.'

The governor was replaced by a young man with a painfully firm handshake and a sharp voice.

'That's the governor's aide.' Prox almost felt the murmur was taking place inside his own head. 'He'd like nothing better than to get your support. Don't let him push you into signing anything until you've rested.'

Other voices came at him from all directions and beat his mind like a gong.

'After your ordeal naturally you'll want to see some justice . . .'

'. . . taken steps of our own which I think you'll find . . .'

'. . . a symbol . . .'

'. . . for too long the Lace . . .'

'. . . the Lace . . .'

'. . . as soon as you're well enough, of course,' the governor's aide was saying to him, 'but I think everybody in the town would like to hear your story. Already feelings are running high about the loss of the Lost, and I think our townspeople have a right . . .'

 163

Talking ceaselessly, the aide showed Prox to his room at the far end of the hall. It was with relief that Prox saw the door close between them.

Prox staggered forward, giving the merest, bleariest look around the chamber that had been prepared for him. Orchids. A yellow nugget of honeycomb in a china bowl. A tall flute of water. A four-poster. A four-poster? Was this room really meant for him? A writing desk. Ah, perhaps it was.

He tottered over and slumped in the chair before the desk. Whenever he was not touching his face, he was bothered by the feeling that it had been coated in wet clay. Examining himself in the scratched little mirror on the desk, it was easy to see why.

He could scarcely recognize himself. Great reddened blisters disfigured every inch of his face. Some of them were starting to harden like parchment. Others had burst, weeping a mess like egg yolk down his cheeks. The damage was worse across his forehead, cheekbones and the bridge of his nose, where it seemed he had no real skin left.

Prox stared, remembering the care he had always taken to be presentable. Once he had nicked his chin shaving and had driven himself mad all day imagining that everybody was staring. *Everybody staring.* His throat was too dry even for tears to swell in it so he reached for the slender bottle of water.

The first day adrift on the boat, there had been little to tell him how the sun was ravaging him. His skin had felt a little strange and tense, that was all. He had been far too busy battling vainly against the current and the storm with his splintered paddle to worry about it.

164

It was only that night he had been woken by a feeling that someone had placed a clammy mask against his skin. He had raised a hand to touch it, and had felt a searing pain as something tore under his tentative touch. Wetting his fingers with water from the shell and dabbing the place had not helped, and when in the madness of desperation he had cupped some sea water and flung it at his cheek, the agony had increased tenfold.

At that point he'd still been trying to ration the water in the shell the little Lace girl had given him. Soon after, though, he'd succumbed to thirst and taken a long drink. Ten minutes later he had been gripped by racking pains, vomiting, dizziness. The second day he'd meant to shield his face from the sun. However he had kept raising his head to look for imagined boats or villages along the coast, and somehow over and over he had woken to find himself staring upwards.

The second night and third day had been phantasmridden. His paddle had fallen from his grasp, he remembered that, and he'd stood to look for it, and then there had been a rushing roar in his ears, stars before his eyes that came and went and came and went and came and came and filled everything until the world went black. And then all the rest had been fireworks in red and gold, horizons twisting like ribbons, voices without owners . . .

He took a gulp, managed to halt himself before he drained the water bottle, then hesitated, the glass rim still touching his lips. Very slowly he set it down and turned around in his chair.

'Who . . . ?' Prox managed through his sandpaper throat. 'Who . . . the hell . . . *are* you?'

The man who had supported Prox into the room, and then seated himself discreetly next to the wall, looked up from his study of the atlas by the bed. His eyes were a patient, pale hazel, with something crisply Cavalcaste about them, like an evening sky with snow behind it. Although he was over average height, he seemed to take up less space than he should, perhaps for the sake of tidiness. His garments were smart but unremarkable, a waistcoat and breeches of good grey wool, a modest knot of cravat.

Only his gently receding hair with its dusting of grey betrayed the fact that he was probably over forty, perhaps even over fifty. At present his narrow face wore an expression that was startled but gratified, as if it made a refreshing and amusing change to be noticed at all. There were bells attached to the back of his boots, marking him out as an official of some sort. When he moved his feet, however, they did not ring out.

'My name is Camber.' The same gentle, cat-footed tone that had murmured in Prox's ear – the same attentive voice that had been Prox's companion, he realized, for the last few days of travel. 'We have introduced ourselves before, but you were . . . not well then, so I hardly expected you to remember. In fact, since you are likely to be peppered with many much more important introductions from now until autumn, you should feel free to forget my name as many times as you need to. My name does not come with a chain of office, Mr Prox. I am nothing. Nothing but a window – my job is to help you get a view on the situation so that you can make the decisions that face you.'

'What . . . decisions?'

'Well, this is unlikely to strike you as much of a silver lining . . . but your ordeal has made you something of a celebrity. You're the "survivor", you see. Politics is all about timing, and you're a highly symbolic figure at a time when emotions are running very high. You have been told about the current crisis, do you remember?'

'Skein . . .' Prox tried to recall what he had been told during the days of fever.

'Not just Skein,' Camber said gently. 'All of them. All the Lost are dead. At first we weren't sure, but word has been arriving from the outlying areas in dribs and drabs, and it's always the same story. The adults died on the same evening, within hours of each other. And then that very night every child known or strongly suspected to be a Lost passed away in exactly the same fashion. Oh, all but one, that is to say.' Camber met Prox's questioning gaze, and gave a short sigh. 'Yes. Yes, you met her. Lady Lost Arilou of the Hollow Beasts cove. Of all the Lost in Gullstruck, only she survived. Strange, that.'

Prox thought of the serene-faced, grey-eyed young seer-ess. It pained him to imagine her a part of the conspiracy that had set him adrift. But her survival was too suspicious to ignore.

'So what are you saying?' he asked bluntly. 'That the Hollow Beasts somehow murdered all the other Lost on the island so Lady Arilou would reign supreme?'

'I am saying nothing,' Camber answered quietly, 'but one must look at the facts. Fact one: thanks to Inspector Skein's letter we know that he was investigating some great conspiracy on the Coast of the Lace, and feared for his life. And his

167

was the only Lost body never found. Fact two: the Hollow Beasts lied about his disappearance. Inspector Skein did not join you in the boat, nor did your mooring rope pull loose in the storm – it was cut. You were not meant to survive, Mr Prox, but you did, and thanks to you we have caught the Hollow Beasts out in two deliberate lies. Fact three: the only Lost left alive in the whole of Gullstruck is Lady Arilou of the Hollow Beasts.

'I think we can be fairly sure that Skein found out a little too much in the cove of the Hollow Beasts, and the villagers had to kill him a few hours sooner than they expected. Which meant of course that they had to get you out of the way as well. Whoever else was a part of this great conspiracy, it seems obvious that the Hollow Beasts were at the heart of it.'

There was a long pause while Prox digested Camber's words.

'You need testimonials from me,' Prox said at last, staring at his singed knuckles, 'for their arrests. Is that it?'

Camber looked down and frowned slightly, as if something pained and embarrassed him.

'If you are speaking of arrest for the villagers of the Hollow Beasts . . . no, we do not. We've just received some news about that. The fact is . . . by the time law and order had mobilized, the ordinary people of the area had taken justice into their own hands. There *is* no village of the Hollow Beasts now. It's upsetting, I suppose, but it happened too quickly to be prevented . . .' Camber spread his hands. They were long and elegant, well suited to the gesture. 'The Hollow Beasts simply had no idea what they were unleashing on themselves.'

168

'They're all . . .' Prox's head was suddenly crowded with images – small fists waving shell necklaces at him, elderly creviced smiles . . . 'Ancestors beyond, are you saying the village is destroyed?! There . . . There were *children* there – you're not saying the children . . .'

Camber left a respectful silence before answering. 'You're a humane man,' he said at last. 'Of course this upsets you. It upsets me. Yes, innocence has suffered in the quest for the guilty, but that does not alter the fact that the guilty are still at large.'

'But . . . if everyone there is dead . . .'

'Not quite everybody. Nearly all of the inhabitants have been . . . accounted for. But their Lady Lost seems to be a very cool and practical young woman. It appears that as soon as trouble loomed she grabbed a companion and abandoned the village. There's a warrant out for them, of course – the governor saw fit to hire an Ashwalker.' Camber frowned for a moment and let the tip of his tongue show between his lips, as if testing the flavour of an opinion he might express and deciding against it. 'But the fact is she's disappeared. Which means of course that our problems are far from over.'

'What do you mean?'

'The Lost are *gone*, Mr Prox, and until it happened nobody really realized what a cataclysm like that would do to Gull-struck. We're an island of provinces, separated by volcanoes, vicious ridges, swamps and jungles. Without the Lost, our communications systems simply collapse. We can't report anything, we can't find out anything, we can't check any-thing. A hurricane could hit the north tomorrow, and *we'd* only know about it when it roared down the Wailing Way

169

a few days later. Soon bandits, smugglers, pirates and cut-throats are going to realize that nobody's mind is patrolling the hills to watch for them. Our fishermen and divers count on the Lost to spot shoals or delve through prime coral. Our merchants depend on being able to bargain with each other through the tidings huts – if they can't, we'll see some of our far-flung towns starving this winter.

'And the dark conspiracy surrounding Arilou clearly counted on all of this. They must have thought that we would have no choice but to turn to the Lace, to their Lady Lost and their farsight fish. Rather a nice chance to trade in their shell necklaces for governors' chains, don't you think? This is more than the actions of one village, Mr Prox. This conspiracy must have had agents in every village, every town, ready to strike down every single Lost, all at the same time. This "night of the long knives" must have taken a great deal of plotting and, whatever the conspiracy plans to do next, Arilou must be central to it. We are looking at a secret organization of Lace who have never forgotten the power their people once wielded, and who thought they saw a way to rise again. And in Arilou they have a leader, a sacred totem.'

'She wasn't more than a child herself,' Prox murmured almost to himself. 'Thirteen, fourteen.'

'I'm sure you know what you're talking about,' Camber responded quietly, 'but I've always found it hard to judge the age of Lace. They're generally so small and slight for their years.'

'Is there no doubt that she was involved? Could she be a pawn in all this?'

'Well, I daresay you can judge that better than I.' Again

a sustained respectful pause which made Prox feel stupid. 'I had heard that the Hollow Beasts had no chief or priest, but if you witnessed someone *other* than the Lady Lost running the village, then that would of course be useful for us to know.'

Camber regarded what was left of Prox's face for a few moments and then stood. 'Mr Prox, I am trespassing upon your rest. Let us leave this until tomorrow.'

'Wait . . .' Prox struggled out of his chair. 'You still haven't told me – what does everybody want me to do?'

'They want you to *take charge*, Mr Prox. Somebody *must*, to stop anarchy breaking out, to make sure that everyone is working together against the Lace threat. Somebody needs to find Arilou, before she can rally her troops and do any more damage. You're everyone's hero at the moment, people will listen to you – and my superiors are impressed by your organizational record.'

'But how? I'd need to check with Port Suddenwind, and . . .' Prox trailed off. It was unnecessary to say more. If he wrote to them asking for authority to deal with the Lace threat, he would probably wait six months and then get a letter giving him permission to add lacework to his saddlebags.

'There's a way. Two hundred years ago, when our ancestors needed to find a way of purging the Lace for the good of Gullstruck, they discovered that the existing Cavalcaste murder laws prevented the purge only if the Lace were legally considered to be *people*. And so they drew up a new law stating that if the Lace became too numerous or troublesome then legally they ceased to be people, and were considered to be . . . well . . . timber wolves. And naturally, if there's a plague of two-legged timber wolves you can declare a Time of Nuisance, and elect a Nuisance Control Officer with immediate and automatic island-wide authority to . . . control it. An officer who can act freely, without needing permission for everything from Port Suddenwind.'

'So you think if I became Nuisance Control Officer . . .'

'Oh, I don't think. I'm merely a channel, a utensil. But right now I'm a utensil dedicated to making sure that nobody bullies you into a decision until you're rested, Mr Prox.'

Prox stared at the mirror again. What kind of face would stare back at him when the blisters were no more?

You were not meant to survive . . . With a pang Prox remembered Camber's words. Again he recalled his vomiting in the boat, and wondered if the water in the shell had been poisoned. Had the village been planning his destruction even then? He tried to recall why he had felt a rush of affection and trust for the girl who had run to him with the water. But his mind was still dazzled by the white-hot madness of the three days on the boat, and he could not remember her features.

'I don't need to rest before making a decision,' he said. 'I'll do it. I'll lead the hunt for the Lady Arilou.'

Camber inclined his head in a small, slow bow. 'Then you will have the papers on your desk tomorrow morning, Mr Prox, ready to be signed. And I'll make arrangements for the town courthouse to be turned over to you so you can use it as a base of operations.'

'We'll need to send armed men to Sweetweather,' Prox muttered to himself. 'No more massacres. No more mob violence.'

'Of course. It will take time, through. Obviously there's

no path through the volcanoes' domain, so from here the shortest practical route is due south, then west through Rogue's Pass, and north up the coast to Sweetweather. Four days' journey at least.'

Prox glanced towards the window and flinched as a lance of sunlight struck his eye. Something was troubling him, something to do with what he had just been told, something to do with the papers promised on the morrow. But he could not work out what it was. 'Where . . . ? Where did you say we were again?'

'New Warkbridge, or so the maps have it,' came the answer, 'but nobody calls it that. You'll have heard of the town as Mistleman's Blunder.'

Hathin was woken by sunlight in her eyes and sat up to peer out of the lava bubble.

The clouds that had cloaked everything had receded before the growing heat of the day. It was as if Sorrow herself and her weird white world had drawn back from them with a hiss of white skirts. The sky was a deepening blue, and the crumbly, creamy earth around them was dotted with small blue and pink flowers and little mounds left by burrowing birds. Somehow, miraculously, they had survived to see the sun again. To judge by its height it must be nearing noon. Dizzily she realized that it could only be a matter of twelve hours or so since she had fled the mob with Arilou.

Hathin emerged blinking into sunlight and found that she was standing on a promontory. Before her lay a vast, flattened vista. There below was the Wailing Way, the long trench that Spearhead had carved in his furious departure, the thread of the river meandering along its base. In the far distance the land rolled and rucked, and Spearhead himself could be seen amid his humpbacked army of hills, his head lost in the grey haze of his own anguish and rage.

But near the base of Spearhead she could also make out a haze of white smoke rising from a hundred chimneys and the brilliant green of fields that had been flooded for rice.

As far as Hathin knew, only one town had ever been built in the track gouged by Spearhead's flight, the track he might retrace if he ever decided to renew his quarrel. Everyone knew it as Mistleman's Blunder, after the name of the founder who had ignored the entreaties and advice of the Lace. Mistleman's own daughter had been one of the first that the local Lace had quietly kidnapped and sacrificed in their attempts to appease the volcanoes and save the town, and so the thick jungle north of the trench had been nicknamed Mistleman's Chandlery, a grimly humorous reference to the many trees and vines from which the district's Lace had been hanged, like tallow candles left to drip. The Lace had never been trusted again . . . but nobody had ever built another town in the Wailing Way.

Mistleman's Blunder, however, remained. It did so with grim defiance, testimony to the triumph over the Lace. And it was after all a fine location, conveniently close to the river, surrounded by flat grazing land and within easy reach of many of the obsidian and jade mining outposts in the ridge of mountains.

Hathin sank into a crouch, and for ten minutes she let herself watch the great eagles while they wheeled above and watched her right back. There were things that had to be

174

done, and so there were things that could not be thought about yet. It was as simple as that.

The Ashwalker had come after them. Not just the maddened crowd and the crowd-witch Jimboly, but the *Ashwalker*. Which meant that he must have a licence. For days, Sweetweather had been waiting to see whether the governor would hire the Ashwalker to chase down the murderer of Milady Page . . . and now he had. Hathin swallowed and stared the fact down. The Ashwalker was hunting her and her sister as murderers. Which meant that even the governor must have believed those strange accusations that Jimboly had used to spark the crowd into frenzy, those poisoned hints that Arilou was the centre of a Lace plot to kill all the other Lost.

It was too late to think of appealing to the law and protesting their innocence. Sentence had already been passed. For now, with the help of the King and Sorrow, they had outrun it. However, in a few days others would arrive from Sweetweather, taking the safe but slower paths that detoured down to the southern passes. They would come and ask after two Lace girls, one of them outwardly wander-witted . . .

Mistleman's Blunder. Of all the places they could have fled to, perhaps the city least likely to look kindly upon a pair of vagrant Lace . . .

. . . and suddenly Hathin was recalling a conversation many years before between Eiven and Whish on the day that Whish's eldest son had left on his revenge quest. Whish's voice had been sharp as a gull's.

'*You persuaded him to go? What, it is not enough for me to lose a daughter, I must lose my son on a revenge quest as well? And*

where is he more likely to be strung from a tree than in Mistle-man's Blunder?'

And then Eiven.

'He will find friends and help at the Reckoning. You know that.'

Yes – Whish's eldest son had left for Mistleman's Blunder in order to find help from the secretive Reckoning, so that he could avenge the death of his younger sister. He had never returned. It was likely that he had died in the attempt, or been imprisoned for his pains. However, hope started to beat its angry little drum in Hathin's chest again. Perhaps he was still alive. Perhaps he could be found in Mistleman's Blunder.

Hathin rose unsteadily and hobbled off to search for one of the bird burrows. The one she found was occupied by its rounded, fuzz-feathered resident and, hungry as she was, she could not bring herself to strike it with a rock as it emerged. Instead she waited for the bird to depart, then dug up the mound with her fingers. She wrapped the eggs in leaves and lowered them into a pool of hot mud until they were cooked. They were still a bit gluey and weepy when she broke the shells, but they took the edge off her hunger. Arilou seemed drugged, perhaps drained by her long journey and her outburst of the previous night. She did not protest when Hathin poured half-cooked egg into her mouth.

Then Hathin found a stream where the water was not boiling or discoloured, and brought the sleepy, stumbling Arilou to its banks.

'I'm afraid we'll have to walk again, Arilou,' Hathin said as she washed Arilou's bruised and bloodied feet. She had no reason to believe that Arilou could hear her soothing tone, but it was a matter of habit and Hathin clung to it. 'But it's all downhill from here. We're heading there . . . Mistleman's Blunder. I've got to find Therott, if he's still alive. I need to go to the Reckoning.'

14
BLOODIED BUTTERFLY

After two hours of leading Arilou through the dry tangle of mountain undergrowth, Hathin fell in with some small, companionable streams, all bound for the river at the base of the Wailing Way.

As the ground levelled, the rough ground gave way to paddyfields, carved into squares by ridge paths. King of Fans and Sorrow gradually fell back behind the sisters, and over the next couple of hours the looming shape of Spearhead became more distinct. When they were close enough to the city to make out the white and black specks of grazing sheep and goats on the outskirts Hathin halted and set about making Arilou a nest amid the ferns.

'I'm going to have to leave you here for a while, Arilou,' Hathin said as she found some heavy rocks and placed them on Arilou's hem to stop her standing and straying. 'I'm nothing to look at, but people will notice you.' Then she beat the worst of the white dust out of her clothes, kicked the sad tatters of her shoes aside, and set off towards Mistleman's Blunder, barefoot and alone.

As she grew closer the town resolved into a sprawling mass of hundreds of palm-thatch roofs, clustered as if some enormous and untidy bird had abandoned its nest half made. In the heart a clutch of crimson clay-tile roofs and walls formed neat rounds about a central tower. Hathin saw these grander houses and knew only that they were Doorsy, no place for her. What she did not know was that they were mostly no place for anyone living.

Like many of the older colonial towns on Gullstruck, Mistleman's Blunder was dying from the inside out. Many centuries before, the Cavalcaste homeland plains had been full of warring, horse-mounted clans fighting each other for land that they could dedicate to their own dead. The Ashlands were commonly placed at the centre of their cities so that they could be protected by the outer ring of the living. The problem was, of course, that once the Ashlands at the centre of town were 'full' of the dead, there was nowhere for the dead to go but into the houses of the living. Families found themselves cohabiting with the urns of their ancestors, yielding them first one room and then another, until the living were squashed into a tiny corner of their own home. Finally they would give up and build themselves a new and smaller house even further out on the edge of the city, surrendering their old house to the dead. And so it would go on. There were many great cities, both on Gullstruck and in the original Cavalcaste homeland, that were thriving at their edges but dead at their hearts. Mistleman's Blunder was just such a city. And so it had grown and grown, swallowing precious farmland, pushing the inhabitants' paddyfields out and out until they were brought up short by the volcanoes and there was nowhere left to till.

As Hathin reached the ramshackle outskirts she faltered,

uncertain. Her only hope of finding Therrot was to make her way to the Reckoning, the legendary revenger meeting house.

The ancient Lace tradition of the revenge quest had been illegal since the Lace purges. However, over time ominous rumours had spread that there were still Lace pursuing such quests, and that the revengers were working together, becoming a formidable and frightening force. The idea of a secret, murderous conspiracy of Lace revengers terrified the non-Lace. And the name of this conspiracy, this nightmare, was the Reckoning.

The governors had taken this new threat very seriously. Ashwalkers at least worked with laws and licences, but Lace revengers operated outside the law and answered to nobody. How could you reason with people like that? What could you do but stamp them out?

For over a century the governors had waged war against the Reckoning. Rewards had been offered for anyone found wearing the revenger's mark, the butterfly wing that was tattooed on the forearm when a revenge oath was sworn. The Lost Council assisted the forces of law and order, scanning the wild places for the Reckoning's hideouts until at last they reported that the secret cult of revengers was no more.

Only the Lace knew that the Reckoning was far from dead. The cult still thrived in the shadows.

The location of the Reckoning's headquarters was never spoken aloud, and Hathin knew only that it was near Mistleman's Blunder. She had to hope that the local Lace would point her in the right direction. And surely there would be Lace working and trading in this town. She need only look in the barren, unwanted places and there she would find their stalls . . .

But where were they? Here were the trains of shambling pack-birds bearing loads of obsidian down from the mountainside mines and the shallow streams that had raged into the Wailing Way from the heights of the King and Sorrow. There should have been a dozen Lace girls selling wares to the workers or stirring through the torrent-borne shingle for tiny pieces of obsidian that had been missed.

The main street was flanked by narrow wooden houses whose planks bore the tide-marks of floods, and whose palm roofs were grey and ragged. The labourers who worked up to their waists in the paddyfields had apparently brought a good deal of the mud home with them, walked it all over the streets and through everybody's expression. But first and foremost, Mistleman's Blunder was an obsidian town. There was something sharp and brittle in the stances and faces of the pale-faced miners queuing before the merchants to have their packs of obsidian weighed. Hathin trembled under cold, hard, curious gazes. There were no smiles here, so there could be no Lace.

Hathin quietly loosed her cloth belt and tied it about her head to hide her shaven forehead. Suddenly she was grateful for the white dust which she had feared would draw attention to her. Now she realized that it was the only thing that might conceal the unmistakable Lace embroidery of her skirt. She let one of her hands hover in front of her telltale Lace smile, as if waiting to smother a sneeze.

From time to time despite herself she felt her heart leap with hope. A young woman scrubbing a table outside a

 181

toolmender's reminded her for a moment of Mother Govrie in gesture and feature. But the woman looked up and met her eye without a smile or any of the silent signs of camaraderie with which even unacquainted Lace greeted one another. A young man polishing amber pieces with a steel brush had a jagged coral cut along his forearm like many of the young divers in her village, but when Hathin got closer she saw that his lower lip was painted with berry juice, showing him to be from the tribe of the Bitter Fruit.

One shack that stood alone smelt strongly of hot, sick fruit, and outside it men of all ages sat and sipped tiny wooden cups of steaming liquid. A white-haired old man grimaced as he tasted his, and for a second Hathin was sure that she saw a wink of jewelled colour in his teeth. She settled down behind a well-pump to watch him.

A previous life leaves marks on the manners, just as floods leave tidemarks on riverbanks. As he drank from his shallow cup, the old man unthinkingly held up a hand on the windy side, shielding his drink from sand that was not there. And then as she watched he wiped the tip of his little finger around the rim of the cup with care. It was one of the many small unexplained rituals that Father Rackan had always performed in mute serenity. *All is well, Father Rackan is taking care of things, everything he does means something.*

Heart pounding, Hathin emerged from her hiding place and approached him.

'Father.'

The old man's face tensed, and the lines about his mouth wore deeper into his face.

'I no father,' he said curtly. He got up and slid some worn

shoes on without looking at her. Perhaps he had already realized his mistake. He had answered her in Nundestruth, but Hathin had addressed him in Lace, using the word that could mean both 'father' or 'priest'.

Hathin watched him toss down a coin and walk away, then followed. He turned to confront her two streets later.

'Got nothing for you! Go!'

She retreated a few steps before his angrily flailing arm, and then continued following. He was waiting for her around the next corner and grabbed her by the shoulder.

'Nothing for Lace here! Wrap goods belong-you, runoff back coast! Go!'

He strode to a shamble-shack of weather-darkened planks and shut a wicker-mat door behind him. Hathin settled herself on the post outside his hut, and after a few moments he came marching out with a couple of flatcakes and a corked leather bottle.

'Take. Get you far as coast. Fill bottle stream, water fine. Go!'

'Father . . .' Hathin spoke softly in Lace. 'I'm looking for the Reckoning.'

He stared at her in angry hesitation, and then took hold of her hands and turned them over so that the soft part of her forearms was uppermost.

'Well, you won't find it,' he muttered in Lace. 'Only the revengers ever can. If you don't have a revenge-quest tattoo to show them, they'll kill you for even entering their jungle.' He retreated into the shack, shutting his flimsy door with an air of finality.

Their jungle. Where else? Mistleman's Chandlery would

 183

be a haunted area avoided by the rest of the town. And it was a peculiarly Lace piece of pride and defiance, to set up a head-quarters in a place linked with their own ignominy and pain. *We shall take everything you do to us and make it into something else.* But Hathin needed more directions than 'the jungle' or she would never find the Reckoning.

She looked down at the flatcakes in her arms, and as usual the pang she felt was not for her own hunger. Arilou would be starving, and had been left too long alone.

A little before dusk the old Lace priest peered through his wicker door again and found not one but two young girls waiting outside.

'You children! You're like cats! Feed one and there's hundreds of you mewling underfoot!' His eye slid over Arilou, taking in her bruised feet and vacant air.

'She's an imbecile,' Hathin said quickly.

'Then use her to beg! You've already emptied my cupboard of kindness.'

An hour later when he looked out again, they were still there, the white ash powdering them like sugared fruits. The smaller girl stared steadily at the door, as silent and stubborn as the settling of dust. When at last he held the door open for them they slipped in meekly and mutely, the smaller stooping to guide the taller girl's faltering feet on the wooden steps.

He picked the cork out of a crock of fish oil, dipped some strips of flatbread into it, then set them in Hathin's hands.

'I know your story, you know.'

Hathin's heart lurched at his words, but then realized that the old man could know nothing of the sisters' flight from the law. Their desperate journey across the mountains had saved them three days' travel. News from Sweetweather would have to tramp the slow route through the passes to reach Mistleman's Blunder.

'It's not an uncommon tale,' went on the old man. 'Your father or your elder brother goes off on a revenge quest and doesn't come back – and so you get the idea that you'll find him and bring him home and everything will be the way it was before.' He sighed. 'It never *is* the way it was before. A revenger always becomes somebody else. When you say goodbye to them you say it forever.' His voice had the harsh tone kind men often use when they are forcing out cruel truths.

Hathin broke up the bread and fed it to Arilou in water-soaked chunks, then stroked her throat to encourage her to swallow.

'You'll have to go home!'

'We can't.' Hathin held one of Arilou's hands in both of hers, kneading it gently as the older girl's head gradually drooped to rest on Hathin's shoulder. 'Father, I haven't come to you for directions this time. I've come to you for the tattoo.'

'What? Don't be absurd.'

'I have cause.'

'Then you should talk to your local priest, someone who knows the rights of the matter. But he'll tell you the same thing. Even if there really was a good reason for a revenge quest, it could never be granted to you.' He sighed. 'Any such quest can be granted to one person and one alone, you understand? If it was given to you, then the burden of bringing justice and restoring balance would rest on you and

185

you alone. Nobody else would be able to take up the quest. So the wrong would go unrighted, because all the strong young men who might have taken the tattoo have been prevented by a hasty little girl.'

Hathin stared down at her hands, intertwined with Arilou's soft one, and said nothing.

'The devil of the thing will be getting you back to your own village,' the old priest added after a sympathetic pause. 'Where exactly are you from?'

Hathin looked up at him, her eyes dark pools above the smile with the nervous ruck.

'My village has no name,' she said. The old priest opened his mouth to answer and then stopped and blinked slowly three times as her meaning swung over him like a searchlight.

'The whole—'

'Nobody in our village has a name but us. We are the village now. We have no priest, no family, no friends. They didn't even leave us our enemies.'

There was a long silence, but for cicadas grinding moonlight into silver dust in the streets outside.

'Daughter, listen to me.' There was a new, careful seriousness in the old man's tone now. 'Think carefully about this. If you take up this quest, you give yourself up to revenge. If you succeed, you become a killer; if you fail, you leave a tear in the world that nobody else can mend. Some day many years from now you might choose to marry. Your husband and children will see your tattoo and know that you have either shed blood or betrayed the world's trust in you. Choose this path, and it will never leave you.'

He left her sitting at the moonlit table next to a bundle of

186

blankets, and retired to his bedding mat in the corner. For an hour there was little sound but the creaking of his mat, which seemed to have become uncommonly uncomfortable to him this night. Hathin made no noise, but remained seated at the table. Stubborn as dust.

Eventually he sat up with a sigh, his hair sketching wild white arcs about his head.

'I suppose you realize that it will hurt?' he said gruffly.

The Ashwalker lay on a stretcher by the road in the moonlight, a strange sculpture in red, white and blue, blood and ash marring the uniformity of his indigo clothes and skin. His eyes were wide white rings showing around the dark eyes in the deep blue sockets.

Prox stared at him, shivering a little in the night air. He had been allowed only two hours of sweet sleep before the excited voices in the street had woken him.

'How did he die?' he asked at last.

'Er, Mr Prox? I do not believe that he *is* dead.' Camber pointed up at the sky. 'I'm not sure, but I think he might be watching the bats.'

Prox waved a hand in front of the Ashwalker's unblinking eyes. But the Ashwalker's chest did indeed seem to be rising and falling. 'How long has he been like this?'

'Difficult to say. He was found by the roadside an hour ago. But, as you see, he's covered in white ash. Our best guess is that he must have dragged himself all the way from Sorrow's domain.'

'Well, if he's not dead, he's had the sense knocked out of him,' sighed Prox.

 187

'Perhaps – but it is rather hard to tell with Ashwalkers.'

They both stared at him for a few moments.

'If he does awaken, he will not be happy if we have removed any of his dye,' continued Camber, 'so we cannot clean his skin, clothes or his wounds. And for all I know he might be fasting so we cannot risk feeding him either. The fact is –' Camber gave a small, rueful smile – 'I am not at all sure what we *can* do with him.'

'Oh, for pity's sake. Well, we can't just stand here waiting for him to wake up and explain himself.'

Even as he watched for the shadow-dance of the bats, Brendril was listening to the two voices passing over him. The actual words themselves did not interest him greatly, but the two men did. Both thought that they could use words to make people do what they wanted, and one of them was right. The younger man with the scarred face tried to gust people along with a fussy logic, pelting them with reasons like fistfuls of feathers. The lean, older man with the plausible smile used words to gloss and slope the ground so that people slithered quite naturally in the direction he wished, not even knowing why.

'. . . is the key,' the younger man was saying. 'I'll help this artist of yours make a woodcut of Lady Arilou, and then we can send messengers with pictures of her back to Sweet-weather and beyond so we can find out if anyone's seen her. She'll probably be heading north along the coast – she can gather support from the villages as she travels . . .'

Brendril's pain had interested him, but now he silently shrugged it off. Human expressions meant less and less to him every year, but he was almost certain that the two men looked startled when he sat up.

'The Lady Lost is not travelling along the coast,' he said. 'She is here.'

The old priest was right. Receiving the tattoo did hurt, a great deal. It was still hurting several hours later as Hathin made her way alone under cover of darkness to Mistleman's Chandlery. She dared not touch the leaves which now bandaged the place, and through which she could see dark stains soaking. As she blundered up the side of the gorge, she held her left forearm protectively against her chest.

The idea of taking the tattoo had first occurred to her when she was looking for ways of reaching Therrot, if he was still alive to be reached. If she turned up marked, the Reckoning could scarcely turn her away. But then the thought had worked its arrowhead into her mind so that she could not pull it out. There was too much feeling inside her, too many dead a step behind her. And so in the end she had run to the tattoo, knowing only that she needed it.

It was a hard hike up the side of the trench of the Wailing Way, but tree roots burst and looped from the soil, offering footholds and handholds. As Hathin reached the top dark and hostile jungle came down to meet her. Tan-coloured vines as thick as her arm trailed across her way, vast spider webs hung like sails and slender shafts of moonlight bored down to glance on the varnished backs of fat mahogany beetles and gaping flesh-coloured orchids.

There was no path, and only the old priest's directions allowed her to pick out landmarks to guide her steps – a butterfly-shaped flourish of roots, along scratch in a tree

 189

trunk, a trailing noose-like ribbon tied to a bough.

A long whistle close by made her jump until she recognized it as a male honeydigger's lovesong. It was answered by an absolute echo a hundred paces away, and it was a few seconds before she realized why the hairs were rising on the back of her neck. Two male honeydiggers would not have been exchanging such calls. The first should have been answered by a challenge or by a female.

The denizens of the forest had noticed her.

'I've come . . .' Her voice sounded tiny in a forest that now seemed to be full of restless motions and trilling calls. 'I'm looking for . . .'

The tree beside her suddenly spat out a chunk of its moss. Staring, bewildered, Hathin realized that there was a sharp stone embedded in the bark. It must have flown from behind her, narrowly missing her head, with enough force to stick in the tree . . . and now there were whistles all around, and something came towards her with a bobbing sway and two heads of different sizes.

A moment of paralysis, and then Hathin was urgently snatching the leaves from her left arm, wincing as the tears came. Even in the darkness she could not bear to look at the bloodied lines that the priest's chisel had cut into her skin. Amber soot dabbed into the wounds sketched one wing of a butterfly. She clenched her eyes shut as she extended her arm, tattoo upwards, so that the moonlit jungle could witness it.

Something struck her softly on the head. She flinched backwards, eyes open again, and found a slim rope of plaited vines swaying against her flank. There were loops at intervals up its length.

190

The two-headed monster drew closer, and the shivering spoonfuls of moonlight showed her a young man astride a muzzled elephant bird. He pointed at the rope and jerked a thumb upwards.

Hathin patted some of the leaves back on to her wound, then carefully placed her foot in the lowest loop and started to climb.

15
FOR THE WRONGED A RECKONING

Climbing loop by loop, Hathin pushed great ferns aside and then watched them swing together below her, cutting out the forest floor. Up through an airy world of gently swaying branches, then into a dense cloud of tapering leaves that slithered over her skin. The moon's rays arrived piecemeal and cat's eye green through the foliage.

At last Hathin's questing fingers felt her rope end in a knot around a bough. Beside her lay a rough platform of boards, nailed along the top of a branch. Gingerly she stepped out on to it, the drop below pushing tingles of panic through her knees.

Where the branch met the vast trunk, it was shrouded by a great shadow-clotted tangle the size of a large hut, made up of leaves, staves and trailing creeper. As she approached it along the branch-platform a tall, slight figure stepped forward out of the darkness and took her by the hands.

It was a young man, not more than twenty, with a face as smooth as quicksand and brows like bands of black velvet. Hathin trembled as he examined her tattoo by the light of a hanging lantern. He nodded briefly, and when he glanced at her face his expression had somehow become less threatening.

'You had this done tonight?'

Hathin nodded.

'Nice bit of work,' he said with an odd gentleness. 'You'll want some more leaves to put on that though, or it'll swell up like a coconut by morning. Dance!'

The last word was much louder than the rest, and for a brief, horrified moment Hathin thought it was a command. But a moment later she realized that his shout had been directed over his shoulder.

The leaves on the nearest side of the great knot of foliage trembled. Then the creepers were pushed aside like a curtain and a woman emerged. A wealth of glossy black plaits tumbled from beneath her brown velvet skullcap fringed with black feathers. She stood over six feet tall, and managed her broad shoulders and large limbs with a leisurely, mannish grace. From head to foot she was dressed like one of the women of the Bitter Fruit, berry juices used to paint her lower lip to a false fullness and to sketch 'veins' across her upper arms in a faint feathering. Her lower arms were hidden in a pair of widow's arm bindings.

She did not look or dress like a Lace, but this was the Reckoning and there could be only Lace here. Evidently this was another Lace who had gone to great lengths to hide her lineage.

The woman came close and looked down at Hathin's upturned face. She did not look like a 'Dance'. Perhaps a 'Quell-With-A-Blow-Or-A-Look'. But not a 'Dance'.

'Who are you here for?' the woman asked in Lace, her voice so deep that Hathin could feel it in her foot soles. Bewildered, Hathin nearly gave Therrot's name, but then understood

Dance's meaning. *Who are you here to avenge?* Hathin opened a dry mouth to begin the catalogue, and her mind crowded with ghosts.

'Everybody,' she said at last.

Dance studied her for a few moments, then nodded very slowly, as if it was an answer she heard every day. She lowered herself to sit on the platform floor.

'Tell me,' she said. And Hathin did, hearing her own voice become a pinched, emotionless rattle of words, counting off unthinkable events. And all the time she watched the woman, trying to see if she was saying too much, looking for the characteristic Lace stiffening or gaze-glitter that meant 'Be careful – who knows who might be listening?' but the woman just kept nodding and watching her between slow blinks.

It was only as Hathin reached the end of her narrative that she started to feel a crushing sense of shame. The old priest was right. What possessed her, tiny and frail as she was, to stand before this giantess and demand the rights of an avenger?

'I . . . I didn't know what else to do,' Hathin added after a long pause. 'There didn't seem to be any choice.'

Dance gave a long sigh and slowly shook her head. 'No. No choice at all, as far as I can see. There may be somebody on this island with a better right to a revenge quest than you, but I haven't met them.' As Hathin flushed with surprised relief Dance stood. 'I had better go and tell Therrot.'

'He . . . He's alive? He's here?'

Dance nodded. 'There's no chance that his family survived?'

Hathin bit her lip. 'I really don't think so. His mother is

dead – I am sure of that. And his younger brother – he was down on the beach . . . I don't think anybody escaped the beach.'

'Right. Right.' Dance sighed again. As Dance turned Hathin found herself thinking of the slow rolling of a whale, muscular and momentous. Dance disappeared back through the creeper curtain, and for a while Hathin sat alone.

When at long last the curtain parted again, the man peering through seemed for a moment to be a stranger. Hathin had remembered Therrot as a taller, more muscular version of his brother Lohan, his laugh a little fiercer and louder, and with strange bulging tensions that moved in his cheeks when he was angry.

The young man before her had slender, wasted limbs, traced with a fine webwork of scars. His hair had grown long, and the little movements in his cheeks were now nervous and continual. He stared at her with something that resembled dread. Therrot had not come home, for there had been no Therrot left.

But his eyes looked like Lohan's eyes, and Hathin felt that the whole of the village of the Hollow Beasts had risen up to reproach her for failing to save them.

'I'm sorry,' was all she could say. 'I'm sorry . . .' Therrot vanished in a mist of tears, and she heard the creepers rustle as he lurched quickly forward. Two arms surrounded her and lifted her from the ground, and Therrot was squeezing her so tightly she could hardly breathe.

'Little sister,' he said over and over. 'Little sister. We'll get them, we'll get them, we'll get all of them . . .'

'Yes!' Hathin held on to him as if she was drowning. 'Yes, we will, we will . . .'

Ten minutes passed before they were capable of saying anything else. Then Therrot set Hathin down gently and led her back towards the vine curtain through which he had emerged. As she followed him she became aware of a grumbling buzz and dark beads of angry life that drew dowsing circles in the air. In among the great tangle of sticks, vines and daub were greyish protruberances like mottled urns.

'Wasps' nests,' Therrot explained. 'The towners won't go near them. There are more on the branches below too, so they cover the sounds of our voices if we keep them low.'

'Don't they sting you?'

'Of course they do.' Therrot sounded surprised at the question.

Beyond the vine curtain was a round 'room' of sorts. The floor was a mix of dead vine, matting, packed straw and board. Around the edges of the room sat little lanterns on broad tin dishes. Hatchin felt Therrot's hand settle protectively on her shoulder as they straightened to face the assembled gathering.

Dance reclined in a rocking chair of wine-red wood, a pipe between her teeth. Around her, eager, angular faces, the glitter of jewelled teeth, Lace voices weaving through one another with a sibilant urgency. The darkness smelt of the oil lanterns, the livid scent of the tree's sap, rotting leather boots, fungus . . . but also something indescribably Lace, like a flavour in the air, something that Hathin had never noticed until she found it missing.

'And here she is,' Dance said. Hathin realized that she must have been relating Hathin's story. 'This woman has volunteered to mend a ragged great rip in the universe. Make space for her.' A lean, long-toothed man with razor-edge cheekbones moved the machetes he was cleaning to make room for Hathin on the rug. A light blanket was wrapped around her shoulders, and a mug of something hot and sweet placed in her hands.

Therrot was whispering in Hathin's ear, all the while gently squeezing her shoulder as if to anchor her.

'That's Marmar – he once killed a man with a pomegranate. That's Louloss – she makes those.' Therrot gestured at the walls, and Hathin glimpsed dozens of hanging faces, all plum-sized and carved from wood. 'They're likenesses of our enemies – we use them to track people down. And you've met Jaze.' It was the young man with velvety black brows who had checked Hathin's tattoo outside. 'Jaze took on an entire gang of smugglers armed with nothing but a conch.' Jaze grinned and held up his arms to show the outcome of the fight. The tattoos on his two forearms were mirror images, the butterfly completed, the universe satisfied.

Therrot ran through the names of the dozen or so men and women in the chamber, proudly listing their revenges like titles, and in turn the strangely scarred and painted faces lapsed into their Lace smiles, uneasily, as though their muscles had lost the habit. Hathin became aware of a warmth stealing over her. It was all new and alarming, but somehow it also felt like a homecoming.

Dance interrupted at last. 'Sorry, Hathin, usually I would not have repeated your story to others until you were ready. But your tale involves the death of Raglan Skein . . . and that affects everyone in the Reckoning.'

'Is it true?' It was Marmar, the pomegranate assassin, a short man with a bulky, boxer-dog frame and a hook-shaped

 197

scar on his brow. 'You saw his body?'

Hathin gave a flustered nod.

Marmar let out a huff of breath. 'Even after we'd heard of all those other Lost deaths, I still hoped he'd survived somehow.' He hissed through his teeth and brushed a wasp off his leg. 'He always seemed to be prepared for everything.'

'Nobody is prepared for everything,' Dance rumbled quietly. 'Not even Raglan.'

Hathin listened, bewildered. Surely a man such as Inspector Skein would be the revengers' enemy of enemies? Surely the Reckoning must have lived in constant fear of being found out by the Lost?

Marmar turned back to Hathin. 'What do you know about the way he died?'

Hathin flushed helplessly before his interrogative gaze. 'It . . . It wasn't us! I mean . . .' Her sentence trailed away. She and Arilou were blameless, but there was still the possibility that someone else from the Hollow Beasts really had killed Skein. That imagined image of Eiven, stalking across the sand with an urchin's spine . . .

'No. We know that, Hathin.' Dance's rumbling baritone again. 'Whatever the law thinks, we know you and yours had nothing to do with his murder.' In the face of Dance's tone of utter certainty, Hathin's nightmare image of a murderous Eiven wavered and melted away, and she suddenly felt sick at the disloyalty of her own imagination. 'Raglan's death was part of something much larger, something that we do not really understand yet. But can you tell what killed him? Any cuts, bruises, anything odd?'

'Nothing. Only . . . he was smiling a little.'

'Just the same as the others,' said Marmar. 'Dance – that's all of them gone. Every single one. The whole Lost Council, Skein and every other ally we had among the Lost. If any of them still had their name, they'd have contacted us by now. We're alone, aren't we? What happens when the governors find someone new to take over the job of hunting down outlaws like us? Whoever they are, they won't be covering our tracks for us the way the Lost Council did. What the hell do we do now?'

'You . . . ?' Daunted as she was, Hathin could not stay silent. 'You mean the Lost Council *knew* where the Reckoning was? They . . . ? They weren't hunting you? They were *hiding* you from the law?'

'Yes, Hathin.' Dance eased her rocking chair backwards, dry vines crackling beneath the runners. 'Understand this: nothing is the way most people imagine.

'To begin with, the great alliance between the Lost and the governors has always been a lie. The two worked hand in hand, but each had their spare hand resting on their dagger hilt. The Lost have always had enemies, powerful enemies – governors who do not like sharing their power with people they cannot control; old Cavalcaste families who despise the Lost for coming from tribal bloodlines.'

Hathin thought of the Sweetweather governor's house and Milady Page's bungalow glowering at each other across the market square.

'The Lost have always needed friends,' continued Dance, 'and at last the Council found us. Or rather . . . one of them found me.

'There was once a man of the Bitter Fruit who loved

arguments. He argued with his neighbours, his family and finally the local governor. So when a young girl in his town went missing, the governor blamed the Bitter Fruit man and hired an Ashwalker to stalk him, and nobody else spoke up for the accused. Nobody but his wife, and no one listened to her. He fled to the hills, but the Ashwalker found him, killed him, took his ash and moved on.' Dance ignored a wasp as it pendulum-swung before her face for a few seconds and then dizzied its way upwards.

'What nobody in the town knew was that although his widow did not look it, she was half-Lace and had been brought up in a Lace cockling village. She took the tattoo, learned the use of sword and sling, and set off to trace the Ashwalker. She had searched for a year in vain when a Lost Council investigator called Raglan Skein approached her and gave her the location of the Ashwalker.'

Dance took another drag from her pipe, and smiled a wide, smoky, mirthless smile.

'Most Lost don't like us,' she said, 'but they like the Ashwalkers a lot less. An Ashwalker doesn't care about justice, only about getting the ash. And it's well known that every Ashwalker secretly drools at the idea of getting the ash of a Lost. They're perfect killers for the men of power who can put a licence in their pockets – you don't have to pay them, or feed them, or give them reasons. They never stop hunting unless you kill them, and nobody's willing to go up against them – except us.

'Men of power hate us because they cannot control us. We are driven by our wrongs, not their orders. And nobody is above *our* law. Not even –' she smiled slightly as if at a private thought or memory – 'not even a governor.'

'Did you . . . ? Did you find the Ashwalker?' asked Hathin timidly. 'The one who killed your husband?'

'Yes,' Dance said. 'The hard bit was luring him on to the wooden bridge I had prepared. As I hoped, he had no magic for detecting sawn-through planks, or powers to prevent him falling into rivers. He scrambled out again, of course, but when the dye ran so did he. It was easy enough to follow the trail of blue puddles up the hillside –' she reached out to tap the ash from her pipe into a metal vase – 'and when I caught up with him the fight itself didn't take long.

'Raglan and I remained friends afterwards. The alliance between the Reckoning and the Lost community was as much his idea as mine. Skein said that the Lost could help point us towards guilty parties, but in exchange we had to promise to keep them informed of our doings and take every care to harm none but our quarry, to avoid burning up everything in our paths, like lava flows. I agreed.

'And so for fifteen years the Lost have lied to the governors to protect us. We have been their secret hand in the world, and in return they have been our shield, our eyes and our ears. And now . . . they are all dead.'

Hathin could only stare at Dance as the world turned itself neatly upside down.

'We can see only a little way into the murk of their murders, but those clues we do have are thanks to Raglan Skein. A few months ago, he told me that the Lost Council had found out something dangerous and important. But he said he would not give me details until he was sure. He said he was afraid I would be . . . upset.'

'Upset' seemed a funny word to connect with Dance. Hathin could not imagine her fainting or bursting into tears. But then again, Hathin suspected that that was not quite what Skein had meant.

'The Lost Council realized that their discoveries had put them in danger, so they invented an "inspection of Lost children" and used it as an excuse to send their investigators away to the furthest corners of the island, where enemies wouldn't find them easily. But Raglan told me that he was travelling to the Coast of the Lace so that he could keep on investigating at the same time.'

Hathin remembered the flurry of panic into which Inspector Skein's visit had thrown the Hollow Beasts. And all the while Skein had just been going through the motions, not giving two whistles whether the Lady Arilou passed or failed her test.

'Think back, little sister.' Therrot had settled next to her. 'Can you remember anything that might help us find out what Inspector Skein was investigating? Dance tells us that you said he was waiting for some sort of message.'

Hathin racked her fuzzy, exhausted brain.

'Yes – he said so, just before he died. That's why he had to send his mind away to look for it. And that letter of his the governor found said that he would be checking the Smattermast tidings hut every two hours for a message from Sightlord Fain.' Hesitantly she recited the wording of Skein's letter as accurately as she could. As she did so, she realized that the mysterious 'D' mentioned in the letter had to be Dance.

After she had finished there was silence.

'This is bad,' said Jaze. Several of the Reckoning nodded

their assent. 'No wonder those townspeople went into a frenzy – that letter makes it sound like Skein was investigating *the Lace*. If that idea takes hold . . .'

'I . . .' Hathin looked from face to face. 'I think it already has – in Sweetweather, anyway. Jimboly . . . well, she made sure of that . . .'

There was a cold, dark silence, and Hathin sensed that a typical Lace conversation-without-words was taking place. But for once she could not hear the unspoken, and it made her feel like a little child again.

'I don't . . . What will happen? What will it mean?'

'Witch-hunt,' rumbled Dance. 'It won't stop with your village, Hathin. They won't be able to back down; they'll have to take another step forward instead. Next thing you know, every governor on the island will be looking for the murderers of the Lost among the ranks of the Lace.'

'This letter.' Jaze frowned. 'You say the governor has it?'

'If the governors' men are pawing through Skein's papers,' growled Marmar, 'then we're not safe here. Skein knew so much about us – what if he's mentioned us in a journal or a letter?'

'Raglan was always careful.' Dance compressed her lips around her pipe stem. 'He would never have set down anything about us in writing.'

Hathin suddenly remembered Eiven flicking through the pages of the book from Skein's travel pack.

'Inspector Skein *did* have a journal,' she said in a small voice.

'Where is it?' demanded Dance.

'We had to give it back . . . but we kept this bit.' Hathin

 203

rummaged in her belt-bag and pulled out the crumpled pages Eiven had removed.

'This is Doorsy writing,' Therrot commented in frustration and disgust. 'Jaze! You were a clerk's apprentice in your last life, weren't you?'

Jaze was passed the pages and squinted at them for a minute through a pair of resin lenses that rested in his eye sockets like monocles.

'You say your Inspector friend was careful about what he wrote down,' he commented at last with a sigh. 'I wish he had been less careful. I can wring *some* sense from these scrawls, but it still reads like a sort of code. The first page seems to be a list of Lace villages, with a few mysterious words after each village name. For example, "Wake's Tail – three eagles, one King, five storms." Or here's another: "Pearlpit – seven cliffs, one eagle, one join R." After each of them there's a string of words . . . that aren't words. No words I've seen before, anyway. Then at the bottom there's a single line by itself. "News from Jealousy – Bridle believes that Lord S will return when the rains end or soon after."

'The second page makes a bit more sense. Listen to this. "Fain's note: C has agreed to cooperate with us, has asked to meet with all the Sightlords, says there is scheme against us, promises to reveal all. Fain says if he does not return I must assume treachery and reveal everything I know in Sweetweather tidings hut."

There was a pause, filled with nothing but the drone of the wasps.

'All right.' Jaze removed his monocles. 'We have a hook in this thing now – let's see if we can pull it up and have a look at it. Somebody, this "C" person, arranged a secret meeting with the Lost Council so that all the Sightlords would be in the same place at the same time. So, either C truly wanted to warn them but did so too late . . . or he led them into a trap.'

'So . . . do we think the Lost Council were ambushed, to stop them revealing this dangerous thing they had discovered?' The speaker was Louloss, a tired-looking, wisp-haired woman in her forties. 'And then somehow Skein was killed, followed by the other Lost, just in case they'd been told something, or discovered the same secret in their wanderings?'

'It's possible,' answered Jaze, 'the Lost always looked after their own. If only some had been killed, the others would have investigated long distance. The only way to kill Lost safely would be to kill all of them.'

'But the murderers did *not* kill all of them,' rumbled Dance softly. 'One of them still lives. Hathin's sister. Arilou.'

Hathin's sister. Arilou. Not the Lady Arilou, no, here she was first and foremost Hathin's sister. This might have meant more to Hathin if ice-spiders had not been tickling her spine. The larger the conspiracy loomed in her mind, the stranger Arilou's survival seemed.

'So why?' asked Marmar. 'Why kill the other Lost and leave Arilou alive?'

'I don't doubt Arilou was meant to die with the rest,' answered Dance, 'but she didn't. Do you have any idea why, Hathin?'

Therrot, who was sitting beside Hathin, visibly tensed, and Hathin could feel him struggling against the engrained habit of talking carefully about Arilou's powers.

 205

'Arilou . . .' Therrot gave Hathin a brief veiled look of apology. 'It was never public, but there's always been doubt . . .'

'I think she's a Lost,' said Hathin suddenly. Therrot closed his eyes and gave a small but impatient sigh. 'No . . . really. I . . . I know what you're going to say, Therrot. It's true, everyone in . . . in our village secretly believed she was just backward. And I'd started to believe that too. We *needed* her to be a Lost, we had to tell ourselves that we *did* believe it, to help us keep up the "lie", and so underneath we were all sure it *was* a lie. But now . . . I don't know, but I'm starting to think she might really be a Lost. She just . . . doesn't bother with people much.'

'Well, it looks like *they* think she's a Lost,' said Dance. 'Whoever is behind this. They must have found out that one Lost had survived. That is why they sent in this Jimboly with orders to stir the town into destroying your village. It had to go, because whatever they did to kill the Lost hadn't worked on Arilou.' Hathin thought of Jimboly throwing a rock at the back of Arilou's head to see if she'd duck. Testing her to see whether she was a Lost and needed to be killed. And Arilou had ducked.

'But why . . . ?' Therrot sounded as if his throat was filling with tears. 'If this conspiracy just wanted Arilou dead, why send a mob after the whole village? They didn't need to kill *everyone*.'

'Think, Therrot,' Jaze said gently. 'A Lost survived. *They* didn't know what she'd seen on the night of the murders or who she'd told. The only safe course was to kill everybody she might have talked to . . .' Jaze trailed off as Therrot scrambled to his feet, shoved his way to the vine door and jumped out into the wasp-filled darkness.

'Let him be.' Dance sighed, and then continued for all the world as if nobody had just thrown themselves out of the hut. 'Hathin, do you truly believe your sister is a Lost? That will affect all our plans.'

Hathin thought of Arilou's horrified frenzy on the plains of Sorrow. She nodded.

'Then we gamble,' said Dance. 'If we *do* have the only Lost left on the island, then we have to try to get some sense out of her. She might be our best weapon and our only hope of finding out who killed the Lost and the Hollow Beasts – and why. Hathin and Arilou must reach the Beacon School. The teachers there might know something, or be able to help Arilou. And perhaps while they are passing through the city of Jealousy, they can find this Bridle mentioned in Skein's notes, and find out about this "Lord S".'

Dance's rocking chair creaked as she rose and stared around the room.

'We're moving out of the Wasp's Nest. All of us. From this point everyone with an unfinished quest will put it aside while we help Hathin with hers.'

One or two revengers flinched and reached towards their covered forearms, as though their unsatisfied tattoos had stung them, scorpion-like.

'Yes.' Dance answered the unasked questions. 'We must all act in this. Whatever it was the Lost discovered, it involves the Lace – and so it concerns us. Raglan virtually admitted as much when he refused to tell me what he knew.

'Besides, the slaughter of the Hollow Beasts was not a freak mob riot – it was planned. Yes, we could go to Sweetweather, rip the hearts out of a few frightened shopkeepers and hope we got the right ones, but justice would still be unsatisfied. We strike at the heart and mind that planned this, or the butterfly will never be complete.

'Jaze, you and Therrot will stay here with Hathin and Arilou until they've recovered enough to travel, then you'll see them safe to the Beacon School. You'll all need disguises – right now anyone who looks Lace will be in for a rough ride. Also, our conspiracy of killers will be looking for Hathin and Arilou everywhere. So will that Ashwalker if he lives, and the law too if anyone guesses that they're still alive.

'Meanwhile, I will take a group and travel ahead making safe houses ready, then push on to Smattermast in case we can find out there what happened to the Lost Council. Marmar, muskets don't grow on bushes. Find out where Jimboly got hers. Louloss, you'll head to the coast and see if any of the other Hollow Beasts survived, then you'll visit all the villages listed in Skein's journal to find out if you can discover what his notes mean.'

And there was no more argument. Dance seemed to hold all the sway of Mother Govrie, Whish and the rest rolled into one, and yet nobody called her Mother Dance or Doctor Dance. Only Dance, a curious name – not a Lace name.

Louloss came and placed a poultice on Hathin's arm. Hathin looked around the room and thought of hands deft with daggers, fingertips dented by tense bowstrings, hands slipping deadly cordials into tankards.

I'm not afraid of them. Why?

Because I am one of them now.

Suddenly a whistle sounded from the jungle outside. The

208

conversation hushed instantly, knives leaped into hands, and Jaze sprang out through the vine curtain. For a long minute there was absolute hush in the tree hut, every ear straining to listen.

At last Jaze re-entered, his face set and tense.

'Hathin, one of the men I sent to collect your sister from the priest's house has just returned. No – it's fine.' He held up one hand to halt Hathin's worried enquiry. 'Arilou's fine, and two of our boys are carrying her through the jungle even now. But apparently they had a hell of a time getting her out of town unseen. Some power-and-the-glory Doorsy pen-pusher newly arrived in Mistleman's Blunder is tearing the town apart – looking for you and your sister.'

'What?' Marmar jumped to his feet. 'That's impossible! Hathin and Arilou left the coast barely a day ago – and *they* only got here so quickly because they took a shortcut across Lady Sorrow's lap! There's no way anyone here could know about the massacre yet, let alone the fact that the girls are here!'

'I know.' Jaze gave a curt nod. 'This pen-pusher can't possibly know they're here, but somehow he does. He even has warrants.'

'But . . . getting a warrant takes a *day* at the very least . . .'

'There's something sour in this,' muttered Dance.

'Hathin, have you noticed that your enemies appear to know things sooner than they should? Arilou alone survives the deaths of the Lost, and within mere days this dentist Jimboly walks into your village. The aide Minchard Prox survives the storm, and a letter about it arrives just in time to put spark to powder. And turns up in Jimboly's hands, no less.'

There was a superstitious murmur, but Dance gave it no time to build momentum.

'You heard the news, boys. The hunt's reached Mistleman's Blunder already. So pack light, and pack tonight. We all move out tomorrow before dawn.'

'But Arilou can't!' Hathin could almost see Arilou's bloody feet, her wan face. 'She's exhausted. If we just had a day so that she could rest, and maybe find her way back to her own body . . .'

Dance shook her head, solemnly unmovable.

'It is too great a risk. I will find a way for her to be carried, but we must move out tomorrow.'

'I . . .' Hathin stared at her feet, crestfallen. 'I'm so sorry . . . We brought trouble here with us . . .'

'Did you? Did you kill the Lost and frame our people? Did you stir up the towners of Sweetweather and murder your own village? No. You have brought us nothing but news and information that we needed. Besides, Hathin, we revengers live in "trouble" the way sharks live in water.

'For years we have been careful sharks, harming none but our quarries, out of respect for our pact with the Lost Council. But now the Lost are dead . . . and so is that pact. Do anything you must, Hathin. Kill anyone you must. Revenge is your only fetter.

'Our enemies think that Lace make good victims and scapegoats. They are wrong. They think that they can strike at us, and we will do nothing but scatter and hide. They are wrong.

'You have been wronged beyond endurance by powerful foes, Hathin. Pity them for not knowing what that means . . .'

That thought lingered in Hathin's mind even after the lanterns were doused and she had lain down next to the other revengers on the plank-and-vine floor. And when at last she slept, her dreams took her to a white, windswept plain. There she ran and ran, and so did the Ashwalker. He left blue prints on the white earth, and her footmarks were red. It seemed sometimes that he chased her and sometimes that she was pursuing him, a dagger in her hand.

16
A GLIMPSE OF A GHOST

In spite of her tiredness, Hathin woke sometime before dawn and followed Dance around with timid stubbornness until the tall woman listened to Hathin's plan to help Arilou find her own body.

'Try it then, but quickly,' Dance agreed at last. 'You must be ready to leave in an hour.'

With Therrot's help, Hathin found a space of soft soil near one of the jungle streams. The pair of them heaped earth into little volcanoes, using stones to stand for towns and villages. It was a clumsy model, of course. Neither of them had ever been to the eastern coast, or cruised cloud-level with the eagles, so a lot of it was guesswork.

Hathin spent the next half an hour crawling around the miniature Gullstruck with Arilou, trying to run her sister's hand over its contours.

'Therrot, if we can't help her find herself before we move on, then it'll be too late – she'll never catch up.' For the fifth time Hathin curled Arilou's stubborn fingers around two tiny stick-dolls and walked them up one side of a double mound and down the other. *This is the route we took, Arilou . . . and this is where we are now. At least this'll help you know where to* start *looking . . .*

'It's already too late.' With a satin swish the monsoon rain swept in, and soon the mud of the miniature Gullstruck was loosening and melting. As Hathin watched, the crater she had fashioned for Spearhead filled with cloudy brown water, which spilled out through the nick in the rim to surge into the model of the Wailing Way.

'All right, all right,' Hathin said gently. 'No more.' She spoke to Arilou out of habit, even though she was increasingly convinced that her sister had sent off her hearing with her sight. Hathin wrapped the older girl's grubby, stream-chilled hand in a fold of her skirt to warm it. Arilou's sense of physical touch was still with her body, of that much Hathin was certain, hence her desperate, blind finger-search.

Where were Arilou's absent senses now? Was her vision wheeling wildly with the gulls above the coast? Was she hearing the crash of waves, smelling the breath of the volcanoes? Hathin put an arm around her, as if she could bind Arilou back into herself, and guided Arilou's head to rest on her shoulder.

'Hathin –' Therrot met her gaze – 'has it occurred to you that somebody might be a Lost and be an imbecile as well?'

Hathin had no answer, nor did she have time to give one. As she stared at Therrot, one of the younger revengers burst from the trees and slithered down to join them.

'Dance says to come back to the Wasps' Nest. A dozen townsfolk with axes have just been seen heading towards our jungle. There's no more time. We're all leaving. Now.'

A very short while later the Wasps' Nest was empty, its erstwhile residents scattered concealed throughout the jungle.

 213

Hathin's group must make it to the road, Dance had said, *and if a distraction is needed to help them get there, we'll give them a distraction.*

Hathin hurried along at a crouch, her new backpack catching on vines. Close behind her came Therrot. Both were disguised as members of the Dancing Steam, complete with indigo-dyed leggings and coats with long cross-laced sleeves that would hide their tattoos. Hathin's hair had been cropped and she was dressed as a boy, for she was to pose as Therrot's younger brother on the trip. However, it had been drummed into her that her disguise would be for naught if she let her distinctive Lace smile creep on to her face and expose her tooth plaques.

If anyone sees through your disguise, strike before they can act, Jaze had instructed her, as he strapped a little dagger in a red sheath to her arm. *You have a duty to avoid being captured or killed. While you're alive and at liberty we can help you, but once you're gone no one can pursue your quest on your behalf.*

Jaze was bringing up the rear of their little group, supporting a half-asleep Arilou. Despite the urgency of the situation, he remained calm, almost too calm. Hathin found his presence soothing, but at the same time wondered whether he had worn the same cool soapstone smile when he had killed the five smugglers who had murdered his mother.

Arilou was dressed as a member of the Bitter Fruit, and the belly of her dress was padded out with rags. The hope was that if she seemed heavily pregnant it would give Jaze an excuse to half carry her.

They reached the edge of the forest just in time to see the last of the townspeople disappear into the jungle, a hundred

214

yards away. There was a distant *chock!* sound, and birds peppered the sky.

'They're chopping down trees,' whispered Therrot. He sounded surprised. Clearly, despite its proximity, Mistleman's Chandlery was not the townspeople's first-choice source of timber. 'They never cut down trees *here*. These jungles – they're part of the Sovereignty Swathe.' The Swathe was one of many areas that had remained jungle purely because some of the first Cavalcaste generals had claimed it for their families, to be used as Ashlands for their dead in the future. It was lifeless space on the map, and the only way to claim a piece of it was to die.

'Not good,' murmured Jaze. 'We'll have trouble getting to the road without them seeing us.'

Hathin peered apprehensively through the undergrowth at the root-tangled slope and expanse of flat ground they would need to cross to reach the main road. Mistleman's Blunder was a major stopping point along the so-called Obsidian Trail, a foot-route down which dozens of men, women and children daily trudged, carrying packs of obsidian, mountain jade and other goods from the mountain mining villages to the richer cities and ports of the north east.

The plan was for Hathin's party to creep down to the road and quietly join the stream of pack-carriers so as to escape attention. Hearts in mouths, they skulked their way down the treeless slope, hunching in abandoned irrigation trenches, until they reached a bush-shielded ditch a stone's throw from the road.

It soon became clear that finding a quiet moment to slip out of the bushes was going to be no easy matter, as the route

 215

suddenly became a thoroughfare for lines of men carrying long, slender tree trunks over their shoulders. The timber was laid down by the roadside and, as the hidden revengers watched, workmen began lashing the newly felled trunks together into tall angular structures.

'What are they doing?' hissed Therrot.

Jaze raised his head to scan the scene. 'Looks like they're making a set of raised platforms . . . Who's that? The man in the blue waistcoat? And what's wrong with his face?'

There was indeed a slightly shorter figure among the workmen, giving orders, stopping from time to time to check a parchment in his hand. Even at this distance it was clear that behind the turned-up wings of his collar, his face was blotched with yellow and plum discolouration.

'Oh, I think I know who he is,' murmured Jaze. 'That's him. The Doorsy who's been turning everything upside down looking for you. Whatever it is he's doing, it's for *your* benefit, Hathin. Take a look – have you ever met him?'

'No.' Hathin raised her head as high as she dared and peered through the foliage. 'I'd remember someone with a face like that.'

'Good,' said Jaze. 'If you don't recognize him, he won't recognize you if you have to walk past him.'

Deep in the forest came the sound of a bang, followed by a chalky trail of echo and a great eruption of birds.

'Damn!' said Therrot, and at the same time Jaze said 'Now!' and scooped up Arilou. His momentum carried the other revengers along, and they lurched after him out of the ditch.

'That came from the direction of the Reckoning! That

216

was a gunshot!' hissed Therrot as he fell into stride with Jaze along the rubbled path.

'I know one when I hear one,' Jaze said through his teeth, shifting the weight of Arilou in his arms, 'and so does everyone else. A gun fires, and everybody looks towards it – nobody looks for people climbing out of bushes. Now fall back – we're not supposed to know each other.'

Therrot slowed his pace, and Hathin slid her hand into his. The nearest wooden platform seemed to be completed and was as high as a house. On its summit stood a man using a telescope to pan across the road, the treeline, the surrounding countryside. Spy-towers then. *Is all of this really to look for us? Surely there is some mistake?*

'Hathin,' muttered Therrot without moving his lips, 'you're smiling again.' She compressed her lips and tried to force down the corners of her mouth.

Her heart beat as ahead of them Jaze and Arilou approached a couple of men who stood on the path, both holding rough cudgels. They exchanged a few words with Jaze, who gave them yawning answers, joked, nodded towards the sleeping Arilou. His mild look remained unruffled as the roadblock guards searched through his luggage with an idle air.

Hathin herself was anything but calm. To keep her gaze from Arilou, Hathin observed the man in the blue waistcoat, who was shouting instructions to the men at the top of the spy-towers. As she watched he raised his head irritably, batting away a persistent fly, and her throat tightened as she saw his face properly.

'Therrot,' she whispered, a squeak of panic in her voice. 'Therrot – I *do* know him.'

'What?' Therrot looked down at her, his face drawn, but there was no time for conference. Their steps had brought them up to the road guards.

'What's your reason for passing through our city?' asked the first, using Doorsy with an air of bored self-importance.

'We're a troupe of travelling parrot jugglers,' Therrot declared wearily. His Doorsy was a little clumsy and had a strong Mistleman's accent. 'Come on – what do you think we are? In case you didn't notice, the bean harvest's over so we're walking the trail and taking packs of black glass to Port Suddenwind to sell. Trope, show the nice men what you've got in your bucket.' Hathin managed to remember that she was going by the name of Trope. She stood by while the guards stirred her tiny scraps of obsidian around with the tip of a knife, and tried not to look towards Prox.

Therrot clicked his tongue in his cheek as if all these formalities were too boring for words, but as the guards started searching their other buckets Hathin could see his eyes glittering with nervous impatience.

Hathin's eyes crept to the face of Minchard Prox, who was studying a map. Horribly blistered, but alive. *Can he really be hunting us? Maybe we should speak to him? He was working with Raglan Skein – doesn't that mean he should be on our side?*

'What's all this about, anyway?' Therrot nodded towards the new scaffolding.

'We've had word that there might be a Lace force massing over on the coast, and looking to sneak through their secret mountain passes. And if they do – well, they're going to attack here, aren't they? We're the people who stood up to them in the first place, and they've never forgiven us. So we're setting up these towers so we can spot 'em if they come skulking through the undergrowth. And we've piled the brush up in those heaps so we can light them as braziers come nightfall, throwing light over the plain.'

The two listening Lace nodded thoughtfully and tried not to meet one another's eye. A Lace force? The only 'Lace force' to have 'sneaked through the secret mountain passes' had been Arilou and Hathin themselves, and they knew of no other waiting to follow the same route.

'What makes you think the Lace would go tramping over the volcanoes in monsoon weather?' Therrot's tone of voice walked the tightrope between idle curiosity and disinterest.

'Because their leader's already here – we're on the look out for her.' The guard pulled out a rough pencil-drawn picture. Its lines were crude, but there was something in it of Arilou, her high cheekbones and serene pirate eyes. 'Look at this – you seen her while you've been walking?'

Therrot examined the picture, gave a snort and pushed it back into the guardsman's hands.

'How the hell am I supposed to know from a picture like that?' He laughed. 'Looks a bit like me.'

'It's no joking matter,' snapped the guard. 'She's the one who ordered the murders of the Lost – so they wouldn't be able to warn us when her armies approached.'

Hathin could not suppress a flinch at these words. She twisted her hands together to stop them shaking. Fortunately the guards' eyes were on Therrot, and they did not notice the flush creeping across her face.

It was happening just as Dance had predicted. The tales of a murderous Lace conspiracy which had infected

 219

Sweetweather like a madness were spreading and had reached Mistleman's Blunder. Seeing towers built to scan the horizons for her sister and herself had been bad enough. But it was only now that the enormity and absurdity of the situation overwhelmed her.

Then, to her horror, ahead she saw Arilou starting to stir in Jaze's arms as if rousing herself from sleep. Would she stay calm when she found herself carried by a stranger? And if she drew attention to herself, how long would it take for Prox to recognize the Lady Lost Arilou?

Prox was folding his map, staring down the road as he did so. He was glancing for the first time at the little huddle of figures on the road . . . he was turning with a start as a young man came running from the direction of the jungle, a swoop of lichen and blood smearing his cheek, and headed straight to Prox.

'. . . were searching the jungle, and . . . gunshot . . . men and a few women . . . Lace, I'm sure of it . . . some kind of treehouse.' Hathin heard only fragments of his panted report.

Suddenly Prox was bristling and terrier-like. In spite of her fear, Hathin stealthily moved a bit closer in order to hear more.

'Lace?' Prox pushed his fingers through his hair, his eyes alive with excitement. 'A Lace hideout in the jungle. I think we've *found* her. Tell me –' he grabbed the sleeve of the lichen-stained man – 'did you see a girl? About thirteen years old? So high, with mix-blood skin and high cheekbones?'

'No . . . I don't think so. Just men and women full grown.'

'Did you catch any of them?'

'We didn't get the chance – there were a good dozen

of them, sir. At least. I mean . . . they were *everywhere*, sir. There was this whistling, and then the trees came alive with them . . . and then there was this creaking crash, and the tree-house came down on us, along with about two dozen wasps' nests. Ten of us went into that forest. I'm the only one who's come out again.'

'What?'

Prox's exclamation coincided with another gunshot from the jungle. Out across the plain workmen could be seen running towards the jungle, axes and hammers in hand.

'Stop!' Prox's voice had no chance of reaching the disappearing figures. 'Will you all stop running into the jungle! Stop it! What is wrong with you all? Here –' he turned to the young man beside him – 'will you please run and tell those idiots to come back, before this town's population is reduced to three!'

Seeing the distressed and perplexed look in Prox's bright brown eyes, Hathin suddenly felt sorry for him despite herself. Then, as Prox listened to a murmur in his ear, his brow creased and became pensive.

'You're right,' he said after a moment or two. 'We can't go in after them, we'll have to cut off their supplies. Someone's been supplying them – someone local. Where are the nearest Lace villages?' Pausing, listening. 'Only ten miles down the coastal road?' He unfolded his map once more and he studied the portion pointed out to him.

'No,' he murmured at last. 'We can't have a bolthole like that for them so close to the town. The risk is too great.' Somebody put a pencil in his hand, and after a moment's frowning he slashed four times at the map. 'These villages will have to go. We'll set up a camp *here* for the inhabitants. If they're not penned, they'll be into the jungles and long grass like snakes and we'll have to burn them out.' He shook his head sadly.

'Trope!' Therrot's voice. 'Grab your bucket; we're going.' Hathin ducked her head and hefted her bucket and pack on to her back. All thought of speaking with Prox had evaporated.

'Look at that!' A snort of uncertain mirth from one of the guards. 'What's wrong with her?'

Arilou's eyes were open, and filled with a happy, dove-grey light. She had stretched out one arm and was stiffly waving it up and down, as if in a stately somnambulist dance. She let her head tip back, and her mouth fell open into a broad smile. A second more and everybody would notice what Hathin could see quite clearly, the distinctive circular tooth-plaques that marked Arilou as a Lace.

But in that second everyone's attention was stolen by a miracle. It was a six-foot tall, scabby-toed miracle covered in dun-coloured feathers. The miracle came upon them so fast that Therrot had to yank Hathin out of its way, and then it was zigzagging wildly among the guards, its flanks huffing and jumping with each long, bouncing stride.

It was an elephant bird, the bit slipped from its beak, a teenage boy clinging to its bristling wings and near to sliding off the back of its rump. He appeared to be cooing reassuringly to it while it rampaged mad-eyed and seemed to blame everybody for the reins tangling its legs.

Once again, Jaze was quick to take advantage of the distraction. He set off briskly, Arilou in his arms. Hathin heaved a sigh of relief, which she had to swallow as the elephant bird made a desultory jab at her with its beak. She leaped away from it, and bumped into a man who had been standing quietly not far from Prox.

'Sorry, sir – I didn't notice you,' she croaked, trying to keep her tone boyish. Utterly flustered, she stooped for the telescope she had knocked from his hand.

'People seldom do; it's all right.' It was a lean, well-dressed middle-aged man, who spoke in Doorsy so smooth and musical that it almost reminded Hathin of Lace. 'You're not the only person who has been too distracted to look right under their nose.' She stared up at him, and saw a narrow, pleasant face gazing over her head towards the mountains. He smiled, and unaccountably she felt the brass and glass of the telescope grow cold in her hands. 'To think, there we were, all ready to scour the Coast of the Lace looking for her . . . And now we are told that she's here! Fancy her coming *here*! That's a quite beautiful piece of cheek.' The stranger looked down and directed a radiant, delighted smile through Hathin and beyond her towards some private thought. And suddenly she felt skinless, fleshless, as if a wall of cold air had raced right through her without noticing her.

The cold feeling would not leave her even when she fell into stride with Therrot and walked past the preoccupied Prox with her head bowed and her heart beating.

'What the hell happened to Arilou back there?' hissed Therrot once they were a little distant.

'I'm not sure,' Hathin whispered back, 'but I think she found herself. Only her body looked different in disguise, so she was swinging her arm around to make sure it was the right one.'

 223

'Brilliant timing,' Therrot muttered. 'If we're going to survive this journey, you will have to teach her something of your gift for invisibility.'

'Yes . . .' Hathin replied after a moment. 'Not being noticed – it *is* a skill, something you can practise, get good at. And sometimes you can spot somebody else who's doing it too. That man back there. That other Doorsy man.'

'What other Doorsy man?'

'Exactly. I didn't see him either at first. But he's just standing there, putting out Mr Prox's thoughts for him like a skivvy laying out his boots and shirt, and Mr Prox puts them on and doesn't even notice where they came from. But *I* noticed him. He didn't see me, *but I saw him.*'

17
KILLER KIND

Retrieving the bloodied, wasp-stung survivors of the battle in Mistleman's Chandlery took Minchard Prox the better part of an hour. Calming them down enough that their reports made sense took more time, and a good deal of rum. The last man to be rescued from under the fallen treehouse had seen more of his attackers than the rest, and came round babbling about a 'giant woman-man with a forest of braids'.

Prox turned to suppress a grimace of exasperation only to find that Camber, the ever-pleasant and unfazable Camber, had gone absolutely white. With an expression of incredulity, he was mouthing a word under his breath.

'What?'

'Dance,' Camber repeated. 'And she's not a what, she's a who. She's supposed to be an ex-who. And this man has just described her.' He shook his head as though trying to shake the thought out. 'It's Dance. There's simply nobody else that it can be. And if she is alive, then the Lost Council lied . . .'

Camber rallied himself, and seemed to become aware that Prox was looking at him with some confusion and concern.

'Mr Prox –' Camber cleared his throat – 'we have, I think, a very serious problem. If Dance is still alive and well . . . then so is the Reckoning.'

A horrified hush spread through the group gathered at the roadside. Prox looked around him, as if trying to reassure himself that Lace armed with obsidian knives weren't threatening that very moment to seethe out of the jungle.

'Bring ink – I need to write letters to Port Suddenwind and every governor in Gullstruck. And fetch me every bird-back messenger you can. This is bigger than we thought.

'If the Reckoning still exists and is involved in this conspiracy, then they have the traditional right to demand help from every living Lace. We must consider every single one of them to be a potential enemy . . . and we must strike before they do.'

Only after the messages had been dispatched did Prox look down at the reports in his hand and remember a detail that had snagged his attention. He caught Camber's eye, and the latter was by his side in a moment.

Moving out of earshot of their companions, the two men strolled along the road towards the town, the little bells on Prox's shoes uttering a silvery defiance, those on Camber's feet clapper-less and silent.

'I've received a letter from the governor of Sweetweather,' Prox began without preamble. 'His own account of the happenings there. There's little more than we've discussed . . . except he makes mention of a woman who was visiting Sweetweather around the time of the Hollow Beasts massacre, a travelling dentist. Some say she seemed very friendly with the Lace, some say she was one of the leaders of the riot against them – the reports are a mess. But she had jewelled teeth. Not quite in the Lace style, but still . . . it might be worth finding out more about her. Just in case she's part of the Lace conspiracy, helping pass messages between them as she moves from place to place.

'I didn't want to mention this too publicly. After all, we've already had one case of riot and massacre, and in all probability the poor woman has nothing to do with the conspiracy, but if you could make some quiet enquiries . . .'

Camber took the reports from Prox's outstretched hand. 'Mr Prox, if she can be found, she will be found. I shall see to it.'

'I'm glad I can count on . . .' Prox trailed off, frowning. 'Now, what in the world is he doing? Should he even be out of bed?'

The crowd by the roadblock had all moved aside, out of wary respect, to allow space to a solitary figure. Amid the midnight blue of its skin and clothes were darker blots of dried blood, but it did not move with the hobbling hesitancy of the injured.

Brendril stooped at the base of one of the towers. One blue fingertip traced the outline of a single small footprint in the rain-softened earth, and then the Ashwalker raised his head to stare down the eastern road.

As the day wore on, the troop of disguised Lace was relieved to see the Obsidian Trail becoming busier. Some of the luckier trudgers had an elephant bird to take part of their burden, and there seemed to be a good number of bird-back messengers speeding this way and that, and so Hathin grew used to the rasping squelch of talons on the muddy road. It was a while before she realized that the same bird-steps had been

227

sounding a little to her left for the last ten minutes.

She looked up, and her 'miracle' was walking beside her, the teenage boy now comfortably settled on the elephant bird's back. He had a round, open face and cacao-coloured eyes which were currently fixed upon the far distance with an expectant look, as if he'd missed something the horizon had said and was waiting for a repetition. He was, however, reining in his bird to keep pace with their gathering.

'Where's Dance?' he asked in Lace. Jaze did not appear to hear him. Therrot's tongue was pushed into his cheek.

The boy did not seem particularly offended at being ignored. 'You know, one of those guards back there cuffed me across the ear. It feels thick as a breadslice. Do you want to have a look?'

'It doesn't count, Tomki,' Therrot growled under his breath. He gave the boy a look of exasperation, but one not devoid of affection. 'He didn't "wrong" you, Tomki. He cuffed you because you attacked him with an elephant bird.'

'Well, *he* didn't know that I did it on purpose.' Tomki shrugged. 'So . . . where are we meeting Dance?'

'We're not! We don't know . . .' Therrot brought himself up short, and met Jaze's eye. It was an uneasy subject, and one that the trudging revengers had been avoiding raising. What *was* happening back in Mistleman's Chandlery? Had Dance and the others escaped? 'Dance has danced off on her own mission,' Therrot continued after a pause. 'And you're not coming with us! This is revengers' business – it's far too dangerous . . .' Therrot trailed off as Tomki's eyes took on a delighted gleam.

'You've done it now,' sighed Jaze.

228

'All Lace should help a revenger in any way they can, shouldn't they?' Tomki asked hopefully.

'That's up to the revenger in question,' Jaze answered swiftly. 'Hathin . . . this young man . . .'

'. . . thinks he's in love with Dance,' Therrot finished curtly. 'He saw her while she was . . . taking care of . . . something on the streets of Mistleman's Blunder, and ever since that he's been trying to get himself wronged so he can get the tattoo and join the Reckoning.'

Hathin could only stare at Tomki, struggling to imagine this sunny-faced boy developing a passion for a brooding giantess more than twice his age. He caught her eye, grinned at her and shrugged.

'He spills drinks on people who look like they might punch him,' Therrot added in an undertone, 'and I've known him spend six hours outside the roughest tavern in Blunder singing the same song over and over again in the hope that somebody would come out and stab him.'

'He was really useful back with the road guards though, wasn't he?' ventured Hathin. 'And . . . sometimes it might be handy to have someone around who *hasn't* got the tattoo.' No tooth plaques either, she noted, as Tomki's smile broadened. 'Not to mention that the elephant bird could come in useful.'

'It's your quest.' Jaze and Therrot exchanged a resigned smile, but neither challenged her decision.

The plan was for Hathin's party to travel throughout each day, except for those hours when savage monsoon rain made walking impractical, and spend their nights in pre-arranged hideouts along their route, or in Lace villages friendly to

 229

their cause. On the first night of the journey they stopped at an old shack concealed beneath a cluster of giant ferns. It smelt of damp soil, and its walls were etched with pictograms from earlier revengers. However, Jaze would not let them enter until he had peered in and examined the earth floor of the hut.

'All right. It's safe.' He tapped a squiggle which had been cut into the floor with a knife. 'Dance's mark. She's been here ahead of us, and this shack should be safe.' There was a general easing of anxiety. Whatever had happened in Mistleman's Chandlery, it did not appear to have slowed Dance down.

The same routine was followed each evening. After a long day's walk, when Hathin was almost tottering with weariness, Jaze would make them wait outside some village or area of unprepossessing scrubland while he checked that all was safe. Then, after Arilou had been installed, the group would forage for food.

Arilou seemed delighted to be reunited with herself. While the revengers took turns to scavenge through the forest, she stared straight ahead and stirred first one limb then another in wondering delight. Her usual stream of musical babble seemed louder than it had been for some time, and Hathin guessed that she was relishing the sound of her own voice as well.

Each evening Hathin was given twine for bird-trapping. Nobody commented when she came back with only berries and mushrooms, but as they sat eating their stew later she found it hard to meet their eyes. By the third night her sense of failure was so painful that she could not sleep.

What kind of revenger was she? If she couldn't bring herself to tug a string and drop a hunk of wood on a wild turkey's head, what good would she be faced by her enemies, with the entire universe waiting for her to right wrongs and make it whole again? She tried to imagine herself with her dagger in her hand, facing down . . . who? Lean and laughing Jimboly? The Ashwalker? Minchard Prox, with his bright bewildered eyes? Or . . . Or that other Doorsy man, the one whose features were already trying to creep from her memory?

Whatever she had to become, she clearly had not become it yet. But she would. With this resolution she slipped out into the forest.

Therrot roused himself an hour later to find Hathin on her knees in floods of tears, her knife-point poised over her cap, which lay on the floor before her.

'Well, the stitching's a bit rough, but I didn't think the hat was that bad.'

There was a small pause, which the cap saw as an opportunity to croak sonorously and nudge its way a few inches along the floor. Therrot crawled over, lifted it and stared into the pearly, fearless eyes of a bright yellow frog.

'It was all I could find,' whispered Hathin. 'I was trying to perform a good-luck sacrifice for the quest, trying to see if I could . . . but it kept looking at me.' The frog was still suiting its action to her words, its throat coming and going in soap-bubble swells. 'And then I heard you waking so I threw my cap over it.'

'So you have trouble with . . . oh. All right.' Therrot closed his eyes and pressed the heels of his hands against them. 'All right, yes. That *is* a problem, isn't it? We'll talk about that in the morning. Right now, I think *you* should go to sleep . . . and

 231

if you don't mind *I* shall take the deadly poisonous tree frog out of the hut. Does that sound fair?'

Many miles away, another person was having a troubled night. Not for the first time, his dreams saw him walking against the wind on a white dust plain. A great, gold-framed mirror was hanging in the air before him, angled slightly away so that he could not see his own image. Even while curiosity drew him closer, a gnawing alarm tightened in his chest. Another step closer, another . . . and Camber woke into a warm and airless darkness.

Why can I never confront that mirror? What am I afraid of? Nothing.

He was afraid that in the mirror he would see nothing but the misty wasteland behind him.

Now Camber looked around his room, but it still felt unoccupied. It suddenly struck him, as it often did, that if he took a step it would make no sound, and if he reached for the door handle his fingers would no more rattle it than if they had been made of moonbeams.

Perhaps I am too good at being invisible, he reflected. *Perhaps I have faded to a shadow of a thought.*

Another idea occurred to him unbidden.

The night could snuff me out, and nobody would notice.

And it was as this notion struck him that he realized he could hear something not unlike the rush of wind that had haunted his dream. A stealthy swishing that came from somewhere out in the moonlit dark.

He opened the front door, and the candle behind him threw out a long finger of light, his own shadow stretched

232

thin as bamboo down the middle of it. He had taken up rooms in the house adjoining the town courthouse, which Prox had now adopted as his headquarters and home. Here in the dead heart of the city the ground was paved with a mosaic of white tiles, puckered by erupting weeds. All around stood the ornate but peeling houses from which the dead had slowly pushed their living relations, windows lightless, balconies untrodden, chimneys smokeless.

For a moment there was no sound but the sleepy throbbing of the pigeons in the loft of the building behind him, then he heard again the furtive noise that had woken him. It seemed to come from the tower at the centre of Mistleman's Blunder itself. Here some of Mistleman's Blunder's most precious and renowned dead commanded the best view of the city, had they only eyes to delight in it.

Camber quietly patted at his own hip and felt the outline of his discreet pistol, then walked cat-footed between the rounded houses until he reached the open arch that led into the tower. The mysterious sound had become harsher, a rain on a bonfire noise. Then all at once it stopped. He waited a moment or two in the silence, then advanced into the dead's most prized residence.

Camber believed ardently, utterly, in the power of the ancestors, and it was for this reason that he knew he did not properly exist. His own family had been late arrivals, sailing into Gullstruck's waters a mere century before. Unfortunately they had timed their arrival to coincide with that of a particularly rapacious pirate, who had promptly sunk their ship. The precious ancestor urns and all records concerning the family had been destroyed. The only survivor had been

Camber's great-great-grandmother, who had crawled up the beach, given birth and died without saying who she was.

Camber's name meant nothing. He could not serve his ancestors, nor could they save him. He was rootless, anchorless, adrift. He was nobody. He was damned. And this gave him a strange sort of freedom.

He halted just inside the first rounded room. Somebody had already disturbed the dust of the floor. The china paving slabs below could be seen through the prints left by a pair of long, lean bare feet. Where was their owner?

She was above him.

Crouched on a sill twelve feet from the ground squatted a lanky figure, a jumble of knees and elbows, but a jumble tensed to become something else. A blood-coloured bandanna bound back a torrent of black hair. There was a bat-like flicker of shadow about her head. The light from the moon was just enough for him to see the knife clutched in her hand.

There was no time for Camber to react as the woman tensed and sprang down from her perch, swinging a dry pig's bladder. Her feet hit the floor less than a yard from him, but even when he found two black eyes staring into his, still he did not react, did not move or flinch. There was a long, dark second of absolute silence.

'I thought,' Camber remarked at last, 'yes, I am almost *sure* – that I told you to get rid of that bird.'

'I couldn't – couldn't do that.' Despite the hoarse playfulness of Jimboly's tone, there was an icy trickle of fear in her voice. 'Couldn't wring the neck of my 'itterbittle. And if he flew off, he'd unravel me into a big loose pile of Jimboly twine.'

'The bird is memorable,' continued Camber. '*You* have

been memorable. You were noticed in Sweetweather.' Under his gaze, Jimboly wilted like a flower in a candle flame. She dropped into a crouch against the wall, her knife now tucked away, her long face stretched even longer by uncertainty and fear. 'You've made good time travelling from Sweetweather though. I wasn't expecting to see you yet. In fact, I wasn't expecting to see you here at all. What are you doing here?'

'I didn't want to hang around Sweetweather.' Jimboly's voice was now unmistakably a whine. 'The town was getting mopey and remorseful. I've got no patience with a town that gets all its powder used up in the first big bang.'

'Well, we'll let that pass. Now tell me – the Lady Arilou...' Camber saw Jimboly flinch. 'I suppose there is absolutely *no* chance that she is nothing but a simpleton?'

'She's Lost all right. Oozy-brained Lost, but Lost.' Jimboly's eyes were hard and bright, but her hands stirred uncomfortably in her lap. 'I've heard people talking in the streets; I know she's passed through here. I can still catch her if you point my nose the right way...'

Camber said nothing. He said it quite loudly as he leaned back against the wall and looked at her with his eyebrows slightly raised. Jimboly squirmed as if he had subjected her to a ten-minute diatribe.

'You'll have to be fast,' Camber said at last. 'You've an Ash-walker three days ahead of you.'

'Are you giving that blue man my fee?' Jimboly's mouth sagged into a scowl.

'I might, if he had the slightest interest in your fee.' Camber let his tone harden, and once more Jimboly's ill-temper melted into unease. 'Fortunately for you, he doesn't, and he isn't on our commission. He walked right out of our physician's house three days ago, spent ten minutes prodding the earth around the towers and then headed off down the road without a word to any of us.

'The Ashwalker will find Arilou. It is what he does. It is all he does. But I will need you a step behind him, to perform a very important mission.' Camber hesitated as Jimboly's eyes went quite mad with greed. For her, important could only mean money. He knew her well enough to guess that she had no ideas for spending it, she was just blinded by a future bright with golden glare. 'The Ashwalker will only strike at Lady Arilou, her companions and anyone else who gets in his way. I need *you* to find out if she has been inconveniently talkative en route. Following the Ashwalker's trail shouldn't be hard – he is *blue*, after all – and he'll lead you to them.'

'And you'd like them "mopped"?' It was amazing how quickly Jimboly could recover her good temper if offered a chance to cause chaos.

'Yes, if necessary. But, Jimboly . . . try not tear too many towns apart. I'd like to keep a few of them on the map, just in case we need them later.'

18
HUNTERS

The next morning Hathin and the other revengers woke to find that the damp of the forest had seeped into their muscles. It was a sodden, stiff, miserable group that rejoined the other walkers along the Obsidian Trail.

Increasing numbers of bird-back messengers overtook them on the road, and Hathin watched them nervously, wondering what message they were carrying to the next town. Pictures of Arilou, perhaps? Warrants for their arrest? Or news of the battle in Mistleman's Chandlery?

Hathin even saw one of Gullstruck's rare horses, a skinny-shanked, fly-bitten nag laden down with packs. As her eye fell on its harness she remembered the name in Skein's journal. Bridle. *Bridle believes that Lord S will return when the rains end or soon after.* Bridle was a Cavalcaste name. If they found him, would he prove a friend or foe?

As the sun started to dry the revengers Therrot fell into step with Hathin.

'I've been giving your problem some thought,' he said quietly. Jaze, Arilou and Tomki were far enough ahead to be out of earshot. 'The killing problem. I was thinking . . . we don't know that it's going to be a problem. After all, that frog never wronged you, did it? It just might make a difference to the revenge you choose, that's all. You might find human beings easier than you expect. Little sister . . . I've never told anyone but the priest who marked me how I completed my butterfly. But I'll tell you – if you like.'

She watched him narrowly, noticing the continual twitch in his cheek. Little sister, big brother. Aside from Arilou, he was all the village she had now, and yet, was he really more than a stranger?

'You must remember what my sister Fawless was like. She was . . .' He gave a painful little smile. 'She drove me mad, running about by herself. One day she ran off to the mountainside collecting blissing beetles.'

Therrot glanced at Hathin and noticed her look of astonishment.

'No . . . you wouldn't know about that, not being a diver.' There was a pause, and Hathin could almost feel Therrot bracing himself to give voice to yet another taboo. It was hard to break the habit of silence, even though they knew that there were no Lost left to listen in, and there was little left to lose. 'It's the way farsight fish are caught,' he said after a few moments, in little more than a whisper. 'You trap a blissing beetle inside a hollowed-out coconut shell and seal it watertight with pitch, wax and resin, then you lower it into the sea on a long string. You see, a farsight fish sends its mind to take a look at anything before it gets close – it can spot a shark, a diver, a hook in a lure, a net sweeping towards it . . . but when it pushes its mind into the coconut to find out what it is, then it hears the blissing beetle and goes to sleep with its gills open. And then a good diver plunges down and grabs it before something else does.

'Anyway, a Doorsy landowner was sitting up on the mountainside with a musket, looking out for Lace moving his boundary stakes. He saw a fourteen-year-old girl in Lace clothes and yelled at her to leave, but Fawless didn't hear him – her ears were stopped up to protect her from the beetles. So he shot her dead.'

Therrot's voice was perfectly level. Hathin knew that it had to be to recount such facts.

'Nobody arrested the landowner,' continued Therrot. 'After all, he'd shot a "trespasser", and she *was* only a Lace. So I took the revenger's mark. Then I ran over to the landowner's house in Sweetweather and gave him a piece of my mind – point first. But the knife missed his vitals and he lived.'

Hathin nodded. She had heard this much in the village.

'When I got out of prison,' Therrot continued, 'I learned that the landowner had run off north. I realized I needed advice, and went to Jaze.

'The landowner knew that a butterfly's wing was beating for him. By the time I next tracked him down he'd spent a year, and half his fortune, turning his house into a walled fortress. The garden had its own fruit and vegetables, its own well, its own cows and goats, even its own beehive. Nobody was allowed in unless he was sure of them.

'One day he hired a gang of men to hack down the creepers and bushes around the walls, for fear of assassins using them to climb over. I still remember the terror on his face when he looked through his barred window and saw me among the workers. I was arrested, and the landowner's word was enough to put me in jail. And then over the next week he wilted, wasted and finally . . . gave up his name.

'They wanted to hang me, but they couldn't prove I'd done anything. They let me cook in a cell for six months, and when I didn't die of malaria they kicked me out, hoping I'd starve. But the Reckoning looked after me.'

'Was it poison?' Hathin glanced sideways at Therrot. 'How did you get it into his food?'

'I didn't.' Therrot gave a thin, confiding smile in which there was a trace of shy pride. 'My little helpers did. I knew I'd never make it over the wall, so I took a serpent smile herb with me and planted it on the verge nearby. A few days later the flowers opened, and bees carried the poison nectar back to the landowner's hive. He always did have a sweet tooth.'

Hathin felt herself go pale.

'You see,' Therrot added in what was probably meant to be a comforting tone, 'revenge doesn't need to be face to face. Maybe you're not made for sticking a knife in someone . . . but would you feel the same way about planting a little fistful of leaves and roots?'

Hathin tried to imagine herself using her sickle to dig root-space for a sly, slow killer. It *did* feel different, but she was not at all sure it felt better.

'It sounds cold-blooded, doesn't it?' Therrot answered her wordless look with a rueful big-brother smile, and gave her a gentle biff on the shoulder as if she really was his younger brother. 'But it won't feel like that when the time comes. I mean . . . if you've got enough anger, then you just go mad. A calm, cool sort of mad. And then it's all easy.'

Perhaps she would try to go mad for her new big brother. She would turn herself into something white-hot, implacable

240

and relentless. And then she would become . . .

The Ashwalker.

'What is it?' asked Therrot as her hand tightened on his.

'It's nothing . . . I just thought . . .' Hathin scanned the low hill, but saw only golden grass waving innocently. It must have been a sun blot on her eye making her seem to see a flash of blue among the trees. 'I know Sorrow swallowed the Ashwalker, but just then I thought I saw . . .'

She gave Therrot an embarrassed smile and he returned it, but a few paces later he switched sides with her, so that he was walking between her and the low hill. Ahead of them, they could see Arilou waving a weak arm, coughing gasps of sound up towards the sky.

For the rest of the day Hathin could not help her eye stealing to left and right, but there was no sign of the Ashwalker.

After several days' hard hike, the Obsidian Trail curved to the east, towards the distant piebald peak of Crackgem the Mad.

In the old stories, Crackgem had been sent far away from the other volcanoes because of the way he laughed. His fits of laughter shook him so hard that it dragged up his maddened stories and dreams and flung them into the air. And the other volcanoes could not hear them without starting to shake, with rage, with fear, with something else too terrible to be laughter. So Crackgem was sent away from the others to play with his coloured mudpools, but there was always a worry that if his laughter grew loud enough the other mountains would hear it and start to shudder in spite of themselves.

However, it was exactly this position away from the other

 241

mountains that had made Crackgem ideal for the Beacon School. A tower like a lighthouse had been built halfway up the mountain, and at night a fire was lit at the top so that it could be seen from nearly everywhere on the island.

The paddyfields had been left behind with the Wailing Way, and the plains were a patchwork of little farms bristling with newly stripped beanstalks and hedged about by stunted banana plants, interspersed with silent, ever-expanding Ashlands. Occasionally the road passed steam-haunted orchid lakes, where green, ginger and golden mud broke the surface in fat bubbles that burst to leave a collage of coloured rings.

As one travelled away from the western coast, Lace villages became rarer and rarer. However there were odd settlements strung out along the road to Crackgem, and Hathin's group hoped to stop at them for shelter and new information. As they were approaching the first such village, however, something halted them in their tracks.

At first Hathin saw only an armed group of men tramping their way from the village to the road. Then she noticed the huddle of bruised and frightened-looking figures hemmed into the middle of the group. They were Lace, and some bore ropes around their wrists.

'Nothing we can do here and now,' murmured Jaze. Hathin noticed that his fingers were biting hard into Therrot's upper arm. Therrot watched the parade of captive Lace pass, his face spasming like a puddle in the rain, but he did not break stride.

Soon they saw other such gangs of armed men, each with their Lace prisoners. They swiftly learned that these were gangs of thugs or out-of-work labourers turned bounty hunter, tempted by the promise of a fee for every Lace they delivered to a camp near Mistleman's Blunder. Non-Lace that passed such convoys stopped to peer at the captive Lace with cold-eyed satisfaction.

The few Lace villages the revengers passed now were eerily deserted.

Hathin remembered Minchard Prox frowning at the map and striking out Lace villages with little flicks of his pencil. But these latest villages were too far away to threaten Mistleman's Blunder. The madness of Lace hatred that had welled up in Sweetweather was seeping across the whole island faster than she and her friends could walk.

Eventually, even the abandoned Lace villages petered out. The Lace did not tend to settle this far east, so far from their fishing grounds and the comfort of numbers. Those very few who did venture into these lands tended to hide their race. But even here there were the roaming bandit-like groups of bounty hunters, stopping travellers and peering into their faces. One such group had clearly captured a Lace in disguise, a worn-looking young woman dressed in towner garb. As the revenger group passed the other way her eyes fixed on them and widened. She made eye contact with Therrot and tapped meaningfully at her own teeth, before looking away.

Therrot swore when they were out of earshot. 'If they've started checking teeth for Lace decorations, we're in trouble. From now on, if we see roadblocks we'll have to duck off the trail and pass them that way.'

It was at this time that they first heard the phrase 'Time of Nuisance'. Nobody seemed to know what it meant, but the words hissed and buzzed in Hathin's ears.

Other worrying news reached them from travellers coming the other way. Crackgem's whims had become more violent of late, and he had taken to flinging up boiling hot geysers under the feet of travellers. The general view was that he should be avoided until his mad fit had passed.

'What are we going to do if Lord Crackgem is not accepting visitors?' whispered Hathin. The 'safe' route up the mountain to the Beacon School was known to very few, but even that was likely to be dangerous if Crackgem was feeling temperamental.

'Hide out in Jealousy, at Crackgem's foot,' answered Therrot. 'It would give us a chance to find this Bridle that Skein mentioned in the journal, and ask him about "Lord S". It'll be all right though – Crackgem will have calmed down by the time we get there.'

But Crackgem, Lord of Maniacs, did not calm down. By the time the revengers reached Jealousy, they found that a host of little camps had formed near the town. The most popular trail towards the eastern ports led between two fizzing, tutting orchid lakes, and many travellers had decided to camp outside Jealousy until Crackgem was in a better mood. The Lost, who might have spied out safe routes for them, were gone.

'It's not so bad,' Therrot insisted. 'Lots of people outside the city – we'll hide ourselves in a big group, get lost in the shuffle.'

Unlike the dour, practical Mistleman's Blunder, Jealousy had been built to show the benighted tribes of Gullstruck all the glories of the Cavalcaste traditions. The simple natives were meant to marvel at the magnificent stables, the family of mosaic-tiled towers, the regal palace for the governor. And marvel they did, as they might have done if they had seen a snow leopard trying to swim the warm ocean tides. To the credit of the founders, not *all* their plans had fallen into flinders. Crackgem's earthquakes had left one of the towers erect, and parts of the palace still stood. Most of the street-houses were squat enough to survive too, even while the weather ate away their balustrades.

The city's complicated Doorsy name meant 'Reflection upon a Greater Distant Glory'. Blunt, practical Nundestruth had no time for such fancies, and translated this simply as 'Jealousy' and, as usual in the battle of the names, Nundestruth had won.

It did not seem wise for the revengers to spend too long in any one camp, in case it gave people time to see through their story, and so each night they joined a different bonfire. Above them glowered Crackgem, but there was no hint of the beacon that should have burned to summon Lost children to their school.

Tomki turned out to be invaluable at helping them blend in. He had a puppy-like way of bouncing up to greet people as if they knew him, and by the time they realized that they didn't he had slotted into the gathering snug as a peg and was halfway through telling everyone a story. There was a camaraderie of the road, and many travellers gave them food out of pity for Arilou's apparent 'condition'.

In the camps, everyone was still talking of how all the Lost had been killed by a secret league headed by the fugitive Lady Arilou. Now, however, it also appeared to be 'common knowledge' that the Reckoning was a part of this conspiracy, and that the rest of the Lace were helping and hiding them at every turn.

Listening, Hathin felt sick. Was this her fault? If she and Arilou had not escaped, would any of this have happened? Perhaps the conspiracy that had really killed the Lost was manipulating the governors at every step, whispering tales of murderous Lace into their ears. But what frightened her was how readily the law and the ordinary people of Gullstruck believed such lies.

Rather than risk all four of them venturing into Jealousy, Jaze offered to slip into the city alone. However, he could discover nothing about the mysterious Bridle or Lord S. Meanwhile, the whole group listened out for mention of the Beacon School, or of anyone who might be able to guide them there between the perilous orchid lakes.

'Nobody seems to know the way,' Tomki told his companions late on the first night. 'As far as I can tell, nobody ever went up there and nobody ever came down. The school kept itself completely to itself.'

'Then I suppose the schoolmasters must have eaten rocks and burned words on their beacon,' remarked Jaze drily. '*Somebody* must have taken them their food and firewood.'

An answer was found to this mystery the very next morning, but it did not help a great deal.

Hathin woke early and noticed that a group of young men had stopped for a rest not far from the road. They were dressed in a 'Dancing Steam' style, except that it seemed a weaker indigo dye had been used on the thread of their clothes, so that instead of midnight blue the cloth was patterned in green and eggy yellow. Large packs of kindling lay beside them, waiting to be hoisted on to their backs once again.

Remembering what Jaze had said about firewood, Hathin approached.

'Friendly,' she called out.

One of the young men stood, but did not return her Nundestruth greeting. He pointed at a bundle of kindling and gave her a questioning look.

'You . . . You carry burnwood Beacon School way?' she asked.

He stared at her, jutting his jaw to one side, then picked up one of the bundles, slapped it and held up five fingers. It took a moment for her to realize that he was suggesting a price. They held gaze in mute frustration for a few seconds, and then the young man gave a rasp of a laugh and turned away. He called over his shoulder to one of his fellows in a language that had no hard edges. Hearing it somehow filled Hathin with a wave of nostalgia for the cove of the Hollow Beasts, reminded her of the downy smell of the clifftop orchids, and the crackle of dry seaweed under her feet. And, yes, this language was liquid like the Lace language, but much less musical and sibilant, so that Hathin could not quite explain the sense of familiarity.

It was not hard to find out more about the green-clad men. They were notorious for being unable to speak Nundestruth. They had arrived in the area at about the time the Beacon School started, and it was thought they had come from the far side of Crackgem, near the coast. Most believed that the Beacon School had deliberately arranged for them to come and ferry their provisions, precisely because they would be unable to tell anyone else the secret route up to the school.

The common local term for them was the Sours. Their green clothing was partly the cause of this, since a 'sour' was a slang term for an unripe fruit, but the name was also a reference to their sullen independence.

While other farmers had fled the foothills of Crackgem, the Sours apparently remained in their village on the mountainside, only coming down to sell timber or green cloth.

'Surely *some* of them must know Nundestruth?'

'Well, if so, they won't admit it.'

On the third night, Hathin's group found themselves in one of the smaller camps, with a big gang of men travelling together. They spoke Nundestruth with a Mistleman's Blunder accent, and it became clear that they were new arrivals and had already clashed with a gang of bounty hunters from Jealousy. 'Poach,' one of them kept saying. 'Like steal rabbit.' He seemed to find this very funny. 'They say if rabbit run on to land belong-them, then rabbit belong-them. Call we penny-pirate, poacher.'

'What rabbit you hunt?' asked Jaze.

'Lace,' answered the man, ending the word with a grinning hiss. Hathin's heart lurched. 'Take Lace Mistleman's Blunderway, dead or live, no matter. *Jealousy* gang over-there –' he nodded towards the lights of a larger camp a little way distant – 'look Lace for takem Superior. But no find Lace, we find all Lace first.' He laughed again, but there was a touch of uneasiness in his eye as he looked out towards the other camp.

'Why Superior want Lace?' asked Therrot, his hand tense in Hathin's. The 'Superior' was the title of Jealousy's governor.

'No can say. Superior want Lace alive. No can say.'

For all their apparent mirth, the men in this group were undeniably jumpy. The general feeling seemed to be that the local bounty hunters had lost their sense of humour about the scarcity of Lace. A tiny sound from the direction of the other camp set half their camp clutching at their knife hilts as they leaned forward to listen.

Into this stillness Arilou dropped a small wandering wail. 'Bad dream,' Jaze said quickly, cradling her shoulders.

Arilou's mouth and eyes were both wide open, as if with fear or effort.

'Ath . . .' she said.

Therrot placed a restraining hand on Hathin's arm, and she realized she'd started to rise from her seat. *But she wants something, she's upset, she needs something . . .*

'Athm,' said Arilou. 'Ath . . . Athern . . .'

And it was not a bubble in a stream of sound, it was a word that Arilou was trying to force her wayward tongue to shape. It was a word so familiar to Hathin that she did not recognize it at first, any more than she would have recognized the taste of air. And then she understood, and for a moment forgot how to breathe.

Hathin.

'Haathh . . .' Shrill. Urgent. Hathin leaped to her feet. She couldn't help it. And in that moment, the wind changed.

Suddenly the smoke from the campfire was no longer in Hathin's nose. Instead there was a strange damp smell of

 249

long-dead fires, and an acrid stench mixed with a reek like rotting meat.

Time came off its axle for a moment, giving the revengers time to see each others' eyes become great moons of realization. Then just as quickly the world recovered from its shock and everything happened at once.

A crossbow bolt hit the log where Hathin had been sitting.

Jaze sprang up, hefting Arilou on to his shoulder.

Tomki flung a cloak over the fire, plunging the area into darkness.

Therrot grabbed Hathin's arm and sprinted away from the campfire, dragging her with him. She threw a hasty glance backwards, and was in time to see a dark, slender figure burst into the middle of the camp. The darkness was too complete to make out the blue of his skin and clothes, but Hathin knew it was the Ashwalker. Sorrow had swallowed him and that had not stopped him. Nothing would stop him.

Behind them there were shouts, gunshots. Hathin and Therrot ran and ran, and then the ground gave out under them and they tumbled into a ditch. Jaze, Tomki and Arilou were already crouched in it, Tomki dragging on the elephant bird's leash with all his strength to stop it raising its head above the brink. Jaze had his crossbow in his hand and was peering over the top of the ditch.

'It's chaos back there,' he whispered. 'Half of them didn't realize he was an Ashwalker, and let fly . . . shh!' He listened. 'Sounds like a stand-off now. They're trying to bargain with him, trying to find out if there's a reward for us and if they can get a cut for helping flush us out . . .'

A calm voice answered the bounty hunters. A light-toned,

rain-on-the-skin voice. It was difficult for Hathin to imagine the Ashwalker speaking.

'He's saying he only wants the ash,' whispered Jaze. 'They're welcome to take our clothes and teeth jewels back to Mistleman's Blunder for the reward.' He glanced around the group, then looked at Therrot. 'Think you can get them to the city?'

'I can buy you time.' Tomki's voice was rapid, a touch of fear amid the eagerness.

'No, Tomki. It's an Ashwalker. Even Therrot here wouldn't slow him enough to do any good. But he'll break stride for me.' There was no bluster or boast in Jaze's voice. Quietly he was handing Therrot his amber monocles, his spare knife, all his most valued possessions. He had taken the situation apart like a clock, and knew that he would not be needing them again.

'No,' said Hathin. 'Jaze . . .'

Figures were now leaving the darkened camp in twos and threes, walking at a crouch and sometimes pausing to run swords into sinister-looking bushes.

'Therrot, you keep Hathin safe,' Jaze muttered, placing a foot halfway up the wall of the ditch. 'Put Arilou on the back of the bird, Tomki, and run with it as best you can.'

'Jaze!' hissed Hathin, a bit louder, and he turned to look at her in surprise. 'We . . . We *need* you. To carry Arilou at least – she'll never stay on the bird, you *know* that.'

'I could carry—' said Therrot.

'No!' snapped Jaze. 'You keep Hathin safe.' He turned back to Hathin. 'There's no time to say this gently. You were brought up to believe that the most important person in the

251

world was Arilou. Well, your village is dead, and what they told you isn't true any more. I'm not even sure Arilou's personality exists outside your imagination. Now it's *you* that matters. This is *your* quest.'

'It is, it *is* my quest . . .' Hathin gripped her fists and drew a deep breath. 'And you're not going to do this, Jaze, because *I'm not going to let you*.' She was shaking, but almost without noticing she had changed to the cold, confident voice she had used for Arilou for so many years. 'You're supposed to help me, but *I* decide how, not you.'

She turned away before she could wilt under Jaze's astonished gaze.

'Tomki,' she said, 'you can move fast on your bird, can't you? I've got something I want you to do. It's . . . very dangerous though.'

A look of barely suppressed delight crossed Tomki's features.

'I want you to ride over to that big camp, the one with the *local* bounty hunters, and tell them that there's a family of Lace here, about to be taken prisoner by the men from Mistleman's Blunder. Don't tell them about the Ashwalker, and be . . .'

The bird lurched upright, and Tomki flew on to its back. A second later they were gone, leaving gouge marks in the earth and a pair of floating feathers.

'. . . careful,' finished Hathin.

Jaze stared at her for a few moments, then carefully removed the bolt from his bow and crouched with a sigh beside Arilou.

'And when they come . . .' he murmured.

'There'll be chaos,' said Hathin. 'And we'll run for the city. All of us.'

There were cries, and the sound of brush hissing in disapproval as it was ravaged by sprinting feet. Evidently Tomki had been spotted. The whistle of slings. A long pause, and then, far distant, a high, piping, excitable voice.

'It's Tomki,' whispered Therrot. 'I think he's reached the Jealousy men.'

The other camp's distant bonfire suddenly gave birth to a litter of smaller lights – torches, with two dozen shadowy figures behind them. An exchange of shouts in different accents. Then the line of torches leaped forward and there was a chaos of cries and rock-ricochets and shots in the blackness.

'Now,' whispered Jaze. It sounded like an instruction, but there was a hint of a question in his face.

Hathin nodded.

Nobody appeared to notice as they scrambled from the ditch and ran, Therrot to Hathin's right, Jaze to her left with Arilou in his arms. As they sprinted across the scrubland, Hathin heard Therrot give a sharp gasp, and suddenly there was nobody running on her right.

She staggered to a halt, and turned. Therrot was face down on the ground. She ran back to him, shook him, found a wet patch on the back of his head. She was trying in vain to drag him into the nearest bushes when the torches rollicked panting out of the darkness and surrounded her.

Torches. The locals had been the ones carrying torches. What if they thought she was with the men from Mistleman's Blunder?

253

'I Lace!' she called out in Nundestruth. 'Look!' She snatched off her cap, and ruffled the short, soft fur above her forehead where her scalp had been shaved. 'Look!' She drew back her upper lip and rubbed her forefinger across her teeth. 'Blundermen try kill, make we no good for you! Pleaseyou, take we to city belong-you or Blundermen find and kill!' She placed both hands protectively on Therrot's back. 'We Lace . . .'

19
THE SUPERIOR'S SOAP

As Hathin and the unconscious Therrot were dragged through the night streets of Jealousy, Hathin could not help remembering Jaze's words.

You have a duty to avoid being captured or killed . . .

What would happen when the Ashwalker worked out who had captured them, and strode up to the Superior's house, licence in hand? Had she led Therrot into an inescapable trap? She looked on nervously as her captors paused to examine him.

Then a couple of men draped Therrot's arms over their shoulders and took him away, and Hathin found herself being escorted by the rest of the torch parade, a heavy hand gripping each of her shoulders. When by chance she met the eye of one of her guards she felt the corners of her mouth curving up into a smile. She was too exhausted to help it, and they shuddered and looked away as if something slimy had brushed their skin.

She was dragged through a heavy gate and across a square courtyard, where white peahens slept here and there on the dark lawn.

It was only as Hathin was dragged into a candlelit hallway

that she realized this did not look a great deal like a prison.

She was manhandled over a mosaic floor, between two suits of gilded armour and into a high-ceilinged room with maps painted on every wall. There was the Gripping Bird-shaped outline of Gullstruck, its volcanoes painted in a cheery cherry-red, and the vivid blue sea around it now apparently populated by several decades worth of insects and bugs that had been swatted against it.

Underneath it sat a balding little man with beautiful long, auburn moustache hairs wound around a curling metal wire. He wore a waistcoat that seemed to have been designed for a much bigger man. As Hathin and the guards entered he looked up with an expression of weary misery.

But when one of the guards moved forward and whispered in his ear, Hathin saw a look of almost pained hope venture cautiously across his features. 'Oh! I see. Ah, yes! Yes, well done. Could you wait outside?' He spoke a crisply accented Doorsy, scrubbing-brush brisk.

As the guards left the room Hathin felt nervously at the bruised places on her upper arm. She could think of several reasons why the little man might be pleased to see her, and none of them were good.

'Let's see your teeth then, young man.'

It took Hathin a moment to remember her boyish disguise and realize that he was talking to her. She obediently bared her teeth, and the man stared at them over his wire-rimmed spectacles before sitting back with a 'huff' of relief.

'You really *are* Lace, aren't you?'

She nodded.

'Now.' The little man moved a jade paperweight, in a

decisive fashion that caused the scroll it was holding down to coil and flip him on the nose. Both of them pretended it hadn't happened. 'You know who I am, I assume?'

'You're the Superior?' She was rewarded by a small, fragile smile.

'Quite right, young man. Superior Pedron Sun-Sedrollo. You have probably heard of the Dukes of Sedrollo.' He waved a hand at the wall, and Hathin noticed for the first time that there were hundreds of tiny framed cameos of men in frilled ruffs and forked beards, and occasional women whose hair swelled up above their foreheads like marrows, reined in by spangled nets. 'You may also have heard of the Counts of Sun.' The opposite wall held a host of similar images.

Hathin started to understand why the little man was so small. Sitting under a hundred needley gazes like those would shrivel anyone.

'You're probably wondering why you've been shown into my presence.' He glanced at Hathin and seemed to be reassured by something he saw in her face. 'You might be too young to understand this, but I have to look after two great towns. There is the living township of Jealousy, which you might already have seen – containing about four hundred souls. But out on the foothills of Crackgem, beyond the orchid lakes, is an entire *city*, with full four thousand souls – an invisible city that is ever increasing its population.'

Hathin remembered the Ashlands near her village, with its forest of spirit houses.

'Sir Superior . . . would those souls be all the Dukes of Sedrollo and the Counts of Sun?'

'Yes,' intoned the Superior, with a note of hollow

desolation in his voice. 'All of them. And their cousins, and their wives, and their wives' cousins, and their wives' cousins' wives' cousins, and many, many more besides. Their ashes were all brought here during the very first landings.' He gave a cramped smile. 'Of course, the Ashlands weren't the wrong side of the orchid lakes back *then*. My predecessors picked out what looked like the best and greenest land, in easy reach of the town . . . but you know what Crackgem is like. Every fifty years or so, bang! Pop! Shudder! And next thing we know there are roasted farmers all over the foothills, and old lakes have suddenly become vales of pitted mud, and new scalding lakes are bubbling up somewhere *totally different*.' He sighed.

'Anyway, I owe my post here to the presence of my ancestors. Who could govern here but the sole heir of all these noble scions? And where could I work but here, so that I might attend to my ancestors' tombs?'

'But . . .' Hathin hesitated. 'Surely your family must help with your reverences, sir – your children, your brothers and sisters . . .'

'I have none!' Poor Superior Sun-Sedrollo waved his hands at the faces on the walls. 'How would I find time for a wife or children? How would I find time to have brothers and sisters? I am even surprised that I had time to be born myself!' Hathin's tired mind grappled with this concept and gave it up. 'Of course, there are many others in Jealousy who have ancestors up there and give them tribute, but nobody seems to think things *through*.

'When I succeeded my father as Superior here, I found that for years uncounted offerings of food had been burned to the ancestors – but nobody had once thought of *cutlery*.'

He shook his head in despair. 'Can you imagine that? For over a century the Dukes of Sedrollo and the Counts of Sun had been forced to eat with their *fingers*.'

It was becoming obvious to Hathin that she had never thought about these things enough, and yet she also had the strong feeling the Superior had thought about them rather too much.

'Of course, everything has become a good deal worse in the last twenty years,' continued the Superior, 'now that everybody burns "dead man's bonds" on the stones instead of even trying to work out what their ancestors need.'

'But . . . doesn't that mean they can buy everything they want in the afterlife?' Hathin had seen only a few of these 'bonds', each promising to be worth 100,000 doubloons of gold in the afterlife and brightly painted with images of famous ancestor spirits.

'How can they? Think about it. The city's inhabitants must have pockets bulging with these notes and nothing else. Who can they trade with? What can they buy, if nobody has anything but money?

'Well, at least now we have comprehensive records of every tribute offered, so we can assess the size of the city and decide what they need. But not a year goes by when I don't find some critical thing I've forgotten. Which brings me to the matter in hand, and the torment of my life.' The Superior adjusted his spectacles and stared at Hathin for a long time. 'Soap,' he said at last.

'Soap?'

'Soap. I did not even think of it myself for four years after becoming Superior – four years! Imagine, a community of four thousand, living in such close proximity for over a hundred years, with no soap at all! I mean, the ticks! The grime! The sweat in their collars!'

The little man slammed his paperweights about his desk in distraction. 'And the worst thing is – *I* cannot possibly give it to them. To give even a beloved brother a gift of soap is to say that you feel his toilette is lacking. How can I give a sackful of soap to the first Duke Antod Sedrollo, who commanded the Imperial Navy?'

Hathin saw the problem and said so.

'This is where you and your friend come in. Long ago a Lace bodyguard gave his life to save his Superior and was uniquely privileged with a grave in my ancestors' Ashlands. The obvious solution is to sacrifice the soap to him, so he can sell it to everyone else. Now, we seldom find Lace passing through the city, but last year I found two brothers who were willing to carry soap up to this grave. Only, ah, that is, ah, one evening while they were making their offering, there was a White Tide.'

Hathin felt herself pale at the mention of one of the deadly waves of white ash and burning smoke that could sweep through and destroy whole villages in seconds.

'And, ah, that left me with the same problem as before, so I have been on the lookout for more Lace ever since.'

Hathin was still reeling from the mention of the White Tide, and so it was a moment or two before she realized that the Superior was looking her over with a gentle twinkle.

'I'm glad to see you've got the right kind of spirit,' he said. 'I'm sorry we can't just load you up with pictures of soap . . . but who can draw soap? We've tried, and you can't tell if it's suet or potatoes. But you're four foot of courage, and that's the main thing.'

Hathin felt that she was four foot of exhaustion, blisters, bruises and ditch-mud. She had intended to venture into Crackgem's domain, but she had not expected this to involve dragging a century's supply of soap up the foothills of a hyperactive volcano.

'Now, I would send someone up with you, but I've had heaven's own trouble getting *anyone* to nip over to Crackgem since he started throwing hot rocks at people. Two weeks ago a group of fellows turned up and toyed with my hopes, promising to take anything I wanted to the mountainside if I would just give them a guide to the Beacon School, where they had business of some sort. Of course I couldn't help them, so I suppose they must have wandered up the mountain on their own . . . and they never actually came back. It was most disappointing.'

The Superior stopped to scrutinize Hathin again, and gave a small approving nod as if he saw something that satisfied him.

'But I can see it would take more than that to daunt you. So – you and your friend will do me this little favour . . . and I'll see what can be done about making sure that you are kept safe from those other Lace-hunters.' The Superior settled himself back in the chair and smilingly dismissed Hathin with a flick of his quill.

As she staggered to the door she could hear him muttering to himself.

'Charming child,' he was saying, 'so bright and cooperative. Not at all what one expects from *them* . . .'

 261

How had she made such a favourable impression? And how had she volunteered for such a dangerous mission without noticing? There could only be one answer. Hathin realized that she must have been smiling throughout the interview.

She was just leaving the room when another guard came in with soft-footed urgency. A letter was placed into the Superior's hands, a letter marked by blue fingerprints. A parade of expressions took turns on the little man's face as he read, ranging from shock to toothache.

'Guards . . . out! I wish to speak with this child alone again.'

The door closed behind the guards, and Hathin reddened under the little man's stare.

'There's an Ashwalker at the gate,' he said, carefully studying her face. 'Tell me, young man . . . are you a young woman?'

Hathin hesitated, and then nodded.

'That is what the Ashwalker gave my men to understand. This is his commission: a warrant to hunt the fugitive known as Lady Arilou and her companions, suspected of complicity in murder of the Lost. And I really do not see why you find that so very funny, young woman.'

Hathin bit her lips together and stared at his hands in a desperate attempt to stifle her terrified smile. It must have worked since when he spoke again his voice was gentler.

'So . . . are you this . . . this Arilou?'

'No . . . she . . . I was travelling with her. But I . . . lost her.' In spite of herself, Hathin found tears of exhaustion and despair welling up in her eyes. 'I *lost* her. I don't know where she is. Sir, I know what everyone is saying, but we never killed anyone, I swear . . .'

The Superior watched her silent sobs with every sign of annoyance, embarrassment and conflict. 'Typical. First Lace I find in months – in *months* – and they are thoughtless enough to be fugitives from justice. Can't they see the position this puts me in?'

For a few moments he sat tweaking indecisively at the blue-stained letter, then he gave a long, vexed sigh. 'Well . . . you don't exactly fit my picture of a marauding assassin. And I don't much like blue people in smelly clothes turning up at my gate and demanding my prisoners. Are you willing to swear on . . . on whatever it is you people care about, that you and the man captured with you had no part in any of this killing?'

A little shakily, Hathin nodded.

'All right then. Now obviously *I* can't get involved in this business, but let us say for now that my men have been fooled by that little disguise of yours. The Ashwalker is asking after a young girl – we can tell him that nobody of that description has been captured. In fact, we might even tell him that a promising-looking suspect was seen heading . . . shall we say north? Up towards Thorn Rise?'

Hathin was shown to a little room with a bed too soft for her to sleep on, and samplers on the walls that she couldn't read.

For a time she crouched by the one small barred window, hands cupped to her mouth, making the owl calls that were Arilou's name. *Arilou, Arilou, find me here.* She only ceased to call when she looked out through the window and saw, beyond the city gate, a single figure sitting on a rock. It was a blot of midnight blue.

When she mustered the courage to look out again an hour later, however, it was gone.

20
THE BLUE CLOTH

Next day two bruised and haggard Lace could be found heaving a barrow of soap up the stony path that led towards the Ashlands of Crackgem.

They had left Jealousy in the late morning, once Therrot had recovered his senses enough to walk. Already their path had climbed and dipped enough that they had lost sight of the city. On either side of the trail the orchid lakes seethed with pearl-clusters of bubbles, fed to the brim by the recent rains. The only landmark that allowed them to keep their bearings was the crinkled outline of Crackgem, which reared up above the crags from time to time.

Hathin and Therrot were not the only people using the path, but they could not help noticing that everybody else seemed to be going in the other direction. Farmers were abandoning their homesteads on the foothills of Crackgem and fleeing to hide in Jealousy until he calmed down.

'So tell me again why we're not making a run for it?' asked Therrot groggily.

'Where would we run?' Hathin asked in a small voice. 'The road past Crackgem to the ports is blocked, the road back is full of bounty hunters looking for us. If we're going back to Jealousy, we need the Superior's protection . . . and we *have* to go back to Jealousy . . . it's where they were heading, the others . . . we were all running to the city . . . they'll be somewhere in the city . . .'

There was a silence, but it was a Lace silence that everybody understood.

'All right.' Therrot said at last. 'Stop a moment; stop striding as if you're trying to grind the mountain to dust.'

Hathin halted and turned reluctantly.

'Your plan last night was pretty good,' Therrot continued, his voice gentle. 'Even if it turns out that the others . . .'

'They'll find us,' Hathin said, too firmly for conviction. 'Arilou will find us. She's Lost, remember?'

Therrot bit his lip and reached out to ruffle the short hair above Hathin's forehead into a fuzz with his palm. The gesture was familiar, and Hathin realized that she had seen him teasing Lohan's hair in just the same way. *Does he really see me at all, or is he speaking to his little brother, his little sister?*

With difficulty the pair of them forced their barrow up a low ridge and then stared in disbelief out across a steam-ridden phantasmagoria. There was no more path. Instead the ground sloped down to a plain of porridge-coloured rock glazed with a thin skin of fast-flowing water. Puckers and spouts broke the dun surface, spewing bubbles and staining the rock with vivid blots of gold, green, red, pink. Occasional great crags jutted up like beach boulders.

To the left and right the plain gave way to steaming lakes. The only way forward appeared to be across the plain's pitted surface.

'Look there.' Therrot pointed, his face grim. There was

a hole in the porridge-like plain, and through it murky blue-grey water could be seen bubbling. 'That's not solid rock, that's barely a span thick. Someone trusted their weight to that, and I bet they didn't come home with a story about it.' The hole was indeed just large enough that a person might have fallen through it. 'Enough.' Therrot set the barrow down. 'The Superior's relatives can go unwashed a bit longer – nobody will know any better.'

Carefully Therrot reached under the cloth that had been laid over the barrow to protect it from the sudden monsoon rains, and lifted out a slithering lump of the soap. He stooped near a convenient little water-filled crater in the shadow of a bush.

'Present for you, Lord Crackgem,' he muttered. 'You don't mind, do you?'

The water in the crater seethed as he dropped in the soap. As he stepped back to the barrow and stooped for some more, Hathin saw the foaming increase and the water start to fountain.

'Therrot!'

He turned in time to see the fountain become a wild, white plume, and to cover his face with his arms as the wind changed, lashing him with boiling spray and scalding steam. The two revengers grabbed at the barrow, and they slithered and tumbled their way down the slope to escape the geyser's fury, stopping just short of the treacherous plain.

'He minds,' whispered Hathin. They had agreed to deliver the soap, and clearly they would make good on their promise. Lord Crackgem in his madness would have it so.

'But how?' asked Therrot, coughing as the acrid steam stung his throat. 'How?'

As they were staring aghast across the plain the answer to their question rose up on a crag as suddenly as a geyser, and flailed white arms. A lone figure, wind-blown hair a scribble against the sky, the padding of her false pregnancy slipped over to one hip . . .

'I don't believe it!' A second figure had joined Arilou on the top of the crag, and was waving frantically at Hathin and Therrot. There was no mistaking Tomki's high-pitched, unguarded tones. 'Jaze! Come up here and look! It's them! She's done it! Arilou's found them!'

Five minutes later, after a frenzy of impromptu hugs and back-slapping, the reunited Lace were starting to recover their breath. Almost sick with relief, Hathin was pulling the thorns out of Arilou's clothing and wiping the dust from the corners of her eyes.

As it turned out, both Jaze and Tomki had spent a sleepless night trying to find the rest of the group. Jaze had made it to the edge of the city with Arilou before finding that none of his other allies had kept pace. Tomki had been cornered by the local bounty hunters, who plied him with drinks in thanks for delivering two Lace into their hands.

'I only found Tomki because he decided to spill candlewax on the toes of the biggest thug of the lot,' explained Jaze. 'I just followed the sound of bellowed swearing, and sure enough – there was Tomki.'

'You know, you really didn't have to step between us,' Tomki remarked mildly.

'Yes, Tomki, I did. Well, at dawn Arilou woke up and started moaning and roaring, so we had to head away from the crowds. We found that if we went one way she quietened, if we didn't she started shrieking. In the end, we gave up and put our faith in her. We've been following her for hours, hoping there was method in her meanderings – even when she started leading us this way, through Crackgem's playground.'

'She found me.' Hathin curled one of Arilou's long paws into a loose fist and wrapped it in both of hers. 'I told you she was a Lost . . .'

'Yes.' Jaze squatted beside her.

'Yes, Doctor Hathin, you did.'

Hathin and Therrot in turn recounted their own adventures, and told of the bargain concerning the Superior's soap.

'So, do you think the Lady Arilou can lead us safely through this steam-pit?' finished Therrot.

The Lady Arilou was certainly intent on leading them somewhere. Her face was set towards the mountain, and any attempt to draw her in any other direction for any reason was met with hoarse squawks of frustration. With some qualms Hathin took her hand and let her lead them across the ominous, multicoloured plain. Behind trooped the others with the elephant bird and the barrow, all following Arilou's path as closely as possible, wincing with each crackle of stones beneath the barrow wheel in case it was the sound of the crust of rock giving way.

On either side of the valley were great splatters of cream and yellow stone that seemed to drip and bubble, as if Crackgem had been poaching vast eggs on the hot rocks but had abandoned them to bleach, harden and stink.

After a while, to the revengers' relief, the fragile plain

 269

gave way to solid-looking ground and they found themselves wrestling the barrow between stone ancestors squinting with moss, their tall hats laden with creepers. These could only be the Ashlands of Crackgem. No wooden spirit houses here – they would have vanished before Crackgem's White Tides like cobwebs in a strong wind.

The Ashlands proved to be vast, just as the Superior had warned, far bigger than Jealousy itself. It took some time before they found a tiny stone figure set apart from the other ancestral memorials. Little circles were etched into its teeth, so this was evidently the dead Lace bodyguard that the Superior had described.

The revengers unloaded the barrowful of kindling and soap, piled them high on a slab and nursed them into flame. A greasy smoke smelling of mutton sweat charged the air.

Jaze took Therrot aside, and the two held a muted conference. Then they returned to the little Lace burial stone and began to dig. Only when they had unearthed the Lace's cremation urn did Hathin guess what they were doing.

'No Lace should be trapped in a pot,' was all Therrot said, as he scattered the dank ashes to the winds.

Hathin looked across at Arilou's pale but serene face and felt a swell of pride. Arilou had *found* her. Arilou had led them safely to the Ashlands. Even as she reached for her sister's hand, however, Arilou lurched to her feet, turned her face back towards the mountain and resumed tottering up the slope.

Hathin was, as usual, a little winded by the impact with Arilou's will. A sudden collision with a stranger, in a pitch-dark room which had seemed empty.

Tomki turned away from the flame to see Hathin setting off in pursuit of Arilou. 'Not *again*! Take your eyes off our Lady Lost for a moment and she's away like a slingshot!'

But Hathin could only think of one place that a young Lost might be heading with such furious determination. The Beacon School. What else was to be found on this desolate and dangerous mountainside? Arilou's urgency infected Hathin. This landscape *did* mean something to her. Perhaps this adventure really would allow Hathin to glimpse something through a chink in the hard shell of Arilou's strangeness.

At last, just as the sun was dropping out of sight, Arilou's chosen path became a recognizable trail, the rain-moistened earth marked here and there by recent-looking footprints. Hathin's heart rose. Dance's hopes had been justified after all then – there *were* still people at the Beacon School, people who might help them.

Another zig, a zag, a short boulder scramble . . . and suddenly Hathin could make out the faint amber glow of a fire further down the path. She could hear the trill of a pipe and the rumble of voices. Clay pots flanked the path ahead, each spewing stunted yellow flames and vast flowers of sooty smoke. Above an unruly cairn an enormous deep-blue flag roused itself slightly in the wind, then fell back against its pole with a sullen slap.

Hathin turned in delight to her companions, only to find that Jaze's smile was thin and joyless.

'Here.' Jaze gently took Hathin by the shoulder and drew her to stand beside him. 'Do you see that? Silhouetted against the moon?'

Obediently Hathin stared out in the direction of his

pointing finger, back the way they had come and upwards. Thrown into relief against the moon was a tapering shape too tall and regular to be a tree.

'The school's beacon tower,' said Jaze.

'But . . . it's so far away!'

'Yes,' Jaze replied under his breath, 'too far away. Whatever it is we've found, I don't think it's the school.'

Has it occurred to you that somebody might be a Lost and be an imbecile as well? Hathin bit her lip hard as she remembered Therrot's words.

She turned back to Arilou just in time to see her break into a stumbling run down the path. Hathin followed with the others in her wake. On either side of the path, crevices in the rocks seemed to deepen and become doorways. A tiny dog ran out and bit red pieces from the night air with its warning barks. People poured from the rock-mounds. The green of their clothes was dulled in the firelight, but Hathin heard the bubble of their anxious, angry speech, and knew that they were Sours.

Oblivious to the dangerous murmurs all around her, Arilou made straight for a little family group near the village's central bonfire. There was a father with a worn, surly face, a wife, an adult son and daughter and two younger children.

Arilou made a trilling, happy sound in her throat, and staggered towards them, her face radiant with recognition, her arms stretched forward. Her tottering steps carried her right up to the mother of the mountain family.

An inexpert pat at the woman's face resounded as the heel of her hand struck the jaw. The woman recoiled from the apparent attack. Arilou crumpled to her knees, took hold of the smallest girl's arm and tugged her into a clumsy embrace. The mother pounced and snatched the screaming child free, then backed behind her husband, face dark with hostility and fear. The family were now in uproar, and as they raised their voices Hathin knew at last why the Sour language sounded so familiar. She had heard words flow in this liquid way a thousand times – from the lips of Arilou.

As the little family backed away from her, Arilou reached trembling arms towards them and her wail rose into a screech of utter desolation. Hathin watched her, feeling a sadness that seemed to belong to someone older.

You didn't come to the orchid lakes to find me at all, did you, Arilou? And you weren't trying to lead us to the Ashlands, or to the Beacon School. No, you were coming here.

The light of the Beacon School drew your mind in, like all the other Lost children, didn't it? And the teachers tried to teach you and the others to go home and practise using your bodies. But when your mind wandered away from your classes, you didn't come back to the coast, did you? No, you didn't go far at all. You found a little village on Crackgem and you watched a family there until it felt like your family. That's why you hardly ever came home to us. That's why you spoke a language none of us could understand. You were trying to speak their *language.*

You were never an imbecile. You've just been busy elsewhere all these years . . . with this *family.*

'But they don't know you,' Hathin said aloud. 'You loved them and they never noticed you – any more than you really noticed me.'

Arilou's face was a picture of hurt, incomprehension and betrayal, and Hathin could only feel pity for her.

 273

Arilou's wail and the dogs' yaps had summoned the rest of the village out of their stone houses and filled the darkness with hostile, uncertain faces. Hathin and the other intruders crouched next to Arilou, sensing that their fate was being discussed all around them.

'Should we try to talk to them?' whispered Hathin. 'I mean, if just *one* of them can speak Nundestruth, maybe we can persuade someone to show us the way to the Beacon School, and then we can leave here . . . before . . .'

'. . . Before they decide to stone us out of the village,' finished Therrot under his breath. Tomki's face brightened immeasurably, but Jaze slowly shook his head.

'It's worse than that. Right now I think they're deciding whether they can *let* us leave. Look around. Look at those pots, the ones with the burning fat in them.'

The pots were made of clay, and as Hathin stared their bumps resolved themselves into blobbed faces . . .

'Oh no! They haven't!'

Jaze nodded grimly. 'Cremation urns. They're using them as candle-holders.'

'But then . . .' Hathin was still struggling with her own horror at the blasphemy, 'what happened to the ash from the . . . oh.'

Their eyes all strayed unwillingly to the great blue flag as it shrugged apathetically in the breeze.

'They *can't* have done!' gasped Therrot.

Jaze shrugged. 'I've seen green cloths hung at the threshold to ward off demons, and yellow cloths to ward off Lace sorcery – and Ashwalkers say they can make themselves invisible to volcanoes if they dye with the right human ash. So maybe if you wanted to make a *whole village* invisible to the volcano . . .'

'. . . Then you'd need a really *big* cloth, which probably means . . . an awful lot of ash. In this case, I guess, a lot of Counts of Sun and Dukes of Sedrollo,' Hathin finished in a small voice.

'We could pretend we haven't noticed the flag or the urns,' whispered Tomki. With difficulty, the Lace contingent tore their eyes from the incriminating evidence. 'I can try talking to the Sours,' Tomki continued in a scared, hopeful voice. 'I can mime.'

'Arilou might be able to talk to them,' Hathin said softly.

'What?'

'I – I think so, anyway. But . . . But she's a bit too upset right now.'

'Then cheer her up quickly!' hissed Therrot. 'They're holding rocks!'

'Arilou.' Hathin stroked Arilou's face to get her attention. Arilou gave a soft, disconsolate squawk.

Tomki was on his feet, both hands raised in a gesture of surrender.

'Friendly!' he was exclaiming in Nundestruth. He illustrated this with a smile, but panic stretched it to alarming dimensions. Two small children wailed and ran off to hide behind a vat of indigo dye.

'Friendly, Arilou . . .' *Come on, Arilou, you spent a little time with us, you checked on your body, you must know a few words of Lace. Please tell me you listened to us sometimes, please tell me we meant* something *to you.* 'Say "friendly" to them.'

An old man squatted beside them and spilled a gargling question. Arilou gaped silently, eyes bulging with effort, then managed a few soft sounds. He looked over his shoulder at his fellows, and shrugged.

Despite herself, Hathin felt a pang. *He asked Arilou a question, and she tried to answer it. And to him that means nothing.*

But now Arilou's mouth had started to soften into a loose pansy-shape. Behind her grey eyes a crystalline dream had softly shattered into fragments.

What was I expecting? She's never had a conversation in her life. Maybe she's learned to understand the Sours' speech, and maybe she's practised making the same mouth shapes, the same sounds. But words are like toy bricks you learn to pick up and put together over years. Did I think she'd just know how to do it?

Poor Arilou. It never crossed your *mind that you wouldn't be able to, did it?*

'There's something ugly about this whole village,' muttered Therrot, 'something dangerous in the mood here.'

'Of course there is,' said Hathin sadly. '*They're like us.* They're so used to protecting themselves and their secret by shutting everybody else out, they can't see how dangerous it is to be so alone.'

Even as Hathin spoke, the village became real to her, became a place where people actually lived. She suddenly noticed the thinness of the villagers' faces, the empty baskets that should have held dried beans, the scarcity of chickens and pigs.

'They're alone up here, and they're running out of food,' she said. 'I don't know why – maybe it's something to do with the school beacon not being lit – but it's true. Look around!

Oh, if only Arilou could tell us why . . . Tomki, do you think you can bargain with them? Persuade them to take us to the Beacon School? There's the Superior's barrow back down in the Ashlands – perhaps we could give that to them to sell?'

'I can try.' Tomki steepled his fingers over his head to make himself into a tower, then pointed in the direction of the distant beacon tower. '*We . . .*' he pointed at himself and each of his Lace companions, 'want to go *there*.' He pointed towards the school again, and mimed walking.

This did not seem to improve the atmosphere at all. Many of the Sours exchanged dark looks.

'We pay!' Tomki rummaged in his belt pouch and produced a single coin. 'Pay! Well, sort of. Pay you to come with us.' He took a companionable hold on the arm of one Sour woman, who hastily tugged it free. 'Protect us from geysers.' He crouched down and then leaped to his feet, waving his arms. 'Whoosh! Geysers!'

There were noises of confused amusement. Various children pushed forward, apparently hoping that Tomki would do it again. When he did, there was a small but noticeable ease in the tension.

'Whooooooosh! Yes! Protect us from geysers! And . . . and rock falls!'

Unfortunately, Tomki decided to mime 'rock falls' by snatching up two fist-sized rocks and tossing them against the chest of a tree trunk of a man. A leathery thump, and Tomki was on the ground clutching his jaw.

'Did you see that?' His delighted squeal was cut short by a brisk foot to the ribs, followed by one to the head. 'Look! Look! I'm being wronged!'

'Wonderful,' snarled Therrot as he scrambled to his feet. 'Now we're all in for a good wronging.'

Jaze did not look towards his belt, but his fingers made idle flicks at the hilt, and the thongs keeping his dagger in its sheath fell loose. Then suddenly the hilt was in his hand, the blade lying hidden flush against his forearm, making Hathin think of a scorpion with its sting folded down under its tail.

Hathin felt sick and dizzy as the crowd surged forward. She could talk to people, but this was Mob. Mob wasn't people. It took people and folded their faces like paper, leaving hard lines of anger and fear that didn't belong to them.

And then without warning a silvery undulation of sound flowed free on the air, and Mob stood amazed. Arilou was speaking, and suddenly the green-clad strangers around them were listening, were people again.

'I don't know what your sister just said,' Therrot muttered out of the corner of his mouth, 'but I'm very glad she said it.'

Whatever it was, it appeared to be enough. No more kicks were aimed at Tomki, and the expression of the old man who seemed to be the Sours' leader grew warmer, more humane. For decades language had been the way that the Sours knew their own and shut out everybody else. By using their words, however clumsily, it seemed that Arilou had broken through their shell and become one of them.

Gingerly Hathin scratched a rough picture of a barrow into the dust, and this time heads clustered round her to observe. At least now the Sours seemed interested in trying to understand.

'Barrow.' Hathin pointed down towards the Ashlands.

'Barrow down *there*. To make it clearer what the barrow was, Hathin added some blobs inside it, then mimed gripping two handles. We *give* to you.' She grasped a large piece of air and presented it ceremoniously to the Sours' chief.

The old man looked quizzically at Arilou, who supplied a single word. Brows cleared, and the word was repeated with expressions of revelation. The Sours seemed happy, and there was a good deal of nodding.

The old man then performed a dumb show of moving something to his mouth and biting down on it. Wondering if she and her friends were being invited to dinner, Hathin pointed to the cauldron of bean soup over the fire with a questioning look and was rewarded with a nod.

'I think we'd better accept,' she said under her breath.

And so the painful conversation went on, even after the sky darkened and soup was served to everyone in hollowed gourds. Using Arilou as translator was rather like trying to sew using a pinecone instead of a needle, forcing big, fat meanings through the tiny aperture that was Arilou's ability to communicate. Hathin was able to pick out one word that occurred again and again amid the flowing Sour sentences. It sounded like 'jeljech', the last consonant a soft hiss at the back of the throat, like the 'ch' in 'loch'.

At last the Sours' leader reached out, took Arilou's hand and clasped it. Bargain sealed.

'Good,' muttered Jaze as he got to his feet. 'Now we'll get out of here . . .'

A chorus of protests. Gentle but insistent hands guiding Jaze to sit back down. Gestures towards one of the rock-pile huts, where clean bedding mats were being unrolled. A stream

 279

of Sour words . . . *something something something jeljech* . . .

'. . . or perhaps we won't,' Jaze finished darkly. 'It looks like we are going nowhere.'

Hathin fidgeted and thought of the Superior, waiting for word from his soap-deliverers. What would he do when the stars came out and they had not returned? Would he change his mind and send for the Ashwalker after all?

21
LESSON'S END

The next morning, the visiting Lace were woken by the mysterious 'Jeljech', who proved to be a seventeen-year-old Sour girl with deep-set eyes and a guarded, self-possessed air. She startled them awake a little after dawn by putting her head through the door of the rock hut that had been allocated to them, and laying down bowls of something hot and herbal.

'Friendly.' It was the gruffest, unfriendliest-sounding 'friendly' Hathin had ever heard, but it was a relief to hear Nundestruth at last. 'Want . . . go . . . tower way?' It soon became clear that the girl's Nundestruth was not good, and that the frown on her face was partly due to concentration and uncertainty.

Jeljech was evidently to be their guide to the Beacon School. Her green leggings were already spattered with mud, and Hathin guessed that she had arrived back in the village only that morning. Evidently the other Sours had decided to delay everything until the return of their only Nundestruth speaker.

As the Lace prepared to quit the village, two things became clear. The first was that Arilou had no intention of leaving. Attempts to lead her to the edge of the village were rewarded by a ragged screech so very like a bird of prey that several villagers ducked and looked about for the great eagle they assumed to be swooping down on them. The second was that the Sours had no intention of letting Arilou leave.

Jeljech hurried to translate.

'*Her* stay here. *We* go tower. *You* go city. You comeback village.' She tapped the slightly trodden sketch of the barrow with her foot. 'Food. You comeback here. *All* you go *after*.'

'That conversation we had yesterday wasn't the one we thought we were having, was it?' Tomki managed a wincing smile despite the swelling of his left eye.

As far as the Sours were concerned, their visitors had agreed to bring them a barrowful of food and other useful supplies in exchange for a guide to the Beacon School. And to make sure that the Lace carried out their part of the bargain, Arilou would stay with them. The Sours were adamant that she had agreed to it.

'But . . . we can't leave her behind!' Hathin felt a surge of panic. 'She can't defend herself! And the Sours don't know how to look after her!'

'I'll stay with Arilou,' declared Jaze. 'And I'll keep Tomki by my side – if there's any trouble or treachery he can get Arilou to safety while I make life unpleasant for people. Therrot, you look after Hathin.'

Still full of anxiety and reluctance, Hathin finally consented to join Therrot in following Jeljech up a pitted, zigzag path. Their route made no sense to her. Sometimes they seemed to be travelling directly away from the beacon tower, and twice they ducked into narrow caves and crawled out through sinkholes. After an hour of this mad weaving, the beacon tower suddenly reared up behind the approaching ridge, so close that they could see the charred timbers jutting from the dead pyre at its summit.

Jeljech abruptly sat down and refused to go further, her face tense and wary. She would say nothing more, but waved towards the tower beyond the ridge, then absorbed herself with plucking leaves and tearing them into strips. Hathin and Therrot took the hint and trudged on without her.

Beyond the ridge, they found themselves on a broad, grass-covered shelf of land strewn with blackened wood stubs from the pyre. All around were little stone huts perched on high granite pedestals, presumably to keep them safe from sudden rushes of lava or hot mud.

Therrot pursed his lips and gave a curling whistle. There was no answer. No sound at all, Hathin realized suddenly, except for the stutter of distant geysers.

'There should be insect sounds,' she whispered. 'There should be birds . . .'

Therrot suddenly stooped to peer between his feet. 'There are,' he muttered under his breath. The burrowing bird that lay in front of him looked unharmed, but was quite dead.

They advanced cautiously to the base of the nearest pedestal, where a few reddish-brown rounds bulged above the grass like oversized mushroom heads. Therrot turned one over with his foot.

'Clay pots,' he said, bemused. 'Look, the cork stoppers are lying on the ground next to them.' He straightened and stared

 283

across at similar terracotta bumps scattered around the other pedestals. 'There's dozens of them. They're everywhere.' He lifted one, upended it and shook it. 'Seems empty.'

'Therrot can you give me a hand with this?' There was a heavy wooden ladder lying on the grass. Therrot helped Hathin raise it to lean against the pedestal, then held it steady as she climbed up. Clambering on to the stone 'sill' before the hut, she put her head in through the open door.

'I think it's some kind of storeroom,' she called down.

She picked up a wooden doll with a long string stretching from its belly button. There was a finger-ring at the back, and when she pulled it the string drew back into the doll, pulling towards it a shiny piece of shell attached to the other end of the string. The doll game. The old way of training Lost children to find themselves.

There were wooden blocks painted in different colours, some with symbols raised in ridges on their surfaces. Candles were stacked next to bundles of pink and yellow incense sticks. Against the walls rested paintings of faces with different mouth shapes, musical instruments. All of these must have been used for the lessons of the Lost children, helping them to master their different senses.

A quick search revealed that there were no less than seventeen of these raised huts. Some were store rooms, some tiny studies, some appeared to be living quarters. In one a set of wooden bowls sat upon a wooden board, and beside them a dried-out cauldron of unserved soup. In another of the otherwise tidy little huts two green glass bottles had been smashed and left.

'Everybody's gone,' said Hathin as she picked up a single ivory hoop earring from the floor. 'It looks like they all just suddenly . . . left.'

'Left, did they?' Therrot stooped to peer at the damp ash that covered the ground around the tower. 'If they left, I don't think they did so willingly. Someone's been dragging something heavy through the ash – dragging it that way, towards the orchid lakes. Yes, here's another trail. And . . . wait.' He stooped and picked up something tiny and metal. 'A crossbow bolt.'

'You think the people here were attacked? And then . . .'

Neither needed to complete the sentence. Hathin knew that, like her, Therrot was visualizing a dozen or so bodies being dragged downhill and dropped into one of Crackgem's seething multicoloured lakes.

While she was thinking about this, a droplet of something hit her above the eyebrow and ran into her eye, making it burn. Shielding her face, she looked up, in time to see another drop swell beneath a crack in the roof and fall gleaming past her vision. She wiped at her brow, and when she examined her wet fingertips they were tinged with red.

The outer walls were rough granite, offering lots of toe-holds to Hathin as she clambered to the roof.

'Therrot . . .' Hathin crawled gingerly over the broad, fragile slabs. 'Somebody's spilt something up here on the roof. Something red.'

'Is it . . . ?'

'Not blood. No. It's some sort of crumbly powder. The rain's washed away a lot of it, but there's still traces clinging.

 285

And somebody spread it deliberately. It's like they drew a big circle or something. No . . . a crescent.'

Hathin sat on the roof, feeling as she had when staring at the Doorsy writing in Skein's journal. She tried to imagine the people who had lived in these tower-like huts, spending their days piling timber for the pyre or painting the strange lesson toys. She thought of them standing every night amid rings of incense, calling lessons aloud, giving their lives to the vapour-like congregation of invisible Lost children who floated around them. Were they like the strange old woman back at the tidings hut? Did they sense the cold touch of hundreds of youthful eyes – brown, black, green, grey – or did they just speak their lines to the empty sky and weird spitting hillside?

What had Hathin hoped to find here? Someone with answers. But the school was just another heap of abandoned riddles.

Hathin climbed down to join Therrot. She found him sitting on the ground, staring into his palm.

'I've found someone to interrogate. Look – it's one of your little friends.' He held up a small, bright yellow object on his palm, and Hathin saw it was a frog, like the one she had hidden in her hat. After a moment she realized that it was made of wood, and that Therrot's face wore a wry little smile. He drew a wooden baton down the sharp ridges that lined its back, and it made a *crrrrk* noise not unlike a living frog. 'Well, that's more answer than we've got out of anyone else.'

'Why's it got shiny silver crescents on its back?' she asked.

'You heard the lady. What do your crescents mean?' A

stroke of the stick, and the frog gave another enigmatic *crrrrrk*. 'Did you get that?'

'Where's everyone gone, frog?' Hathin glared it into submission.

Crrrrk.

'Who dragged them away down the hill?'

Crrrrk.

'Why do we always get everywhere too late?'

'Why did the Lost die?'

'Why does everyone want to kill us or send us up volcanoes?'

Therrot and Hathin looked at each other, and their mock stern expressions suddenly spread into grins of helpless, hopeless hilarity. Everything was *too* grim, *too* horrible. They dropped eye contact, but it was too late. In her peripheral vision Hathin could see Therrot shaking with helpless laughter.

'Soap!' spluttered Therrot in a small, high-pitched voice unlike his own. 'They sent us up here with *soap* . . .'

'A blue man wants to turn me into a sock!' squeaked Hathin. They looked at each other, threw themselves on to their backs and cackled.

And it was wonderful to let go, to unbraid her mind and let it blow loose. There was a lightness in Hathin's head and a warm throb behind her breastbone. All her usual worries melted away. Just for once she could almost ignore the tiny, tyrannical part of her brain that still yanked at her worry-leash, trying to pull her together, to tell her something . . .

There was a rising rushing sound like a cauldron coming

 287

to the boil but she barely noticed it, and so the echoing bang took her completely by surprise. Reflexively she slapped her hands over her ears, and watched uncomprehending as a boulder the size of her head bounded down the slope past her. The next instant her face was tingling and she was dragging in her breath in great squeaking heaves, suddenly realizing that her lungs were desperate for air. Desperate because only moments before she had not been breathing, and had forgotten that she even needed to do so.

There was a warm throb behind her breastbone, and at last Hathin could remember what that meant.

'Therrot! Cover your ears!' In desperation she stood and kicked out at his ribs while he giggled at her. 'Therrot! Can't you feel it? In your chest? *There are blissing beetles here!*'

Seriousness seeped back into his expression. He hastily stopped up his ears, and immediately gasped for breath. As he staggered to his feet, Hathin was suddenly aware that the land and sky were pulsing and wavering with each beat of her heart.

They sprinted and scrambled and tumbled down the mad, flexing mountainside. They hurdled a pile of kindling, leaped steaming streams, and finally lost their balance to slither into a heap on the rough ground. There they lay panting until their blood was no longer thunder. Hathin felt drained and sick.

'Poor frog,' she said after a long time. 'He told us everything he knew – we just didn't understand. He had the answer: crescents. It's so obvious what a crescent means really – it's the moon. Untrained Lost follow light, so one of the first things you teach them is not to fly towards the moon or they'll be wandering in darkness forever. For Lost, the moon is *danger*.'

'So the frog was marked with crescents because it was poisonous. But then the crescent on the roof . . .'

'I think someone managed to hide when the school was attacked, saw what was going to happen, and had time to get on to the hut and draw the symbol, hoping it would be visible by the light of the beacon pyre. But I guess it wasn't.' Hathin hesitated and wound her arms round one of Therrot's. Once again she felt a sadness that seemed to belong to someone much older than her. 'The Lost children's minds would have flown in from above – the symbol was meant to be a warning for *them*.' She sighed, and rested her cheek against Therrot's rough sleeve.

'The enemy must have brought the blissing beetles here in those clay jars, all the way from the Coast of the Lace, and then set them free. The Lost . . . you kill them like farsight fish. You can't get to them all, but you don't have to. You just need to know where their minds will be.

'The night the adults died, everybody knew they'd be checking the tidings huts for news. You'd only need to fill one hut with beetles, and then, all over the island . . .' Milady Page tumbling from her hammock. Skein lolling back with a smile on his face. 'But that still left the children.'

All over Gullstruck, children receiving goodnight kisses from their parents, then lying in bed or sitting cross-legged on wicker mats and sending their minds out to the Beacon School . . .

'But then, Arilou . . . why not her?'

'She can't have been at school. I shouldn't be surprised

289

really. School would have been full of people telling her what to do and giving her homework, and I guess she didn't like that much. So maybe she just stopped going and stayed with the Sours instead . . . I don't know, I don't know. I ought to cry and I want to, but most of all I just want to go to sleep. Is that horrible?'

'No, no. You sleep, little sister.' Therrot stared up at the sky with a look at once distant and dangerous, as if warning it against troubling her.

'Therrot? Whoever did all this . . . they're so much cleverer than we are.'

'Maybe. But we're still alive, still breathing.'

'Only because Crackgem threw a rock at us to wake us out of the beetle-trance.'

'Yes.' Therrot almost smiled, and ruffled the tufted hair above Hathin's forehead. 'Lord Crackgem has a soft spot for those with weak minds.'

She drifted into sleep, but the breath of Lord Crackgem seemed to have drugged her dreams into madness. She tried to stagger away from him down the hillside, while underfoot crescent-marked rocks snarled like jaguars.

Far below Hathin could see the people of her village gliding silently into a cave, heads bowed. She called and called to them, but they did not respond. *Do not worry*, said the giantess beside her. *I will go after them for you*. And Dance was bounding away down the slope towards the cave of Death, heedless of Hathin's desperate cries behind her . . .

Hathin jerked herself awake, almost knocking heads with Therrot.

'Therrot, we have to get word to Dance! She's heading to the Smattermast tidings hut! That's the hut Skein was checking for messages when he died – *that's* why he died before the rest of the Lost adults! She's running straight into a pit of blissing beetles!'

22
DANGEROUS CREATURES

When Therrot and Hathin staggered down to join her, Jeljech scrambled to her feet. There was, Hathin noticed, a touch of wary defensiveness in her frown. Their shaken and dishevelled state did not seem to come as a complete surprise to her, but there was undeniably a question in her hard, defiant eyes.

'Jeljech? We go village belong-you. Scamperfast.'

When they reached the village, the Sour that welcomed the revengers wore the same expression as Jeljech. Inquisitive, cautious, slightly furtive. In return they received two haggard but unflinching Lace smiles.

'We speak friends belong-us. Yes?'

When all of the Lace contingent except Arilou had formed a huddle at the edge of the village, Therrot and Hathin quietly spilled the news of the blissing beetle murders. There was a horrified silence.

'It's too big,' Tomki said at last. 'It's so big I'm standing on it and I can't see the edges. I can't even look at it properly.'

'Dance,' said Jaze. It was the first time Hathin had seen Jaze look almost frightened. Dance was his idol, his guiding star.

'Yes,' agreed Hathin. 'We have to warn her – but first we need to warn the Sours.' She tried not to let her gaze flit to the villagers standing barely out of earshot. 'They clearly know *something* . . . but not that they're sharing a mountain with a horde of blissing beetles. They'd never have let Jeljech come with us to the school if they'd known. Come to think of it, they'd never have let *us* go there either, if they really want their barrow of food.'

'You're right.' Tomki looked horrified. 'We can't have them dying, now that I've finally got myself properly wronged.' He ran fingertips over his bruised eye with an air of pride. 'What would I do if I came back with the tattoo and they were all beetled? I'd – ow!'

Hathin had grown better at spotting Therrot's danger signs. However, on this occasion there was simply no time to react before Therrot gripped Tomki under the arms and flung him aside like a bundle of straw. Tomki stared up at him, his eyes round but not yet afraid.

'Wronged?' erupted Therrot. 'You threw rocks at them, and nearly got us killed!'

'Jaze!' Hathin looked to the taller man, but Jaze held back. Evidently he saw no reason to stand in Therrot's way.

'You really want to be wronged, Tomki? You want a wrong that'll keep you awake at night?' One could almost hear the self-control hissing out of Therrot like grain from a split sack.

Hathin ran forward to place herself between Therrot and Tomki, who was gingerly getting to his feet. Then, before Therrot could move or speak another word, she turned her back to him.

 293

Tomki flinched too late, and Hathin's slap caught him across his nose and upper cheek. He sat back on a rock, clutching his eye and looking at her like a pained puppy.

'It's not a game!' All the others flinched as Hathin's voice echoed with cold clarity from the surrounding crags. 'The tattoo isn't something you wear to impress girls, like a . . . a . . . a hat! You see this?' Hathin pulled off the wrapping around her forearm. 'You see these? These?' She dragged back the sleeves of Jaze and then Therrot to show their tattoos. 'We didn't *want* them, Tomki. They mean we're . . . we're *broken*. Broken so badly we can't ever be fixed . . . and . . . and all that's left to us is breaking something else.

'You want to be with Dance? *Go* then. Find her and warn her. Then you can show your bruises to your priest and ask for your tattoo and do whatever you like. Just don't bother coming back to us afterwards. If all you care about is getting the tattoo, then you've got no place with us. And you never will have.'

After a shellshocked Tomki had ridden off on his elephant bird, it took a few minutes for the Sours to overcome their alarm at seeing their visitors smiling broadly while yelling and hitting each other. But Jeljech and Arilou were brought out again, and with painful slowness the dangers of the blissing beetles were made clear.

The Sours boggled and scowled at the news and argued bitterly among themselves. At last they seemed to come to a decision, and after an awkward pause Jeljech began a slow, defensive account of the night the Beacon School's fires went cold forever.

A group of heavily armed men had turned up unexpectedly at the Sours' village, having followed an elderly Sour woman whose twisted leg left her unable to outpace them. These men had brought a map with them, but there were no paths drawn on it between Jealousy and the Beacon School. They held out a quill, inviting the Sours to fill in the blank space. When the villagers shook their heads and pretended ignorance the strangers had pointed to the flag, and then out to the Ashlands to show that they knew where the ash had come from.

The implied threat was clear, and two of the villagers had shown the men the way to the Beacon School. That night the beacon was lit as usual, but when the Sours dragged their timber to the school the following day, they found it deserted. Their main livelihood had literally vanished overnight, leaving only sinister traces. And so they had withdrawn distrustfully like a hermit crab, certain that whatever had happened, they would get the blame.

Those men you showed to the School – were they carrying anything?

Yes came back the answer. Backpacks of corked jars. Some of them carrying so many jars it seemed their legs should give way.

'The jars were probably sealed with nothing but air and the beetles inside,' murmured Jaze. 'No wonder they were so light. And then when the men reached the school they must have pushed plugs in their ears and pulled the corks out of the jars . . .'

'Wait!' Hathin was suddenly struck by a recollection. 'I've just remembered – the Superior talked about some men who came to him asking for guides to the Beacon School. Perhaps he'll know something about them.'

There was one other person who might know something, Hathin realized, and that was Arilou.

Poor Arilou. Hathin no longer held out much hope that Arilou would be able to cast light on the fate of the Lost Council or the end of the Beacon School. It was all too clear that in her wilful way she had taken no interest in either her studies or her Lost comrades. However, it seemed she had been watching the Sour village religiously all her life. There was the tiniest possibility that she had seen these ominous armed visitors, and that her strange Lost perspective had allowed her to notice more than the Sours had.

Hathin cast her mind back to the day of the storm, of Skein's death, even though her soul flinched from the task. The men had visited the Sours in the late afternoon, at about the time Skein was trying to test Arilou. Yes, she recalled with a throb of excitement, Arilou's behaviour *had* been a little stranger than usual. During the test of hearing, Arilou had not been pouring out the usual indistinguishable babble but a particular phrase, repeated over and over.

'Jeljech, what mean "Kaiethemin"?' asked Hathin. She had to repeat it a few times before the Sour girl understood. Then Jeljech linked her thumbs fingers and flapped the rest of her hands as wings.

'Bird. Bird many fly.' Hathin's excitement subsided into tender, bitter disappointment. The infamous Lady Arilou, hunted all over Gullstruck by a league of killers, all for fear of what she might have seen or heard. And what had she been doing while a deadly trap was laid for Lostkind? She had been watching birds, watching their flight like a fascinated infant.

'I can't believe the Sours *still* won't give us our Lost back,' muttered Therrot darkly as he bounced their barrow back down the path towards Jealousy.

'She'll be safe there,' Hathin said in a small voice. Leaving the village, she had seen the two daughters from Arilou's 'other family' settling down to comb the seed husks out of Arilou's hair, and had felt a sting of something like jealousy. 'Besides,' she added sadly, 'it's where she wants to be.'

'The Sours have decided that she's kin,' Jaze summarized calmly. 'As for the rest of us, they *want* to like us, they *almost* trust us, but we know a dangerous amount about them. Holding Arilou is the best way to make sure we come back with that food.'

'Yes, that food.' Therrot sighed. 'How *are* we going to find that?'

'Um . . . I think I'll have to go back to Jealousy and talk to the Superior,' Hathin suggested timidly.

Therrot said nothing, but the colour drained from his face.

'I *must*, Therrot. It's our only chance of keeping the Ashwalker at bay. And of finding out more about the men who brought the beetles. The Superior met them, and he might be able to remember something about them, or other people might have talked to them . . . I . . . I *have* to go and find out more. It's my quest . . . it's why we're here . . . so I think . . .

297

I think I'll have to tell the Superior that I'm willing to carry on taking his sacrifices to the dead.'

Therrot did not look at her, but took her hand. *If you do this, then you will not do so alone.*

'Risky.' Jaze looked meditative, but did not discard the idea out of hand. 'And the Sours won't be pleased if we turn up with soap and tell them to eat that.'

'No . . . but, you see, we can give them the soap to sell . . .'

'What if they can't sell it? What if there's nobody in Jealousy who wants to buy a big barrowful of soap?'

'Um . . .' Hathin looked up at him with the tiniest of smiles. 'Well . . . I've thought about that and there *is* someone. There's the Superior.'

'Wait.' Jaze's velvet brows twitched slightly. 'So . . . You're saying we carry the Superior's soap *up* the mountain and give it to the Sours. And then they carry it back *down* the mountain to Jealousy. And then we buy it off them using the Superior's money, so they can buy food. And then we carry it back *up* the mountain . . . and they carry it back *down* . . .'

There was a long pause, and then the sound of three Lace snorting and snickering helplessly.

'It could work,' Therrot said wonderingly. 'Providing Lord Crackgem doesn't decide to boil us alive for impudence, that is.'

'They say Lord Crackgem loves anything crazed and crooked – if it's true we have nothing to fear.' Jaze wiped his eyes and his smile opened like a razor. 'You're a dangerous creature, Doctor Hathin.'

*

Hathin and Therrot arrived outside the Superior's palace a little before noon, and were admitted despite the dust in their clothes and the tufts of foliage in their hair. Perhaps because she had acted as spokesperson before, it was Hathin once again that was shown to the Superior.

'You're alive!' The little man seemed astonished and exultant. 'The mountain farmers have been fleeing the foothills and bringing with them the most frightful rumours – landslides, rocks bursting from crannies, steam erupting and cooking farmers like lobsters. You were gone so long I started to fear the worst . . .'

Hathin hurriedly reassured him that his sacrificial soap had been delivered safely into the ghostly hands of the ancestors. However, the news of the blissing beetles on the mountainside came as a severe blow for the Superior. Reflected in his welling eyes, Hathin seemed to see a calamitous future in which wave after wave of living underlings slumped over their barrows of ritual offerings and joined the ranks of the demanding, toiletry-less dead.

'But you and your . . . friend . . . brother . . . survived?'

'By the grace of Lord Crackgem,' Hathin answered, with a degree of truth. 'I . . . I think His Lordship's taken a liking to us. Perhaps it's been a while since he had someone to talk to, someone who spoke Lace. Anyway, that's why we took so long to come back – Lord Crackgem didn't want us to go.'

The Superior's face took on an expression of surprise and something like avarice.

'You can talk to volcanoes! I'd heard that the Lace could, of course, but I thought it mere folklore. And just when I

really need somebody who has a way with volcanoes . . . So –
what did Lord Crackgem say?'

Therrot was kept waiting in his little room for three hours.
By the time Hathin reappeared, he was pacing like a caged
jaguar.

'What happened to you?' He took a step back and looked
her up and down. 'What *did* happen to you?' His wondering
gaze took in her new leather boots, her red hat with braid
on the broad brim, the satchel slung from her shoulder, the
boyish jerkin and neck-smock.

'I talked to the Superior – and this is my new disguise.
He's got one for you too. He says that now we're working
for him we can't "shamble around looking like vagabonds".'
Hathin reddened. 'I'm . . . I'm a diplomat.'

'I'll say,' murmured Therrot.

Hathin was not simply the Superior's new diplomatic
envoy to Lord Crackgem. While the land around Crackgem
was too dangerous for his people to venture into at all, she
was to organize hit-and-run missions between the orchid
lakes to bring supplies to the now-stranded community of
dead. In exchange, the Superior would shelter them and
remain blind to their identity.

Therrot was also fitted with new clothes. He looked
younger and more ill once the villainous sprout of stubble
had been shaved from his narrow chin. He glowered his way
after the Superior and Hathin as the little man led them
through room after room of his palace, trying to decide what
else to send to the dead.

'And so you think that, suitably equipped, the Lace body-

300

guard might be able to lead an expedition to another city of the dead to trade? What would they need?'

'Good boots and travelling clothes,' Hathin said quickly. 'Maybe elephant birds to carry packs. Tents. And provisions, lots of provisions.' Who could say when she and her friends might find themselves on the run again?

'And armour, maybe? Just in case of dead brigands out on the heights? Perhaps . . .' The Superior faltered before a suit of armour that seemed to have been designed for an elephant bird, complete with beaked helm. Above it a tapestry showed a stormy-browed duke at the head of a wave of sabre-wielding cavalry, all straddling armoured birds. 'Artistic licence,' he murmured under his breath. 'Sadly, the birds could never run in that armour. Or walk, actually. In fact, anything beyond lying on their side and clanking was a bit of a triumph.'

When the Superior handed Hathin one of his signet rings and told her to walk through the market and collect further emergency supplies for the ancestors, she guessed from his smile that this was a great honour. Perhaps all 'honours' were like elephant bird armour, and looked better from the out-side.

Hathin cleared her throat. There was no obvious way to lead into the questions she wanted to ask.

'Sir, I was wondering. Those men who came here, asking for the Beacon School. You . . . You don't remember what they were like, do you, sir?'

'Like?' The Superior wrinkled his brow in perplexity. 'How would I have time to notice what anyone is like? They were just . . . fellows . . . usual number of arms and legs . . . rough clothes . . . but spoke decent Doorsy, thank goodness.

I told them to talk to Bridle, of course, but I doubt that he'd have helped them.'

Bridle. Amid all the dangers and discoveries of the last couple of days Hathin had almost forgotten the mysterious entry in Skein's journal. What was it? *Bridle believes that Lord S will return when the rains end . . .* Another trailing clue in the mystery of the Lost deaths – a clue in the hands of someone named Bridle.

'Who is Bridle, sir?'

'The best mapmaker in Jealousy.' The Superior looked inexplicably annoyed, but not apparently with Hathin.

'Could you . . . ? Could you tell me where he lives?'

'Lives? Drat the man, he does nothing of the sort. Bridle was a Lost – do you think I would hire a mapmaker that was anything less? He wouldn't have helped those men – the Lost were always so secretive about their precious school – and now he's no help to anyone.' There was a small pause during which the Superior fiddled with his moustache. 'Maps. Young lady, do you think our dead Lace will need maps for his trading expedition?'

'Er . . . yes! Yes, sir. Yes, I'm sure he would. Perhaps . . . Perhaps my friend and I could go to Mr Bridle's house and look through his maps.'

Five minutes later Hathin and Therrot were slipping through the streets, suppressing their smiles, the military cut of Therrot's new jacket causing the crowd to part before them.

'At least we're safe for now,' Hathin murmured, as much to reassure herself as Therrot. 'Well, as safe as anybody can be while running up and down a volcano every couple of days.'

The Superior had told them that Bridle's house and shop were to be found in the craftsmen's district, and so the two revengers wove their way in that direction, Therrot pushing their barrow. Very soon it became clear that finding Bridle's house would be no easy matter.

The craftsmen's district was huge, bigger than Sweetweather in its entirety. Although Hathin and Therrot did not know it, for years Jealousy had drawn in the finest craftsmen and artisans on the island. Thanks to the Superior's obsession with his demanding ancestors, there was a thriving market in exquisite offerings for the dead. Not just intricately painted 'dead man's bonds' of different values, but all manner of luxuries reproduced in miniature. Little sedan chairs carved from bone, beautiful moon-faced courtesans made of jade, sumptuous banquets painted on to banana leaves.

'We should probably buy some things as we go,' whispered Therrot, 'just to look more natural.'

They did so, but managed not to get carried away, despite the novelty of having money. After all, even though they did not have to pay for their purchases, they knew they would certainly have to push them up a mountain.

At last they found a street in which maps hung like flags. Bridle's house was the largest, and easily identified by the shield that hung over the door. On it a bridled horse's face was painted. Therrot unlocked and opened the heavy wooden door, and the two revengers stared into the shop beyond.

Bridle had clearly been a very busy man. He had not, however, been a tidy one. Maps hung from every rafter. Every flat surface was a litter of half-painted maps, pestles and mortars tinted with different dyes, brushes, sticks of charcoal, ink bottles and banana leaves. At the back of the room, bundles of papers were stacked like hay bales.

The maps were drawn with the accuracy of one who can float above the land and see it laid out before him. The paintwork had a finesse unusual for a Lost, suggesting that Bridle had had good control over his own body. One map showed the back and wings of an eagle in the foreground, making you feel as if you were looking down past it at the land below. It made Hathin giddy.

There was a chair set before a low easel. Hathin ran her fingertips over the worn wood, and wondered whether Bridle had sat there with his sight sky-high, sketching what he saw by touch alone.

Therrot hefted down one of the bundles of parchments stacked against the back wall.

'They're all pictures of Crackgem seen from above – and they're all the same. Why paint dozens of identical maps?'

'Perhaps that particular map sold really well?'

'Perhaps . . . wait.' There was a long pause, interrupted by occasional rustles of parchment. 'Wait. They're not all the same. Come and look at this.' As Hathin joined him, Therrot pointed at the bottom-right corner of the map at the top of the bundle. 'You see those squiggles? They're numbers. And this symbol that comes before them means the numbers spell out a date. There was a symbol like this on the papers they gave me when I got out of prison. So each of these maps has a date on it, and it's a different date each time. Now look at this.'

Therrot turned the stack upside-down, and turned over the first map. A picture of Crackgem amid his iridescent lakes, his long crinkled line of joined craters like the mouth of a clam slightly agape. Then with swift fingers Therrot slapped the next map on top of it, and the next, the next, the next, and on, and on. Before Hathin's eyes the clam-mouth gradually opened, tiny cracks and furrows appearing and tracing their way down the mountain's sides.

'Stop!' It was almost too much, watching a volcano changing shape before her eyes. 'Therrot, what does it mean?'

'I don't know.'

The other bundles also held sequences of maps, depicting the other volcanoes. As before, the same view had been painted over and over, the sequence of maps revealing almost imperceptible changes in the volcanoes' outlines. Sorrow seemed unchanging for dozens of maps, and then her crater suddenly altered its shape and became larger. New speckles kept appearing on the flanks of the King of Fans. More disturbing still, Mother Tooth developed strange blots and blemishes, like bruises on a fruit, several of which looked oddly rectangular.

The pictures of Spearhead were generally very indistinct, doubtless because of the cloud that nearly always wreathed his head. Peering at the smudges of charcoal, however, Hathin was sure the vague pattern of light and shadow within his crater was changing slightly. In some, she thought she glimpsed a dim bulge like a puffball inside the crater.

'Perhaps it means nothing,' suggested Therrot. 'After all, is it so strange if the volcanoes stir in their sleep?'

But his words convinced neither of them, and they were glad to leave the house, despite being not much the wiser for their visit.

They had just locked the door behind them when it happened. Two men who had been dawdling by a resin-worker's stall abruptly plunged into the crowd. There was a scream, and they emerged dragging a twisting, kicking, scratching, reed-like woman. Her beaded bowler fell off her head to show the shaven place above her forehead, and the crowd pulled back murmuring dangerously as they realized that she was Lace.

For a moment Hathin's eye clouded with the memory of a darkened beach, the murderous pinpricks of torches . . . but the crowd held back out of respect for the two men pinning the woman to the ground. Hathin recognized them as two of the bounty hunters from Mistleman's Blunder. Of course, now that the Superior had his pet Lace, he had probably paid off and discharged his own bounty hunters, allowing the visitors to hunt Lace freely in his city.

One of the men placed a knee on the woman's back and tied her hands behind her with a piece of cord. Then, to his own very great surprise, he flew backwards and lay on the dust clutching his nose. The other man's hasty leap to his feet proved to be a wasted effort. A well-swung mutton joint caught him on the side of the head and dropped him to the dust again. One could almost feel the air of the marketplace thickening and crackling with stares, and every stare was fixed on Therrot, who now stood over the bound woman, the mutton joint still in his hand.

There was a strange expression on Therrot's face, almost a look of relief. *I'm falling*, said the expression. *No more decisions. All I can do now is fall.*

'Stop!'

As Hathin ran forward she could feel the stares crystallize on her skin like salt. Flushed and desperate, she held the Superior's ring at arm's length towards the bounty hunters. Their hands paused on the hilts of their knives. Hathin revolved slowly, holding out the ring so that everyone around her had a chance to see the seal.

'We're claiming this woman.' Hathin cleared her throat to rid it of its nervous croak. 'She . . . She's a necessary supply. We're – we're stockpiling all the Lace we can find.'

The woman, who was doing her best to spit out a mouthful of dust and her own hair, twisted her head to look up. Her eyes lost a little of their wildness as her gaze locked with that of Hathin. Behind both pairs of brown eyes a thousand Lace ancestors raised shields in salute and shouted a silent greeting across the void between.

And if any of the crowd had stopped to look closely at the girl who stood before them in the plainest of sight, they too might have detected in her every feature the whiff of the sea, the glitter of centuries of smiles. But they were hypnotized by the ring, and Hathin was invisible again.

A second barrow was fetched, and as the crowd receded Hathin and Therrot retraced their steps towards the Superior's palace. Behind them walked a middle-aged man and his adult daughter, who had without comment taken on the task of pushing the barrowful of Lace captive along. Therrot cast a glance back at the pair of them, then gave Hathin a meaningful look. Hathin nodded slightly. She too had noticed the coral cut on the father's chin, the pebbley snubness of their features.

At the governor's gate the little convoy paused, and

mumbled thanks were exchanged in Lace.

'You'd probably better go back before anyone wonders why you're helping us,' whispered Hathin.

'Wonder is already abroad. We moved here fifteen years ago in search of work and have lived here ever since, but I don't think anyone quite believed us when we said we were from an east-coast cockling village. And since the Lost died, our neighbours' friendship has been curdling. We're living on borrowed time.

'If you'll have us – we'd like to join your Stockpile.'

23
A LITTLE LIGHT

The next morning Hathin had to break it to the Superior that he was stockpiling Lace. At first anxiety rippled his forehead.

'But, sir – there's always a chance that we'll die from the blissing beetles, and I wouldn't want you to be left without some . . . *spares*. And more people heading to the Ashlands means we can take more barrows.'

These words had the desired effect. Five minutes later the Superior was very pleased that he had come up with the idea of the Stockpile and was willing to put aside a small building to house it. Two hours after that Hathin had to return and ask for a larger one since his Stockpile had increased by three: two children who had been living in the irrigation ditches and eating wild birds' eggs crept into the city and turned themselves in; a ragged young man singed by geysers staggered through the gates with a wounded bounty hunter hanging off his back, and claimed his right to join the Stockpile. Word had apparently spread fast.

Hathin could only pray that the Stockpile would actually be the refuge its members seemed to imagine.

'Therrot,' she asked as she walked through the palace with her 'big brother', 'have I done something terrible? What if

I've drawn people into a trap, making them think they're safe there?'

'Nobody's safe,' said Therrot, 'and everyone knows it. If the Superior changes his mind, we're all dead. These people know they're taking a risk, but it's a risk that means they get to eat.'

Later, however, when they secretly met with Jaze by the city gates and told him about the Stockpile, he did not seem completely convinced.

'Well, *I* won't be joining it. I think I would be better placed at the Sour village, keeping an eye on our Lady Lost.' He peered at Hathin speculatively for a few moments. 'I just want to be sure you know why you're doing this, Doctor Hathin,' he said quietly. 'What is it that you want? Are you making yourself a new village and hoping that you can protect it this time? Or that maybe if you wait long enough some of your own village will turn up here to be "Stockpiled"?'

'What harm if they did?' Therrot's stare was defiant.

Jaze sighed. 'Blissing beetles were used to kill the Lost,' he said softly. 'You do know what that means?'

'Yes.' Therrot stamped an angry little hollow in the dust with his heel. 'It means we're going to have to kill some very clever people.'

'Worse,' said Jaze in the same cool tone. 'At least one of the people we'll have to kill is probably a Lace. I suspected it when Hathin told us that Jimboly knew about the Path of the Gongs. Doctor Hathin's right – the Lost were killed just like farsight fish, and farsight fishing has always been a Lace secret.

'Don't start fingering your knife hilt, Therrot. I'm not

insulting the memory of your nearest and dearest. But if someone from your village suddenly turns up alive and well . . . don't go happily throwing your arms around them.'

A shocked silence followed. Perhaps one of the Hollow Beasts *had* played a part in the Lost killings after all. Hathin remembered her dream of the string of Hollow Beasts walking into the cave that was their death. This time she imagined one figure turning a furtive, venomous look upon her and scurrying from the line, but its face was featureless, an expression and nothing more.

The next two days were tense and frustrating for Hathin and Therrot, despite the luxury of regular meals and a roof above their heads. Their mornings were spent in the palace, their afternoons in the marketplace, all too aware of the curious eyes of the townspeople. In vain they waited for word from Dance, some hint that she had received Tomki's warning in time. Besides this, Hathin was desperate to visit the Sour village and check on Arilou. However, the Superior wanted to see all preparations made for the 'dead trading expedition' first and his will was law.

On the third day, Hathin and Therrot finally had leave to take their barrows of offerings up the path to Crackgem. At the point where the path petered out they found Jeljech sitting on a boulder, waiting to escort them to the Sour village.

On the way, Hathin could not help deluging Jeljech with questions. How was Arilou? Was she eating? *What* was she eating? Was somebody keeping her clean? Had she said anything?

'Laderilou well,' Jeljech told her, over and over. 'Laderilou',

 311

a distortion of 'Lady Arilou', was apparently the name that the Sours now used. 'Laderilou want bee-wine.' 'Bee-wine' was the Nundestruth term for honey. That request, at least, did sound a good deal like Arilou.

This time the welcome at the village was more affable.

Arilou was found in one of the huts on the edge of sleep, her eyelids drooping, a sheepskin swaddling her. Hathin sat beside her and made a quiet inventory of her sister's limbs, then curled one of her hands inside Arilou's larger one. It felt at home there, like a mouse in a burrow.

'Jeljech . . .' Hathin spoke at last. 'Men come here gun-slung, want go school. Friends belong-you remember men, remember colour hair? Eye?' She tugged at her own collar. 'Wear-withel?'

Jeljech puffed out her cheeks doubtfully, turned to one of the other Sour girls and loosed an interrogative stream of words in her own language. Halfway through it, Hathin's attention was abruptly snagged by a familiar phrase.

'Stop! Er – wait!' Hathin blushed as Jeljech turned back to her. 'Jeljech, say that word! Say . . . kaiethemin?' Hathin could almost swear that she had overheard the peculiar phrase Arilou had been repeating on the beach just before the death of Skein. 'Mean . . . many bird fly, yes?'

Jeljech seemed perplexed. She engaged in a muffled con-ference with the other Sour girl, and then the brows of both cleared.

'Kaithem ano.' Jeljech pronounced the words carefully and slowly for Hathin's benefit. 'Mean bird . . . no.' She closed her eyes tight in a wince of concentration, then opened them again. 'Mean pigeon . . . pigeon man. Many pigeon man.'

They stared at one another as once again the conversation fell screaming into the language chasm.

'Pigeon?'

'Pigeon.' The Sour girl mimed herself a rounded front, waggled elbow wings and managed a serviceable coo. 'Pigeon man destroy school, yes?' There was no doubt about it. Jeljech was talking about the mysterious beetle-carriers. But pigeon? Was this some weird slang?

The Sour girl smothered a giggle at Hathin's expression, and shrugged. 'Nocansay. Laderilou name gang pigeon man. Now allwe name gang pigeon man.'

So it was *Arilou* who had given the beetle-carriers that strange name, and the Sours had simply followed her lead.

Arilou, watching the men. Arilou, watching the birds. There was a connection after all. What was it? A glimmer of a possibility formed in Hathin's mind, and overwhelmed her for a second so that she could barely force her thoughts into Nundestruth.

'Jeljech, pleaseyou ask Laderilou *why* name pigeon man.' She fidgeted in impatience as Jeljech stroked Arilou's forehead and translated the question. Arilou gave a sleepy moan, then offered a string of molten sentences. Jeljech listened with a scowl of increasing bewilderment, and at last turned back to Hathin to translate.

'Laderilou tell us she here. Up . . .' She pointed at the sky and fluttered her hands to mime a hummingbird hover. 'She look, see all strange man come down mountain. Man got pigeon in coat. Look.' She slapped her own chest. 'Man.' She mimed writing on something invisible, which she then care-fully folded. With her spare hand she reached around behind

313

herself and brought it back clutching a second invisible something the size of a cup. She held it up for the inspection of Hathin's mind's eye. 'Pigeon.' The folded writing was apparently placed into or on to the pigeon, and then she flung her imaginary bird into the air.

'Laderilou follow pigeon!' Hathin could barely contain her excitement. 'Laderilou follow pigeon where?'

More Sour questions from Jeljech. More sleepy answers from Arilou.

'Pigeon go, Laderilou follow, follow over mountain . . .' Jeljech fluttered her hands in an upwards, outwards arc, like a bird leaving the ground and flying away. 'Pigeon find other man. Man put writing in desk, lots other writing. Other man make writing, throw other pigeon. Laderilou follow pigeon, find man three.'

Hathin dropped to a crouch next to the Sour girl, who was now stooping to move stones on to the path. 'Many man,' she explained, pointing to them, then started drawing lines between them in the dirt. 'Pigeon . . . pigeon . . . pigeon . . .' she murmured as she did so. 'Pigeon . . . pigeon . . . pigeon . . . pigeon . . .' At last she looked up at Hathin with a flushed but triumphant smile. 'Many many pigeon man,' she summarized, and shrugged.

Hathin covered her mouth with her hands and stared at the network that had been drawn in the mud. It was true, then. Her hazy, newly formed suspicion had been correct. *Have you noticed that your enemies appear to know things sooner than they should?* The question had lurked in the shadowy corners of Hathin's mind for the last week, leaving her imagination to shape theories of demonic

314

familiars, uncanny powers.

No. There had been a simple daylight answer all along. Messages sent using pigeons. She had heard stories that they had once been used so in the old Cavalcaste lands.

A large, secret network scattered across the island, in touch with each other through pigeons. Ordinary messengers would travel too slowly along the mountain paths, and any message sent by the tidings huts would be read by the Lost. A message system that would not be affected by the deaths of the Lost. The little caged pigeons Jimboly always carried were probably meant to be dropped off with her contacts so that they could use them for messages later.

All this while, the murderers of the Lost had feared what Arilou might know or have seen – the killing of the Lost Council, perhaps, or the slaughter of the Beacon School. But while all that was happening, Arilou had been busy chasing pigeons.

She had seen 'her' village bullied by some strangers with weapons. She had sent her mind to follow the nasty men. And then she had seen a funny man take a pigeon out of his coat and throw it in the air, so she had followed it to see where it went. Perhaps she had forgotten her initial worry and even made a game of it, chasing messenger pigeons from contact to contact in the secret network.

This wasn't what Hathin had originally expected or hoped to hear. It was quite different, and it was *better*. Arilou could spy on the secret network – had spied on it, without realizing it. She could tell the Reckoning where its members lived, what they looked like, where they hid their secret papers.

Breathless with excitement, Hathin ran to Therrot

 315

and recounted her discovery. 'Therrot, we can track these murderers back using their own messengers! We're going to find out who killed the Lost, who sent Jimboly to our village and why! We're going to chase after *them* for a change!' Just for a moment she felt an excited tickle in her right forearm, as though the hidden butterfly tattoo sensed that she had taken a step on the path to revenge.

And Therrot squeezed her hand in the same excitement, but when he looked in her eye his smile was uneasy, as if he saw something there that troubled him.

The next day, a handful of Sours appeared in Jealousy's marketplace. Apparently by chance, Therrot and Hathin encountered them, and bargained in mime for the soap, trinkets, wooden goats and coconut rum in the Sours' barrow. Both sides were stony-faced as if they had never met each other before.

Among the items handed over by the Sours was a map of Gullstruck, finely painted but marred by five small holes. Most were in the provinces, but the largest hole was in Mistleman's Blunder.

'Pigeon man.' Jeljech murmured softly. There was nobody but Hathin close enough to overhear, so Jeljech tapped each of the little holes in turn, and for each gave a short description of the 'pigeon man' they represented. One was 'no-hair, beak-nose, black smock', another was 'sing always, slow leg'. Last of all, Jeljech prodded Mistleman's Blunder. '*Thisere* one many many pigeon.'

Hathin stared at the last hole. If the 'pigeon man' in Mistleman's Blunder was sending so many messages, did that mean he was the hub of the conspiracy, the mastermind?

'Pigeon man here how face?' she asked, touching Mistleman's Blunder as Jeljech had done. If she could only get a description of their greatest enemy!

'No face.' Jeljech shrugged. 'Laderilou say he none face.'

Jaze set off with the marked map within the hour, in search of the Reckoning.

'I'm more likely to find them than either of you are,' he explained as he provisioned himself with goods bought for the Superior's ancestors. 'You can leave the job of tracking down these underling "pigeon men" to the Reckoning. We may not be able to strike at Mistleman's Blunder with it fortified the way it is, but let's see how well the octopus throttles once it's had some tentacles cut off.' He hefted his pack on to his back, and prepared to brave the afternoon's onslaught of rain. 'Therrot, look after Hathin. And, both of you, try to keep a low profile from now on.'

Hathin had to agree that, in terms of keeping a low profile, setting up a haven for fugitives from the law probably hadn't been a great start.

But at least we're unlikely to get any more Lace joining the Stockpile, she reassured herself. *You just don't get many this far east.*

She was wrong. Over the next three days a further two Lace families arrived. Before the week was done, the Stockpile had doubled in size once more. And, as it did so, the new arrivals brought word of the lands they had fled.

Pearlpit, Knotted Tail, Seagrin, Eel's Play, Wild Man's Cradle and dozens of other Lace villages on the Coast

317

of the Lace were gone, the houses torn down, most of the inhabitants chained by the neck and dragged off to camps like the one at Mistleman's Blunder. Many bandits had turned bounty hunter, now that selling Lace brought in more money than brandy-runs and storehouse raids. So those few Lace that had escaped the bounty hunters had fled east. Once far inland, the lucky ones had heard rumours of a sanctuary in Jealousy . . . and had trekked for days to the Stockpile, the one place in Gullstruck where Lace might still be safe.

And when they spoke of the persecution of the Lace one name was spoken again and again, always with a bitter venom.

The Nuisance Control Officer, Minchard Prox. A man without a face.

24
STRATAGEMS AND SURPRISES

Prox had never known happiness like this.

It was like a sort of fever, in the sense that he could not think *outside* it. Clocks spun their gleaming hands until they blurred into golden discs. Prox ate and drank what he found beside him but tasted nothing.

Only after working at his desk for fourteen hours at a stretch did he sometimes notice the cramps in his back, the iron clamp behind his eyes. He would stand and pace, pausing automatically before the mirror. He ran his fingers down the senseless leather of his face, but now he no longer saw himself, nor remembered what he was supposed to see. Looking away from the mirror, he would see that somebody had scattered stars carelessly like corn outside the window, and would long to rake them into lines.

It had waited for him all his life, this challenge. There was not a second to waste on doubt. The scrolls on his desk were wands he could wave to drag towns across valleys, fell forests, erect bridges. It was not the power that dizzied him. It was the stature of the problems and disorder facing him that filled him with a battlefield glow.

You took hold of one problem, and found that another

was knotted to it. Now that the Lost were dead, organizing things was so *slow*. News took so long to reach everyone. Camber was the magical exception, of course. In his calm, orderly way – somehow information always seemed to find him first.

The death of the Lost had left the merchants in chaos. Nobody knew how to buy and sell from other towns. Whole granaries of food rotted in some places, while elsewhere people starved. But, looking into this, Prox started to realize how little food there really was on Gullstruck.

'We're looking at a harsh winter.' He was speaking to himself, but was not surprised when he received an answer.

'It was looking bad even before the Lost died.'

It no longer seemed strange to Prox to find that Camber was standing right behind him. Camber seemed to have moved into Prox's mind, his voice now ringing like one of Prox's own thoughts.

'The new camp for the Lace will be the very devil to feed,' Prox continued. It was his latest brainchild, a large and permanent camp to replace the scattered temporary stockades where the Lace prisoners were currently being held.

'Not necessarily.' The map of the camp slid away from beneath Prox's fingers, to be replaced by another, a map of Spearhead. 'It rather depends where you build it.'

And the stubborn problem that Prox had been wrestling in his mind slid into place with a click and all was well. The blank, lush upper slopes of Spearhead stared back invitingly. Clear the jungle there, and you'd have farmland ready for use, a plantation in the making. Spearhead did not have the King of Fans' eagles, Sorrow's landslides and barrenness, nor

320

Crackgem's earthquakes and geysers. And yet this land lay completely unused . . . why? Oh, of course, the old superstitions about Spearhead returning to wreak vengeance. It was criminal to waste that land, and if the workers had no *choice* but to tend the land there . . .

'It's the only way to feed the Lace camp,' he said under his breath. 'We can't have them starving.'

'It's the only way to feed everyone,' said the other voice, weaving in among his thoughts. 'There are too many of us, living and dead. Between them, the dead and the volcanoes have all the best land. We cannot rob the dead – so that leaves the volcanoes. Some farmers have already started tilling the lower slopes – with the help of the Lace we can make use of the upper.'

'But . . . they can't *all* work the plantation. What about the old, the crippled, the very young?'

'They can be found other, gentler, duties.' A long, delicate finger tapped a point much further down the mountain, a large shaded patch marked 'Ashlands'. 'The spirit houses must be cleaned, offerings made, candles lit. And if families are divided, then the strong adults will be less likely to rebel for fear of what will happen to their parents and children. There will be less bloodshed. This is kinder.'

'Yes . . . yes,' murmured Prox, but he hardly knew what he was saying. Already his imagination was designing stockades, rotas, roll calls.

He worked until the stars tired of waiting for him to order them, and went out one by one. He worked while the sun rose, peaked and started to descend. When it distracted him by peering into his room he walked to the window and stared nonplussed at the parade of tiny figures struggling along the brow of the hill towards the distant Spearhead.

He blinked hard until he could make out their arms and legs, the heavy baskets of candles and incense on their backs, the brushes, hoes and brooms in their small hands.

'Mr Camber, why are there children on that hill? Did I order any children?'

He needed sleep, he realized. He could tell by the way colours changed after he blinked, and the way that Camber's face seemed to rise like steam without actually moving. The constant throb of pigeon coos from the neighbouring loft distorted in his ear, and he almost thought he heard voices in them.

'They're just part of the Lace project, Mr Prox. You remember? In a time of emergency it is all important to have the support of the ancestors, so due tribute must be paid to the dead. The advantages of a workforce that can attend to the tombs full time . . .'

'Oh yes, that was it. Mr Camber, do my eyes seem blood-shot? There are blots in front of everything, and somehow those children look very . . . small.'

'Lace children often do,' Camber remarked calmly, watching as Prox peered into the mirror. Camber drew the shutters closed, and the vista of the struggling children was crushed to a sliver and then extinguished.

'You should rest, Mr Prox. Go and sleep the sleep of the just.'

And yet, while Minchard Prox slept, things were happening across the island which he had not guessed at as he reshaped the world with his pencil.

What did he dream? He did not dream of a Lace man with a cool smile and black velvet brows trekking through hidden jungle paths with a marked map in his pocket. He did not see this man showing his tattoo at a sliver of lighted doorway and being shown into a back room where a gigantic woman with dreadlocks and widow's arm bindings was waiting for him, larger than life and very much alive. He did not see them planning until dawn, voices low and eyes bright as knives.

He saw nothing of the bird-back messengers that ran through forest and swamp, moonlight dappling their stilt-legged shapes, carrying word to the scattered Reckoning.

In the nights to follow, there would be consequences. But compared to the great project that obsessed Minchard Prox, these events were small, and he would not notice them.

Camber, however, noticed everything.

There had been a sudden fire at a courthouse in Port Hangman, in which it was supposed that the chief clerk had perished.

The magistrate of Haleslack, who had always insisted on hunting wild turkeys in the forests before dawn, had apparently fallen prey to a jaguar, to judge by the tattered state of his abandoned cloak.

Robbers had become bold and broken into the house of a merchant in Simmerock, stripping it of all valuables. The merchant himself was missing and the worst was feared.

The High Custodian of the Ashlands at Chillford's Drop had apparently absconded with the coffers of money

323

for the upkeep of the Ashlands.

Four disappearances in as many nights. Four of Camber's contacts. He could not imagine it to be a coincidence.

Worst of all was the reported testimony given by the seven-year-old daughter of the missing merchant's house-keeper.

. . . and I heard a squeak like a door so I went to shut it so the rats wouldn't get in and there was a giant lady with snakes for hair and a big club in her hand but she told me she was just a nightmare and I should go back to bed and wait to wake up . . .

The local authorities had made nothing of this story and seemed ready to believe that it *had* been the girl's dream. But Camber knew better.

Dance. This was the work of Dance, which meant it was the work of the Reckoning. But how did the Reckoning know where to strike?

Somebody somewhere has noticed me. Somehow my finger has left a mark, my foot has left a print.

I have been seen.

Even as the thought rolled through Camber's mind, it brought a certain sense of recognition, of inevitability.

It was the same feeling he had experienced when he learned that Lady Arilou, Jimboly's so-called 'oozy-brained' Lost, had escaped from the cove of the Hollow Beasts. The same feeling that had struck him when he discovered that she had not fled up the Coast of the Lace, but had dared the volcanoes and turned up unexpectedly in Mistleman's Blunder. A sense of a glancing blow against another will.

Camber had taken great pains to terrify Gullstruck with the idea of a deadly Lace conspiracy. He had depicted Lady

Arilou as its calculating leader, and then the dreaded Reckoning as its scorpion sting, capable of striking from darkness without warning. Now he faced the alarming possibility that this story might actually be true.

Then there were the other worrying reports. Whole Lace villages had started disappearing overnight before the bounty hunters could find them. There were rumours of a secret trail, by which Lace who were willing to dare the hazards of volcano and jungle could make their way undetected away from the Coast of the Lace and off towards the east. If this was true, perhaps the Lace had found themselves a stronghold, somewhere for Lady Arilou to rally her supporters.

Lace. Trying to pin them down was like grabbing a fistful of eels. Slithering, unaccountable, endlessly elusive. Even their names could not be pinned to paper, for they were musical imitations of natural sounds, never meant to be written, never meant to outlive those who had heard them spoken.

What could he do? Strike back. Strike back hard. End forever this terrible sense that perhaps he, even *he*, was being watched, was being *seen*.

Quickly he wrote a letter, and the next day a pigeon fluttered into his loft with an answer. It was in scrawled and spattered letterings and was marked with the inky footprints of a flickerbird.

Sir,
> *Did like you said and told blue man to look for Lace trail, follow them east to their secret hidey-hole. Found a family*

 325

trudging through jungle, slow and easy to follow. All simple as slurping out an oyster – they never knew we were there.

Led us straight back to Jealousy. One little word me and Ritterbit go mopping. Send word to me at Palm Point on Jealousy road.

He was still reading the note when a second pigeon alighted on the perch beside the first. The letter it had brought was also unsigned, but again the handwriting was well known.

Most Honoured Sir,

You promised me that nothing more would be required of me, and that nobody who knew me would be left with a name. Now I find both are untrue. You ask me to act as your spy once more, looking for signs of Lace in Jealousy, and when I do so I see that a man from my own village is alive and well and walking through the craftsmen's district, working alongside a boy who carries the signet ring of the Superior himself.

I hear rumours that they have been seen walking on Crackgem, and talking to the Sours. Furthermore, all of a sudden everybody knows that there are blissing beetles at the Beacon School.

Worse still, common talk has it that the Superior is collecting Lace. Some even say he is building a private army of them. If anyone guesses my ancestry, I will surely be dragged to his Stockpile. You must move me somewhere else. I call on you to honour your promise.

It was Jealousy, then, that had become the secret Lace power-base. Worse still, it seemed the Superior of Jealousy was involving himself on the side of the Lace. This was a terrible blow.

How had it happened? What had the Superior been told to win him to the cause of the Lace? Camber could report the Superior for obstructing an Ashwalker and ignoring the official edicts issued by Minchard Prox, but if Lady Arilou *had* been able to tell the Superior something incriminating, then the Superior might respond to official charges with some devastating accusations of his own.

With a sigh Camber borrowed a little of Prox's paper and wrote an answer to the first letter.

He walked back to the map of Gullstruck and spent a few moments in quiet scrutiny. Then he placed his thumb over the town of Jealousy, just to see how the map looked without it.

All of this is done because it must be done, he reminded himself, *for the sake of the island*. Compelled by habit he set about wiping the quills, laying the papers exactly where Prox had placed them, erasing even the tiniest hint of his own presence.

Perhaps he himself could learn something from the Lace after all. Did they not also work hard to make sure that they left no footprint, that posterity did not know them? Some heroic deeds lived on in story, but the names of the heroes were forgotten. Camber had a private theory that in time all such tales were told as stories of the Gripping Bird. The Gripping Bird was nobody, he was a thousand men, he was the place stories went when they were lost. But, Camber realized, he was doing something very similar.

Gullstruck would change – was changing – and already

 327

Camber had decided that the glory for this should go to Minchard Prox. He had surprised himself with a real affection for the younger man. There was, he reflected, a greatness that came only with a certain kind of blindness. Prox had a mind that clung to order, a world of properly folded napkins, account books, modes of address when meeting a duchess. Papers were his servitors – he could make them perform and pirouette.

Prox's brain was a pleasure to manipulate, a strange mix of fire and precision, logic and madness.

History shall not remember me, Camber reflected, and the thought filled him with a melancholy calm.

That night, the moonlight saw a single bird-rider sloping exhausted down the road towards Jealousy. His rounded, naturally sunny face was marked by fading bruises and traces of tiredness.

Tomki was passing a shamble-shack when a chorus of throbbing coos caught his attention. There was a congregation of pigeons inside the shack, he realized, pushing their beaks through the wooden lattice at the front. Even as thoughts of roast pigeon chased across his mind, he heard a loud long whistle and realized that he was not alone. A raggle-tag, loose-limbed woman was bounding down the slope towards him, a piece of parchment in her hand.

'Hail Brother Gripping Bird!' she called out cheerfully in Nundestruth. The rider looked down at his long shadow and laughed. The silhouette of rider and steed greatly resembled a giant bird with human arms, just like the legendary Gripping Bird. 'Pleaseyou lend star for light lantern belong-me? Tinder damp.'

Tomki grinned, found his own tinder and lit the candle in the woman's lantern. In the candlelight her bandanna became red, and a piece of the night frayed away from the rest and flickered about her head, its tiny tail opening and closing like a fan.

'Thankyou well, Brother Gripping Bird.' A grin of tin and garnet. 'Where travel?'

'Jealousy.' A sigh.

'Ah, travel Jealousy also. But Brother Gripping Bird no reach Jealousy before dry season, if draggle so.' The woman drooped her head, imitating the elephant bird's weary pace for a few steps. 'Why so slug-foot? Someman wait there for hang you?'

'Close.' Tomki gave a rueful grin. 'Somegirl. Need say sorry. Lastime see girl, slap me goodbye.'

'Ah . . .' The lantern was raised to illuminate Tomki's bruised face. 'Blackandblue you, no kind girl. Listen, forget love, bird belong-you droop and drop. So stop. Rest bird. Sit twinsome here talk awhile. Thisere road lonely, company better.'

'Travel lone?' Tomki dismounted, and led his wilting bird to the roadside.

'No lone, but lonely.' The woman gave a jerk of her head up the hill. 'Other sleep up there. Companion, no company. No talk, no smile, no laugh.'

And so the two strange figures sat cross-legged by the benighted road as the stars brightened above them, chatting as if they were the oldest of friends. Only when the boy roused himself and continued on his way did the lanky

329

woman unfold her new letter and pore over its last paragraph once more by the light of her lantern.

'I enclose a message from our Lace friend, who has become frightened. Frightened people sometimes make mistakes. Save our friend from making mistakes in any way you can. In the meanwhile . . . Jealousy is yours.'

Jimboly's grin opened like a ravine.

25
THIEF OF THREADS

Until the moment she found the message in her hand, Jimboly's week had been very dull. For one thing, her blue-dyed travelling companion was not a great one for conversation, and since Jimboly had no intention of leaving the chirruping to the birds this meant that she had been forced to supply both sides of the dialogue. She had tried to rile him into responding by delivering his lines in a range of squeaky voices. Most of the time he had ignored her. Occasionally he had glanced her way without malice, as if calculating how he would skin her to cover a drum.

'Half a mind not to let you join in the fun, my darling.' Jimboly's smile glittered like a dragonfly conference. The surviving Hollow Beasts were clearly hiding in Jealousy – she no longer needed the Ashwalker to track them down. The next moment, however, her expression became pensive. Perhaps he could still be useful. 'What do you think, Ritterbit, do we need the blue boy?'

She smiled at the tickle of Ritterbit's feet against her collarbone.

'*You'd* peck him up, wouldn't you? He's a thread worth playing with. All right ittle-rittlebit, we'll peck him.'

331

Morning brought a good strong breeze, so Jimboly had no trouble following her nose and finding the hollow that Brendril the Ashwalker had chosen as a makeshift bedchamber.

Generally there was nothing Jimboly liked better than creeping up on dozing people, but Brendril seemed to make a practice of sleeping with his eyes open, which took a lot of the pleasure out of it. Jimboly was not afraid to approach the living or the dead, but it was unfair of him to leave her wondering which of the two he was.

She picked up a piece of twig and flicked it at his face. 'Wake up, the day's as pretty and blue as you are.'

The fragment of wood bounced off Brendril's temple. He sat up smoothly, showing no sign of anger, then stood and readied his travel pack. As usual he took pains to make sure that Jimboly and Ritterbit were on the sun-side of him, so the flickerbird would have no chance to snatch threads from his shadow.

'I've brought you a titbit.' Jimboly fell into her lanky barefoot stride beside him. 'Better than bread. Even better than rat pie. It's a titbit of news – listen. The Superior sent you away from Jealousy. Want to know why he did that?'

Brendril slowed and stopped. He turned to look at Jimboly. There were crumbs of earth on his cheek and in his eyelashes, but he did not seem to have noticed. For the first time in two days he spoke to her.

'Yes.'

Jimboly grinned. 'He's hiding your prey. *That's* why all these ragamuffin Lace are creeping to Jealousy. He's set up his own little camp for them to skulk in. There's even a couple of Lace running around town carrying his signet

332

ring. Lace from the Hollow Beasts, they say.'

Once more Brendril started to walk, his tireless lope taking him in the direction of Jealousy. He did not look at Jimboly, but she knew he was still listening.

'Running around bold as a beacon. Nothing to fear – like they had *protection*. That's how it sounds to me, but what do I know, you're the –' Jimboly had to execute a lolloping skip to keep up with the Ashwalker. 'You're the bloodhound, *you tell me* what it looks like.'

Without apparent effort, Brendril's lopes lipped into a leaping run, and soon even Jimboly was struggling to keep pace.

'Commission in your pocket!' she gasped. 'Gives you the right to cut through anyone who gets between you and *her*, doesn't it?' Out of breath, Jimboly gave up and stooped to lean her hands on her knees, while a scrap of night sky leaped and bounded along the rugged route towards the town.

'Oh, we've set him rolling like a rock down a ravine. There'll be no stopping him now.'

Jimboly set off again at a more measured pace, for she did not have the Ashwalker's relentless energy. For hours the road rolled past beneath her jaunty stroll. Only as the road dipped and Jealousy came into view did her steps start to caper and dart, as if she was her self a flickerbird. As she entered the outskirts her black eyes flitted to and fro looking for threads, threads that she could tangle and pull.

A group of seven-year-olds playing. This was a thread.

One gilded weathervane in a street of stark thatch. Also a thread.

A group of bored, scarred men whose stares clung to

 333

passers like hot tar. A Bitter Fruit soupery. A stall full of good-luck charms. All threads.

Jimboly's jaunty walk faltered and altered. She started to hop. Hop left-and-forth, hop right-and-forth, to and fro and ever on, leaving a zigzag of prints behind her. Soon the children she had seen stopped their game of dirt-chequers to stare.

'Ankle broke?' called out the boldest in Nundestruth.

'No.' Jimboly laughed and pointed at her tracks behind her. 'Want folk think person got two left foot walk down road.' Her laughter was a disease, and the little gang immediately caught it. Soon that part of the street was empty but for the tracks of a woman with two left feet, and the prints of her six similarly afflicted children.

In their secret den in the hollow under the stilted granary, the gang showed Jimboly their treasure trove of little thefts and findings, bird skulls and bodice pins and broken goblets. And Jimboly's quick fingers also sorted through the other scraps they offered her – tattered pieces of overheard conversations, shiny shards of gossip, mouldering patches of rumour.

Out of the ditch with straw in her hair, fastening some new bronze pins into her kerchief. Hop-hop, hop-hop, down the street with Ritterbit's tail flish-a-flash.

She paused to pore over the stall of good-luck charms. She ran the tips of her fingers over a line of wooden bells, painted with spirals and eyes, and whistled regretfully through her teeth at the bubbles in the paint.

'It is just the heat,' the woman at the stall said quickly. Jimboly smiled at the woman's thick-tongued Doorsy, a sure sign of a businesswoman trying to sound respectable. 'Look, the bubbles have not ripped, they are still holding the good luck in.'

'That is no ordinary heat.' Jimboly prodded them. 'You've used good paint here – ordinary heat would not blister it.' The woman opened her mouth and closed it again, not wanting to disagree. 'That's *volcano breath*, that is. I've seen it before, back west. When a volcano gets bored with just rumbling and starts taking interest in a *town*, then it leans over and *breathes* on it. And at first the only signs are yellow fringes on some of the leaves, and a couple of chickens laying eggs baked in the shell, and good-luck charms rippling in the heat. But when the volcano leans closer for a *good* look . . .' Jimboly gave a grim laugh. 'Then *everyone* notices it, all right.'

'Wait!' The woman looked distressed as Jimboly moved away. 'Aren't you buying anything? Where are you going?'

'You think I'm staying in this town with Lord Crackgem breathing down on it? You will leave as well if you've a spoon of sense, and quick.'

As Jimboly walked away she noticed the woman staring nervously towards the volcano, then pushing some of her wares into a shoulder-yoke bucket. She seemed to be readying herself to run rattling from the town if the mountain made one false move.

Jimboly lingered long enough to push one of her new pins into the door of the house with the gilded weathervane, then strolled on, fingering the painted bell that the stallholder had been too flustered to reclaim from her. She walked up to the bored-looking loiter of men, calling a greeting as cheerily as if she knew they had been waiting for her.

It took only five minutes for her to prove to them that they owed her a drink, and a mug of rum and crushed pineapple was brought to her. She dipped her smile into it, and then gestured with her head towards the charm stall.

'What do now luck leave town?'

What did she mean?

'Mean luck lady. Overthere stall. Lady got *gift*. Got *sight*. Sense illthing before happen. Lady say go runoff, leave town. Say volcano angry with town.'

'Angry? Why mountain angry?' Seven or so accusing stares were levelled towards Crackgem, followed by a series of half-reverent, half-defiant warding gestures.

Jimboly shrugged, then narrowed her eyes. 'Back west, angry mountain sign of Lace whisper, Lace fireup mountain. But Jealousy too east. No Lace here, eh?'

One halting description of the Stockpile later, and Jimboly was staring at them bug-eyed as though she had never heard of such a thing before.

'Superior protect Lace here?' She gave a long, low whistle. 'No wonder mountain angry. If Lace got powerful friend, wager Lace gather here long time. Wager many, many Lace in town. Look around. Lookout folks got strange accent. Lookout folks got more money than should. Lookout house got pin stuck in door – sign Lace safe haven. Findem easy . . .'

And away strolled Jimboly, sipping through her grin from her borrowed cup, and pausing now and then to push a pin into a door. At the Bitter Fruit soupery she halted and her smile slipped from her face, leaving her looking pained and uncertain.

336

'You hear about the fight up the street?' She slipped into the Bitter Fruit dialect, her tone rapid and urgent. 'Couple of bounty hunters saying the Lace are all disguising themselves as Bitter Fruit. It's getting out of hand – these hunters have started pulling people out of their houses and smashing up their stalls. The neighbours sent me to call the guards, but I don't know where to find them . . .'

The stallholder paled, left the stall in the hands of his children and ran off down the street. *Oh, so* that's *where the guardhouse is*, thought Jimboly as she continued walking.

Outside a forge she found a monkey tethered to a hook on the wall by a rope. It hobbled over on its knuckles when she held out a palmful of crushed pineapple, and its blush-coloured fingers delicately scooped the pulp into its mouth. Doped by rum, it did not notice Jimboly cutting its rope and slipping a noose about its tail.

People erupted from their houses as a tawny ball of screech and snarl bounded off walls and stalls, knocking pots, rolling bowls, scattering ducks.

'What go pass? What matter monkey?'

'Monkey got bell tied to tail, look!'

The monkey swiftly vanished from sight, and Jimboly strolled through the suddenly full streets, asking everyone she met what the fuss was. Out of the corner of her eye she noticed the raised voices drawing in people from other streets, adding to the confusion. Her erstwhile drinking companions arrived, and quickly became the centre of fierce debate.

'. . . pins in doors . . . volcano breath . . . Lace . . . Lace . . .'

Jimboly tugged at a sleeve. 'I just arrived here – why's

 337

everybody gathering? Is it true that there's going to be a march on the Superior's palace?'

'What?' answered the first dozen people she asked.

'That's what I've heard,' answered the next dozen.

'Yes – didn't you know?' came the answers at last. 'Are you with us?'

'I'm just an outsider,' said Jimboly. 'But I'll come along if you want me.'

She sauntered in the midst of the crowd, rubbing her palms as if at a well-stoked fire. *Ah*, she thought when the road widened and she saw a whitewashed and gabled house ahead, *so* that's *where the Superior lives.*

Jimboly looked all about her, and then up at the roofs. And, sure enough, perched amid the dust-coloured thatch she spotted a familiar inkblot of a figure.

'About time he spent some time following *us*, isn't it, Ritterbit my gobblesome?' Jimboly fell back in the crowd, then climbed up the pedestal of a statue of the first Duke of Sedrollo. She settled between the stone duke's great buckled shoes. From the side streets the Superior's men were pouring in and completing the confusion of the march.

On his roof, Brendril saw Jimboly wave across at him and point towards the Superior's palace. He did not see her as a woman. She was a great voracious flickerbird with a jewelled beak, pulling loose threads of souls and tangling them together. He respected her as he might a scorpion or a precipice.

But most of his thoughts were upon the palace, iced with marble peacocks and stucco suns. He did not know whether the Lady Arilou could be found inside. But he did know that somewhere within the palace was a man – a man mistaken. A man who thought he would stand between a fugitive and an Ashwalker. A man who thought his heart was beating. A man who did not understand that he was nothing but ash.

26
THE SUPERIOR'S STAND

It was during lunch that Hathin heard Mob baying at the palace gates, and suddenly sensed the fine cracks in the yellowing ivory of her sanctuary. It was one voice at first, but a rabbling roar of them soon followed, like a landslide triggered by a solitary rock.

The palace was suddenly full of running feet. A valet ran in and whispered furiously to the Superior.

'What? At the gates?' The Superior's face took on a hopeless look. What was he to do if even the living were determined to spoil his lunch? 'No. Yes. Wait. I shall talk to them.' He felt gingerly at the wires that supported his elaborate moustaches.

'Can I recommend that you do so from the balcony, sir?' suggested the valet.

Having changed his dressing gown for an oversize silk-lapelled frock coat, and his lace morning cap for a full-bottomed wig, the Superior ascended to the first floor. As the shutters were opened for him, angry noise poured into the room.

'What's wrong with you?' The Superior stared at Hathin, who had doubled into a crouch and was flinching at each raised voice. Nobody and nothing could stop Mob. She could not speak, but in her wide eyes the Superior seemed to see something of the blind white panic that filled her mind.

'Here.' He held aside a fold of the curtain. 'Hide in this if you must.' She gratefully hid herself in the curtain's folds, and he let it fall around her.

Through the worn places in the curtain, Hathin saw the Superior step forward on to the balcony. There was a surprised hush, and then the sound from the street instantly became deafening.

'Citizens of Jealousy – Citizens of – this is ridiculous. You, sir, in the white waistcoat, kindly stand next to me and do my shouting for me. Tell them that their Superior stands before them, and that he will not bellow to a rabble like a fishmonger. They must choose *one* spokesperson.'

As his instructions were called out the Superior drew himself up as if to prove his Superiority. Strangely Hathin thought this made him look all the smaller and more frail. His words, however, did seem to cause some confusion. Clearly the crowd was not sure who its leaders were. But then a voice from near the back pealed out with gull-like clarity.

'Hey, Bewliss, speak Doorsy, don't you? Bewliss, everybody! Push man forward!'

A broad-shouldered young man was pushed forward amid slaps on the back, but Hathin's eye had lodged not on him but on the person who had called out, the person who now playfully punched his shoulder and whispered into his ear. The velvet of the curtain smothered Hathin's croak of horror.

A red bandanna. A grin studded with coloured stars. A bird on a string, with its tail ever in a flick-knife twitch. It

 341

was Jimboly. And suddenly her appearance had a dreadful inevitability.

'We want the Lace!' came the cry in a rough-cut Doorsy, amid a chorus of approval. 'We want an end to them quarrelling with the mountains and making soup out of our children and squeezing the strength from our goats and making our wells dry up. We want the Stockpile.'

The Superior murmured in the ear of his spokesperson, who listened, nodded, then repeated his words more loudly.

'The Superior has no intention of handing over his supplies to a riotous multitude. Within Jealousy, wrongdoers will be punished by process of law, not in the street. Anyone who tries to do so is a simple murderer.'

'Don't fiddle with the velvet, child,' the Superior murmured quietly as the roar of protest rose, and Hathin realized that she was clutching the folds of the curtain tightly. 'You are fretting loose my great-grandfather's crest.'

The crowds in the street knew that they outnumbered the Superior and his men five to one. What they did not realize was that they in turn were outnumbered by the thousands of ancestors who stood behind the Superior, watching to see that he did not disgrace their line. What was the threat of a few brute moments with a cosh-carrying mob compared to the danger of an eternity of steely disdain from a thousand high-born relatives?

'My good girl, kindly stop quivering. Get yourself to the Lace quarters . . . and have all my Lace brought into the main building. Put them in the trophy room – we will be better able to protect them there.'

Hathin ran to the Stockpile to find the Lace readying

themselves for fight or flight. Enough of the cries outside the walls had been overheard for panic to set in. Jaze, who had arrived back in Jealousy a couple of days earlier, was already giving curt orders. The Stockpile's numbers had now swollen to about three dozen, including some entire families.

Hathin stared mutely at the terrified smiles of the children, and the gulls above sounded like Jimboly's laughter. Hathin had made things easy for Jimboly and her friends, gathering all these Lace in one place when they might have scattered to the winds . . .

Grim and desperate resolution was legible in the faces of Therrot and Jaze as they shouldered children and shepherded the terrified gathering out of their hut. A few of the young men had skinning knives out and wore dazzled looks as if they were already running through imagined fights in their heads. The stragglers were halfway across the courtyard when there were shrieks, and Hathin turned to see heads and shoulders appearing over the courtyard wall.

The Lace broke into a sprint, but bottle-necked at the door of the main building. The Superior's men had all been drawn to the front of the palace, and there was nobody to call to as figures hauled themselves over the wall and dropped into the garden.

All thought was burned away by brute terror. Everything was animal – the gaggle of Lace turning its knives and teeth outwards, their young in the middle, while the attacking figures lurched in like wolves. Somewhere in the crush a little child gave a scream, a white, raw, naked sound like a gash of chalk. Therrot turned to face their attackers, brutally shoving Hathin behind him.

She was caught in a crush of tall bodies and did not see the first blow struck, but she felt the crowd flinch one way, then surge the other like wild water, nearly dragging her off her feet. The screams striped her mind and confused her, and it took a while for her to realize that one of the screams was hers.

'Get inside!' she was screaming. She could feel the crowd yielding as the Stockpile looked to flee down the side of the palace wall, into the bushes, towards the walls. 'No! Everybody inside!' She could just glimpse the Jealousy men grappling some of the Lace away from the group, trying to break up the defensive line.

Oh no, thought Hathin. *Oh no, no, no you don't, Jimboly. Not again. Not this time.*

A blunder of fists, a snick, a cry, and then a wary space opened suddenly around Jaze and his knife. Through a gap between shoulders Hathin saw a brutish-looking local go down in a flurry of Therrot.

'Everybody *in*!' Hathin's voice found a space in the noise and seemed to galvanize the crowd. Suddenly the Lace were not tug-of-warring to and fro, they were pushing through the door into the dim-lit hall.

'Follow me! *This* way!' Hathin stooped to scoop up a small child whose parents' arms were already full of infants, and ran as fast as she could down the mosaic-floored corridor. The vaulted passages had no idea what to make of children's screams, the patter of wicker shoes, frightened cries in Lace, and they threw the sounds back in confusion.

The Lace fugitives erupted into the great trophy hall, their entry watched by stuffed deer, peacocks and dust-matted jaguars' heads. The hall had a heavy oak door with black iron bolts. But when to slam it? Should they wait for all the Lace to be within, or should they close it after the children and the old, and leave the rearguard with no retreat from the growing mob? Hathin's heart plunged as she realized that Therrot was nowhere to be seen.

'Shut the door! Shut the door!' Jaze's voice from down the hall.

Too late. Even as the Stockpile tried to force the door shut, half a dozen shoulders arrived to heave against it from the other side. The gap bristled with hands, knives, feet, elbows. Helplessly Hathin watched as it started to gape once more.

Then something changed in the tone of the combat outside. The Stockpile all felt the change, and tensed to it, but could not understand it. They stared into the dark mirrors of each other's eyes and listened as the baying outside was suddenly punctuated by sharper, higher cries of surprise and betrayal. The door lurched, buffeted against the defenders' weight, then the clustering hands and feet were withdrawn and the door crashed to. The nearest Lace quickly flung down bars, drove home bolts. The door shook and jolted a few times, and then there was a pattering of receding steps and the cries took on a watery distance.

A battering at the door. 'Open up!' It took a moment for Hathin to realize it was Jaze speaking. 'It's me – open the door!'

When the door swung open, Hathin's heart jumped as a stream of unfamiliar people burst in, drawn knives and bone coshes in their hands. However, instead of setting upon the flinching huddle of families, the newcomers scoured the room, hurried to windows or posted themselves like guards by the door. It was a moment before she was calm enough to recognize Marmar, Louloss and others she had met on that first night in the Wasps' Nest.

'Any of them make it in here?' Jaze hurried in, clasping a bloody arm, Therrot a step behind him.

The Stockpile roused itself from paralysis and shook three dozen heads. Two bear rugs humped themselves ominously, and the frightened faces of small Lace children peered out from under them.

Hathin stared down the passage beyond the door. It was a mess of broken vases, bloody palm-prints and hastily abandoned clubs. Not a single rioter, however.

Jaze allowed himself a smile. 'Funny, they lost their taste for a fight once they were trapped in a narrow passageway between a locked door and us. As soon as they saw an opening, they fled for the wall again.'

The calls in the passage were more distinct now.

'. . . he's not in the ballroom. You two – any sign of him?'

'Nothing in the minstrels' gallery . . . anybody see which way he . . .'

Marmar caught Hathin's questioning glance.

'We weren't the only ones to follow that mob over the back wall,' he said quietly. 'I saw an Ashwalker vault in and vanish among the figs. And now we can't find him.'

While most of the Reckoning continued their search for the Ashwalker, much to the confusion of the Superior's guards Hathin learned the reason for the Reckoning's well-timed

346

appearance. As it turned out, the maker of this miracle had been Tomki.

'He tipped us off,' explained Louloss, the head-carver. 'He'd stayed with us a few days but was returning to Jealousy on Dance's orders. Half day's ride from the city he ran into a woman on the road. He'd never met her before, but he'd seen that little wooden head I'd carved to your description, and when he caught sight of a flickerbird on her shoulder he realized that this was Jimboly the tooth-puller, the crowd-witch.

'So he stayed to chat with her, and found out that she was heading to Jealousy, travelling with an Ashwalker, and that she'd heard that Jealousy was "Lace-infested". Apparently he had half a mind to ride straight back and warn you all, but the nearest Reckoning safehouse was closer, so he rode there like fury for reinforcements. By the time he got there, he'd nearly shaken his brain loose with galloping. His bird flopped right down, drank half a lake of water and hasn't let him on its back since.'

Hathin felt a twinge of remorse as she imagined Tomki tumbling exhausted from his resentful bird.

'What in the name of . . . ?' The Superior had just appeared in the doorway to the trophy room and stood boggling at the scene before him. 'How . . . ? Who . . . ? Who are all these people?'

'They're . . . They are *yours*, sir.' Hathin gingerly advanced, feeling self-conscious in her use of Doorsy before so many Lace. 'They're your Lace Stockpile.'

'*What?*' The Superior's jaw wobbled about for a few seconds like a cork on a stream. 'What – *all* of them? How can we possibly need this many to push barrows up the mountain?'

347

Hathin could only hope that he had not noticed the weapons being tucked away as he entered, or the suspicious number of people with covered forearms. 'Where did you even *find* them? And what are they all looking so happy about?'

Hathin's spirits wilted before the prospect of explaining the Lace smile to someone with such a short attention span for the living. But the Superior was already occupied trying to shoo a pair of Lace children from riding his stuffed gazelles.

'All right!' he was shouting. 'All right, these people can stay for now, but no more, you understand! Not a single Lace more!'

So it was perhaps just as well that neither the Superior nor his guards noticed when Dance of the Reckoning arrived with the dusk and let herself in through the kitchens.

27
DEATH DANCE

Nothing was to be found of the Ashwalker. He seemed to have melted into the palace like a drop of ink losing itself in a glass of water. By dusk, everyone said that he must have left as silently as he arrived. Yet an air of unease remained.

Hathin had no doubt that the Ashwalker who had been spotted must be the same one that had hunted her all the way from the coast. At the back of her mind she had always known he would return. Her only consolation was the fact that Arilou at least was safely tucked away in the Sour village. And yet, unreasonably, she felt that Arilou could not be really safe without Hathin herself to watch over her.

Hathin felt a fear of herself as she walked the nocturnal passages, the clap of her boots on the marble tiles too loud for her liking. She had started the Stockpile, and now the fates of dozens of innocents, even the fates of Dance and her Reckoning, all seemed to be teetering precariously on that one small decision, like an inverted mountain perched on its peak. How had it happened? Her revenge quest seemed to have taken on a very strange shape.

As she clipped through the passages figures detached themselves from the shadow to give her a small, lazy raise of the hand before concealing themselves again, so that she would not be startled by coming upon them suddenly. Despite their hell-for-leather run to Jealousy, many of the revengers had chosen to eschew sleep and stand watch throughout the palace that night in case of trouble.

It had seemed best not to bother the Superior with this plan. He had been flabbergasted enough at the discovery that his personal stash of Lace had increased to an army of nearly fifty souls. If he found that his Lace were leaking out of the trophy room and lurking fully armed in corners of his palace, Hathin felt that he might be downright upset.

In the ballroom Hathin found Dance, but only because she knew to expect her. Dance sat there alone with the patience of a mountain, her slow-blinking stillness rendering her unobtrusive despite her size. Around the room marble biceps bulged, painted armour gleamed and woven horse haunches flexed as the dead dukes paraded their victories on wall and pedestal.

Hathin took off her hat and sat down next to Dance, feeling like a rowboat beside a ghost galleon.

'I expect,' Dance said quietly after a few moments, 'that your Stockpile have told you about the secret trail? It runs from the coast through the jungles and marshes all the way to Jealousy. Among our people, the whisper is spreading that in Jealousy there's a haven. Right now there are probably dozens of Lace on the trail, all on their way here.'

Hathin swallowed and said nothing.

'Whatever we choose to do, it is too late to stop them coming. Wave after wave of them will arrive.' Dance rolled her shoulders slowly, easing out cramps. 'What has your

Superior promised? How sure is his protection?'

'I . . . don't know.' Rather hesitantly, Hathin explained the peculiar nature of her agreement with the Superior. It sounded flimsy and foolish in the retelling.

'We have two choices,' continued Dance. 'The first – we can all leave Jealousy, and abandon the town to this crowd-witch Jimboly. Scatter ourselves like sparks, so we can't be stamped out easily. Take as many of the Stockpile with us as we can, and leave them on the Obsidian Trail to fend for themselves. The other choice – we stay. We make this the haven our people want, a headquarters for pursuing your quest and a new base for the Reckoning. We gamble everything.

'If we choose the second . . . the Reckoning won't take to it easily. We're hawk-soldiers, we stoop, strike and fly. We don't stand guard like dogs. Our strength has always been that daylight only borrows us – we come from darkness and return to it again, and nobody knows where to find us out. If we choose to remain here – we might as well be standing by a great pyre like the Beacon School.'

'It's . . . If we could stay here a little longer . . . perhaps the Sours can get more information out of Arilou. It could help us find out who our enemies are . . . or why . . .'

Dance turned her head slightly and looked down at Hathin.

'Those little children in your Stockpile, do you know their names?' Dance listened as Hathin falteringly recited a few names, then quietly interrupted. 'Don't learn any more of them. They're becoming too real to you, and their protection is not your quest. If the Reckoning leave tomorrow, we take you with us.'

'Tomorrow! But—'

'Hathin . . . thanks to you and your sister we now know how our enemies have been trading messages with each other so quickly. And we have been having interesting conversations with four very frightened men who never thought they would find themselves our guests.

'They're all officials.' Dance sounded neither outraged nor surprised. 'All Doorsy men, instructed to report on Lace and Lost activity. They claim they did not know that the Lost would die, but they admit on the night of the deaths they were ordered to stay away from their local Lost and find themselves alibis. What is remarkable is how little they *do* seem to know. They do not even know the identity of their immediate leader. But they all seem certain of one thing. He is an agent of Port Suddenwind.

'Until now, we've been thinking ourselves faced by two bands of foes. On one hand, the secret killers of the Lost. On the other, the forces of law and order. Now we have to face the fact that they may be one and the same. Small wonder this woman Jimboly turned up at the same time as the Ashwalker.'

Hathin's skin went cold. Was it possible? If Port Suddenwind was behind the murders of the Lost, then what hope did she or her friends have? Powerful enemies. Men with warrants and Ashwalkers at their fingers' ends. Perhaps even the 'Lord S' mentioned in Skein's journal was one of them. *Lord S will return when the rains end or soon after.* Return for what? Another grand strike? Another wave of deaths? What had poor Bridle tried to warn against before he died? She had nursed some frail hope that once they'd unravelled the mystery she and Arilou could prove their innocence to the authorities, stop the Lace being used as scapegoats and complete her quest by having the culprits brought to justice. If the authorities were the true murderers, then even this was hopeless. The butterfly wing on her arm suddenly seemed absurd. How could a twelve-year-old Lace fugitive avenge herself on the government itself?

'Dance – was there nothing else the pigeon men could tell you? Did they know anything about the lists in Skein's journal, or who "C" might be?' Hathin could not quite keep a touch of desolation from her voice as Dance shook her head. 'Well . . . they must have had orders from their leader from time to time. What did he ask them to do?'

'They did receive orders, yes. In particular, they were told to gather carpenters, masons and mining experts to be transported west in secret. Also gunpowder, picks, shovels . . . everything you would need for a mine. But these supplies were not delivered at the usual mining outposts. They were taken to the Coast of the Lace and then north somewhere. That was all they knew.'

They still had no answers.

'One of our prisoners told us something else,' continued Dance. 'He seemed very sure that there is a Lace spy working for the organization. And that is the other reason that your Stockpile troubles me. They are all Lace, and all strangers.'

Hathin was silent for a moment. The suggestion of a spy again called up the phantasmal image of her village filing into the cave of death, but for one furtive figure . . .

'Dance,' Hathin said carefully, 'the Lace spy might not

 353

be a stranger. Jaze . . . Jaze thinks that someone else from the Hollow Beasts might be alive. Someone who told Jimboly about the escape route through the caves. Someone who didn't die because they were expecting the attack. A traitor.'

There was a long silence.

'If there is such a one,' rumbled Dance at last, 'and we find them . . . they are yours.'

'Mine?' The marble tiles chilled Hathin's bare calves. 'Yours. Whatever happens to Jimboly and her masters, it is fitting that you are the one to take away the traitor's name.'

Hathin felt as if she had promised to leap a ravine, and had just now halted breathless at the precipice, feeling her stomach tumbling down and away towards water-chilled rocks.

'Dance . . .' She could barely squeeze out a whisper. How could she tell this giantess that the Reckoning had risked all for nothing, because she, Hathin, could not bring herself to crush even a cockroach? The revengers were her only friends – how could she see their eyes cool as Eiven's had when Hathin had failed to find a way round the Lost Inspector's tests? How could she be less than they expected? 'I . . . I will take the traitor's name.'

Dance put out a hand and rested it on Hathin's boot. For a moment Hathin thought it was a gesture of acceptance, camaraderie. The next instant, however, she noticed the sudden tension in the older woman's posture, and heard what Dance had already heard, the tiniest metallic creak from the next room.

Dance's eyes were plum-blood moons. There was barely a sound as she stood, and Hathin realized that her feet

354

were bare. The painted veins on her arms wove darkly, as if rivulets of blood had trickled down from her shoulders and then dried.

The tall woman stooped, carefully lifted the lid of an ottoman and pointed within. Hathin obediently climbed inside and took the weight of the lid on her hands as Dance lowered it so it wouldn't click shut.

The lowered lid allowed her a sliver of vision, and through it Hathin saw Death walk into the room, man-shaped but midnight blue. Her first thought was that he must be searching for Arilou and herself, and she watched bewildered as his steps took him in the direction of the door that led to the Superior's quarters.

The Ashwalker was halfway across the ballroom before he seemed to sense Dance. Hathin saw his head turn to look towards her, and the tapestry behind her fluttered as Dance launched herself from the wall.

From one of her hands drooped a wood-handled club. As she circled the Ashwalker she let it twirl slightly, so that the loose leather bandage around it unwound itself and spiralled on to the floor, revealing a long row of obsidian blades jutting from either side of the long wooden shaft that formed its core.

With a lurch of her heart, Hathin realized that she was looking at something that few had seen since the time when the Lace were purged, their priests executed and their temples left to ruin. Once in a long-dead time elite companies of black-feathered Lace bearing such weapons would have hissed out of the darkness to storm strangers' camps and carry off prisoners for sacrifice. The obsidian blades were volcano teeth, and blood shed by them was drunk by the mountain.

Rings of white appeared around the Ashwalker's dark irises as he stared at the weapon. He was a head shorter than Dance, but his form seemed to drink light out of the dim hall. Now there were two figures slowly circling one another, one muscular and momentous, the other slender and deadly as a garrotte wire.

They swung into battle like leaves on a water eddy, and Hathin knew suddenly why Dance had been given her name and why she had no other title. There was a stillness even in her swiftness, a rolling agility as if she was a sea thing underwater. She *was* a dance. Each time she swung her weapon, the air buzzed between the obsidian blades with a sound like a dozen people humming.

The Ashwalker was also a dancer, but one full of hummingbird-like darts and retreats, a sliver of steel gleaming in each hand. Hathin held her breath and watched a waltz older than the ballroom, older than the dukes it honoured.

The pair vanished behind a pillar, and Hathin heard a rending, a thud, a release of air. When they reappeared at the other side, one of the Ashwalker's knives was too dull to catch the light, and new dark rivulets were coursing down Dance's arm. Only then did Hathin remember that although Dance had killed an Ashwalker previously, he had been river-dunked first, washed of his powers.

The Ashwalker made a brief lunge, which Dance seemed to dodge, but then Hathin heard the tall woman give a low growl in her throat and saw a dark patch forming on her thigh. When the moon started to peer its way in through one of the high windows Hathin could see that both combatants were leaving stained footprints on the white marble tiles. Those of the Ashwalker were faintly blue, but Dance's were red.

Only as the Ashwalker slipped across a stripe of moonlight did Hathin realize that Dance's broad swipes had not missed entirely. The serrated teeth of her sword had missed skin but caught cloth, and his garments now sported rents and ragged tufts like feathers. That was why the indigo was marking the tiles. Dance was losing, but the Ashwalker was at least perspiring.

An image flashed into Hathin's mind – a blue figure crouching beneath his waxed parasol on the volcanic hillside, hiding from the rain . . .

There was a raised gallery that ran along the wall behind her, some ten feet above the ballroom. And on the gallery were small shrines to the ancestors, complete with offerings in ornate pots. Perfumes. Wines. Water.

Teeth clenched with concentration, Hathin eased up the lid of the ottoman, and winced as it came to rest against the wall with a faint clunk. She clambered out, feeling painfully exposed, and scampered along the wall to the wooden steps that led to the gallery. Every creaking step sent an ice needle of panic through her heart.

At the top of the steps she snatched up two tall pewter flasks from a little altar and leaned over the balustrade of the gallery. Where was the Ashwalker? Had he heard her? Was he following her up the stairs?

No. The dance was continuing below, and now the unheard music had increased in tempo. And yet, maddeningly, the dancers did not move beneath the gallery, beneath the two flasks that Hathin now held over the drop in her trembling fists.

A leap, a lunge, and a pedestal tottered, dropping the chalices entrusted to it. The silence shivered into fragments and lay with stars of glass and china upon the floor.

Two guards ran in from the corridor, summoned by the smash. From her eagle-eye view, Hathin saw them rush into the deadly shaft of moonlight, then fold and fall, their drawn swords clattering to the tiles. The Ashwalker had barely favoured them with a look as he killed them. His attention was entirely fixed on Dance. So he did not notice the way that the guards' ill-fated charge had pushed him back a critical few paces, bringing him closer to the gallery. And he did not notice two arcs of perfumed water sluicing down from above until they struck him in the head and shoulder-blades.

A shiver went through his whole frame, as if it had been a blade or arrow that had hit him in the back. Dance swung in again with new energy, and the Ashwalker stepped aside, but now his footwork was less sure, his motions more hasty. He was blinking blue dribbles out of his eyes, and puddles of indigo marked his wake as though he was melting.

The heavy door to the Superior's quarters swung wide, and three guards strode out, swords at the ready. Two steps behind them hobbled the nightcapped Superior himself, moustaches unwound and trailing down to his chest, a candle in his hand.

The instant the Ashwalker saw the Superior, it was as if he had been unleashed from a bow. He broke from the skirmish and sprinted for the small, yellow-robed figure, barely seeming to register the three guards that stood in his way. With a sick feeling in her stomach, Hathin saw the guards falter and then each step neatly aside, parting like curtains to allow him passage to their master. They had no will to stop Death going about his business. The Superior's eyes widened, appalled.

Then something broke upon the Ashwalker like a wave, something horse-heavy that landed behind him with a whirl of dreadlocks. A black-toothed blade keened downwards through a shaft of moonlit, and at last choked on more than cloth.

The Superior stared at the knife which the Ashwalker's lunge had pushed point first into his breast pocket, then watched as the dead weight of its owner dragged it down, rending the cloth as it went. Only when the midnight-blue figure collapsed to the floor did anybody release their breath. Still nobody dared speak or take their eyes off the fallen figure. The Superior's hands fluttered helplessly up and down his chest to make sure that the knife had left no holes in him.

'Wha—?' he said at last. 'What . . . ? Who . . . ? How did this . . . ? Why did nobody . . . ?'

He jumped immoderately when Hathin tottered down from the gallery steps, hands raised to show her harmlessness. The guards, clearly feeling that they had to make a belated show of valour, promptly presented their weapons towards her.

'Oh, blood belied, put those things away! How dare . . . ? What's wrong with you, men? You stood aside, you would have let . . .' The Superior stared at Dance, who now had one hand clamped to the gash in her thigh. 'You men – run for my barber–surgeon! Now! If this woman hadn't been

 359

here . . .' He trailed off. 'Wait – who *are* you, good wife, and why *are* you here?'

'Stop!' bellowed Dance in Nundestruth as one of the guards neared the door. 'Milord, call man back. If leave room, ten ticks all palace know got dead Ashwalker here. Dead Ashwalker dangerous, much as alive.'

'But he made an assault upon my person – upon a governor of Gullstruck!' exclaimed the Superior. 'Without a commission!' He stared at Hathin. 'He was supposed to be after you! And your friend!'

'And anyone brave enough to protect us,' Hathin explained quietly but firmly. All eyes strayed back to the figure on the floor. Brendril's face was utterly peaceful. The Superior gave a small, impatient gesture, and the guards closed the door and returned to the centre of the room.

'Blood of my blood!' the Superior continued in a quieter tone. 'Just imagine – what if he had come in through my window?'

'I wouldn't have allowed that, sir,' came a voice from behind the Superior. The little man started, marched back into his room followed by the others and pulled back his shutters. Jaze, who was crouched precariously upon his moonlit sill, raised two fingers to his forehead in salute.

The Superior flung open the next set of shutters, and boggled as Louloss's deferential smile met his eye.

'And we've a man and a woman up on the roof, in case anyone tried to slide down the chimneys,' Jaze added helpfully.

The Superior looked around aghast and astonished at the

respectful glitter of jewelled smiles.

'Since when have I had a Lace bodyguard?' he stammered at last.

'Since you decided not to throw a young girl to an Ashwalker,' Jaze answered calmly. 'In these poison times, a little kindness goes a long way.'

28
WITCH-HUNT

Even after they covered Brendril with a rug, Hathin could not take her eyes off his shape on the marble floor. He seemed to have shrunk, and yet she still felt that at any point he might shake himself, get up and look around with white-ringed eyes. He had existed so long on the cusp between the living and the dead that it seemed quite plausible he might slip back across the divide without effort.

Of the three guards that had so singularly failed their master, two were now on their hands and knees wiping the floor of all evidence of the death-dance, and the third and youngest, who was receiving the brunt of his employer's opinions, looked as if at any moment he might faint or cry.

In the end it was Hathin who went for the barber–surgeon, as the only trustworthy person who could trot invisibly through the darkened corridors of the palace without drawing comment. She knocked on the surgeon's door, and told him that he was needed to attend to the Superior, which by that point was certainly the case. The Superior had reached a pitch of hysteria where he was convinced that only blood-letting would restore his mind.

The Superior's personal barber–surgeon was a mild-faced

young man with a cleft chin. When Hathin roused him he pulled his coat on over his nightgown with an air of weary good humour, as though accustomed to such interruptions.

'I'm surprised he has any blood left in him,' was his only comment as Hathin led him swiftly back towards the ballroom. His expression became less mild and drowsy as the vista within was revealed and he turned to find that Jaze had shut the door behind him and was standing against it. He walked over to the fretful figure of the Superior, keeping his tread steady but allowing his eyes to flit to the armed Lace lurking to each side. Kneeling beside the Superior's chair, he started rolling up his master's sleeve.

'Are you a prisoner, sir?' he asked in the softest of Doorsy whispers.

'What? Don't be an idiot, Staunch – these people are the only reason I'm still alive.'

'And,' Hathin whispered almost inaudibly, 'some of us speak Doorsy.'

As if to prove the fact, Jaze cast a glance towards the barber–surgeon, who was now fitting a crescent-shaped little bowl against the Superior's arm, to catch the blood from the 'breathing' vein. 'Can we . . . ?'

'Oh yes. Mr Staunch has had a razor to my throat every morning for the last two years – if I could not trust him I would know by now.'

'Good. Milord, who else would you trust with this secret?'

Precious few, it appeared, once the Superior had had time to absorb the severity of the situation. An Ashwalker pursuing a commission had been struck down in the palace. This breach of the law was bad enough, but if the dead Ashwalker

363

was identified as the man hunting Lady Arilou, this would spell disaster for all of them. Everyone would assume that some clue had led the Ashwalker to seek Arilou in the Superior's palace, and that once there he had fallen foul of Arilou's secret conspiracy. The fact that he had been struck down by a weapon that had been illegal for two hundred years was unlikely to help.

And the Superior, despite his many years of dedicated and dutiful service to Jealousy, had few among the living that he could call friends. He faltered as he realized this, then had Hathin run for his secretary, his captain of the guard and one other close advisor. Dance gave orders that the Reckoning should be told what had happened. However, the Stockpile and the rest of the Superior's staff and advisors were to be left ignorant. The three guards, who it was decided could not be trusted to be discreet, were stripped of their weapons and confined in one of the old butteries.

At about two in the morning, the ballroom hosted a very peculiar council of war. Chairs were set up for the Superior and his people, mats laid down for the Lace to sit upon.

It was Jaze who spoke for the Reckoning. Beside him Dance sat in silence, an inscrutable, uncertain hulk, crippled by language. Dance did not speak Doorsy.

The Superior sat in silence as Jaze recounted the story of the Hollow Beasts, the strange demise of Skein, the destruction of the village at the hands of Jimboly. He gave Hathin occasional troubled glances as he heard of her initiation into the Reckoning. Then, as he heard of the Reckoning's discoveries, the murder of the Lost using the blissing beetles and the clues linking the assassinations to Port

Suddenwind, he gradually went pale.

'So,' he began with a slightly tremulous attempt at brisk-ness, 'why would Port Suddenwind sanction the murder of all the Lost? Why would the government plunge the whole island into chaos?'

Murmurs and shaking of heads.

'We still do not know,' answered Jaze. 'Our only guess is that the Lost Council found out something so incriminating that they had to be killed, and the rest of the Lost along with them.'

'And who exactly do you say has been marshalling these activities?' asked the Superior. 'Who is giving orders to these "pigeon men"?'

There was a pause, filled with subdued mutterings and the exchange of glances.

'We can hazard a guess,' Jaze declared after a moment. 'Lady Arilou says their leader is in Mistleman's Blunder – and that he has no face. And we know of a man who fits that description. Minchard Prox. The "Nuisance Control Officer". He's a mass of scars with no face worth the name, and there's nobody in Gullstruck chasing our people down as ruthlessly and tirelessly as he.'

Several of the Lace silently showed their agreement by turning their heads aside to mime a spit upon the floor. Hathin could not quite bring herself to do the same. Her first impressions of Prox were being eaten away, poisoned by everything she had heard of him since. His original features in her memory were distorting, marked by the scars she had seen on his face that day on the road outside Mistleman's Blunder, but she still recollected a pair of bright brown eyes, thoughtful, exasperated, flustered and not unkind.

'The Nuisance Control Officer . . . appointed specially by Port Suddenwind, they say. Well.' There was a long silence, during which the Superior fretted at his own buttons. 'Well, this traps me between two stories, doesn't it? One story from you people, and a completely contradictory one from Port Suddenwind. But –' he took a shaky breath, and then released it – 'on balance I am inclined to believe the storytellers who are *not* actually trying to kill me.'

The tension in the room noticeably relaxed, and Hathin guessed that a number of the Reckoning had been bracing themselves in case they needed to fight their way out of the palace.

Disposing of the Ashwalker's body was the first priority, but while all agreed that it should be burned, they couldn't settle on where or how. Jimboly was still somewhere in Jealousy, and nobody knew if or when the palace would find itself under siege from another mob, so trying to smuggle the Ashwalker out could be a dangerous procedure.

'If we burn the body on the grounds, everybody will smell the smoke and know that somebody here is dead,' fretted the Superior. 'Besides, the only suitable furnace we have is the one we use for the scions of our line. That would *hardly* be suitable.'

After Jaze had translated, Dance leaned across and murmured something in Jaze's ear. Hathin watched his velvet brows rise slightly and then smooth as he listened.

'It might,' Jaze said with every sign of restraining an uncharacteristic excitement, 'be very suitable indeed. Milord, nobody outside this room knows that the Ashwalker is dead –

nor do they know that you are alive.'

The Superior stared from Jaze to Dance, as if wondering whether they meant to make him less alive.

'Think about it,' Jaze went on. 'All anyone knows is that there was some confusion in the direction of the Superior's quarters. The surgeon was called in and has not returned.' He glanced across at Mr Staunch, who was now attending to Dance's injuries. 'Five guards are missing. And nothing has been heard from the Superior since.'

'Are you suggesting I circulate a lie?'

'Trust me, sir, circumstances have already laid a young lie in people's heads,' Jaze answered calmly. 'We're just suggesting that you don't kill it in the egg. Listen, sir, you're a marked man. Whoever our enemies are, they killed all the Lost but one and are hunting the last in case she saw something to incriminate them. Now that they see you as her protector, they will assume that you must know all she does. They cannot afford to leave you alive. More assassins and more bounty hunters will come. But if they believe you're *dead* . . . that is a different matter.'

'But the city! It needs a strong leader! It will fall into anarchy!'

'I do not think so, sir. Your rioters wanted to string up Lace, but if they fear one of their number has assassinated a governor, that'll put ice-water on their fire. They'll back away from their battle-lines and look for someone to blame.'

Something uncomfortably warm was flowering in Hathin's chest. She stooped and whispered into the Superior's ear, 'Sir . . . I know who we can give them to blame.'

*

The next morning the charade began. Jealousy woke at dawn to find the flag with the Superior's heraldry was missing from the palace flagpole.

'It has been taken down to be washed,' was the official answer. Nobody believed it.

At nine Hathin ate alone in the long, dark breakfast room, the Superior's chair empty at the head of the table.

'The Superior will be eating breakfast in his room today,' Hathin explained, and the maid looked at her doubtfully and cleared the Superior's plate away.

After breakfast a set of letters and decrees went out, each signed and sealed by a different deputy, instead of with the Superior's distinctive scrawl and signet.

'The deputies are taking on some of the Superior's duties for now,' was the emissary's explanation as he handed over the letters. Rumours started to run on rat-feet all over the city.

While Hathin and Therrot sent out orders to craftsmen for ornaments that might suit the richest of burials, the captain of the guard marched a troop of men down to arrest Bewliss, the young 'spokesman' for the riot the day before.

'Let's just say that that riot you led has caused a death,' was all the captain grunted as Bewliss was taken into custody. Once he found himself in the jail without a crowd at his back, Bewliss's fire did indeed seem well and truly dowsed.

'Now,' said the captain, when they were sitting face to face. 'I know you – you're good timber, from your clumsy feet to your wooden head. So what makes you fall in with murderers? What makes you turn traitor to your most honoured lord? Or should I say, who? Come, boy, don't hang your head like you want me to slip a noose over it; we know it wasn't your fault.

There's a vagabond woman with a flickerbird – folks say they saw her lay a hand on your arm and a strange light come into your eyes.

'So . . . just tell us straight, boy. Was this rebellion of your making, or did she 'witch you somehow? When she had her hand on your shoulder, did you feel something strange shadow your mind and make you act against your nature?'

Blind with tears, Bewliss stared about him, and like many trapped animals decided to fight his way towards the only chink of light.

'Yes,' he said. 'Yes – she 'witched me. I felt my arm tingle and my brain swoon.' As he said it, he might even have believed it.

A little after lunchtime what seemed to be a young boy wearing good leather boots and a smile with a nervous ruck left the palace and walked through the Superior's private gardens to where a teenage boy with a rounded, sunny face and an enormous limping elephant bird was waiting.

Hathin sat down next to Tomki rather self-consciously, feeling again the unfamiliar sting of her fingers when she had struck him across the face.

'They said you wouldn't come into the palace until you had permission,' she began timidly.

Tomki noticed her gaze creeping towards his forearm, and held it up with a bright but serious smile. No tattoo marked the skin.

'You were right,' he said. 'The Sours meant no harm – they were just frightened. If I'd taken the tattoo for that, I'd have been unworthy of it. I'd have been unworthy of *her*.'

369

'You . . . You really do love Dance in your way, don't you?'

'Yes,' said Tomki simply. 'She's . . . so . . . *big*.' He stood up and spread his arms wide, staring up and out, as if he was standing on a promontory and embracing the view. 'She's so big she pushes back the horizons – the world is smaller when she's not there.'

After a few moments Tomki sighed, sat down and continued cheerfully feeding roots to his bird.

'We do need you,' Hathin said gently. 'We need some rumours spread in town. You don't look Lace and you're good at talking to people.' Tomki listened attentively as Hathin explained.

'So Dance wants me to do this?' he asked hopefully.

Hathin bit her lip, wanting to say yes.

'It was my idea,' she admitted.

It was dusk the next day when Jimboly started to notice the mood of the town changing. Until that point she had been listening to it pop and crackle, warming her hands at it and occasionally stopping to throw another log on the fire. Now, however, there was a change of tone in its spit and roar, as if it was devouring new fuel or the wind had changed without warning.

Her first hint of danger came when she drew near to the hideout of her new child friends and heard a whispered conversation suddenly hush. She stooped to peer under the house, and there was a sudden flurry of scuffles. She found herself looking into an empty ditch, mud gouged crazily by small bare feet.

She walked into the market and knew that something was

wrong. She could almost sense rumours weaving from mind to mind, whining like mosquitoes on the edge of her hearing. And yes, the town *should* have been full of rumours, but *her* rumours, not these strange scraps that floated to her ears.

'. . . tear many city apart . . .'

'. . . bird servant, send bird gofetch gossip and secrets . . .'

'. . . death rattle in pack . . . can kill with thought muchas knife . . .'

'. . . yesterday bewitch Bewliss . . .'

'. . . flickerbird witch . . . flickerbird witch . . .'

What? *What?* Jimboly's smile faded. The great, sleepy eye of the city had suddenly turned its baleful gaze upon her. Why? How? This was rumour-magic, mob-craft, *her* game – and somebody was playing it against her.

She suddenly felt exposed. It was the flickerbird making her obvious. She tried to coax Ritterbit into her coat by sprinkling seeds in her kerchief, but he was restless.

'Please, 'itterbittle, I don't want to have to wring your pretty neck. I really don't.' She tucked him into her collar again, and wound his leash tight about her hand.

'Over there witch!' Jimboly's erstwhile drinking companions, headed by Bewliss, were stamping their way towards her through the rain-churned mud. At a glance she took in their tinderbox mood, their air of resolution.

'Keep away! Murderer!' she screamed. Best to keep them on the defensive. Sure enough, the new arrivals' pace faltered. 'Trick me yesterday, make me join march! I no join march if know Bewliss plan climb wall to kill Superior! Murderer!'

Bewliss's party halted in confusion, then dissolved into simultaneous bellowing, some at Jimboly, some at Bewliss, some at those who had been drawn from their houses by the noise.

'Hey! What gopass?'

Poor Bewliss could not understand what had happened. One minute he had been the leader of a plucky gang of crusaders, and now he was surrounded by noise and dangerous faces.

'Thisere woman witch!' he shouted. 'Can prove! Folk say death rattle in bag, fullof teeth belong-dead. Grab pack! Lookin pack!'

'No let Bewliss near! Want kill me!' *A little more confusion*, thought Jimboly, *and I can run*. But at that very moment Ritterbit's leash unhooked from her necklace, and he flew up into her hair from which he used his tail to signal to the world.

'Flickerbird! Look! Is her! Everyone talk of woman got flickerbird! Flickerbird witch! Flickerbird witch!' The cry was taken up by the whole crowd. 'Grab pack! Lookin pack! Empty pack!' Jimboly was seized, and her pack rent from her shoulders. Off came the two underslung cages, and four scrawly miserable pigeons suddenly found that they were free. Out fell the children's toys, the stones painted to look like frogs and fish. Jimboly's tooth-pulling tools hit earth with a silvery clatter. Her hideous dolls with real teeth were passed from hand to hand in horror.

'Look! Here rattle!' The yellowing rattle was brandished aloft. 'No shake rattle! Set down gentle, break open!'

A man with a machete strode forward, knelt beside the rattle and then hacked it apart. There was a brief hush as everybody peered into the split husk.

'True! All true! Rattle fullof teeth! Grab flickerbird witch!'

'No touch!' screeched Jimboly as she leaped away from them and stood gripping Ritterbit's leash. 'Bird belong-me got thread from many soul, from all soul in Jealousy, from soul belong-*allyou*. Take step closer, bird go free, unravel all you! Keep back!' And before any of them could recover their presence of mind, Jimboly was darting away between the houses. Only when she was hiding in the wreckage of a house that had been destroyed during the riots two days before did she stop to recover her breath.

Somebody had known about her death rattle. How? Who? Had she ever told anyone about it? She chewed softly at nothing as she tried to remember, and then a gradual look of disbelief and venomous rage spread across her face. Yes. There was one person who knew.

29
A NEW SISTER

Barely a day after his rumoured death, the Superior called another meeting of his new secret 'council of war'.

Death transforms everybody, but in the case of the Superior the change had been very much for the better. After the initial shock, he had taken to being dead with zeal.

At first he had blushed at the idea of erecting a tomb the equal of his predecessors', but Hathin had kindly suggested that his grieving people would insist upon it. As if to prove her right, anonymous tributes started turning up at the gates of his palace. Scented herbs, sticks tied into man-shapes to act as servants, shards of obsidian, model carriages. So he had flung himself delightedly into devising epitaphs, commissioning statuary and assembling an interminable list of what he would require for the afterlife. It was as though he had become real to himself for the first time.

It was a new, brisk Superior who confronted the council of war, a scroll clutched in his hand, voice raised to compete with the rumble of rainfall on the roof above.

'I would like to know,' he began without preamble, 'what I, as a dead man, am supposed to do in response to *this*.' He flourished a scroll of rich, apricot-coloured parchment and stared a challenge about him before realizing that the assembled company had no idea of its contents. 'Ahem. This letter has just arrived from Mistleman's Blunder, from Minchard Prox, Nuisance Control Officer, Agent with Special Powers Relating to the Lace Emergency and so forth. You know, I *do* wish you people had chosen your enemies better, perhaps someone who *didn't* have free rein to create and enforce emergency laws.

'Anyway, this letter reminds me that, according to the latest decrees, all Lace are to be placed in the new permanent "Safe Farms", where the greater population will be safe from them and vice versa. All those harbouring or supplying Lace may be arrested and their holdings confiscated.' The Superior did not seem to notice the Doorsy elements of the 'council' exchanging swift, anxious glances. 'One of these Safe Farms already exists, near Mistleman's Blunder, and he asks – no, demands – that my private store of Lace be delivered over to the proper authorities at this Farm. There's even a map.'

'Safe Farms . . .' One of his deputies cleared his throat and directed a suspiciously bland look towards the Superior and then around at the assembled Lace. 'Sir, these do not sound so very bad. Perhaps it might indeed be better . . . rather than risk more riots . . . after all, there are children here who might get hurt . . . it might even be kinder . . .' He trailed off as Jaze translated and he felt two dozen Lace eyes fixed upon him.

'Can we see the map?' Jaze asked suddenly. After a moment's hesitation the Superior held it out, and Jaze donned his amber monocles and unrolled it. He said nothing, but his head gave a small upwards flinch. He passed the map to Dance without a word. She did not move, but something in her whole aspect seemed to change, and Hathin thought of mountains blackening beneath a sudden sweep of cloud-shadow.

The scroll passed from hand to hand like a spark down a fuse, and reached the gunpowder that was Therrot. The deputy who had spoken winced before a hissing, spitting onslaught of Lace swearwords.

'*Safe?*' Therrot spluttered into Nundestruth at last. 'Safe? Safe Farm *here*.' He turned the scroll about and held it above his head. 'See? Here. Spearhead. High Spearhead. Just under Spearhead mouth.' Half disbelieving, Hathin followed the jab of his forefinger with her gaze. Yes, there it was, right under the red-centred blotch of Spearhead's crater, a green space neatly bordered with ruled lines. Something about the stark lines of it reminded Hathin of the painted maps in Bridle's workshop, but she could not pin down why the memory left such an ominous impression on her mind.

'But –' the deputy was trying to recover his feet – 'your people always claim to have a special relationship with the volcanoes . . .'

'And our young friend over there attends upon his lordship the Superior,' Jaze said icily, gesturing towards Hathin, 'but she does not march into his bedroom beating a drum. No lord likes trespassers, and Lord Spearhead is unforgiving. *That* –' he gestured towards the map – 'is not a farm. It is an oven. Sooner or later it will cook hundreds of men, women and children to white ash.'

There was a horrified hush.

'And the other Safe Farms . . .' The Superior broke the silence. 'Are these also to be built on volcanoes, in accordance with this highly original definition of "safe"?' The question was addressed to nobody in particular, and nobody in particular answered.

'If I send back a refusal, we'll have a militia on our doorstep in no time,' said the Superior curtly, 'but since I am currently dead for the sake of my health I can at least buy us time. Prox's messenger will be made comfortable and told that I am "indisposed".' The little man drew himself erect. 'I see right through their game. They mean to soften me up and scare me by turning my city against me, then bully me into giving up my supplies. But I am neither a coward nor a fool – I am the Duke of Sedrollo.' He seemed to become aware that the simple magnificence of this statement was rather diluted by the way the long sleeves of his century-old robe drowned his hands.

'Now – we all have more urgent matters to consider, do we not? This woman, this rabble-rouser . . . Jumbly . . . has she been found yet?'

Rumours of Jimboly's flight from an angry mob had reached the palace, and Tomki related the story with visible relish and a hint of modest pride.

'Gone to ground, eh?' said the Superior. 'That's good, young man, but not good enough. She's still at loose in my town, and she must be found.'

There were some murmurs about the difficulty of searching every house, the ease with which a single woman could hide and the dangers of sparking another riot if armed guards started beating doors in.

'What the devil are you all talking about?' The Superior waved a wild hand, which was instantly engulfed by his

 377

enormous sleeve again. 'Beating down doors? Are you all mad? Surely the very crux of our situation, the cause of all our dilemmas, is the fact that *we have a Lost*. A Lost! Who can send her mind anywhere in the town she pleases!' He stared about him at the rows of gaping faces. 'Can she not? Am I missing something?'

'No . . .' Jaze's startled face had slipped helplessly into a broad Lace smile. 'No. I rather think *we* were. It's . . . It's worth an attempt, sir.'

'Good. Well, put Lady Arilou on to the job immediately. And . . . And send me my tailor!' The Superior clutched impatiently at the dragging skirts of his ancestral robe. 'I should have had this robe taken in years ago.'

It seemed unwise to send the Sours visitors they would not recognize, so an hour later Hathin, Therrot and Jaze were picking their way gingerly up the path to the Sour village.

As they walked Hathin wondered at the way one could become used to certain kinds of danger. While everyone in town cringed in the face of Crackgem's current excitability, Hathin had come to accept it. Crackgem might destroy them if they bored him, or he might not. She had grown as used to that thought as she had to the smell of sulphur.

'Want see Laderilou?' Jeljech appeared by their side. She seemed to have become an honorary member of Arilou's 'second family'. Hathin nodded, and the older girl took her arm and led her further up the path, to a shelf of rock where another Sour girl was sitting with her legs dangling over the edge, five or so small children seated around her.

Hathin's first thought was that she must have misunderstood her guide's question. Where was Arilou?

There. There on the shelf, dressed in the greens and yellows of the Sour village, her legs mannish in thick cloth leggings, her expression distant but radiant with delighted concentration. One of the smaller boys stood with his back to Arilou, and as Hathin watched he steepled his hidden hands together, fingertips touching. The other children watched Arilou expectantly, and after a few moments in which her jaw wobbled with effort, she clumsily moved her hands to imitate the gesture, to the delight of her audience.

Hathin could only stand and gape. She waited for the surprised joy to come, but it did not. Instead she felt a sudden desire to sit down right there and bawl herself hoarse. This was a mockery of all the years she had spent in attendance on Arilou, trying to coax the tiniest response from her, the slightest acknowledgement of her existence.

'She . . . You're not looking after her right!' Hathin turned on their guide, surprising herself. 'She doesn't like to sit like that, there's nothing supporting her back, you've left her where she can fall, and . . . and the stone there is all hard edges; she'll cut herself!' Hathin's tirade was met by a look of bewilderment, and she realized that she had been babbling in Lace. She dropped her gaze, face burning, took a deep breath and was glad that she had not been understood.

'Is everything all right?' Therrot jogged into view, perhaps drawn by Hathin's shrillness. Hathin nodded mutely.

'Ath'n,' said Arilou. To judge from her face, she was still gazing at the horizon, but now she was smiling. Not a Lace or a Sour smile, a broad, loose monkey grin with a lovable shamelessness to it, a hint of childlike guile. Another instant and it pulled apart like a bow and was gone. But it was enough. Suddenly Hathin was warm from toe to tip and she forgave Arilou everything, everything.

The smaller children made room for Hathin to sit beside Arilou. As she began to go through all the little grooming gestures that had become as much a part of her own life as blinking or breathing, she felt her restive mind fill with calm and a sense of completeness. Arilou's hair was free of burrs, but Hathin combed it with her fingers anyway.

Arilou. It was as if Hathin had always known she had a sister and was meeting her for the first time in this strange landscape. The combing motion was achingly familiar, but the sense of Arilou's awareness, the spider-thread of connection, was new. Had it been quietly weaving into place as they travelled? Or had the tiniest strand of it always been there?

It was five minutes before Hathin could bear to break the silence.

'Arilou . . .' She hesitated. For those few minutes the sense of link to Arilou had been so strong that she had quite forgotten the language gulf between them. She glanced across at her erstwhile guide, who was fidgeting at a respectful distance. 'Um . . . Pleaseyou tell Laderilou I want her look town. Lookout Jimboly. Bird lady.' Hathin scrabbled in her pouch and brought out the little carving that Louloss had made of Jimboly's head.

Arilou listened to the Sour girl's translation, but when she was handed the wooden head the corners of her mouth drooped in a child-like expression of distress. Hathin remembered Jimboly slyly throwing a rock at the back of Arilou's head and did not wonder at her sister's reaction.

380

'Tell Laderilou I no like Jimboly too,' Hathin added, giving Arilou's long hand a squeeze. Something in Arilou's expression changed very slightly, and Hathin sensed that her sister's mind had flitted away.

While Therrot and a couple of the other Sours sat with Arilou, Jeljech insisted on showing Hathin around a hut, patting the blankets on the bedding mat and showing her a bone comb, a wooden water jug shaped like a bird. It took a while for Hathin to realize that these were Arilou's living quarters, and that her guide was watching nervously to see if Hathin approved of them. She beamed as best she could, and nodded, fighting the temptation to be jealous of Jeljech in her role as one of Arilou's new Sour 'sisters'. Perhaps sensing her conflict, Jeljech seemed determined to defer to her, despite the difference in age.

'Laderilou practise say . . .' The Sour girl faltered, then gave the sentence another run up. 'Practise say . . . Hhatph-hin.'

Non-Lace often had trouble with Lace names. They were not simply based on natural sounds, they were supposed to imitate them, even in ordinary speech. Strangers were often baffled at hearing a stream of Lace interrupted by impressions of bird calls, fire-like crackles and rushing sounds of wind and water. Jeljech's attempt at speaking Hathin's name made her sound as though she was choking on feathers.

Hathin laughed to cover the mistake as she would have done when talking to another Lace, then winced as Jeljech looked offended. The Sour village was so much like her own in some ways that it was easy to stub one's toe against the hidden differences.

'No matter.' The girl shrugged, a little hostile. 'You got new name. We give name.'

Hathin bit her lip as the Sour girl carefully spoke a phrase in her own language, trying to gauge whether her 'new name' would be a veiled insult. The names non-Lace threw at Lace were seldom kind.

'Name mean . . .' The translator bent her arms, so that her spread hands were level with her shoulders and seemed to strain against an imaginary boulder. 'Mean push . . . push . . .' She straightened, raised her arms and brought them down and outward, her fingers describing two symmetrical slopes. 'Mountain. Push mountain.'

It was her turn to laugh at Hathin's expression.

'Laderilou tell us you two rabbitrun away coast. She have none eye, none ear. You carry Laderilou. You push . . .' The girl furrowed her brow and made broad elbowing motions, as if shoving her way through a crowd of giants. 'Push many mountain to side. Laderilou feel mountain tremble, rock give way.'

Hathin ducked her head to hide the fact that her eyes had filled with tears.

That terrible chase across the King of Fans and Sorrow had taken every ounce of her will and courage. Thinking back, it had felt a lot like she was struggling against the very mountains themselves. And Arilou, the dead weight in her arms, had not been oblivious to it after all. She had known; she had cared.

Their feet had taken them in a circle. The rocky shelf came into view. The children were squatting on its edge, leaning over to spit. There was no sign of Arilou.

'Where Laderilou?'

Jeljech repeated the question in Sour. An answer was given by a young man whom Hathin had seen sitting next to Therrot when she left.

'She go with friend belong-you.'

'What?' Why would Therrot and Arilou leave the village without her?

Jeljech continued questioning the young man. It emerged that some time after Arilou had sent her mind down to the town, she had suddenly given a joyful noise of recognition. All she had said was 'friend from beach home' over and over in Sour. Then she had made a strange noise which seemed to mean a great deal to Therrot, for he had leaped to his feet, his eyes bright. His tone was fiercely questioning and he pointed down towards the city repeatedly, but of course the bystanders had not understood a word.

Then he had taken Arilou's arm, heaved her to her feet and led her quickly away down the path towards Jealousy.

Hathin listened in horror. Had Therrot gone mad? Why would he drag Arilou down into the tinder-tense streets of Jealousy in broad daylight? Dazed, she listened as the young man tried to imitate the sound which had had such an intense effect on Therrot.

It was a soft rasp of sound, half sigh, half surge. This time Hathin knew immediately what it was meant to be. The next moment she was sprinting through the village to find Jaze.

'Jaze! Therrot's gone! He's taken Arilou to Jealousy! She was searching the town with her mind, and she didn't see Jimboly, but she found somebody else – somebody from the

 383

Hollow Beasts. Alive and in the city, just the way you said. Arilou tried to tell everyone who it was. The Sours heard her making a strange sound, like a wave stroking sand. Only Therrot realized it was a name.

'I know who it is now. I should have known before, but I was *so* sure she was dead. And now Therrot knows she's alive he's running down to find her before we do, probably because he's afraid we'll kill her as a traitor. And she *must* be the traitor, and he's taking Arilou *right to her*.

'It's his mother, Jaze. It's Whish.'

30

THE SOUND OF WAVES

The young man who had witnessed Arilou's conversation with Therrot had not heard much, but what he did remember was useful. When trying to describe the place where she had seen the 'friend from beach home', Arilou had been talking of 'red houses' and 'black goat go round-round on top'.

'I know what that is!' Hathin exclaimed. 'It's in the craftsmen's district. One of the Dukes of Sedrollo built it as a stables, but then all his horses died of fly-plague so now it's just shops. It has a black weathervane shaped like a horse on top.'

Jaze flicked impatiently at his knife sheath as they began the scramble down the mountainside, looking all the while for their missing companions.

'So . . .' Something had set in Jaze's face, like a new blade fixing in a haft. 'Tell me about this Whish.'

Scrabbling breathlessly over the treacherous rocks, Hathin told Jaze all about the old feud between Whish and Mother Govrie, and then, reluctantly, about finding Whish ready to dash Arilou on the rocks of the Lacery.

'On the day all the Lost died,' Jaze said with icy gentleness, 'somebody tried to kill the one Lost who ended up surviving, and you didn't think it was worth mentioning?'

'I thought Whish was dead! There was this drowned hand in the Path of the Gongs, and it was wearing her shells . . . it was like I'd seen her body. Only of course I never did. And there was Therrot . . . I couldn't rip through his memories of his mother. I couldn't bear to.'

'No,' said Jaze simply. 'You're a child.' There was no venom or anger in his tone, but Hathin knew that in his mind she was no longer Doctor Hathin. 'You haven't spared Therrot anything by your silence. He has worse coming to him now.'

'What . . . ?' Hathin's throat tightened as she was overcome by a new fear. 'You're not going to hurt him, are you?'

'That depends what he's done,' Jaze said grimly, 'and what he does when we find him.'

The coloured mud pools of the volcano's lower slopes had been drying out and cracking, and now they seemed to stare at her with the frightened faces of old men. Jaze's countenance in contrast was smooth and untroubled. Fractured youth has its own special kind of cruelty, and looking into his face Hathin understood it better than she ever had before.

Therrot had that cruelty too. He had tried to teach the art of it to her, so that she could kill anyone who stood in her way. But now the one standing in her way was Therrot.

He can't hurt me, Hathin thought desperately. *I'm his little sister.* The wind roared down in ragged gasps about her, as if Crackgem was laughing.

The Superior's supposed death had galvanized the thoroughfares of the craftsmen's district. Outside every workshop a blanket was strewn with offerings suitable for his tomb. Miniature soldiers, less-than-grand pianos, diminutive musicians, their reddish varnish sticky as blood. Hathin and Jaze had to push through the crowds of people haggling over the models with sombre eagerness.

There were the 'stables', a long building cobbled from rounded red bricks so that its walls looked like slabs of bubbling meat. During a long-forgotten earthquake the stable had shrugged its front facade into rubble. Now you could see inside, where every stall of the stable had been converted into a tiny shop. At this moment the weathered wooden door of each stall was pulled to, for the sky had deadened to a deep violet-grey, and the daily onslaught of rain was expected at any moment.

Jaze strode to the first door and stooped to peer in between the cracked slats. Hathin tensed for the door to be flung open, but Jaze passed to the next door and peered again, then the next, and the next.

The rising wind blew grit into Hathin's eyes. As she turned her head to shield them she suddenly caught sight of two figures hugging the wall of an adjoining building, perhaps once the treasured home of some Master of the Stables. She knew in an instant Therrot's jacket with its coarse twine braid, Arilou's Sour garments, her loose green belt given life by the wind. Therrot was trying to guide Arilou around the corner when he looked up and saw Hathin.

The expression on his face told her instantly that she was no longer his 'little sister'. She had been a small floating spar for him to cling to after the shipwreck of his life. Now she was simply a threat.

There was a bigger threat for him to face, however. Therrot's eyes widened as Jaze sprang past Hathin, and he sprinted off around the side of the building, pulling Arilou after him.

 387

Hathin raced to keep up with Jaze, and turned the corner in time to see Therrot drag Arilou in through a door and try to close it behind them. Jaze had his foot in the gap before it could shut. Both men were shouting, but Therrot was a helpless storm of noise, while Jaze's words organized themselves into tight, angry rows like teeth.

'Let me in, Therrot! You know it has to be done—'

'Leave us alone, Jaze! I mean it! You touch her – you touch a hair of her head and you're dead!'

'Dead! Yes, I'm dead! You're dead! Listen to me – a dead man has no family, no mother! We all gave up being alive for something greater that had to be done.'

'What do you want from me? I can give up my family, but I can't give up loving them. I can't give up killing or dying for them! What if it was your mother?'

When Jaze spoke again, something sharp had curled out of his seeming calm like a cat's claw from the dead grey skin of its sheath.

'I would drive a knife through her throat if my mother mysteriously survived a trap laid by a traitor. If her shell bracelets were found planted upon the corpse of another woman. If I knew she had always hated Arilou and her family. *If I knew that on the very day of the Lost deaths she had lured Arilou to the water's edge and tried to dash her brains out on the rocks . . .*'

The door opened abruptly, catching Jaze's face. It was closely followed by a tidal wave of Therrot. The suddenness of his attack bore Jaze backwards. A blot of blood on his shoulder reminded Hathin that Jaze was already injured.

Then Hathin's breathless, horrified helplessness was extinguished by a single thought.

388

Arilou. Whish must surely be somewhere in this house, and so was Arilou.

She scrambled past the two thrashing revengers and in through the door, which promptly blew shut behind her, unsettling her and cutting out the daylight. She blinked the sudden darkness into meaning and found that Arilou was nowhere to be seen . . . and that the room around her was at the bottom of the sea.

Tiny windows with blue-tinted diamond panes gave the whole room a dusky ocean glow. Along the wall-shelves glowed elaborate pink-and-gold conches. Before her lurked a great turtle, its shell a gleaming mosaic. Above her floated shoals of iridescent angelfish and pouting trumpet fish, all hanging motionless as if sheltering from a strong current.

For a dazed moment Hathin could only wonder what magic ruled this place. Then she saw the threads suspending the shoals, the wood-grain in the turtle's shell. More models, more shrine offerings.

Her chest was tight as her trembling hands worked her knife free from its hidden sheath. No more time to prepare. No more time left to become the killer everybody needed her to be. She had promised to take the traitor's name herself, and the traitor was here. And so, somewhere, was Arilou.

Hathin advanced cautiously through the crowded work-shop. Shadowy benches, anvils . . . lean, angry Whish might be skulking behind any one of them, perhaps with her hand over Arilou's mouth.

There was a faint sound from the other side of the room, a shuffle like that of wicker shoes against stone. Hathin snatched up a murderously realistic swordfish with her free hand and spun to face the noise.

There was a great tree of creamy coral near the opposite wall. A shadow-patterned face was peering through its lattice, straight at Hathin. As she recognized it, suddenly she felt she was back in the cove of the Hollow Beasts.

She could hear the rasp of the waves. Coming in with a *whish*, and going out with a . . .

Larsh.

Poor Arilou had tried. She had opened her unpractised mouth and made a sound like waves. Therrot had heard what he wanted to hear, Hathin had heard what she dreaded to believe, and both had thought it the same name. But it was Larsh, not Whish, who now skulked in his cave of coral like a scorpionfish and watched Hathin with unblinking, unfriendly eyes.

There was a pause, and then the traitor stepped out from behind his coral screen. He was every bit the distinguished tradesman now, in his dark blue waistcoat, his poor pink-lidded eyes hidden behind wire-frame spectacles, a novice moustache waxed to curling points. Even the jewels seemed to have been removed from his teeth. But for all that, it was still Larsh the fishmaker, with whom she had shared secrets on the night of the mist.

A memory flashed across her mind. Larsh standing on the beach alone, freeing a pigeon from its cage. Not out of pity or kindness. No. Those birds must have carried his secret reports to the men who would mastermind the destruction of everyone he knew.

Larsh, with a look of recognition dawning in his eyes. Boyish disguise or no, he knew her now.

'Where's Arilou?' Hathin's voice was louder than she

expected, and shook as if tugged by a fiddle bow.

Larsh flinched as she opened her mouth. Then as the echoes died he seemed to relax. Perhaps he had been expecting her to call for help. Perhaps she was shrinking before his eyes into a small girl with a patch of troubled water on her forehead, a girl who had stumbled into his workshop alone.

'Please put that down,' he said calmly, nodding towards the fish.

'Where's Arilou?'

'I never thought I would hear *you* shouting. It doesn't suit you. It makes you ugly.'

Grief was ugly. Rage was ugly. Fear was ugly.

'*You* made me ugly, Uncle Larsh.'

'Oh, I never had any quarrel with *you*, Doctor Hathin.' He gave a short but weary sigh. 'If things were different, I would be very glad to see you alive.'

Beyond the walls, a sound like the fizz of a wavelet, rapidly swelling to a rumble. Outside, sky had declared war on earth and flung down a million spears of rain. The noise filled Hathin's brain so that she could not even hear the words in her own mouth.

'What?' Larsh's brows twitched. 'What did you say?'

Shakily, to strengthen herself, Hathin was whispering the names of the Hollow Beasts: Mother Govrie, Eiven, Lohan, poor maligned Whish, each a little louder than the last, until Larsh blanched under his greyish tan.

'What makes those names so sacred? Why shouldn't I sacrifice them? They sacrificed *me*. They sacrificed *you*. They took the best years of our lives and gave us nothing in return, not even recognition. Look around you – I can create fish-eyes from mother-of-pearl that will swivel to follow you. I can paint silk so like a moon wrasse's scales that the gulls are fooled. I have always been the best craftsman on the coast – perhaps the best on Gullstruck – but I had to pretend to be a failed fisherman to protect the secret of the farsight fish. I wore the lustre off my eyes working in darkened caves, when I should have been the king of master craftsmen.

'Everything you see about you I fashioned in secret, and had to hide. They are all I have to show for forty lost years. I am an old man, Hathin, and my life has been stolen from me. And then one day somebody gave me a chance to take back just a little of what my life should have been. All I needed to do was betray the village that had betrayed me.'

'I understand.' Hathin had found her voice again. 'I understand it all now. *We died for fish.* Not even real fish that somebody needed because they were starving. Wooden fish. Shrimps made of clay.' She stared down at the silvery lacquer of the swordfish in her hands. 'So who died for this one? Eiven?'

The swordfish's fragile blade splintered as she swung it against the heavy workbench. Larsh gave the shriek of a man that had seen his own child gutted.

'And who was this? My mother?' A cream-and-mauve conch smashed against the wall. 'What about this one? Lohan?' A delicate squirrel fish shattered into red-and-white shards. 'And where's Whish? This one?' A high-swung stool knocked a tiny turtle from its string. 'Father Rackan?' Tinkle, skitter. 'And where am *I*, Uncle Larsh? What was *I* worth? A prawn? A limpet shell?'

'*Stop it!*' All the colour had leeched from Larsh's face, and he had snatched up a metal-headed mallet. Hathin knew that he meant murder, but somehow all her fear had abandoned her.

'You'll never live to enjoy it! You're no use to them any more and you know too much – they'll silence you, even after everything you've done for them!'

Larsh ran at Hathin, but she ducked the swing of his hammer and darted behind a table. She grabbed a huge lobster carved from ivory and blushed with paint. It lolled over her arm with a domino-clatter of intricately carved joints.

'Get back! Not another step, or I'll . . .' She lifted the lobster as if to smash it, and Larsh halted. She had years of his life in her hands.

'Now – *where is Arilou?*'

'I have no idea,' said Larsh with a new caution and meekness. 'Why do you think that she's here? If you'll just be calm and . . .' He was keeping his eyes rigidly on Hathin's face. Rather too rigidly.

Too late Hathin heard the scrape of a sandy heel on the floor behind her. Two long, strong brown arms were flung around her, pinning her own arms to her sides.

'Careful! Careful of the . . .' Larsh's face was frozen into a grinning wince, his eyes fixed on the lobster.

'Hit her with your hammer, you dolt!' Jimboly's voice was hoarse but unmistakable. 'She won't be such a wriggly little fish with her head knocked in.'

Hathin's knife was still in her hand. She aimed a slash at Jimboly's elbow, and the older woman squawked and loosened her grip. Hathin turned about, just in time to be grabbed by the collar and pushed down backwards on to a workbench. Reflexively she lashed out with her knife towards Jimboly again, and felt a brief resistance, but only brief. She had missed. Or had she?

There was a long, desolate scream. The dentist's hands were no longer pinning her down.

'Catch him! Catch him!'

Trailing his severed leash, Ritterbit was flickering about the room, occasionally spreading a taunting tail. Hathin's wild knife had cut through his rein.

'Close all the doors, the windows!' Jimboly croaked. Hathin seized her moment and sprinted for the back door of the workshop, ducking a swing from Larsh's hammer. *Arilou. Where are you?*

Hathin found herself in a Doorsy little parlour. No Arilou behind the dresser. Still clutching the lobster, Hathin sprinted to the next room, a study with a woven grass sleeping mat spread on the floor. No Arilou in the oaken chest.

'You search the hayloft; I'll go through the workroom again!' Jimboly's voice, urgent but distant.

Up some stairs, Hathin found a bedroom with its own balcony. No Arilou in the garderobe. No Arilou in the four-poster bed, which smelt dusty with disuse. No Arilou under it.

The door suddenly swung wide, and Hathin scrambled up off her hands and knees.

'Look what I've found.' Jimboly's smile was a multicoloured parade. 'Down in the workroom. Hiding inside a giant clam. Does that make her a pearl?' One of her arms was curled around Arilou, almost protectively, but her other hand held a sharp-looking saw to Arilou's throat. Arilou's eyes were misty with tears, not distance, and her mouth made soft panicky shapes.

Hathin raised the lobster.

'I'll . . . I'll smash it . . .' Her voice weakened as she spoke. Her angry strength had burned itself out. She felt herself pale and become paper-frail before Jimboly's grin. Jimboly was tidal wave, vulture beak, wet-weather fever. There was no pity in her. There was no stopping her.

'Good,' said Jimboly. 'Smash it. Smash everything in this shop. Smash everything and everyone in this whole town. I'll stop you when I start caring.'

'You should start caring right now.'

Both Jimboly and Hathin lost their eye-lock and looked towards the voice. Larsh was standing in the doorway, a string in his hand. At the other end of the string fluttered Ritterbit. Jimboly reached eagerly for the leash, but Larsh stayed back, watching her with mute, wary enmity.

For a long moment all three stared at each other, Hathin still poised to shatter the lobster, Jimboly with her knife to Arilou's throat, Larsh with the flickerbird's leash in his fist.

'Now this is just getting silly,' Jimboly said at last.

31
A LOST LOST

'What's got into you?' hissed Jimboly in Lace. Hathin watched the lines in Larsh's face deepen. Clearly the animosity she had always sensed between Larsh and Jimboly had not simply been an act to hide the fact that they were secretly working together. No, they genuinely despised each other.

'A little cloud of dust just told me that there was a plan to silence me,' said Larsh.

Hathin felt the hatred of Jimboly's dark glance slide over her skin like the flat of a blade.

'Friend of yours, was it, this little cloud of dust?' snapped Jimboly. 'Somebody you trust? Somebody who wishes you well?' But her voice was shaking. Her eyes were on Ritterbit, and her face twitched each time he fluttered, as if she could feel an invisible thread tug-tug-tugging, pulling it loose one row of stitches at a time.

'And who's Jimboly then?' Hathin echoed her enemy on impulse. 'Somebody you trust? Somebody who wishes you well?'

'She and her friends want you dead, fish-wizard. I'm the only thing keeping you alive.'

'Wrong.' Hathin could not prevent her eye straying to

Arilou, whose arms were stiff with panic. 'You've served your paymasters' purpose. Now you're just a danger to them. We're the ones that need you alive. It's your masters we're after, and you can help us find them.'

'You'd hardly think two minutes ago she was smashing your damselfish, would you?' Yes, it was undeniable – Jimboly's words had lost some of their confidence, some of their sly, serpentine power. 'Listen – if that brat leaves this house, she'll bring the whole Reckoning down on us. If not, then we have Arilou and her little nursemaid. The reward's ours. All you have to do is keep your head.'

'The Reckoning's already coming,' said Hathin, praying it was true. 'But they'll do what I say.' Very carefully she pulled back her arm binding. Both Larsh and Jimboly stared in astonishment at her tattoo. 'It's *my* quest. If I say you live, nobody else can say otherwise. You'll be safe. All you have to do is keep Jimboly's bird away from her – and give it to me.'

'Larsh?' Jimboly's voice held a warning as Larsh advanced into the room. He hesitated, then took a rapid step towards Hathin, slipped Ritterbit's leash into her hand, scooped the lobster from her willing arms and placed himself behind her.

'Now . . .' Hathin stopped to swallow, a little apprehensive at having an enemy of Larsh's size behind her. 'Now *we* swap, Jimboly.'

Jimboly's eyes flickerbirded around the room, over the bedroom door by which they had all entered, across the balcony door opposite. They flickered up and down Hathin's diminutive figure, making plans, appraising.

'No,' Hathin said as Jimboly took half a step forward. 'The three of us are leaving *that* way.' She pointed to the bedroom door. 'You leave Arilou next to it and step away from her, and I'll tie Ritterbit to this bedpost. Then you'll walk to the bed and we'll walk to the door.'

Jimboly scowled, but nodded. Slowly she guided Arilou to the doorway, then took two paces backwards. Heart beating, Hathin tied Ritterbit's leash to the bedpost, her knife ready to slash the leash if Jimboly jumped at her.

'Now –' Hathin's heartbeats felt almost like sobs of hope, of relief – 'we walk past one another . . .'

Within the house there was a sudden crash of furniture overturned. Jimboly's scowl was instantly replaced by a look of panic. She leaped forward, grabbed Arilou about the waist, placed her knife against her belly and dragged her backwards on to the balcony.

'No!' screamed Hathin, even as Jaze burst into the room. 'What . . . ?'

'Jaze, guard him! And – and that! Both of them!' Hathin pointed madly at the cowering Larsh and the startled Ritterbit, then bolted after Jimboly. She burst on to the balcony and found it empty. Wooden steps led down to street level.

Even with the protection of her hat, the rain was blinding and deafening, a savage grey curtain of falling sky. Hawkers ran past in search of shelter, their wares on their backs. The roadway was a milky red soup, frothing and leaping with the falling water.

And where, amid this frenzy, was Jimboly? Where was Arilou?

It was a desolate Hathin that returned to Jaze a little later to report that she had failed to find Jimboly and Arilou. He listened to her story of events without interrupting.

'So why keep this man alive?' he asked when she finished, looking at Larsh.

'We need him for now,' Hathin said wearily. *And because I promised him I'd let him live*, she added in her own head. *But I promised Dance I'd kill the traitor . . . Oh, I can't think about that now.*

No, now they had other work. The unconscious Therrot, whom Jaze had left lying on the workshop floor, had to be revived and told that he had been cruelly cheated in his hopes of finding his mother alive. On Hathin's insistence they made a quick search, then climbed to the hayloft to claim the four pigeons roosting there.

'If we take them, Jimboly can't report back to her masters just yet,' Hathin explained. 'According to Tomki, *her* pigeons all escaped from her pack when the crowd broke her rattle.'

They were an unhappy little group as they walked back to the Superior's palace. Therrot looked bruised both in body and mind, and could meet nobody's eye. Larsh winced each time a passer-by greeted him sunnily as 'Master Craftsman, sir', his hard-won glory already slipping through his fingers. Hathin fidgeted helplessly, tears in her eyes and a furious flickerbird in her pocket.

Uncharacteristically, it was Jaze who offered her some comfort.

'We'll hear from Jimboly soon,' he murmured. 'She daren't hurt Arilou or you'll release her bird. And she can't go far, or she'll start to unravel. And that means that Arilou can't go far either.'

As it happened, he was only partly right. And the news of

 399

Jimboly and Arilou that arrived next morning was in fact even worse than Hathin had feared.

Tomki, who seemed to have ears in every camp and alley, brought the Reckoning the story.

Arilou still in tow, Jimboly had fled to the edge of the city, where the shacks on its outskirts mingled with the new camps of the Obsidian Trail walkers waiting for Crackgem to become more peaceable. Here Jimboly had unexpectedly bumped into an old enemy. It was Bewliss, the man she had tricked into leading the riot against the palace.

He and his two friends had been delighted to have another chance to deal with the flickerbird witch. In the hope of winning allies, Jimboly had called out to the nearest gaggle of lounging ruffians, who happened to be Mistleman bounty hunters. They had taken no interest in her plight until in desperation she had yelled that she'd come out to bring them a Lace, at which point their sense of chivalry had made a miraculous recovery.

'Once Bewliss and his friends were chased off, it sounds like she tried to backslide and say she wasn't selling Arilou,' explained Tomki, 'but the bounty hunters weren't having any of that. So she got a thank-you and a little money, and off they trotted before anybody could tell them their Lace belonged in a Stockpile.'

'"A Lace?" That's all Jimboly called her?' Jaze frowned. 'That's something then. She may be in the hands of bounty hunters, but *they don't know who they've got.*'

'They will,' Hathin replied, with a miserable sense of urgency and helplessness. 'Even if they don't work it out, once they get to Mistleman's Blunder Minchard Prox will recognize her. We have to go after them, rescue her . . .'

'According to Tomki, there's more than a dozen of these bounty hunters, and they'll be heavily armed,' Jaze said levelly. 'We'd need to send a large part of the Reckoning after them – too large to go easily unnoticed. Also, the bounty hunters have a day's head start on us, and they can walk in the open. With all the new roadblocks and checks, we'd have to take big detours, travel at night, skulk our way along ditches.'

Hathin hung her head, but was touched to notice Jaze's 'we'. He evidently took it as a matter of course that if such a dangerous mission took place he would be a part of it.

'We'd have no hope of catching up with them before they reached Mistleman's Blunder itself,' Jaze continued. 'And everyone there is coiled, waiting for a Lace attack. You can't take a step without somebody checking your teeth. If that wasn't so –' he looked around with a hint of ruefulness on his face – 'then I think half of us would be there already, trying to spirit people from the "Safe Farm" . . . or hunting down Minchard Prox to help Hathin finish her quest.'

Hathin felt sick. It was all true. She had an ugly choice. She could flounder in indecision while Arilou was taken ever further from her, and ever closer to Mistleman's Blunder, or she could send half the Reckoning to their deaths.

But then, quite suddenly, the king of tricks hatched in Hathin's brain, like a baby dragon.

For a while she could do nothing but stand absolutely still while she peered at the idea from every angle, tapping at it with her mind to test its soundness. At last she sidled up to Tomki.

 401

'Um . . . Tomki?' She glanced at him shyly, then whispered the idea to him and watched his jaw drop.

'Dance!' he declared, rallying himself. 'Hathin's got an idea.'

Hathin swallowed, her skin prickling as the assembled Reckoning turned their gaze upon her.

'If I'm right . . .' she began slowly, 'then the Reckoning *can* follow the bounty hunters. *All* of the Reckoning, or as many as we want. They can march by day, and they can use the road. And nobody will stop them. Nobody will even try.

'What we do is this: the Superior sends one of his deputies to talk to the messenger from Mistleman's Blunder, the one who's waiting for an answer to Mr Prox's message. And –' she took a deep breath – 'and the deputy will promise to do exactly what Prox wants: deliver the Stockpile to the Safe Farm. So if they see a big group of the Superior's men setting off with lots of guns, and "guarding" a large number of Lace, they won't be surprised.

'Only the Lace they're guarding won't *be* the Stockpile. It'll be us.'

32
SOUL-STEELING

From the moment Hathin spoke the idea aloud it took on a life of its own, as if she really had loosed a baby dragon. Within an hour it had become a full-grown-dragon idea, and she could see the flame of excitement reflected in every face as it caught and held. Even the Superior, after performing a few pendulum swings between bravado and panic, declared in favour of the plan.

Hathin was present in the great reception hall when Minchard Prox's messenger received his letter of response.

'The city of Jealousy is glad to assist in this time of emergency,' read the letter. 'Our Lace prisoners will be brought under guard to the Safe Farm of Spearhead forthwith. We would be grateful if nothing were to impede our passing.'

As the messenger put away the letter, Hathin felt her stomach lurch. The Superior, the Reckoning, the Stockpile – everybody had now heaped their stake on Hathin's plan, and the die was cast.

But nothing was fast enough for Hathin. While orders were sent out for provisions, Hathin's mind was on Arilou, Arilou, Arilou. Hathin was like a tiny cog in a great clock trying to spin twice as fast and force the rest of the mechanism to do likewise, and so of course she did nothing but rattle herself loose and get in everyone's way.

In the end she gave up and went out into the courtyard with the caged Ritterbit to practise throwing knives at a cloven log.

Louloss had made her the cage, but had insisted on keeping her distance as Hathin cupped Ritterbit's tiny, docile form in her hands and slipped him into it. She had told Hathin to be careful of Ritterbit, and had shaken her head when Hathin promised to keep her shadow away from him.

'That's not what I mean,' she had answered. 'I think he likes you.'

Hathin pondered this as she aimed at the log, threw, recovered her knife, threw it again.

'You're getting better.' She turned to find Therrot slumped on the edge of a fountain. His tone was odd, a mixture of apology and accusation.

'Yes.' It was true. It was so much easier today. Before she had always imagined herself facing an enemy, with her friends' gaze tingling against her back, waiting for her to strike the avenging blow. Now there was just a knife, and a target, and a thing she had to do with her arm, and a cold black marble in her stomach that told her to think of these things and nothing more.

Where had this cold little ball of obsidian come from? Suddenly she remembered struggling with Jimboly in Larsh's workshop, and blindly lashing her knife towards Jimboly's face and neck. And it had not been hard. She had not even needed to think about it. Was that when she had become a real revenger?

'It's about time, isn't it?' She walked back and took aim again.

'Little sister . . .' Therrot flinched as soon as the words had escaped him and seemed to be bracing himself for her outburst. Hathin realized that she did not have one to give him. With a deep sense of loss she realized that the little ball of cold would let her feel no anger towards him, and no fondness either. There was only exhaustion and impatience.

'I'm not your little sister,' she said, as kindly as she could. 'Your little sister is dead.' She sighted up, and her knife shocked cleanly into the heart of the log's rings.

'You sound like Jaze.' Therrot's voice was dazed.

'I know you want to explain about running off with Arilou. I know you feel like you're carrying around this big heavy rock until you can talk to me about it . . . only if you do then you'll be giving *me* the rock. And it'll squash me flat. I have too much to carry in my head already, Therrot. So please, don't.' She could be calm, she could be kind. But how could she make him go away? 'There's so much I have to . . . I have to be ready. I have to be all those things you told me a revenger has to be.'

If you've got enough anger, then you just go mad. A calm, cool sort of mad. And then it's all easy.

'I have to be *good* at this. For when the time comes.'

'No, you don't,' Therrot said quietly. 'You're fine the way you are. Hathin . . . I want you to forget everything I ever tried to teach you. You're not a killer like us . . . like me.'

She stared rigidly at her knife for a few seconds, then sneaked a glance towards Therrot. It was too late, he was already striding away. For some reason she found herself

405

remembering the moment when she had been too slow to wave at Lohan, just before he had dropped out of her world and gone to his doom on the beach. If it had not been for the tight little marble in her stomach, and the comfort of Ritterbit's black bead eyes, Hathin might have burst into tears.

It was very lucky that Jealousy lay in the lap of Crackgem. In Jealousy it was believed that madness was something that came upon you like hiccups, because you had breathed in when Crackgem was breathing out. If you behaved oddly, everyone just tutted and waited for it to pass.

And so when the palace guards were sent out to confiscate every pigeon in the city, people simply muttered, 'Crackgem's breath,' and went about their business.

If Jimboly could not be found, she could at least be prevented from contacting her masters to tell them of Arilou's capture, Larsh's defection. The pigeon coop where Tomki had first seen her had been raided, but nobody knew where she might have another stash of little messengers, so the guards searched haylofts, shacks, even the belfry of the stubby clocktower.

Everywhere the Superior's guards asked after the flicker-bird witch, but Jimboly was nowhere to be found.

Meanwhile, from a hiding place beneath a raised hut, a burning mind pictured Ritterbit's blunt smiling beak accepting seeds from new, young hands.

Jimboly imagined Hathin and Ritterbit walking blithely through palace and town, the invisible gossamer of her own soul tangling in trees, slamming in doors, getting caught in the long legs of elephant birds, each step yanking loose a little more of her spirit.

She thought she could feel herself unravelling already. She lay on her stomach and peered out at the palace.

'I'll wring your sweet little neck,' she muttered. A listener would not have known whether she spoke of Hathin or Ritterbit. 'I should have done it a long time ago.'

She lived in dread of the bounty hunters working out Arilou's identity. If any harm came to that oozy-brain, then her sister, her precious little sister, would think nothing of letting Ritterbit off his leash. And then Ritterbit would forget all about Jimboly and fly right off to the growling, steaming forest of Mother Tooth, where nobody lived but the birds and where axe never swung and sling never whistled.

But what could she do? She could not go after the bounty hunters to retrieve Arilou. She would unravel even more with every step away from Ritterbit.

'Well, neck-wringing it is,' she whispered to herself, then wormed her way out of her hiding place and headed around the wall, looking for somewhere to climb. Her lean brown hands found easy purchase on the flowering creeper, and soon Jimboly was peering over the top of the wall, bright eyes a-flicker with malice.

Ah – but there were guards standing by the palace, guards who would certainly spot Jimboly if she tried to clamber into the courtyard. She was about to drop back down outside the wall when a curtain was tugged aside at a top-storey window of the building, allowing her a glimpse of a small man. His arms were stretched out to either side, and tailors fluttered around him, pinning a lavish travelling robe. One had clearly pushed aside the curtain to let in more light.

'Well, why shouldn't I come?' the little man's voice floated down from the window, with a curiously tremulous bravado. 'I never travelled more than twenty miles from Jealousy while I was alive. What good am I doing here? I can hardly govern the city while playing dead. Besides, what if another assassin should come here and find me without my Lace bodyguard and with half my guards missing? No, heroically leading this endeavour sounds like the only safe and prudent course.'

Jimboly's face broke into a grin and she let herself drop from the wall.

'Oh, there's fun and games being played here!' she muttered as she fled back to the safety of her ditch. 'There's a ghost being measured for new clothes, is there? You crafty old toad! But I can scotch *you*. You're *easy*. You're a thread I can use, old man.'

Crackgem seemed to have noticed that madness was afoot in Jealousy and had woken up to watch it properly. His geysers went off all at once, throwing little rocks so high that they fell on the town, clattering on the roofs like birds in clogs. And at last the volcano trembled so much with laughter that he shook the village of the Sours to pieces, and sent them hurrying with frantic stealth down the mountainside, their precious flag rolled into a sausage and thrown over the shoulders of three strong young men.

The Sours were quite sure that their flag had not lost its power to hide them from Crackgem, but what good was it being invisible to him if he kept fidgeting like that?

There was nothing for it but to come down and join their Laderilou in the valley.

Therrot took it upon himself to tell them where Arilou had gone, and why. He came back with a bruise above his eye, and Jeljech by his side. She had taken custody of his sleeve, as if afraid he would break into a run, and was frowning like thunder.

'I told Jeljech what happened to Arilou, and she . . . she hit me with a pestle. Then their village had a big meeting, and apparently they decided that Arilou's one of them and they want their Lost back. So now Jeljech says she's coming along with us to rescue Arilou. She keeps saying that Crackgem's laughter will wake up the other mountains and that there's not much time.'

It was late afternoon, and the Superior surveyed the massed ranks of the counterfeit 'Stockpile'. There was no way to disguise Dance's prodigious build, but she had been dressed as a man, and grubby bandages covered her face and concealed her wealth of dreadlocks. Some other members of the Reckoning were too recognizable to join their ranks, and it was decided that they should stay behind in Jealousy with the bulk of the 'real' Stockpile.

Nonetheless the numbers in the false Stockpile were impressive. The persecution of the Lace had swollen the Reckoning's numbers overnight. For every village burnt, a handful of fugitives sought the tattoo. For every child or parent lost, a revenger had been born. Minchard Prox might have trembled if he had seen how his decrees had fed the Reckoning, given it new passion and strength.

The 'Stockpile' practised looking woebegone, hunched in their ragged clothing.

'But how are we to conceal weapons under such meagre clothes?' asked the Superior after looking them up and down.

'Actually, sir, they already *are* carrying their weapons.' There was a percussion of clinks, scrapes, rattles and hushes as knives slid from wrist straps, bracelets became garrottes, swords and machetes emerged from back-mounted sheaths.

'Ah . . . ah good,' mumbled the Superior, glancing around at the pictures of his ancestors for reassurance.

Evening came, and Hathin strayed restlessly among the true Stockpile. Even though they had not been told of the Reckoning's plans, they seemed to have picked up on the excitement and tension in the palace, and they all wore apprehensive, curious expressions.

The Superior's secretary, presumably on the instructions of the Superior, was trying to take an inventory of them, a task that seemed to have driven him almost to the end of his tether.

'My good fellow, all I need to know is how you spell your *name*.'

An elderly Lace man frowned slightly and shook his head.

'Look – a pictogram will do. Your mark. *Anything.* How do you write your name?'

'He doesn't.' Jaze had appeared at the secretary's shoulder. 'None of us do. Our names are not meant to be written down. Our names are meant to be forgotten when there is nobody alive who remembers us, so they must never be written down.

Paper has too long a memory, you see.'

'But how am I supposed to keep records? How can I keep track of them all and make sure none of them go missing?'

Records. Missing.

Hathin covered one hand with her mouth, then tugged timidly at Jaze's sleeve, and drew him aside.

'He's right,' she whispered. 'That's what we do. That's what we Lace are always doing. We *go missing*. Jaze, do you still have those pages of Inspector Skein's journal?'

The papers were quickly retrieved from Jaze's pack, and at Hathin's request Jaze consulted the list and found mention of his own village.

'"Seagrin – two eagles, three storms, one join R, one smugglers."' Jaze looked a question at Hathin.

'And the words afterwards – the words that aren't words – can you sound them out? Please?'

Jaze struggled in mouthing the unfamiliar syllables. Even after he had pronounced the final, short word, it took a moment or two before either of them recognized it. It was a mangled version of his own name.

'No wonder you couldn't read those words,' breathed Hathin. 'They were never meant to be written down at all. They're names. *Lace* names. And Inspector Skein was trying to spell them out with Doorsy letters. Jaze, I think you're in the list because you disappeared to join the Reckoning. "One join R" – that's you.

'Carried off by eagles, drowned by storms, killed by smugglers, joining the Reckoning – they're all reasons why people might vanish overnight and never be seen by their village again. Poor Inspector Skein's letter to Sightlord Fain talked about deaths and disappearances on the Coast of the Lace – and that's what the Inspector was looking into. *Lace* deaths. *Lace* disappearances. He was visiting all the Lace villages, making a list of everyone who'd vanished suddenly, and even noting down why the village *believed* they had disappeared.'

'So,' Jaze said, very quietly, 'you're saying that there's another reason for these disappearances? That our enemies were behind it all along, and the Inspector was investigating them?'

'I think we need to talk to Uncle Larsh,' said Hathin.

Master Craftsman Larsh was kept locked in a buttery, partly for his own safety, for there were many among the Reckoning who were sickened by his continued existence. He looked up as Jaze and Hathin entered, his eyes very tired and old.

'Disappearances,' said Jaze, without preamble. 'Disappearances on the Coast of the Lace, these last few years.'

Larsh sighed, and his gaze dropped to the floor.

'I never had much part in it,' he said wearily. His hands fidgeted, tweaking and plucking at his bread ration, fashioning a little figure from it. 'They came past the Hollow Beasts cove sometimes at night, convoys with Lace prisoners. Sometimes I hid them in the caves. Once during some bad storms I had to guide a convoy up the coast, but only as far as a quay at Pericold Heights. I don't know where they went after that.'

Pericold Heights, the place where the Lost sent their minds so that they could judge the coming winds by the

412

wavering of the banner of steam from Mother Tooth. The closest point on the coast to Mother Tooth . . .

'I know where they take them,' breathed Hathin. 'Mother Tooth's island.' In her mind's eye she was remembering Bridle's map of Mother Tooth, with its strange rectangular shadows. Not rocks, not lakes – no, shapes made by the hands of man. No wonder the charts of the Safe Farms had reminded her of them so strongly.

'Dance told me the pigeon men were sending mining supplies to the coast. Those shapes on the map of Mother Tooth – I think they're *mines*.' Mother Tooth, more fitful and dangerous even than Crackgem. Nobody would live there, let alone dig into her shuddering rock by *choice*. But what if the miners had not gone there by choice? What if they had been stolen from their villages in ones and twos? What if they were Lace, who were *expected* to go missing, who would never be missed? And for how many years had this been going on before a man named Inspector Skein got suspicious and started taking notes? Was this discovery the reason for the deaths of the Lost?

Jaze's face reminded Hathin of a naked blade, and she guessed that his thoughts were running parallel to her own. She wondered what expression she herself wore.

She looked at Larsh and felt only numb. He had shrunk – she could look right through him; there were much bigger foes to find.

'You can't follow the trail back,' sighed the craftsman. 'My orders came from Port Suddenwind, and if you try to trace anything back there you go mad. Even the man I report to in Mistleman's Blunder is nobody. Suddenwind is a mountain of paper laws and orders, full of faceless people.

Faceless people.

Faceless. A man without a face had done all this.

Hathin thought of Minchard Prox and realized that she could remember only his scars, and the flick of his pencil as he struck out Lace villages. He no longer had a face. At last she felt something through the numbness. At last she knew the calm madness of the revenger.

33
THE KING OF TRICKS

The next morning everyone woke to find that Lord Crack-gem had stopped laughing. The very air felt as if it was caught in that half-second between a breath and someone starting to speak. Everything including the volcano seemed to be waiting, listening.

The early-morning streets were hushed when the palace gates swung wide, letting out the bleary guards with their unfamiliar muskets and their red-looking, newly shaven chins. The Superior was riding in an absurd little carriage like a giant perambulator, pulled by three elephant birds, all of which seemed to have strong but different navigational viewpoints. He too seemed headachey and sluggish.

In contrast, Hathin felt restive, unable to settle on anything. The other Lace seemed just as bad. There was also a fitful stirring within Ritterbit's cage, and a warning fidget in the songs of the birds in the hedge and brush. The package train of elephant birds continually shrugged and huffed their flanks, bouncing their packs. This was a day when the earth might open as silently as a fish mouth and pour out mysteries.

Hathin herself had been given a new disguise, though still a boyish one, and slunk along beside the Superior's tottering carriage. A rough hooded cape covered her face, her form and the flickerbird cage in her hand, so that they could not be recognized by Jimboly. Not far away she could see Jeljech, her hand still resting on Therrot's arm as though he was her prisoner, her green Sour garments traded in for less distinctive clothes. They walked with the other members of the Stockpile, flanked by guards.

Overnight, the rain-pitted mud of the track seemed to have cooked into lizard ridges, and the irrigation channels were all dry. It was strange to walk the Obsidian Trail against the flow of heat-dazed families staggering past with their buckets of black glass. Roadblocks melted before their party's liveries and muskets, questions evaporated before the petulant authority of the Superior. Granted, at the road blocks nearest to Jealousy some consternation was caused by the appearance of a Superior who showed no signs of being dead. As the convoy travelled further from Jealousy, however, the guards they met seemed less startled by this. Clearly news of his 'death' had not reached everywhere.

Afternoon came, but the heat and oppression of the air remained relentless, and the sky unclouded. For the first time in weeks, the monsoon rain missed its daily appointment.

All the while, the Reckoning kept an eye out for traces of the bounty hunters that had taken Arilou. Near evening they found the remains of a campsite. On a slab of black stone, Hathin found the white imprint of a long-palmed hand. Instinctively she recognized its shape, and saw a meaning in the way it had been laid so carefully, so cleanly, against the rock.

'It's Arilou!' Hathin felt a pang, amid her excitement and

pride. 'Look – she must have used bonfire ash. She left it for me. She knows – she can see me coming for her.'

That night, in spite of her weariness, Hathin sat up for many hours, close to the campfire. Arilou's mind would come looking for Hathin, she was sure, and be drawn to the light. Over and over Hathin performed the same mime, while staring upwards towards the stars. She pointed to her sleeping companions one after the other, counting them, and then held up a stick and made the same number of notches with her fingernail. When at last she slept, a pile of such tiny sticks pillowed her head, and etched grooves into her cheek.

The second day was hotter than the first. The air trembled and the shadows blackened, and now the invisible denizens of the world of mysteries seemed almost as real as the palpable.

And was Jimboly out there too, scampering alongside the road with the half-seen imps of Hathin's imagination? No, surely not – hopefully she would not know that Hathin and Ritterbit had left the town with the convoy; Hathin had changed her disguise for exactly this reason. Jimboly would be lurking in Jealousy, watching the palace, fidgeting with the uneasy sense that loop after loop of her soul's cloth was pulling away from her.

Sometimes Hathin almost thought she saw the fine scarlet thread of Jimboly's soul stretching from Ritterbit's cage. At other times she imagined a thicker, duller purple strand tethered to her own heart and pulling her down the road. At the other end was Arilou. She knew now that however angry, frightened, tired or despairing she became, the tug of that thread would always bite through the numbness, pull her across plains and over mountains and through rivers.

Could souls become entangled? Could she have somehow snagged a soul thread from a man called Minchard Prox, a woman called Dance, a lost brother called Therrot? It was as if they were all caught up in a great web and could feel each other's motions as tremors through their own spirits. Fate was starting to pull the threads taut, drawing them all towards one another.

That evening the revengers discovered their quarries' next camp. By the bonfire lay a single green stem, clumsily scored with seven thumbnail creases. Arilou had marked it as Hathin had shown her. Arilou had seven guards.

The Reckoning made camp, the sun went down, and for hours Hathin had a new dance. She would pluck rough seed heads from their stems and then advance, taking care to drop them so that each head pointed in the direction she was walking. She might have gone through the same motions all night if Jaze had not intervened.

'Get some sleep, or you'll be no good to your sister when you find her.'

Just after sunrise on the third day the cloud bank that had been sliding towards them split and they could see the barbed and blackened tip of Spearhead. It appeared to rip upwards like a claw through gauze. Before now only Dance had filled Hathin with the same awe, the same sense of something momentous and unforgiving.

At first the jungle was a distant smear of murky green, but by mid-afternoon the road had curved close enough to its tangle for the travellers to make out plaited vines, orchids fading like wrinkled silk, and occasionally a monkey flinging itself so fast from bough to bough that it seemed to fly through the green. The jungle could easily have offered cover for a dozen spies or attackers, but it was not this that kept every hackle raised, rather the continuing sense of blood-level strangeness.

Once Hathin thought she saw a shadowy figure waiting for them by the road ahead, a creature with a bird-like head and long black fingers. But half a mile became a quarter of a mile, and as she drew closer the shape pulled itself apart like a cloud. Its slender body became a carved black tethering post, its fingers and the plumes on the back of its head became wavering fern fronds, its beak two leaves rubbing tips. And yet as she passed it she felt her skin tingle as if the Gripping Bird really was standing right there in the light of the sun, too bold to be seen, and watching her pass with eyes of sapphire blue.

Miles passed without conversation. No Lace could help twitching a glance about them every couple of seconds, as if their wits were flea-bitten.

'What is it? What? What is wrong with you all?' asked the Superior at one point, his voice squeaky with tension. His face was flushed and queasy from the jolting of his little carriage.

To do Jaze justice, he really tried to explain what every Lace was feeling, although there were hardly words to describe it, even in their own language.

'This sun is not our sun. This sky is not our sky. Behind all this gold and blue and green there is the jet blackness of the deepest caves. We cannot see the ancient things that walk alongside us . . . but we can feel them licking our faces.'

 419

The Superior did not ask for another explanation.

The roadblocks were now more frequent and better organized. Each time they halted, Hathin kept her mouth bitten into a narrow line. It was becoming easier to suppress her smile. Now the questions were more searching, and there were precarious moments when someone looked as if they might search the 'prisoners'. Hathin could see the Superior's own guards swallowing and exchanging looks, clearly unsure how they had found themselves in this situation. Although the guards did not know about the plan to rescue the infamous Lady Arilou, they were quite aware that their prisoners were not real prisoners, and that for some reason they were playing a part in a strange charade.

The Superior's presence saved them. Soldiers who might have caused problems stood cowed by the ancestral lace of his sleeves, the dusty embroidery of his silk travelling cap, the mildewed campaign tent bundled on to the backs of the pack-birds. Even the fact he was so tiny and crabbed seemed to speak in his favour. The pressure of his inheritance had squashed, like a blob of warm, pink wax beneath the cold weight of an ancient signet ring.

Just after sunset they found the remains of the bounty hunters' camp, but this time there were signs that it had merged with another, larger camp, spreading across the crushed grass like a double-yolked egg. Hathin swallowed drily and stooped to pick up a green stick. She tried to count the thumbnail creases that striped it, but they were too densely packed and her eyes blurred.

Jaze knelt and prodded at a stripped stem with only the

420

seed head left untouched. The seed head did not point along the well-trodden track, but along a narrower path.

'It looks as if they took her straight to the Safe Farm, not to Mistleman's Blunder. This is last night's camp – she'll be there by now.' Jaze looked up at Hathin, and the evening light shifted in his eyes in a way that resembled sympathy. 'It might buy your sister a little time. If Minchard Prox is in Mistleman's Blunder, perhaps nobody at the Farm will work out who she is . . .'

Hathin could suddenly feel every ache of her journey, every blister from her new boots, every lost hour of sleep. She staggered over to a roll of cloth that had been unloaded from the Superior's carriage, sat heavily upon it and dropped her face into her hands.

She did not raise her face again until bonfire smoke stung her eyes. She looked about her, and found that there were only a handful of Lace still sitting up around the fire. The Superior had retired to his tent, his guards to the perimeter of the camp. Jeljech had apparently fallen asleep against Therrot's shoulder, her face locked in a frown, one of his arms still imprisoned by hers.

'That's right,' Therrot said gently as Hathin came closer. 'You've got to eat. Come and join us . . . Hathin, what are you doing?'

Tears streaming down her face, Hathin was scooping up the loose earth, making a mound.

'She's watching me, she'll be scared, she'll want to know what to do, what I'm going to do, what's going to happen . . .' Hands trembling, she was fashioning a little mountain, just as she had when she was helping Arilou find herself. She gave her little volcano a crater, with a kinked lip and a barb like a spear's head.

She stood up and spent a few seconds staring at it. Spearhead in miniature, the mountain that had carried off Arilou. She recovered her breath, and then kicked her mountain so hard that she staggered and fell over sideways. She scrambled to her feet again, stamped in the lip of the crater, started avalanches with her heel, ground crags to rubble. She kept kicking until the mountain scattered into the undergrowth.

Arilou, I am coming for you. The mountains themselves will not stop me.

She walked back, shaky and muddy, and dropped into her previous seat. Although she had said nothing, she sensed that the other Lace had guessed the meaning of her mime as clearly as though she had shouted her thoughts.

She looked defiant, and braced herself for the tidal wave of her friends' common sense. The wave did not strike.

'It's time,' said Dance. Her words were met with a silence that was agreement, and Hathin realized that a conversation had been hanging in the air, waiting to be had. All the Lace had known. Hathin alone had been too distracted to notice it.

'I know,' Jaze said carefully. 'We'll never get this close to the Farm again – not so many of us, not so well armed and provisioned.'

'Let us look at the map.' Dance reached into her pack and pulled out a rather familiar-looking picture of Spearhead seen from above. Evidently she had responded to Hathin and Jaze's information by raiding Bridle's shop. Hathin glimpsed a Bridle map of Mother Tooth in the backpack as well, complete with the telltale rectangles of the mine huts and compounds. Hathin wondered whether Dance was planning a rescue raid there as well.

'How many are we thinking?' whispered Louloss, casting a glance towards the barbed black hulk that Spearhead had become. 'Arilou, of course – but how many more?'

'Who deserves to stay up there?' asked Therrot, folding his arms. Everyone else stared into the campfire and nodded slowly.

'They are not just prisoners of Minchard Prox,' murmured Dance. 'The Lord –' she nodded towards Spearhead – 'won't like it. He dislikes intruders, but now they're there he'll see them as his to sacrifice or punish.' Her tone was antagonistic but with a hint of affection, as if the volcano was a cantankerous uncle.

'There *is* a way of getting up the mountain without the Lord noticing us,' answered Therrot. 'In fact – Hathin's sitting on it.'

Hathin jerked herself forward on to her knees and peered over her shoulder at the long sausage of rolled cloth she had been sitting upon. For the first time she noticed its faint smell of smoky damp. She snatched back a corner of the sacking cover and found herself staring at an inky cloth that left shadowy blue stains on her fingertips.

She stared around her, and found her flabbergasted look mirrored in every face but two. From under Dance's bandages, a single dark eye was staring at Therrot, a little orb of storm.

Therrot looked rueful and gave the tiniest of shrugs. 'The

Sours insisted – they thought we might need it to get their Lost back.'

Faces locked in a wince, half a dozen Lace turned to peer towards the Superior's distant tent. Everybody's mind was busy with the same image: the Superior riding along in his little carriage, unaware that his esteemed ancestors were bouncing above him in a bundle of blue cloth.

'It's just a *flag*, all right?' hissed Therrot. 'He can't tell how it was made by looking at it, can he?'

'Therrot,' said Jaze, 'when you pass through the Cave of Caves you might find a great number of angry people waiting to talk to you about this.'

'All right.' Dance pulled off her bandages and pensively gave her dreadlocks freedom. 'We use the protection of the flag. But this is a task for those who have finished their quests, and those alone. The others have work still to do before they pass through the Caves. They will remain with the Superior for now.'

A slow nod from Jaze, Therrot, Louloss, Marmar. Nothing more need be said to make it clear that those who climbed the mountain were probably not coming back.

'What about me?' Hathin asked. Nobody answered. Nobody met her eye.

Suddenly inspired, she fumbled at her belt pouch. Yes, inside there was still a piece of cloth twisted into a tiny bundle. She pinched it, and it gave a little between her fingers with a grainy lumpiness.

'Wait, you can't go without me . . . I'm *meant* to come. Even if the flag hides you all from the Lord when you're climbing, he will surely notice when his prisoners start to disappear down into the valley. Dance, I think *I* can distract him. I have *this*. It's a gift, sent to him by his Lady.'

It was her pocketful of Sorrow, the keepsake that the white mountain had told her to take to Spearhead. Spearhead was unforgiving, but he had a weakness, like the chink in his crater rim. Unlike the King of Fans, he had not chosen to forget the past. Instead he burned with the memory of it, and the heart of that memory was his love for Sorrow.

It was Tomki who broke the astonished silence.

'I think Hathin can do it. You know what she's like when she's possessed.'

'When I'm *what*?' Hathin stared at him, stupefied.

'Oh . . . sorry.' Tomki wrinkled his brow amicably. 'Not possessed then . . . but, you know, when that other spirit takes over your body and makes everyone obey you.'

'Oh, *that* spirit.' Therrot's forehead cleared. 'The one that took control in the ditch outside Jealousy, and again in the market place when Hathin claimed that woman for the Stockpile, and again when the palace was under attack, and . . .'

'And when you hit me.' Tomki smiled at Hathin with a hint of embarrassment. 'You know, when your voice changes, and your personality changes, and the little worried crinkles in your forehead disappear, and you're suddenly eight feet tall . . .'

'I've never been eight feet tall—'

'Not *eight* feet, certainly, Tomki,' Jaze corrected Tomki gently. 'Anyway, let it be. If Hathin does not want to talk about the other spirit, we should respect that.'

Hathin was about to protest again, but Dance was leaning

forward. Red specks of firelight wandered lost in her eyes like the torches of benighted travellers. 'Do you really believe that this is your path?'

Hathin's sleep-starved world tipped and bobbed as she nodded.

'Then come, Hathin.' Dance stood. 'We shall talk to the Superior about a parting of the ways. The rest of you, sleep. I will wake you when the night is darker.'

The Superior's tent was perched on the edge of the forest, and about it fireflies surged and spiralled like mind-stars before a faint. As they grew closer Hathin's numb mind suddenly realized that there were other lights, candles and burning brands. These were held up by a handful of guards who stood rigidly before the Superior's tent, as if enchanted. Even then she might have sleepwalked into the midst of them if Dance's large hand had not settled firmly on her shoulder and squeezed it, commanding her to remain still and silent.

Candle-pale, the Superior stood among his guards in the same spellbound state. He was talking to a tree. The tree had a face. The tree spoke back.

It was a wicked bride vine, she realized, the sort of creeper that covered every inch of a tree, then remained as a hollow vestige when the real tree had been throttled and rotted away. Like other children she had sometimes used them as hiding places, climbed up inside them using the side-winding vines like rungs.

The face in the tree was longer than a sleepless night and more bitter than a broken dream. Its black eyes gleamed with a frosted madness. Even the smile that opened in its face was not really a smile, just a jewelled multicoloured gash.

426

'All you need to do,' the Jimboly-tree told the Superior in a rough-cut Doorsy, 'is get me that bird. The little bird in the cage. Otherwise . . .'

A lean brown hand reached out among the vines. It held a pot, shaped like a pot-bellied dignitary. It was one of the cremation urns from the Ashlands where the Superior's ancestors were buried.

34

A TOOTH FOR A TOOTH

Hathin's mind snapped out of its dream-like acceptance and understood what she was seeing. Jimboly must have been following them every step of the way, flanking them along the ditches, waiting for a chance to speak to the Superior when the Reckoning were not listening. Jimboly could have given them away to any roadblock they passed, but had probably been afraid that in a scuffle Ritterbit might be loosed from his cage.

The Superior's guards stood poised, uncertain, staring at their master. The Superior had one hand raised as if he had held it up to halt his men, then forgotten about it. Dance hung back in the darkness, frowning at the strange confrontation, and Hathin remembered that Dance did not speak Doorsy.

'I hope you have no ideas about attacking me up here,' continued the Jimboly-tree, its face some twelve feet above the ground. 'I think this is –' she turned the pot and scowled at it – 'the fifteenth Duke of Sedrollo?'

'. . . Glorious-Victor-of-the-battle-of-Polmannock-Order-of-the-Silver-Hare-Vice-Admiral-of-the-Rainhallow-Expeditionary . . .' managed the Superior in a wispy, breathless squeak.

428

'Really? Well, if you guards take one step towards this tree, then the Vice-Admiral learns to fly. He goes away to explore the world, carried on the wind and the backs of beetles. He is swallowed by pitcher plants and is ground into the road by the boot-soles of soldiers. Besides, there are half a dozen more of your ancestors hidden in the forest. Some of their pots are missing their lids. Without me you have no chance of finding them before some spider monkey pokes his finger in to see how they taste.'

'Whu-heu-nerp,' commented the Superior, his face grey.

'The girl will be sleeping. Send someone to knock her on the head and bring the cage to me. Then you can have a family reunion.'

'I . . .' The Superior stared shakily up at the little pot, which Jimboly was tilting dangerously so that the lid slipped to one side. 'I gave my . . . my word to the girl . . .'

The pot upended, and the lid fell away, followed by a flurry of fine powder that dusted leaves and pattered on ferns. The Superior gave a wail of anguish and ran forward to clutch at it, trying to cup it in his hands. He fell to his knees, staring at his grey-freckled fingers, his face so colourless that it appeared he too might crumble to ash.

'Now.' The lean brown hand had reappeared among the vines, holding a second, slightly bigger pot. 'The *sixteenth* Duke of Sedrollo . . .'

'Stop!' Hathin could not contain herself. Ritterbit's cage still in her hand, she ran out into the circle of torchlight. 'Listen! Sir, your ancestors are not in those pots! There has been no human ash in them for years!'

'Whu-what? But where . . . ?'

429

'Don't listen to her!' screamed Jimboly. 'Grab her! Take the bird!'

'Oh, someone fetch a flask of water! He's going all blotchy . . .' Hathin knelt beside the Superior. 'It's true, sir. All the ash was stolen years and years ago and . . . and used to make dye . . .' Too late Hathin was regretting sliding off down the toboggan slope of truth. '. . . And someone, um, filled the urns with animal ash. Sheep. And goats.'

The Superior whimpered faintly and stared out into the twisted madness of the jungle. Hathin wondered if he was imagining a spectral landscape obscured by mounds of rich velvets, toothpicks, hair combs and paper money, amid which scrambled ghostly goats and sheep, uttering soft, confused bleats as their hoofs slithered on vast cascades of mutton-fat soap.

'Sheep?' he remarked in a tiny, choked voice. 'Goats?' he added, then fell over on to his side, gurgling for breath.

'You fool!' screeched the Jimboly-tree. 'What good is he to either of us now? Stamp your foot through the drum of his existence, why don't you? Well, I hope he dies from it!'

'Please, sir,' Hathin put a tentative hand on the Superior's shoulder. 'It's not . . .' Not that bad?

'All these years I've been . . . I'm . . .' He still seemed to be choking. 'I'm . . . an *orphan*. I'm . . . I'm *alone*. I'm . . . I'm . . . I'm . . . *free*.' He pushed himself up on one elbow, staring at his hands as if for the first time they had become his own. 'I can . . . I can do *anything*. I can leave Jealousy! I can break my spectacles and run off barefoot to become a . . . a . . . cobbler! I can . . . I can marry my housekeeper! Do I have a housekeeper? I never had time to notice! But now I can get a housekeeper! And marry her!'

He struggled to his feet and staggered away wild-eyed, presumably in search of a housekeeper.

As more of the camp came running in, drawn by the sound of raised voices, the spellbound guards remembered themselves and set about slashing at the wicked bride vine turret. Jimboly's face disappeared, and a turbulence rippled downward through the leaves. Two ferns at the base thrashed asunder, and then Jimboly's lean figure could be seen sprinting off into the jungle.

'Stop her!' Hathin called out in Lace. 'She knows who we are! She knows who Arilou is!'

Dance lurched out of the darkness in pursuit of Jimboly, past the startled guards, all of whom had sufficient presence of mind to get out of her way.

Hathin snatched up a lantern and gave herself no time to think before plunging into the jungle too. She stumbled on with the lantern in one hand, Ritterbit's cage in the other, while great leaves slapped at her face. Other lanterns bobbed around amid the trees like overgrown fireflies. Eventually the giant fireflies convened, illuminating a dozen grim faces. Nobody had found Jimboly.

'She will not have gone far,' said Jaze. 'She cannot.' He pointed towards Ritterbit, whose wings were now flickering so fast one expected him to whittle himself out of his cage. 'But our eyes are still full of firelight – we need time for the darkness to clean them before we have a hope of seeing her.'

'We don't have time,' said Therrot, who was still catching his breath. 'We don't have the time to search an entire jungle for one dentist.'

'Then . . . Then I have to climb Spearhead *now*, don't I?' faltered Hathin. 'If I take a curved route up the mountain through the jungle, steering away from the roads and the Farm, she'll follow me, and she won't be able to run off and tell anyone we're here or get in your way. I can draw her off, and distract Lord Spearhead like we planned when I reach the top.'

'I can go instead,' Therrot said quickly. 'It doesn't have to be Hathin. I can take the bird and the gift for the Lord—'

'Hathin is Sorrow's chosen messenger,' Dance cut in. 'But . . . you can go with her, Therrot. Keep Hathin safe, and report back to us if she is granted an audience with Lord Spearhead.'

Spearhead did not have Crackgem's spitting madness, Sorrow's barren beauty or the King of Fans' rock-strewn majesty. Spearhead wore his jungle like a ragged wolf's pelt. He bristled like a wounded beast. A cloud of rage cloaked his head, and he could see nothing beyond it.

Hathin was still carrying her lantern, for if she did not, how would Jimboly see her? The canopy above was dense and cut out a good deal of the light. Therrot had been ordered to follow under cover of the shadows, the better to surprise Jimboly if she attacked. Even though Hathin knew that he must be behind her, matching his step to hers to hide the crack of undergrowth beneath his feet, it was hard not to feel alone, hard to resist the temptation to look for reassurance.

For reassurance? But what was Therrot? He was not her big brother. He was just a shape behind her in the darkness,

432

a man with blood on his hands, somebody she did not really know.

Her eye dropped to Ritterbit's cage, and a smile crept on to her face despite herself. She felt a little throb of fellowship every time his fantail bobbed between the bars. A black bead of an eye gleamed in the darkness within, and found an answer in the black bead in her stomach. Perhaps Ritterbit was her little brother now.

A few of the trees seemed to fold and ooze like raw pastry, and had great holes in them. Climbing through one she laid her foot down, only to feel the ground tremble beneath it, like the flank of a vast animal. Occasionally there was a hint of panicked motion in the trees above, a monkey's trapeze swing, a bird belting through the foliage like a slingshot. But they did not seem to be fleeing from her, rather she thought they were all moving past her towards the lower ground.

She walked and walked, and her chest tightened as she started to see occasional blackened trees. They seemed to stand as warnings to the others around them, like courtiers who had said the wrong thing. Warnings to the other trees, and to Hathin herself.

The ground grew steeper, the going more difficult, the air colder and harder to breathe. The mist-clouds came down and softly surged through the trees to meet her. Was Therrot still behind her? She dared not look back.

A mist-filled ravine gaped unexpectedly to her right, trees leaning over it dangerously with their roots splayed as though it had just opened and they were bending over to peer in. From its depths came a fluctuating hiss and the damp, stinging fragrance of singed greenery.

 433

She began edging along the side of the crack, but flinched into a crouch as she felt the ground shift slightly again beneath her feet. There was a distant sound, which to her bewildered ears sounded like some great beast coughing, and then suddenly the leaves around her were shaking as some-thing fell upon them like rain. Tiny grey rocks the size of birds' eggs were falling and bouncing, light as hazelnuts. They stung her back and neck, and she ducked beneath one of the tipping trees.

Lord Spearhead had noticed her. He would not let her talk; he would not even let her approach.

To her right, away from the ravine, a phantom forest of stencilled grey ferns and boughs twitched and jumped with the stony downpour. And it was from this dancing, ghostly forest that Jimboly came leaping, her red bandanna like a war-flag.

As the dentist's weight slammed into her, Hathin lost her grip on the lantern and it bounced to the ground to light the world lopsided. It was all Hathin could do to throw one arm around the nearest stooping tree to stop herself tumbling backwards into the chasm. There was now only a frail net of dry vines between her and a long, dark fall, and these were creaking and starting to give as Jimboly's weight forced her backwards. One of Jimboly's lean, strong hands dug into Hathin's face, forcing her back, and the other grabbed at the handle of Ritterbit's cage. With a strength born of desper-ation Hathin yanked the cage free and beat Jimboly across the face with it, seeing her enemy's eyes fog.

Just as Therrot burst from the ferns behind Jimboly, the vines supporting Hathin finally gave way. She lost her grip on the tree, her nails gouging furrows in the lichen and breaking against the wood. The fall welcomed her, it had been waiting for her, her insides were become air already . . . then she felt a thick, woody, vertical vine graze her arm and snatched at it reflexively, ripping the skin from her hands and struggling to twist a leg around it.

Below her she was faintly aware that she could see a curling green creeper quietly hissing itself to death, wrinkling and wilting as if time itself had grown impatient. Lower still she thought she glimpsed a dull, hungry glow of red.

She could hear sounds of struggle over her head, but could see only maddened shivers of the leaf mosaic above, and beyond it the pale bar of the leaning tree. Hathin clenched her teeth, took a deep breath, then smashed Ritterbit's cage against the rocky wall of the abyss.

The scattering of wood was almost musical, a chorus of surprised plinks and patters. A wicked bit of shadow flew free, his wing-tricks quick as a whiplash, his path as changeable as a traitor's smile. Up flew Ritterbit to land high on the tilting tree above, where he fanned his feathered cards and hid them, fanned them and hid them. There was a scream from Jimboly.

The sounds of combat abruptly ceased. At the same time she noticed Jimboly creeping along the slanting tree towards the taunting, twirling shape of Ritterbit. Again and again he waited for her imploring hand to come within inches of him before hopping out of reach.

The vine had never intended to bear something of Hathin's weight. Queasily she sensed it giving, pulling away from the wall of the ravine. *Therrot, Therrot.* But the woman who had killed his family was up there, vulnerable, distracted.

435

And Hathin was not really his little sister.

A chip of bark fell into Hathin's eye. Something *was* coming down towards her with a slither and crack, showering her face with leaves. She peered up and there he was. Therrot, his face mask-like with concentration, one of his legs hooked over a knob of roots, leaning down towards the vine that held her.

Hathin's grip slipped a little, and as the dry stem rasped in her fingers it caught Jimboly's attention. For a moment the dentist turned her head to look at her. There was hatred in her dark eyes, and madness, but also a hint of incomprehension.

You are dust, her eyes said. *You are dirt. You are nothing. Why do you bother surviving? Why are you still alive?*

I am the dust in your eyes, was the answer in Hathin's look. *I am the dirt that will bury you. I am the nothingness waiting to open up under your feet. And I can hold on longer than you can.*

Hathin opened her mouth and screamed. It was not a scream of pain or fear; it was the explosion of the little black egg in her core which had been waiting to hatch. As the sound split the air Ritterbit bulleted skywards, and disappeared into the mist. And Jimboly, giving a croaking echo to Hathin's cry, groped wildly at him as he passed, lost her balance and fell into the chasm.

Crash followed crash followed crash, and then there was silence but for a long, hungry hiss. And not another sound rose from the earthy throat that had swallowed Jimboly whole.

Therrot said nothing as he scrambled precariously down the side of the ravine, finding footholds and handholds among the splayed roots. At last he was on a level with Hathin, and could pull her vine towards him so that she could climb up him like a ladder to the top. He clambered up after her, and she could see for the first time the fingernail marks on his cheeks. She did not resist when he crouched next to her and almost crushed her with a hug.

It took a minute or so for Hathin's head to stop spinning, and for her to realize why the forest was so silent.

'The stone rain's stopped.'

'Yes. I think the Lord's willing to talk to you now, at least.' Therrot glanced over his shoulder at the ravine into which Jimboly had fallen. 'He understands vengeance. And revengers.'

Hathin stood rather shakily, and Therrot followed suit. The mist had cleared a little uphill, and they could now see that they were approaching a steeper slope where the jungle thinned away. They had taken a few paces towards it when both halted and looked at each other.

'It's up to you.' Therrot answered the unasked question. 'I'll walk with you to the crater's lip and beyond if it means I can protect you. But if my presence would endanger you . . .'

The same thought had dropped into both their minds at the same time. If Spearhead had been watching the destruction of Jimboly he might approve Hathin as a revenger, but Therrot was a different matter. The village destroyed by Jimboly's machinations had been Therrot's, just as it had been Hathin's. And yet when he could have killed the murderess of his family, he had made another choice. He had left the fight to save Hathin. He had chosen his 'little sister'.

Hathin threw her arms around him again and squeezed with all her might. When she looked up his face was hesitant and expectant.

'The Lord might not understand,' she whispered, and saw a look of desolate anxiety steal across his face. 'And somebody needs to go back to the others and tell them that I'm near the top. But you'll listen out all the time, won't you? And if it sounds like he's angry . . . will you come and get me?'

Swallowing drily, she did her best to pull the leaves from her hair and rub the tree sap from her clothes and, having wiped her boots and done what she could to make herself presentable, Hathin walked up through the fraying forest to talk to Lord Spearhead alone.

35
LORD SPEARHEAD

As the upward slope became steeper, the living trees gave way to the dead. Solitary bone-white trees that time had stripped of their bark. The cloud breathed by Lord Spearhead was chill and blinding, for it was revenge that he exhaled.

After an age the broken trees became sparser, and she no longer needed to clamber over fallen trunks. The tangling roots were replaced by a shifting, sinking slope of tiny rocks, puckered with holes like ocean sponges. Every footstep sank and slid into the slope, pebbles slipping into the lip of Hathin's boots. One false step could send her sliding back, bringing down a torrent of tiny rocks to bury her entirely.

She was high now – she could feel it through the singing in her head, the way her lungs heaved helplessly at the thin air. Spearhead was taller than any of the other mountains she had climbed. His cold mist bit through her thin clothes, and her face burned with effort.

But then at long last she felt rock under her hand, a crumbling crag of it. She scrabbled for purchase and pulled herself upward, finding fingerholds and toeholds by touch. Finally she heaved herself on to the top of the crag with such determination that she nearly lost her balance. With an internal yelp, Hathin found that she had run out of 'up' and there was nothing but the sheerest drop before her.

Hathin screwed her eyes shut, until she became aware of a brightness behind her lids. She looked around to find that the cloud on all sides had thinned to a gauze, leaving everything around her soaked through with moonlight. She could even make out the deep, meaty red of the stone on which she sat, and the tulip-shapes of blackened rocks that fluted steam into the air near her feet.

Below and about her was a rolling landscape of thicker cloud, and jutting up from it a vast scattered ring of prongs and peaks. Hathin herself was perched on the highest. Her mind reeled as she realized that she must have clambered to the very tip of Spearhead's 'spear' and now teetered on the brink of the Lord's crater.

The vapour beneath her swirled, and Hathin saw that there was a large lake down in the throat of the crater, turned by the moon into a ragged-edged mirror of mother-of-pearl. It was like finding a single perfect tear in the eye of a great and terrible beast, and for a moment Hathin could only stare entranced by the beauty of the scene. The next, the earth shook beneath her with a growl that she could feel vibrate through the marrow of her bones.

Hathin was the first to feel the slight tremor, but not the last. The ripple passed onward and outward, making its dark and secret way through the earth.

As it moved down the slope through the forest, flock after flock of birds erupted from the trees like soft-winged bombs, and monkeys filled the air with shrieking. The chasm that had swallowed Jimboly gaped a little wider, and two trees toppled into its darkness.

Fence posts hiccuped out of their sockets. Down in the Superior's camp, a servant trying to mop the Superior's forehead ended up poking his employer in the eye. In Mistleman's Blunder, diamond windowpanes rattled in their frame so that the moonlight scintillated in them like dragonfly scales.

Working late in his study in the courthouse, Prox had to swoop to save his inkwell, and watched his rebellious pens skipping away from him across the table. He glanced at a stoppered bottle on his windowsill, and relaxed slightly. The quaver of the ground had barely stirred the reddish sediment in the base of the bottle. The pendulum on the stand beside it was swinging only with a slight and lazy motion. Spearhead stirring in his sleep, that was all. Nothing more.

In his own study, Camber looked up as though somebody had knocked, and continued staring out through his moonlit window long after the tremor had passed.

And down on the lower slopes of Spearhead, nine revengers who had been creeping through the darkness threw themselves flat and waited, a dark blue cloth shrouding their prone forms.

Hathin held on tight, feeling the vast crag beneath shift slantwise a few inches. Then there was only a faint throb in the rock.

Was it a growl of warning? She could only hope not. She could only hope that in his basalt tones Spearhead was talking to her.

Face clammy with cloud and her own cooling perspiration,

 441

Hathin raised herself to her knees and tried to wipe the caked dust from her cheeks with her trembling, bleeding hands.

'Lord Spearhead!' It was the voice that she had always used as 'Arilou', for she knew no other way to make her voice ring out far enough to fill the great crater. But this time she spoke in Lace, for that was the tongue the volcanoes understood, and she drew out her words, for volcanoes' thoughts were slow as lava. 'I come with a message and a gift – from the Lady Sorrow.'

'The Lord has seen us,' whispered Louloss through a mouthful of undergrowth. 'He knows.'

Dance responded only with a short hissed intake of breath, an injunction to silence. The revengers hiding beneath the flag all tensed and listened for a while. The music of the forest had been given over to new instruments. No longer did the crickets rasp like saws through wood, nor the cicadas give their rising maraca echo. Now everything was bird-siren, monkey-roar.

'No.' Dance pushed herself up on to her hands and knees. 'If he knew our minds, the sky would be bellowing and half a hundred broken crags would be rushing down the slope to meet us. Are your bones ash, Louloss? No? Then the Lord doesn't know what we intend. Come on.'

And so up they crept, a core few bearing the flag on their backs, the rest melting into the shadows. Above them, guards from Mistleman's Blunder stood in the light-pools from their lanterns, scanning a dark countryside that was no friend to them. Below them, the city itself slept, dreaming centuries-old dreams of Lace – Lace creeping through darkness with unseen smiles and blades. Mistleman's Blunder slept, not knowing that it had called its own nightmares home.

Spearhead's rumble had left the guards alert and troubled, listening for the telltale clatter of rocks above them that might warn of a landslide. But they heard nothing except monkey-roar, bird-siren. They were not ready for the land below them to come alive with knives. They were not ready for a vast woman to dance into their fragile pools of light, a tornado in worn leggings, her long dreadlocks falling against her back with a soft thump like a heartbeat.

Two of them had just enough time to grab the poles on which their lanterns were perched and shake them as a signal to the town. But the lanterns were already swinging after the tremor, and it made little difference. Dance's swords knew their path through the air, just as a gull's beak knows its way through water to fish flesh. And, behind her, silence closed like a wound.

The jungle had been cut back to make space for the Safe Farm, and the hewn wood used to make a fence around its perimeters. The guards fidgeted in their wooden guard-towers, and the wall of the stockade threw a long, toothed shadow across the slopes of the farm, the piles of battered pails, the heaps of mud-caked hoes, the raw ridges of the dry, ploughed soil. Deep in the shadow lay the 'farmers' them-selves, Lacemen, women and children, most with their cheek pressed to the ground as if listening for footfalls. They dared not speak, for fear that the waking volcano would hear them. They dared not move for fear of rattling the long chains that linked them.

443

Only one prisoner shakily pushed herself up into a sitting position, grey eyes wide and full of strange moonlight.

'Athh,' she murmured. 'Athn . . . Hatthhn . . .'

'What?' A guard walked over. 'What was that?'

'Me,' answered a woman who sat next to the girl who had spoken. 'No speak. Sneeze.'

The guard looked down at the mosaic of sleepy, stubborn, bruised faces, their wide-apart eyes reflecting the lantern in his hand, and then stooped to wave his hand before the face of the grey-eyed girl.

'What wrong her?' he asked in Nundestruth. 'Clutter-skull?'

'Sun,' answered the woman bluntly. She slapped the top of her own head, then rolled up her eyes and lolled her head to mime dizziness. 'Work too hard.' She picked up one of the girl's hands and opened it like a book to show the blisters on the palm.

'Hey!' A call from an officer in the guard-tower. 'What are you doing, socializing with the smilers? Keep your eye to your arrow slit.' And so the guard returned to his post, watched by all the prisoners. Everybody was jumpy. A scout had sprinted back to the Farm, babbling of a blue creature with no head that ran on a dozen legs and whose back rippled like the sea . . .

All the while the Lace held their tongues. Long before they reached the Safe Farm, the grey-eyed girl's fellow prisoners had noticed her drifting eye and her stumbling walk, and had seen that they had a Lost among them. There was only one Lace Lost – the much-sought Lady Arilou. Voicelessly the news had spread through the Safe Farm, and the guards never noticed the way that one prisoner was always shielded from their view, always had her pail of rocks lightened by stealthy hands, always had new rags tied around her injured feet.

Lady Arilou had come to the Safe Farm, and that could mean only one thing. She had come to rescue them. And so in silence they watched her, waited for a sign.

Ath, mouthed Arilou to herself. *Hathin*.

Swallowing, Hathin held up the little pouch of white dust. Some instinct told her that she should not give it immediately, despite the terrible impatience of the gaping crater. After all, she was there to keep the mountain talking.

'Milord . . . Lady Sorrow . . .' The smell of volcano breath was thick in the air. She felt her voice die inside her, and her stomach plummet in panic. 'Lady . . .' She could not form the words.

Afterwards she could not be sure whether it had been wishful thinking, but she suddenly seemed to feel a coolness against her face, like the touch of silk against fevered skin.

Eyes like ice. Hathin remembered the old woman from the tidings hut who had spent her life waiting for the chill touch of a certain gaze. Was it possible that a familiar pair of moonstone eyes was resting on her? She clutched the idea and would not let it go.

If it was so . . . then she was not alone. Arilou was there.

And so Hathin took heart, swallowed down the panic in her throat and found her words again. She spoke of Lady Sorrow's emerald-and-sapphire eyes, the satin whisper of her landslides, the chalky perfection of her slopes. She continued

445

speaking, even when the cooling sense of Arilou's presence slipped away into the cloud.

The wind rose a little, as if Lord Spearhead had softly sighed.

'What's wrong with them?' The officer strode along the ranks of the chained Lace, itching to kick them, just to make them look at him. He was sure he had heard a faintly musical sibilance of whispering among them. Now, however, their heads were bowed, their eyes lowered, watching one slack-jawed girl trailing her fingers through the dust. 'What's wrong with them all? What's wrong with . . . ?'

What is wrong with the earth, why does it shudder like a fevered animal, what is wrong with the air, why does it fill our lungs with pins? What ancient thing smiles through your smiles, and why can I feel it breathing on the back of my neck?

The lolling girl spread her hand flat on the dust and gave a slight pat with her palm. She patted it again, a third time, and then let her head loll back to show her eyes, sleepily intent slivers of grey. It was only as she drowsily raised her hand again that the officer noticed a pictogram traced in the dust before her. A clumsy outline of a boat. The symbol for salvation.

Slap.

Her hand struck the ground, and dust erupted between her fingers. As one, the massed ranks of the Lace leaped to their feet and sprang upon their captors. Chains were thrown around the guards, pinioning their hands to their sides before they could reach for weapons. Others were borne down by sheer weight of numbers.

446

The guards in the guard-towers were not slow to turn their muskets and bows about and aim down into the compound. Before they could fire, however, there came a whirr of slings from the surrounding slopes. Stones rattled through the towers, breaking skulls and lanterns with equal ease. In the darkness an atlatl gave a soft 'whoomph', and an officer suddenly thought better of firing his musket into the prisoners and toppled slowly from his tower with a short spear through his sternum.

After the silence settled, the guards both living and dead were searched. The officer wearing a spear through his middle turned out to have a ring of keys on his belt. Within a minute the keys were off the ring, and manacles were rattling discarded to the ground.

A deep growl passed through the earth, and all heads turned to look towards Spearhead's peak, almost lost among the cloud. When the ex-prisoners turned back to their rescuers, their faces held a scared question.

Whispers, whispers. Gestures towards the great blue flag. Nods. And now the prisoners were shedding jackets, cloaks, coats, and padding them out with straw, leaves, dirt. By the time the clouds started to part, a strange community of fat little figures could be seen crouched by the wall in the compound. Cloth bodies, earth bellies, heads made of buckets, legs made of sticks, feet of stones. If the Lord Spearhead looked closely, he would see that these were not his prisoners, but Lords seldom look closely at those beneath them.

Meanwhile a large, crouching gaggle of frightened Lace crept down the hill, all trying to remain as close as possible to the great blue flag which those at the heart of the crowd carried spread on their backs. Their only hope was to reach the safety of the plains before Lord Spearhead realized that he had been tricked.

The clouds were parting again. Looking down into the crater, Hathin could saw a ripple passed across the lake as the volcano softly growled.

Hathin's voice was becoming hoarse, and she dared not try the volcano's patience longer. She could only hope that she had bought enough time for the rescue attempt. Once again she raised the pouch high above her head.

'Lady Sorrow has sent this token, so that you may know she has not forgotten you.' She hesitated, then flung the little pouch out into the crater. It dropped away and dwindled to a pinpoint splash and ripple.

As Hathin hesitated, breath held, she became aware that she could see something else, a dusky, rounded growth on the inside of the crater on the far side. There was something about its outline that frightened her, like a bunched fist, or the bulging of a frowning brow. And then she realized that what really frightened her about it was the familiarity of its shape. She had seen it before on Bridle's murky maps of Spearhead, seen it swell from a speck to a shadow to a bulge. But she had never guessed that it would be so huge. Half of Sweetweather would have fitted on that great buckling of the rock.

Bridle believes that Lord S will return when the rains end . . .

And now at long last Hathin knew what Bridle had meant. 'Lord S' was not a human being at all; he was Lord Spearhead. And it seemed Bridle had been right. The mountain upon whose shoulder Hathin perched was not murmuring in

448

half-slumber the way the volcanoes always had. The rains were ending, and Spearhead was awake, ready to return, ready for revenge.

Wetting her dry lips, Hathin cast a glance over her shoulder and almost overbalanced at the sight that met her eyes.

Now that the clouds had parted, through the gap she could see the downward slope of Spearhead, just beneath the jagged nick in his crater rim, all the way down to the long trench of the Wailing Way.

She stared at the dizzying vista for several spellbound seconds. An ancient legend somersaulted in her head, and when it landed on its feet it wore a new and terrifying aspect.

Never build in the Wailing Way, for that is the trench left by Spearhead when he roared away from his fight with the King of Fans. Some day when he is overcome with wrath and the need for revenge he will return along the same route for another battle with the King . . .

A mountain on the move, grinding its way south-west towards the coast, hauling the skyline behind it. No. That was not what the long-dead storytellers had meant. The story had been a poetry hiding a truth, like those tales with secret directions concealed in them.

From where she was sitting, Hathin could see that the surface of the secret lake touched the bottom of the nick in the crater rim. And through this nick and below it, centuries of waters had carved a deep twisting groove down Spearhead's flank, a dozen small rivers and streams threading into it. It was a perfect channel, and anything flowing from the crater would run right down it. Again Hathin seemed to see the miniature mountains she had made for Arilou filling up with rain, the little Spearhead's crater filling and overflowing down the groove in its side, into the trench waiting at its base . . .

Never build in the Wailing Way.

Soon Spearhead would rouse himself from his memory of his lost love. Soon he would think to look for his prisoners. Soon he would wonder what had happened to the little messenger that had brought his gift.

For the moment that messenger could be found slithering recklessly down the scree amid a deafening *hisshhh* as the slope slid giddily away beneath her. She had no time to lose.

36
RESCUE

Moving *down* the scree was certainly easier than *up*, but a lot more frightening. In some respects it was like running in slow motion, but there was nothing slow about Hathin's descent. Her feet sank helplessly among the pebbles, and she slid down the slope with ever growing momentum, her arms flailing as she tried not to fall forward.

Thus she sailed down at the heart of her own private landslide, thanking the Superior with every breath for forcing her into boots.

When the slope at last flattened she celebrated by falling on to her behind and tobogganing to a gentle stop, then dragged herself to her feet and ran until the dead trees rose up to meet her, followed by the living.

Find Arilou. Find the Reckoning. Tell them to get out of the gorge from the crater. Make them keep out of the valley, stay away from Mistleman's Blunder.

For what seemed like hours she struggled down through the jungle with these thoughts alone in her head. She had lost all bearings. *Down* was the only compass point left to her, so she followed it blindly.

*

In the end, Therrot very nearly shot her. He was a little nervous at finding himself in possession of a musket at all, and dealt with this by waving it at everything that alarmed him. The sudden eruption of a small, hooded head amid frenzied undergrowth caused a near-fatal twitch in his trigger finger, and he barely stopped himself in time.

As soon as he recognized Hathin, he recklessly threw his weapon aside and charged into the undergrowth, scooping her up into a hug. Immediately Hathin felt herself slump with weariness, as if she had finished a long journey and fallen in through her own home doorway.

'Arilou?' she asked.

Two of the revengers had made a seat of their crossed hands, and riding upon it was Arilou, leaning against her carriers, her face slack with exhaustion, her eyebrows plaintively raised. Her expression did not change when Hathin threw her arms around her, but Hathin did not care. Arilou was alive, safe. Eyes squeezed shut, she held her limp sister tight.

She wanted to fuss at the blisters on Arilou's hands and feet, but Therrot picked Hathin up like a small child and carried her. And it was thus, half lulled despite herself by the rocking of his stride, that Hathin gabbled everything that she had seen and heard.

She was not the only one being carried. Many adults had small, round-eyed children in their arms, a lot of them weak from hunger and fatigue. Intentionally or no, Spearhead's tremors had done his fellow revengers a service. When the volcano had first growled, most of those guarding the Lace children in the Ashlands of the foothills and lower slopes had abandoned their posts, and the remainder had fled when they found themselves facing the Reckoning.

'We'll move through the jungle,' rumbled Dance. 'We'll come out on the mountain's eastern side. We must be out on to the plains before dawn.'

'*Long* before dawn,' remarked Jaze. 'As soon as the sky lightens the Lord will notice that his prisoners have buckets for heads. And when that happens I for one hope to be a long, long way away.'

'What about . . . ?' Hathin fought against the numbness of her exhaustion. 'What about Mistleman's Blunder?'

Her own voice sounded small and distant, even to herself, and the slash of machetes through the vines and the crunch of trodden undergrowth became a lullaby. She could not help closing her eyes, and when at last an answer came she barely recognized Dance's voice. It held the solemnity of prophecy.

'It is too late for them. Perhaps it was too late the first time they laid brick on brick in the Wailing Way. Hatred of the Lace was born in Mistleman's Blunder, and hatred of the Lace will destroy it. The story has been waiting to end this way for two hundred years.'

And Hathin thought that she stood in the streets of Mistleman's Blunder, looking up at Spearhead. The mountain roared with a wide red mouth like that of a jaguar, and from its crooked lip poured a tide of light. As it drew closer she realized that it was not a sheet of fire, but a racing army of flaming figures, each holding a torch from which blazed a quivering blackness. All around them grass fizzed and wilted, timber walls burst into flames, glass windows popped and tinkled. People ran before the army, but it caught them and

453

they flared and were gone in an instant with a sound like paper tearing. Their coins and keys and watch chains fell to the ground and lost their shapes, becoming gleaming puddles like molten butter. Hathin was immune. The flame men ran past on either side, and Hathin felt nothing but a cool breeze as they did so. Not far away she saw a man collide with one of the fiery strangers and fall to his knees, screaming and clutching his own cheeks. Her feet took her closer, and he looked up at her with a pair of familiar brown eyes, letting her see the terrible burns to his face. He reached out trembling, imploring hands towards the great shell of water she held . . .

'Hathin, stop wriggling!' said Therrot. 'You'll make me drop you.'

'I can't – I have to . . .' The little patch of troubled water was back in Hathin's brow as she tried to disentangle herself from Therrot's arms and her own sentence. 'His face – I remember what he looks like,' she chirped hopelessly, and then tailed off and stared desolately down the slope towards Mistleman's Blunder. 'There's . . . There's a whole town . . . Please understand.'

Hathin could feel Jaze's eyes boring into her face, and had a feeling that perhaps he *did* understand, and did not like what he understood.

'There's no time to go back,' he said, his tone decidedly cold. 'The Lord won't stop to listen to you a second time. And the towners won't listen to you at all.'

'Hathin, how many of them do you think would cross the street to help a Lace in trouble?' asked Dance.

'I don't know. Maybe none. But maybe one or two. And there only needs to be one. Put me down, Therrot. *Please.*' As he set her down, his expression almost broke her heart. He looked as if he had discovered her bleeding to death and could do nothing about it. And Hathin, who seemed to have used up all her words on the volcano, turned from her friends and pushed away through the jungle.

Something crashed after her, pushing aside the tree ferns she ducked, stepping over the leaning logs she crawled beneath.

'*Stop.*' There was such velvet authority in that one deep word that Hathin's weak legs halted against her will, and she turned to face the speaker.

'Dance,' she said, 'I'm going to talk to Mr Minchard Prox.'

'No,' said Dance, with soft but absolute firmness.

'We set him adrift on a little boat, Dance, and when he came back he was different. I don't know – I don't understand – but when I first met him he was *kind*.' Hathin thought of his pink face, his bright, bewildered eyes. 'Kind, but lost. Like a coconut rolling to and fro in the brine, tossed about and not knowing why. I have to hope maybe he's still like that, still kind underneath, only . . . lost.'

'If anyone can make Minchard Prox listen, I think it would be you. The mountains themselves bend their ears to you. And that is why you will not stir another step towards Mistleman's Blunder.' There was no mistaking the menace in Dance's tone now. More than ever she reminded Hathin of a volcano, her movements slow and relentless as lava. Until now this inexorable force had been behind Hathin, supporting and protecting her. This was no longer the case.

'I can't help it,' whispered Hathin, feeling about as inexorable as straw.

'I will not see you rescue *these people*. These are the same people that hanged our priests in the Chandlery two hundred years ago, the same who killed your village, the same who have hunted us throughout the island. Different faces, different names, but the same souls. No. They have turned a blind eye to our fate – we shall do the same to theirs. That is *justice*, Hathin. That is the meaning of our quest.' The vast woman stooped beneath a balcony of vines and drew closer, ferns throwing shark-tooth shadows down her cheeks. Her eyes were ink.

'It's not *our* quest, Dance,' Hathin said in a very small voice. '*It's mine*. I can't be a warrior like you. This *is* my way of questing. Your quest was over years ago.'

Even while the words were still in her mouth, Hathin seemed to taste something odd in them. And then when Dance reached for her left-hand widow's arm binding, Hathin knew suddenly what she would see when it was peeled back.

The fractured moonlight shone on the unblemished skin of Dance's left forearm. It bore no second tattoo.

'But. . . you killed the Ashwalker who killed your husband! And the governor!'

'It was never enough for me. My husband had two hundred assassins. Everybody who refused to speak up for him or hide him. Everybody in Mistleman's Blunder. Cruel, frightened little people. Well, I have given them lessons in fear. I have given flesh and steel to their nightmares of the deadly Lace that will come for them in the night. And I have waited fifteen years for something like this, Hathin. This is my night, Spearhead's night. Do not stand in our way.'

The black bead in Hathin's stomach seemed to have torn itself apart in the scream that had sent Jimboly to her death. Hathin's legs would not hold steady, but would not buckle. She could not take a step, could not slump. What was left for her to do but stand?

'So how many deaths do you need, Dance? Will a town be enough? Will that make the pain go away? Or will you still need the Reckoning so you can live through other people's revenges? There *is* no "enough". Nothing finishes with this night. If we let Spearhead eat up the people of Mistleman's Blunder, then the story doesn't end, *it goes on retelling itself.* Their revenge and ours, feeding each other, rolling over and over like fighting cats forever. And my village will die again and so will your husband, over and over and over. Different faces and names, but for all the same reasons.

'No revenge will ever be enough for us. All we can do is try to stop others dying like those we lost. Even if that means taking up arms against the volcano.'

It was a strange stand-off, like a staring match between a mountain and a sea poppy. The jungle stirred restlessly around them, but neither woman nor girl moved, even when a brown snake slithered hurriedly between the feet of one and then the other.

Only the jewelled cicadas were witness when one of the two combatants lowered her eyes and bowed her head in consent.

There was always a clock on Prox's mantelpiece. It broke up his time, and served it to him once an hour in tiny silver pieces. It was his only companion, and so he felt a sense of betrayal when, just after it had 'tinged' its way through its four o'clock greeting, it juddered sideways and threw itself on the floor.

Reflexively he looked up from his papers towards his sediment bottle and pendulum to judge the severity of the earthquake. He was just in time to see them both plunge off the sill.

His chair bucked, as though resentful of his weight, and he stood, steadying himself against his desk, only to feel it galloping under his palms. And then, just as he thought the spasm was ending, the whole house began to shake around him, the floorboards jumping like xylophone bars.

In his ears there was a colossal roaring as if his head was being held under water, but it came from outside the house. He staggered, falling against the window frame, and saw through his window a dawn like the end of the world.

Spearhead was alive with light. One of its hunched peaks was missing, and in its place was a vast, leaping flame-coloured orchid. Over the volcano an enormous black cloud was forming, under-lit by the coppery light of the torn mountain below. From time to time, flaming balls fell out of the cloud and bounced down Spearhead's slopes.

'No . . .'

There were maps under his hands. Carefully shaded with parallel strokes. The Safe Farm. Safe. The camp for the children up in the Ashlands. Once again he seemed to see a troop of tiny figures walking along the hilltop, carrying pails, but suddenly they had faces.

'Pull yourself together!' he hissed at his reflection, which hissed back at him aghast, then shattered as his candleholder fell sideways and smashed the mirror. He had just time to watch what was left of him go to pieces before the slopped wax drowned the wick and left him in darkness.

Prox groped his way to his study door and opened it. Beyond lay the courthouse's hearings chamber, which he had been using as a reception hall and meeting room. This too was lightless.

'Camber!' It was the desolate cry of instinct. Camber had been the cushion for his mind for months. Who else would he cry for now the world had disappeared? Who else did he have?

He heard the great door that led to the street swing open on the far side of the hall. A lantern appeared in the doorway, and swayed unsteadily through the room towards him. A hand holding it, a limber, elegant figure behind it. Camber, his gait weaving like one walking the deck of a ship.

'Camber! The children . . .' Prox gestured towards the window, the mountain.

'It's too late,' Camber said gently, but firmly.

'I sent . . . up there . . .'

'And for good reasons you sent them. Come on, we need to leave.' Camber took Prox's arm and some of his weight, and pulled him towards the door. The candle made golden question marks in his eyes. 'How else were you to keep the parents docile? Follow me – we'll be safer in the old store-house.'

There was a crack from above like a cannon shot, and plumes of plaster dust dropped towards them. Then the

459

nearest window exploded into shards of metal and crystal dust, and something vast and bullock-black erupted into the room.

The great figure seemed to fill the space like a whirlwind, throwing tables against walls, knocking Camber back into a chair. The guttering lantern light caught a long blunt-tipped sword of wood, fanged at the sides with black glass shards. Camber, who had at first struggled to regain his feet, now froze at the sight of the weapon and carefully eased back into his seat, his hands raised an inch or so above the chair arms as if to soothe the new arrival, his face a picture of studied calm.

Prox was hypnotized by the sight of the toothed sword. It was an ancient Lace weapon. He had seen them in pictures. Prox had sent the Lace children to fiery death on the mountainside. The invading figure needed no face, it was vengeance incarnate. Prox could only stare stupefied at the sword, trying to make sense of what would be the last moments of his life. How had he got here? And what would he be in death, a martyr or a monster?

'All right,' he told the faceless figure, unable to manage more than a whisper. 'All right.'

But the dark shape did not move, and Prox became aware of another smaller figure climbing in through the window. It picked up Camber's dropped lantern and tinder, and a spark revived the spent wick. The weak flame revealed a small, boyish figure with badly grazed hands and knees, skin all but deathly in colour from caked dust. As he watched, it tugged back its hood to reveal a snub little face, with wide-apart eyes glazed from weariness. The corners of the small mouth curled upwards in a smile, an anxious little ruck appearing at one side. A thumbprint-sized patch in the centre of its forehead wrinkled uncertainly.

'Mr Prox . . .' The voice was breathy and hushed, with the familiar sibilance of the Lace accent. 'Mr Prox, I've come to save you.'

37

THE MAN WITHOUT A FACE

'To save me?' croaked Prox.

How could he be saved?

I give up on this life. Where is my next life so I can try to do better?

And the child before him had the wrong face. A face taken from someone else, somewhere else.

'I know you,' he said, 'don't I?'

'Child,' said Camber, his voice quiet and carefully unemotional, 'you speak Doorsy, yes? And to judge from your large friend's expression, she doesn't. How much are you being paid to work for the Reckoning, and how much would it take to change your mind?'

Instead of answering him, the small figure turned to the vast shadow beside her, and musical Lace murmurs flowed between them, a duet between a piccolo and a cello.

'Dance says I should tell you that I do not work for the Reckoning,' the child answered in Doorsy at last. 'She says I should tell you that the Reckoning is working for me.'

'Aah.' Camber gave a slow sigh of revelation. He looked at Hathin with a new and acute interest, before giving a slightly rueful smile. 'I see. Lady Arilou. So sorry not to have been faster on the uptake. You're . . . rather shorter than I was expecting.'

'I know this girl.' Prox stared at Hathin, taking in every detail of her face. 'But this is not Arilou.'

Taken aback, Camber turned to stare again at the small Lace girl before him. He narrowed his eyes, then slowly shook his head.

'I've missed something important,' he said, 'haven't I?'

'You're from the Cove of the Hollow Beasts,' said Prox. 'The girl on the beach. You gave me a shell.' The shell full of poisoned water . . .

And the eternal Lace smile, which had been hiding exiled in the compressed dimples of her mouth, emerged and lit up her face.

'You remember me,' she said. There was no hesitancy, no furtiveness in her eyes, and for the first time in a long while Prox was touched by doubt. Was it possible that she had not known the water was poisoned, that she had really meant to do him a kindness? Or . . . could it even be that it had not been poisoned at all – that he had just drunk from it more quickly than his sun-racked body could stand?

'Yes,' she said, 'that's me. I'm Hathin.'

Outside there was a rattle, a bit like rain, but this rain broke tiles, smashed windows. There were screams, and the continued cavernous roars of the wakened mountain. The hulking woman called Dance murmured something impatient, and the girl nodded.

'We don't have much time,' she said in a polite but hurried tone. 'You're going to die if you don't get out of Mistleman's Blunder. You have to leave the Wailing Way. All of you.'

'We'll die if we *do* leave,' Camber countered mildly. 'Those are rocks falling out there. Our only hope is to stay in our houses until it stops. If your people are out on the plains, then the best thing you can do for them is persuade them to surrender. They'll be safe in the guardhouse. Out there they don't stand a chance.'

'Please listen to me. By dawn there will be no guardhouse. There will be no Mistleman's Blunder. There will be flat plains, and black rock setting like treacle over your heads.'

The same old Lace warnings, the same old Lace threats. And a child coming with a poisoned offer in the guise of a friend. And yet Prox could not help raising his head and looking up at her with an expression of appeal.

'Up on the hillside – the farm – the Ashlands – you wouldn't have come here first, not if the children – there are children –'

Hathin nodded. 'They're all safe.'

'Thanks be to . . .' Prox slumped, felt his insides melt. He stared at the lantern in Hathin's hand and did not know who to thank. Groggily he tried to pull himself upright again. 'Look – I can see that I am not going to leave this house alive. But I will not betray the people of this town. I cannot lead them from the safety of their homes into the jungle so that they can be slaughtered by the Reckoning. If you need a sacrifice, well, you've found me. Leave it at that. Let that satisfy your need for vengeance – or your volcano, if you want to put it that way.'

'Oh no, you don't understand!' Hathin looked flustered. 'Spearhead *will* destroy this town, not because of anger, but because *things roll downhill*, Mr Prox, and they do it the easiest way they can find. Nobody should have built in the Wailing

464

Way – not because it's sacred, but because that gorge out there down the mountainside, *it's a pipe*, and when the crater spills over, everything will rush down it. My people knew all this once, but then we made up a story about it and forgot everything but the story.'

'You're asking Mr Prox to stake hundreds of lives on a story from a less than friendly source,' Camber offered gently, as though trying to point out a spot on her jacket without embarrassing her.

The girl looked from one face to another, her expression stricken. When she started speaking again it was in an urgent monotone, her Doorsy stumbling in her hurry.

'Mr Prox, I can't stay. My people are heading to safety, and I have to join them. But first there are some things you need to know.

'We didn't kill Mr Skein or the other Lost. When Mr Skein died, my village panicked – we lied, and we hid the body, and one boy went off without telling the rest of us and cut the rope to your boat.

'The people who really did kill the Lost are scattered all over the island. They send each other letters using trained pigeons. That's how they've been getting word to each other since the tidings huts went down. We know their leader's connected to Port Suddenwind, but all Arilou could tell us about him is that he lives in this town, and he . . . hasn't got a face.

'My friends all thought it was you, Mr Prox, but *I* don't. I don't think you're one of these people at all. Because if Skein had died when he was supposed to die, you'd have been with him, back at the inn in Sweetweather, and you wouldn't have had an alibi. All the conspiracy members made sure they were as far away as possible from the victims when they died.'

'How . . . ?' Prox cleared his throat, as the facts slid about and clicked into place like the lock and catch of a pistol.

'They put blissing beetles into one of the tidings huts, and released them in the Beacon School as well. We've already been there – you can go and look for yourself. My sister Arilou only survived because, well, she has a really bad attendance record.'

'And . . . their leader?'

'I think the man without a face isn't someone whose face is missing or . . . covered in scars; it's just a face that's hard to see, almost impossible to remember. The sort of man that you can meet and hardly notice, and when you think back you can remember that somebody was there, but . . . he has no face.' There was a pause, during which Hathin stole a wary glance at Camber, who had suddenly become entirely impassive. 'I think it's your friend here, Mr Prox.'

Prox stood gripping the top of a chair back and stared at the carpet.

'Prox . . .' began Camber.

'I'm counting!' Prox responded sharply. 'There's one little thing that has always bothered me. I just never gave it the thought it deserved because it happened while I was still half crazy from the brainfever. We arrived here together, do you remember? And you told me all about the slaughter at the Cove of the Hollow Beasts. Maybe the sun did addle my brain . . . but I can still *count*, Camber. And when you gave me that news it was only twelve hours old. Even the Ashwalker, who took a short cut through the mountains, hadn't reached us then. How *did* you know about it all so quickly? And how did you happen to have all the papers ready for me to become Nuisance Control Officer?'

An unruffled Camber opened his mouth as if to offer up a confident answer, but there was something in Prox's gaze that seemed to silence him.

Camber. Hathin could hardly drag her eyes from his face. C for Camber. A suspicion formed in her mind that this was the very 'C' that had been mentioned in Skein's journal. The 'C' who had arranged to meet the Lost Council and betrayed them to their deaths.

'And all those pigeons.' Prox continued not taking his eyes off Camber, 'the ones filling our loft, the ones that come and go all the time. I wondered why we put up with them.'

'Inspector Skein wasn't on the Coast of the Lace to test Lost children,' Hathin went on quickly, 'or to investigate the Lace. He was looking into *Lace* deaths and disappearances over the last few years. And there were a *lot* of them, Mr Prox.'

An exchange of murmurs between the Lace, and the great woman with the spiked club pulled out a crumpled map.

'That's where the Lace go when they vanish,' explained Hathin, pointing to the dim painted rectangles near the centre of the map. 'Mines. Secret mines built on Mother Tooth. The missing Lace are taken there to work, and nobody ever sees them again, and nobody misses them – because they're Lace. It's been happening for years.

'And then a Lost mapmaker called Bridle noticed. He'd been watching the volcanoes, Mr Prox, painting a new map of them every week, because he'd seen them starting to move, changing shape. And so he spotted the new buildings on

 467

Mother Tooth. I think *that's* the reason the Lost were killed. They found out that there were secret forced mines on the volcanoes . . . and that the volcanoes were waking up.'

'There are some things you need to understand,' Camber said softly but hurriedly as Prox peered at the map.

'Yes,' said Prox, as he scanned the smudged rectangles. 'Yes, I rather think there are, Camber.'

'There was never anything selfish in this.' Camber was speaking faster now, as if he could see Prox sliding away from him and was pattering to catch up. 'Losing the Lost was more than regrettable – in some ways it was cataclysmic – but it could not be avoided. I would have told you about all of this sooner or later, but you were not ready. Most people are never ready for the most unpleasant kind of truth; they simply cannot see that *some things have to be done*. It's a sort of selfishness, really. To say no to something, without offering any alternative solutions. That is exactly the way the Lost reacted.'

'Forced-labour camps . . . ?' Prox rounded on Camber. 'You *knew* about this? How many people knew about this?'

'I am not *quite* sure why you are looking so shocked, Mr Prox,' said Camber with an air of infinite patience. 'Have you forgotten why you set up the Safe Farms? Do you remember us talking over the problem of feeding Gullstruck, and saving it from famine? And you do remember what we – what *you* – decided?'

'Yes,' said Prox faintly. 'Yes . . . yes, I do.'

'You saw, as we did, that the volcanoes needed to be mined and farmed,' Camber went on quickly. 'Can you condemn us for realizing it years before you did, and for seeing that we could tackle the island's Lace infestation at the same time? Of course, we only started to see the *true* potential of our situation after Lady Arilou survived the Lost purge, and we realized instead of a "Lost plague" the Lace could be blamed and dealt with even more effectively. But *you*, Mr Prox – your Safe Farms have gone further in addressing the land shortage and curbing and harnessing the Lace than we ever dreamed was possible. Better still, we could create a Nuisance Control Officer, who could act freely, unshackled by Port Suddenwind, and *do what needed to be done*.'

Prox flinched, and stared at the map in his shaking hands.

'Our ancestors never meant Gullstruck to be a home for the living,' continued Camber. 'It was supposed to be an enormous cemetery, so they gave the best farming land to the dead.' He sighed. 'And year after year, the new dead take a little more and a little more. But the ranks of the living have been increasing too.

'Everyone talks about the "bad harvests" we've had for the last few years, as if a good summer will sort everything out. It will not. The soil of our farms is tired out, and the dead are pushing us into the barren places. Even most of our jungles are already promised to the dead. People are hungry. If the volcanoes are not farmed properly, or mined for their treasures, then next year or the year after everybody will starve.

'Gullstruck's farmers were slowly overcoming their fear of the volcanoes, and building farms on their lower slopes. But it was *too little and too slow*, not enough to stop the island starving.

'So, yes, we took drastic measures. A labour camp on

 469

Mother Tooth, mining sulphur which we could trade for food for the island. And, yes, we took Lace from their villages to work there for the good of Gullstruck, and to pay back their ancestral debt. After all, the worst that could happen if the Mother erupted would be a temporary reduction in the island's Lace infestation. That tribe breed faster than mice anyway.

'But the Lost Council noticed our . . . little projects. And they were convinced the volcanoes were waking. So they came to us with an ultimatum. Our secret mines had to go, and worse still – we had to declare the volcanoes unsafe and move everybody away from them.

'The conflict was of their making. In the end, my superiors had no choice. If the Lost had told what they knew, the mines would have been closed, the farmers would have fled the volcanoes, and the whole island would have starved. As I said, some things have to be done.'

'That's what our priests thought two hundred years ago,' said Hathin quietly. 'And they were wrong too.'

'And I hate to break this to you,' said Prox, raising his voice against the roar of the stone-shower outside, 'but as far as the waking of the volcanoes is concerned, I think the cat's out of the bag.'

'Mr Prox!' A cry from outside in the street. 'Are you all right?'

'Break down the door!' Camber called out before anyone could stop him. The door burst inwards, and as Prox, Hathin and Dance turned towards the crash, Camber slipped deftly back into Prox's study, closing the door behind him. They heard the 'ting' and 'spang' of glass being kicked out, and

470

when they opened the door the room was empty and one window a jagged wreck.

'What . . . ?' The two men who had burst in wore singed nightshirts under their coats, and their hair was full of grey dust. They stared in bewilderment at Dance and Hathin.

'Never mind, it's all right.' Prox wiped both hands hard down his cheeks, trying to force his mind to work. 'These people are all right. Get everybody ready to leave the town. Everyone. Immediately. And if you see Mr Camber, he's under arrest. And . . . don't let him even start to talk to you, or he won't be.'

On any other night, the people of Mistleman's Blunder would not have liked being kicked out of their beds and told to leave their houses. They would have liked it even less if they had known that they were doing so at the behest of a small Lace girl and the leader of the Reckoning. However, tonight the world was ending around them, and everybody wanted orders.

Soon they were appearing in their doorways, shielding their heads with tea trays, upturned chairs, thick blankets. Obsidian buckets were handed out and used as makeshift helmets. Everywhere, small grey stones dropped from the sky and danced on the road, skittish and oddly light, like foam turned rock.

Prox struggled to organize things above the clatter of the falling pebbles. People had to be told to leave things behind; one old woman had to be carried in her own wicker chair. Dance had spoken of overgrown temples in the jungle foothills that might shelter them. But would there truly be room for all these people?

471

It was nearly time for dawn, but the sky was darkening, not lightening, and the wind was changing direction.

'Stop! What are you doing?'

As Prox stormed up like a short bristling tornado, a local goldsmith and an obsidian foreman looked around without loosening their grip on the barrow with which they were playing tug-of-war. They shouted contrary explanations over the rain of stones. Both were trying to pile the urns of their household ancestors into it, flinging the other's dead into the road to make space. Further down the street Prox could see families struggling to carry great chests away from the dead heart of the city, each bearing funereal seals.

'That's it! We leave the dead! All of the dead! No exceptions!' There were gasps and then howls of protest. Prox stooped next to a small girl who had fallen to the ground nursing a scalded ankle, grabbed her beneath the armpits and held her up to the goldsmith's face. 'Your ancestors can't be reduced to ash a second time, but *she* can. Leave that barrow, or you'll all be ash by morning.'

The girl began to wail and the goldsmith reluctantly released his barrow.

'Good. Now carry her.' Prox thrust the girl into the man's arms. She threw her arms around his neck. In her mind, he had clearly just rescued her from the scary man with the scarred face.

Through a deepening twilight the crowd struggled from the town, Prox bellowing himself hoarse at those who wanted to flee the easy way down the road, along the base of the treacherous valley. His face was red and his hair rebellious, but nobody was in the mood to laugh. The panic-stricken fugitives began scrambling up the tree-covered slope, out of the valley.

Far, far above in Spearhead's crater, ash had frosted everything, and turned the surface of the steaming lake to porridge. Occasionally cart-sized rocks that had been flung high dropped from the sky and smashed into the lake, leaving gashes in the gruel-like surface, the naked water gleaming like burnished copper as it reflected the hectic clouds above.

Half submerged in the lake jutted the great bulging mound of rock that had frightened Hathin. Each time the mountain shuddered, the bulge deformed a little more, a divide starting to appear in it like a cleft in a chin.

And then, somewhere deep below the surface of the lake, the great bubble of boiling rock split.

There was a hush-half-second like a gasp, a sense of some tiny but momentous change, of something cracking silently like a heart. The next instant, through that hidden crack beneath the surface, an oozing, millennia-old fire met dark, lucid water. And in that meeting, water and fire loved each other to destruction.

Something was born in the moment of their touch. It roared, and flung half the lake towards the hidden stars. It kicked a deep gash in the crater rim, then tore free and crashed its way down the narrow gorge that led to the Wailing Way.

Hathin felt the change before she heard it. A moment of weightlessness, as if the world had decided that down was up, and then changed its mind before anything could move. A

 473

crescendo, a great door swinging slowly open upon a world of roar.

Hathin turned her head to stare towards the mountain. There was no tide of fire. No, it was far worse. A raging, roaring wave of nothingness, a blackness denser than shadow, surged down the mountainside with unimaginable speed. She watched it reach ridge after jungle-cloaked ridge, and each vanish, eaten by the darkness. As she stared, paralysed, the wind changed and a searing wall of force flung her backwards to the ground. From all around her came the cannon-cracks of trees bowing and snapping before the same unseen shock, hissing with heat and dropping their branches.

She had taken up arms against the mountain, and the mountain had struck back. Before she could draw breath the world around her was swallowed by a hot and stifling darkness full of screams and the choking taste of ash.

38
THE WAILING WAY

For a second or two Hathin thought there was no more Hathin, no more world left to save, but the screaming all around brought her back to herself. Then something bounced off her shoulder, which a second later started to burn. Her lungs scalded and she throttled, throwing one arm across her mouth and stinging eyes. Everything remained pitch black.

'Keep going! Keep going up! Follow my voice!' It was Prox. She thought it was Prox. His voice was high and harsh and it was hard to be sure. 'Keep climbing!'

Eyes clenched shut, Hathin scrambled towards the sound of his voice, struggling through the mesh of invisible fallen trees. All around were other cries, threatening to drown out Prox.

'Somebody, please help me . . . my leg, there's something on my leg . . .'

'Alyen, where are you? Alyen! I let go of her hand, I let go . . .'

'I can't breathe . . .'

And somewhere else a young child's despairing cry drew its serrated edge across Hathin's soul. Perhaps Camber the Ghost had been right, perhaps these people would have been safer in their houses . . .

'Quiet!' Prox's bellow was almost a scream. 'Everybody! Quiet!' Hathin could hear him taking a few ragged gasps, then he began to shout again, his voice so strained that a squeak crept in now and then. 'I'm going to call out names. Answer your name, so we know where everyone is, and who needs help. Jelwyn family? Good. Crayfools? Good. Blackmire? All right, all right, don't try to move it, keep talking, I'm coming to you.'

But now there were new voices sounding from the choking darkness, a sibilant music that seemed to come from all sides at once. These strange voices had much the same effect on the frightened refugees as the stink of fox has upon a chicken coop.

'Fathers protect us!' Hathin heard one of the women scream. 'We're surrounded! They're coming for us! Lace! Lace in the forest!'

To judge by the scrape of steel, several of the beleaguered refugees had actually drawn blades. All they knew was that they were ringed about by the hiss and lilt of Lace voices. Hathin, however, could understand what those approaching voices were actually saying.

'Hathin! Dance! Are you there?' Therrot's voice.

'Here, keep hold of my belt so we don't get separated.' Tomki.

'You heard that? They're drawing knives.' Jaze's voice, a pool of cool in the raging chaos. 'If they make a move on Hathin or Dance . . .'

'It's all right!' Hathin screamed in Lace before Jaze's own knives could leap to his hands. 'I'm here! Dance is here! We're

476

all right! These people will not hurt us!' As if to contradict her, incoherent exclamations of terror and hostility erupted from the refugees around her. Was this surprising, given that someone in their midst had just started shrieking in Lace? 'Mr Prox!' She switched quickly to Doorsy. 'Mr Prox, *please* tell everyone to put away their weapons, or my friends will think they're under attack! They can help us to the temples – we *need* them. You have to *trust* us, Mr Prox.'

'All right.' A muffled murmur from Prox. Then, much louder: 'Quiet, all of you! Put your weapons away! These Lace are our guides – they're taking us to safety. Now anyone who's trapped or too hurt to walk, raise your voice . . .'

Someone had been forgotten, and sat thanking all his nameless ancestors for that fact. He had mastered the art of sliding from people's minds, and as the others fled the town he could almost feel the thought of him slipping away from them. He too had seen the raging nothingness surge down from the crater top, but he had the walls and roof of the stone storehouse to defend him from the clouds of ash and strange gases, the rain of stones and embers. He was safe.

From the abandoned houses he had taken all he needed for a siege against the elements. Candles, tinder, water, blankets against the cold, a spade in case the little rocks mounded up outside his door, even a couple of pigeons in case he needed to summon someone to dig him out. And of course the storehouse already held the town's supply of jar upon jar of olives, raisins, flour, wine.

He was truly sad to have lost Prox. He felt he had been working for months painting a masterpiece, only to see

 477

someone pick it up with clumsy, innocent hands and mar the wet colours before he could shout, *No, don't touch it! It's not ready.* A month or two more and Prox's mind would have been tough enough to deal with such truths, if weaned on to them like a child or a kitten. But coldness was the only way to deal with such cataclysms. Prox had been spoilt by the untimely interference of that strange little girl, and would have become a danger if he had lived.

He cleared his mind of all unpleasantness and decided to think of the mountain doing the same thing outside the walls. A great hand smoothing away Prox, the Lost girl, the Reckoning and anyone they might tell, like letters drawn in sand. Then he could begin his good work again.

It's nothing personal, he told their memory. *I'm not a personal person.*

But he was not alone. There was another figure standing in the room, tall but insubstantial. Camber blinked and realized that the ghostly column was a cloudy gush of ash, falling from some hidden hole in the roof. He was not safe after all. The volcano could get in.

He dragged over some boxes, stood on them and found the little sliding wood panel that had been left open to let the hay breathe. And while he was balancing there, the roar of the mountain seemed to change. He could not resist raising his head out through the trap door. One quick glance, and then he would duck down and shut it.

He straightened, gazed out across the roofs, and saw It coming for him. He did not drop back into the storehouse. He did not fumble for the catch, or throw his arms over his head. There was no point. He watched as something vast, deafening and gloom-grey fought its way with a battlefield bellow out of the false twilight of ashen clouds. A house-high wall of dull, mashing foam, devouring the road to the town so fast that his clinical mind had time for only a single thought before the deluge was gnashing buildings to flinders.

I am a dead man.

The dead do not blink. Death was just another cataclysm to be met coldly, and with eye contact, even as the winds went crazy around him and his head filled with sound.

History will not remember me. I have not been missed, and I never will be.

The trees were the first to hear the rumble from the valley, and they began to tremble. Then the bass bellow became audible to the fugitives, and grew louder and louder until it swallowed all other sounds.

The winds shifted again, the ashen clouds puckered and plummeted, and everyone glimpsed something enormous plunging through the valley and the town below, sleek, grey-brown and muscular like an enormous serpent, its back strewn with timbers and trees that it did not notice. Not fire but water, a dragon of scalding, murky, terrible water. As they watched, chunks of the slope below them vanished as though bitten away by a vast, invisible maw. Bite after bite, working its way up the slope . . .

Hathin turned away from the carnage as the clouds closed again, and slipped, falling to her knees. She tried to stand but the ground was giving under her feet, sliding down towards the gorge. She fell on to her stomach, grabbing at tussocks to stop her slide, her ears full of the

479

roar that swallowed her own cries.

Hands grabbed her arms and dragged her back up the slope, then heaved her on to her feet. She barely managed to remain upright as she was bundled along through the darkness. Ash was falling now, like hot insistent snow, settling on Hathin with an insidious, slumberous weight that threatened to bear her to the ground.

Someone leaned her against a wooden wall. She found herself sliding down it, ash-laden. But now she was being helped through a door, which swung to behind her, muffling sound, completing the darkness. Ash was no longer falling on her.

A little flame guttered into life, and then a lantern glowed. The hand that held it was shaking. The face it lit was a ravaged map of pink and yellow, Hathin recognized the scarred face of Minchard Prox. Her gaze took in the curling, heat-wrinkled papers and crude mud-red pictograms that covered the walls around them, and realized that they were in a tidings hut.

As if by unspoken consent, both slumped to the floor, Prox tentatively touching a trickle of red from his temple, Hathin retching against the ash in her mouth and throat.

They sat without speaking for a long time, until the roar outside faded enough for them to hear the complaining creaks of the rafters above them.

'The timbers won't hold forever,' said Prox at last, his voice rough as sawdust with effort. 'It's not the rocks, it's the weight of the ash. It'll be the ash.'

He might as well have said, *It'll be the ash that does for us.* There was a pause.

'Others be well,' Hathin said quietly in Nundestruth. It

480

didn't seem like a Doorsy moment. 'Others reach temple. Hidemhole for night.'

Prox looked up at her, then nodded.

'We win,' Hathin said. 'We save them. We beat mountain.'

There was a pause, and then Prox nodded again and smiled. His seamed face softened and rounded, and his eyes seemed to brighten and become his own again. That small smile was the last thing Hathin saw before the roof caved in on them, smashing the lamp.

39
ALL CHANGE

Dawn came grudgingly, and several hours late. A dull sun parted the clouds of steam and ash nervously, afraid perhaps of what it might find.

It found Spearhead biting a new and jagged shape out of the sky. The spear in his crater rim had blown itself apart, leaving a crinkled gash. The nick in the rim had become a gaping V shape, through which steam still billowed. He had seared away his fury, and now stared bleakly at what he had done.

What had he expected? Had he thought to see this, a world cloaked in soft, all-smothering grey? No birds circled in his sky any more. The jungles were gone, flattened by winds, burnt by giant falling embers, drowned in ash. The lush patter of leaf on leaf, the hoot and howl of monkeys, the drill and whirr of insects, all choked into a slumberous silence.

Mistleman's Blunder was gone. The roaring dragon of lake water and boiling mud had swept it away, leaving only here or there a blue-crusted brass bell from a clock tower, an anvil adrift, the broken wall of an old storehouse. The rest was a slick of drying, steaming mud, dotted with black, pockmarked rocks like burnt loaves.

There was a silence, but for a crackling rustle deep within what had been the jungle. Dozens of white-faced people were still struggling out of forgotten stone temples, pushing their way through the curtain of tough, straggling vines that had saved their lives. Now there were no Lace, no towners. The ash that covered their faces made them one race, bleached them into kinship.

And then there was another sound. It was a terrible keening, croaking cry with the true ugliness of pain that does not care how it sounds.

Arilou lay full length on the earth, wailing and thumping the ashen ground with the heels of her hands. The Reckoning stood in a circle around her, and did not know what to say to each other.

They were all certain in their heart of hearts that Arilou was mourning the loss of her sister.

As a matter of fact, Arilou was not doing anything of the sort.

Dip down. Dance like a midge just above the earth, waver with the strain of make-myself-do-it. Charred shards of tree, spiralling white vapour, thick wind-rippled dunes of ash, getting closer closer closer almost touching. Feel roughness of stones. Flinch don't want to. Want to send down eyes and ears but won't do. Too dark. Have to feel the way.

Rocks full of tiny foamy holes. Push into the ground, through the rocks, feel each raking through my mind as go into darkness. Want to thrash, want to scream, want to not do it. Deeper. Shard and shingle, splinter and spike, feel them all pass through.

Like swallowing coals with mind.

Ash gets in my thoughts, forget which way is up. Panic! Panic and plunge! Somewhere body I cannot feel any more is flailing. Plunging mind onwards, darkness, darkness. A strangling cord nearly cuts mind in two. Tree root. Follow tree root down and down, to mud, hot mud. Hot, hot, hot.

Scramble back to the air, bruising mind on stones. Can't do it again can't can't can't.

Do it again.

Must find Hathin.

Afterwards, when people talked of the day following the great rage of Spearhead (or Broken Brow as he was afterwards known), Arilou's name was spoken with reverence. It was she, the last Lady Lost, who searched through the earth with her mind and found many who had taken refuge in cellars or hollow trees and been buried alive. No longer Arilou the treacherous, Arilou the murderous. Now she was Arilou the heroine.

She was tireless, sleepless. Again and again she staggered to her feet like a new calf, and led the way at a lurch to some other buried victim, her mouth hanging loose and forgotten. Every time someone was found alive there was celebration, and yet behind the eyes of every would-be rescuer lurked a question. *Where is Hathin?*

By the end of the second day, however, the few bodies that were being dug out no longer held the spark of life, and it seemed probable that the rescuers had saved all who could be saved. None of the Reckoning would say as much out loud, but they shared a fear that Hathin, child of the dust, had quietly slipped back into dust. It was as if she had held centre stage only as long as she needed to, and then had shyly crept back into invisibility, this time forever.

And yet nobody was willing to give up the search. Lace and townspeople alike struggled across the grey plain, calling out, looking for prints, shifting the fallen trees, their footprint trails furrowing the deep ash.

On the second evening, as Arilou rose unsteadily, eyes red from the sting of the ash, Therrot sprang to his feet, only to find his legs unwilling to support him. He was caught by Jaze, who carefully lowered him to the ground.

'Therrot . . .' Jaze's tone would have been gentle if it had come from someone else.

'I know what you're going to say. Don't tell me to prepare myself. I don't want to be prepared.'

Jaze studed Therrot's face and then gave a long, deeply saddened sigh.

'There might be a time when you have to let go. You still haven't learned how to do that, have you?'

'No,' said Therrot bluntly as he staggered to his feet again, cupped a supporting hand under Arilou's elbow and let her lead him away for the twentieth time along the colourless plain. And Jaze, for all his talk of letting go, followed them, as did Tomki and Jeljech.

Hathin was nowhere. Hathin was everywhere. Everything in the deathly landscape had her secretiveness, her careful blandness, her quietness, her stubborness. *Hathin*, whispered the wind-borne dust as it settled on the slopes. *Hathin*, lisped the ash as it rained upon the plain.

'You hear that, Arilou?' Therrot muttered with fevered

intensity. 'Your sister must be still alive. The mountain is still talking to her. All the mountains talk to her.'

Exhausted and stumbling, Arilou led them along the route the fugitives had taken from Mistleman's Blunder, up the side of the valley. There, quite abruptly, she slumped as if in a faint. Nothing that anyone could do would make her rise from where she lay, resting her chin on a ridge sticking up from the ash. And for a while everyone was too glazed with exhaustion and frustration to realize what the ridge was. It was the angular spine of a half-buried slanting tiled roof.

An instant later, willing hands were scooping away the ash, lifting fractured timbers, picking out tiles. Jaze called down to the plain and soon more figures were struggling up the incline to help. At last a small boot became visible, then another, and everyone picked up the pace until a diminutive figure was uncovered. Hathin was half-curled, as though she had made herself as small as possible so as to be no trouble to anyone.

They almost failed to notice Prox at all. At the instant that half the roof had collapsed he had flung himself across to push his small companion out of the way, and the worst of it had fallen on to him, burying him completely. But by chance Jaze noticed some pale fingers through the rubble at a little distance from Hathin, and they set themselves to clearing the rest of the debris away. And if there were some among the Reckoning who recognized him and suggested that he should be left there under the wrecked hut . . . perhaps it is best if such words lie buried.

Hathin looked for all the world like a child of dust, white and still, as if a careless hand might crumble her. For once she had the serene, angelic strangeness of her sister, the ash powdering her face like the chalk dust Arilou wore for formal occasions. But Therrot rubbed at the ashen face and found pinky brown skin underneath, and poured water over her clamped mouth until it went up her nose and resulted in a far from angelic sneeze. And then Therrot flung himself backwards on the slope and howled at the hills, for true joy like true pain does not care how it looks or sounds.

When someone thought to check a little while later, it turned out that Minchard Prox also had a pulse.

It was not a good time to be Minchard Prox. Half the island wanted to blame him for everything, half of them wanted him to tell them what they should do. Everybody wanted answers from him. And the answers he had to give did not really make anybody happy.

There has been a colossal and terrible mistake, and I have made it. Lady Arilou and the Lace are innocent. Every Lace who has died at our hands was murdered. Those who killed the villagers of the Hollow Beasts and other innocent Lace must be found and put on trial. All the Lace who have been held prisoner in Safe Farms and secret labour camps must be set free. All the Lace villagers who were robbed of their homes must be built new ones. And I, who am the most guilty, will make sure this happens, and then submit myself for trial.

Those who truly murdered the Lost and framed the Lace must be tracked down. They killed the Lost because they did not want them to tell us that the volcanoes are waking up. They were afraid that if we did not build on the mountains we would starve. They were right. We will. Unless we do what we should have done many,

 487

many years ago, and start reclaiming the land from the dead.

There was utter uproar. Prox was a blasphemer, a murderer, a defamer, a rabble-rouser. But what could be done about him? After all, who had set up bird-back messenger networks to take the place of the tidings huts? Prox. Who was even now setting up a new carrier-pigeon post and a system for food distribution? Prox. Who had been organizing patrols to round up bandits now the Lost could not look for them? Prox. And who was working with the last Lost left alive? Prox. There was no point in looking to Port Suddenwind for such things.

So he remained at large, but abhorred by many. He grew used to the sudden jab of a flung stone against his cheek, to the lowering of voices when he entered the room, to hearing his own windows smash. A few attempts were even made on his life, but somehow none of them quite reached him. A man who had been squatting on a roof with a pistol aimed at Prox's heart somehow managed to fall two storeys on to his own head. Two attackers who broke into his house with hatchets fled again almost immediately with bleeding crowns. Prox thought as he peered out of his bedroom window that he glimpsed a third figure in pursuit of them, a large figure with long loose dreadlocks thumping against her back as she ran, a spiked club in her hand.

Dance had disappeared shortly after the discovery of Hathin and Prox, taking with her Jaze and many of the other revengers who had survived the rescue raids. After a little thought Prox had thought it best to record them as 'lost during the events of the Spearhead eruption'. It was not quite a lie.

Prox did find support from an unexpected source. The Superior of Jealousy, still exulting in his new freedom, declared that he was quite willing to move his ancestors' urns and let his people farm the Ashlands. But others were slow to follow suit, and the Superior himself was too busy with wedding preparations to offer Prox any more practical help than this. He had discovered to his delight that he *did* have a housekeeper. And his housekeeper, who had patiently and loyally looked after the irascible little man for decades without him noticing her, had been surprised but pleased by his offer of marriage and had accepted immediately.

The only person who suffered as much as Prox was poor Arilou, everyone's heroine. No longer could she retreat into her private world to flit her mind where she chose like a butterfly. Everybody had found her out. She was no imbecile, she was the only living Lost, and suddenly all the problems of the island were laid at her feet for her to solve. Someone had to watch for storms, hunt down the rest of Camber's allies . . .

And there was no Hathin to help her. For Hathin seemed to be capable of nothing but sleep. From time to time she would wake, look up from her bed at whichever room or tent she found herself in, and feel nothing in particular. It was not unpleasant, but her body felt empty, like a kicked-off slipper. And so she would close her eyes and go to sleep again, to wake up on another day.

Then at last one day she woke up and she felt she might get up. She stood, and ducked her way out of the tent, and found herself watching blue silk waves lollop and sparkle, rending themselves softly on the hidden reefs. She did not need to see the dark-stained sand, the tooth-like fragments of coral in the shingle. One taste of the air was enough to tell her that she was on the Coast of the Lace.

And so it happened that on a bright morning some two months after the destruction of Mistleman's Blunder a young man with a scarred face and a small girl with snub Lace features could be found sitting on a clifftop, watching soft blue waves frothing through a limestone lacework full of ins and outs and twists and turns and sleeping lions pretending to be rocks. Both looked tired, because putting the world back together is very hard work.

'He was extremely clever,' said Prox. He had been spending a lot of time with the Lace over the previous weeks and had fallen into their hesitancy when naming the dead. But Hathin, with her Lace gift for guessing the hardly spoken, recognized the combination of recoil and admiration, and knew that he was speaking of Camber. 'He made himself invisible. The government knew of barely any of the things he ordered in its name. He sat in the middle of the paperwork like a spider, sending out an order this way, a request that way, always making it look like it came from someone else. He claimed to be just a middleman – but everything was really being run *from* the middle. And nobody noticed. So many people knew a small piece of what was going on, yet nobody but he knew all of it. We're still discovering arrangements he had in place, with the help of Lady Arilou.'

Arilou had been able to track down most of the other 'pigeon men', many of whom had continued sending desperate messages to one another after Camber's death.

'Nobody else will come after you, will they?' he asked after a moment.

'I don't think so.' Hathin sighed slightly. 'The Ashwalker is gone. The dentist who wanted me dead is no more. She . . . The volcano took her name.'

If Prox picked up something odd in her voice, he said nothing. *Yes*, thought Hathin, *he's almost becoming Lace.*

'And the traitor? Is it true about the traitor?' He glanced across at Hathin's profile and saw the little patch of troubled water briefly crease her brow as she ducked her head to tuck some stray hairs into her hat. Her other forearm she carefully turned over so that the fresh tattoo on the skin was hidden from sight.

She watched two butterflies waltz, and wondered if Prox would smile at her so kindly if he had seen her two weeks ago, standing in the dark cavern at the far end of the Path of the Gongs.

Larsh kneeling at her feet, and all around them the white of stalactites, the green gleam of glow-worms, the watching figures of the Reckoning. Larsh gazing in alarm as Hathin dropped a cord with a wooden amulet around his neck. Her knife was out before he had time to react, and he could only watch as she cut through the cord so that the amulet dropped into her hand. She lifted it up before his face, and he blinked, bewildered, at the cluster of Doorsy letters carved there.

'It's your name, Uncle. I've cut it away.' His face, confused by the sadness and pity in her voice. 'I told I'd make sure nobody killed you, but I promised Dance I would take your name myself. Now you have no name. You will be nobody until you die and join those others who have no name. Nobody will know you or speak

491

with you. You will be invisible forever.'

'Yes.' Hathin snuffled the answer into the back of her hand. 'It's true.'

Prox watched the sea for a bit. 'I suppose we had better have a description of him then. So that if we see him . . . we don't see him.'

Hathin gave him a sideways glance, watching how the youthful brown hair flickered in the breeze and brushed against the scarred forehead. Prox's blisters were healing, but he still looked like he was wearing a mask.

'Will it . . . ?' Hathin waved a hesitant hand towards Prox's face. 'Will it ever get better?'

'This?' Prox ran his fingertips over one puckered cheek. 'Probably not – that is to say, I'll be scarred. It doesn't matter. The important thing is, when I look in a mirror now at least I can recognize myself. It's the eyes – they belong to someone I know. They didn't for a while.'

Both of them stared down at the beach. The last time Hathin had crouched here, she had seen her world dying in flames. Now with gentle cruelty the sea had washed away every trace of her village and the tragedy that had claimed it.

The beach was not empty, however. After all, there was good fishing in the cove in spite of the current, there were pearls to be dived for, there were caves to offer shelter. The people of Sweetweather had avoided the beach out of guilt and superstition but, as if following some silent summons, families of Lace had turned up over the last week, bearing their stilted homes on their backs. Leave a hole in the Lace, and the hole will quietly fill again, like mud oozing back into a footprint.

492

But these newcomers knew what was due to the living and the dead. On the beach Arilou sat enthroned in a litter, face painted with powdered chalk and sapphire feathers in her hair, her face crumpling with fatigue and the heat as she watched the dances in her honour. Around her stood a perplexed gaggle of Sours, who had travelled to the Coast of the Lace with her, and who would escort her back again when she returned to live with her Sour family in the mountain village.

The new Lace were performing the Dance of Change. A dozen or so seriously smiling dancers took it in turn to wear a wooden bird mask and become the Gripping Bird of legend. It was an unpredictable dance, for whoever wore the Gripping Bird mask could change everything just by clapping.

Clap! All change! A new tempo.

Clap! Clap! All change! A new direction.

Clap! Clap! Clap! All change! New partners.

It was a dance of joyful new beginnings, but also a tribute to the dead, to the village of the Hollow Beasts.

Hathin thought of the old legend of the cunning of the Gripping Bird, who had frightened attackers away from the village with grass jaguars on the clifftops, while he led the villagers to safety through the caves. She imagined a bird-headed figure with a human body dancing into the cave of the Scorpion's Tail, with a queue of familiar figures following behind him into the darkness. This time, however, as they reached the darkened opening, each turned and seemed to look up at Hathin just for a second.

Mother Govrie, beaming with a berry-swell in her lower

 493

lip that spoke of stubbornness, warmth and true affection. Eiven's knife-slash of a smile, her angular face softening for an instant as she looked at her younger sister with something like pride. Then came poor, sad, foolish Whish with her narrow, scarred face, and even she managed a real smile, like one that Hathin half remembered from the time before Whish lost her youngest daughter and eldest son and sank into bitterness. And a step behind his mother came Lohan, who had liked Hathin so much that he had helped bring destruction down on all of them, Lohan still looking stricken and aghast. And Hathin gave him the wave and smile that she had been too slow to give him that last night on the clifftop, and saw his face smooth with the relief of forgiveness.

They walked into the darkness, and something tight in Hathin's chest loosened, leaving her feeling suddenly weak, cold and alone. She collapsed into sudden helpless tears and felt Prox's concerned gaze on her.

'It's gone . . .' She tried to explain. 'They've all gone . . . I think I was carrying the dead around with me, and they were so *heavy*, with everything they wanted me to do. But now it's over, and I did it, and they've gone . . . and . . . I . . . don't know what to do any more . . . I mean, Arilou doesn't . . . Arilou doesn't *need* me any more . . . . What do I do if nobody needs me?'

'What do you want to do?' Prox asked quietly.

Hathin opened her mouth, took a breath and managed only a small uncertain cheep. It didn't seem to answer much, but she couldn't think of anything else to say.

'Hathin!' Therrot appeared on the cliff path. 'Will you come and get Tomki out of my hair before I "wrong" him with a rock? It's always, "Where's Hathin? Are we going to meet Hathin? Hathin, Hathin, Hathin."' Therrot's expression changed as he saw Hathin's face, and he came to sit next to her.

'There now, little sister.' But Therrot was not her brother, and he was going to travel back to Crackgem with the Sours. At first he had thought he would vanish like Dance and Jaze, but when he had said so, Jeljech had hit him, twice as hard as she had when he had let Arilou fall into the hands of Jimboly. And she had run away, and he had run after her, and she had hit him again but less hard, and now Therrot, who had never been very good at being dead, was likely to give up on it altogether. He would go to the Sour village and wear green, and fling himself into life as he had into battle, until his nightmares started to fade.

'I'm fine,' Hathin said, and gave her two companions a rainy smile, 'but I'm going down to the beach – is that all right?'

She stood up gingerly and picked her way down the sloping path. The two men on the clifftop said nothing until her wide-brimmed hat had bobbed out of sight.

'She says she's not needed,' Prox said at last, with the slightly apologetic tone he often used with Therrot and many of the other Lace. The atmosphere between them was still tense, and Prox could not blame the Lace man for disliking him.

'Not needed?' Therrot stared at him. 'I suppose you pointed out that she's the only person *everybody* trusts now? The Lace, the towners who know what she did in Mistleman's Blunder, the Superior of Jealousy, the Sours, not to

495

mention the mountains – how does she think everybody's going to keep talking to each other if she's not there?'

'No. No, I didn't tell her that. I thought I'd give her five minutes without people *needing* her to do something, even if the idea scares her.'

A slow dawn spread across Therrot's face, and then he gave a curt nod.

'She doesn't know who she is, does she?' said Prox. Therrot shook his head, and the two of them sat and watched the Gripping Bird dancing from face to face down below.

Hathin skulked in the Lacery for some time, waiting for Arilou and her retinue to leave the beach. At last the litter moved to the pulley chair, and Arilou was helped into it, her new Sour sister sitting beside her to stop her falling, just as Hathin had once done.

Arilou the Lady Lost, floating upwards with her white robes flickering around her, as if she was a cloud that had visited earth and was returning to her kind. *Goodbye, Arilou, goodbye*. Arilou no longer needed Hathin, and Hathin could not bear to be with her and be unneeded. It was right that Arilou was rising in the world, becoming all that she might, taking her place as the Lost of Gullstruck. And Hathin would not cling to her, would not slow her ascent.

'Athn,' said Arilou. She was too far away for the sound to reach Hathin, but the movement of her mouth was unmistakable.

Hathin felt a brief and curious sensation, like cold silk slithering over her skin. The gaze of a Lost – why were their eyes like ice? Was it because there was something lonely in

496

their spirits? Knowing that Arilou was watching her, Hathin raised one hand in a small wave.

Arilou put out a hand, palm forward, and dabbed it at the air, as though patting at an invisible face. And there it was, that oh-so-rare, wise-wicked monkey smile. Then the pulley chair reached the top of the cliff, and Arilou was helped out and vanished with her entourage along the precipice pathway.

Hathin sank back against the rock that hid her. Now at least she had the beach to herself. But no, she could hear two voices murmuring, voices of children younger than herself. She ducked down behind her boulder so that she would not be seen, and listened.

'. . . heroine of Spearhead,' one of them was saying. 'She's beautiful, isn't she? But scary.'

'Yes,' agreed the second voice. 'She's descended from a pirate – you can really see it when you look at her, can't you?'

Hathin smiled a little despite herself. Poor Arilou, her legend rolling out in front of her like an eternal carpet.

'. . . hunted her all over the island but she was too clever for them . . .'

'. . . tricked them into letting her come all the way to the Safe Farm . . .'

'. . . leading the Reckoning . . .'

'. . . saved everybody . . .'

And that was how everyone would remember things. People all over the island would be speaking of Arilou like this for centuries. Arilou, who been hunted across Gullstruck, but who had led the Reckoning to victory and saved everybody. *Well, what did I want, recognition? No,* Hathin realized, *I did everything I did because, well, I'm me.*

Quietly, so as not to be noticed, she got up and slipped off to the brink of the Lacery, where the shallow water slopped gently at her feet. She glanced down at her reflection, and stopped dead.

A pirate was looking back at her. The pirate wore a broad-brimmed hat with a sun-bleached crown, good boots and a torn tunic. It wore a green-dyed sash around its middle and carried a sheathed knife at its belt. Two ominous-looking tattoos marked its forearms, a lacework of tinier scars freckling the knuckles and bare arms. Its face had been burnt gipsy-dark by long days in the sun.

Hathin looked over her shoulder, just in time to see two small heads duck sharply down behind a rock. They were watching her. With the same sense of weightlessness she had felt just before Spearhead erupted, Hathin realized that they had been watching her all along. They had not been talking about Arilou at all. They had been talking about her.

For the first time she wondered if her pirate ancestor had not been beautiful and fine-featured like Arilou. Perhaps he had found himself lying on this beach amid the flinders of his ship, and looked around with wide-apart eyes and a patch of troubled water in the middle of his brow, and thought, *Well, this is the way the world is. Let us make the best of things and set about surviving here, shall we?*

The two younger children, awed by their own presumption, were running away up the beach, and Hathin turned back to her reflection.

Who am I? The shell-selling Lace girl, the attendant of Lady Arilou, Mother Govrie's other daughter, the thing of dust, the victim, the revenger, the diplomat, the crowd-witch, the killer, the rescuer, the pirate?

I am anything I wish to be. The world cannot choose for me. No, it is for me to choose what the world shall be.

Slowly, watching her reflected smile in the water, Hathin raised her hands and gave them two rapid claps.

'All change!' she whispered.

And all around her, with a soft golden roar like a lion waking, the world was changing.

GLOSSARY

Gullstruck

The island of Gullstruck rests in splendid isolation, with no other land for hundreds of miles. Seen from above, its outline looks a lot like a hurrying hunchback figure with uncannily extended fingers and toes and a twisted, gaping bird beak. It is said that Gullstruck was fashioned by the Gripping Bird, a capering bird–man trickster, who shaped the island in his own image.

Much of 'him' is inhospitable, his head and shoulders racked with giddying ravines and choked with cloud forests, his belly and legs barren land. But between these, in the region of his waist, lies a band of verdant land, the playground of the volcanoes.

A long ridge of mountains divides the mad, frilled western coast from the rest of the island, and the tallest and middlemost of these mountains is the King of Fans, cloud-shrouded and momentous. Beside him to the north-east sits his wife, Sorrow, the white volcano. Twenty miles further north of them sulks Spearhead with his barbed summit, standing at a sullen distance from the file of other mountains. Far towards the eastern side of the island steams Crackgem the Mad, amid his wildly coloured lakes. And out amid the hiss of scalding sea off the west coast, vapour twisting like wild hair, crouches Mother Tooth.

The Tribes

The original denizens of Gullstruck. According to legend, the Gripping Bird fashioned the original tribes of the island from anything he had to hand. He used berries for making the Bitter Fruit, who dwelt in the northern jungles; geyser vapour for the Dancing Steam, who lived on the hills and lakes around Crackgem; resin for the Amber, who kept to the barren southlands; and coral for the Lace, who had once been scattered all over the western half of the island but now scratched out a living on the ragged western coast.

The Cavalcaste

Originally from a distant land of plains and snow, the Cavalcaste put to sea to find new lands that they could divide up and dedicate to their sacred ancestors. They soon dominated Gullstruck, and although the majority of people are now of mixed race, most of the governors and men of power have a lot of Cavalcaste blood.

Port Suddenwind

The first landing point of the Cavalcaste fleet, where a 'sudden wind' blew their ships into a small bay allowing them to drop anchor. A popular joke has it that nothing sudden has happened there since. Port Suddenwind is now the home of the government of Gullstruck, a grinding, monolithic heap of useless laws that nobody can throw away.

The Lost

The Lost are born with the ability to move their senses out of their bodies and send them abroad. They are scarce and are highly respected, providing their local communities with news, communication with the rest of the island, warnings of storms and other dangers, and a roaming watch for bandits.

Led by the Sightlords of the Lost Council, they are in many respects as powerful as the city governors who follow the orders of Port Suddenwind.

The Volcanoes

The tallest and middlemost mountain in the long western ridge of the island is the King of Fans, his cratered head forever lost in the clouds. Beside him to the north-east sits his wife, Sorrow, softly and perfectly conical, sweet and treacherous as snow. Twenty miles further north of them sulks Spearhead with his barbed summit, standing at a sullen distance from the file of other mountains. An old battle with the King of Fans has nicked his crater rim and left a long gouge in his flank, down which fierce streams rage. At Spearhead's base these streams become a river which over the millennia have worn a long valley towards cold, beautiful Sorrow, and past her to the south. Far towards the eastern side of the island, isolated by universal consent, steams Crackgem the Mad, piebald in black and green, amid his wildly coloured orchid lakes. And out amid the hiss of scalding sea off the west coast, vapour twisting like wild hair, crouches Mother Tooth.

A Note from the Author

Neither the tribes of Gullstruck nor the Cavalcaste are designed to resemble or comment upon specific real-world races. Here and there I have worked in elements taken from various different cultures because they suited the story, but the world of Gullstruck is basically fantastical.

ACKNOWLEDGEMENTS

I would like to give my thanks to the following: my editor Ruth, my agent Nancy and my housemate Liz for persuading me that this book should not be dropped into a lava spout and forgotten; Martin for running up and down volcanoes with me; the museums at Rotorua and Te Wairoa for details of the Tarawera eruptions; a New Zealand fantail who followed me down a path pecking at my shadow and the beetles my footsteps had disturbed; the hill tribes of Sapa, where foreheads are shaven, cloths are hung in doorways to keep out evil and the Black Hmong's faces and hands are stained with indigo from their smoke-scented clothes; Helen Walters for her first-hand account of baking alive on a drifting boat; Profound Decisions and the superlative Maelstrom; the Escuela Sevillain Antigua, Guatemala; the Maori legend of the rivalry of Taranaki and Tongariro for the beautiful Pihanga; Carol for kindness and hospitality; *The Maya* by Michael D. Coe; Taranaki, Tarawera, Tongariro, Ruapehu, Whakaari, Ngauruhoe, Baldera, Mount St Helens, Arenal, Fuego, Pacaya and, last but not least, my favourite volcano, Felix Egmont Geiringer.

I should also mention a young girl who appeared quite suddenly in the middle of a jungle temple in Cambodia and followed me around with quiet stubbornness until I noticed her. She had wide-apart eyes, a faint whisper of a voice and a civet-like creature perched on one shoulder. She wanted me to blow up her balloon. This done, she vanished again among the trees. I will never know who she was.

ABOUT THE AUTHOR

Frances Hardinge spent a large part of her childhood in a huge old house that inspired her to write strange stories from an early age. She read English at Oxford University, and then got a job at a software company. However, a few years later her first children's novel, *Fly By Night*, was snapped up by Macmillan. The book went on to publish to huge critical acclaim and win the Branford Boase First Novel Award. She has been nominated for, and won, several other awards, including being shortlisted for the prestigious CILIP Carnegie Medal for *Cuckoo Song* and winning the coveted Costa Book of the Year Award for *The Lie Tree*.

Read on for an extract of

a FACE LIKE GLASS

FRANCES HARDINGE

SHE WAS ALONE, THIS CHILD.
THIS ODD AND TERRIBLE CHILD.

In the underground city of Caverna, the people are unlike any other: they have faces as blank as untouched snow. Expressions must be taught by the famous Facesmiths – at a price.

Into this dark and distrustful world tumbles Neverfell, a girl with no memory and a face so incredible to those around her that she must wear a mask at all times. For Neverfell has a face that shows her emotions as transparently as glass. A face incapable of lying. A face that is a dangerous threat and an irresistible treasure – a face that some would kill for . . .

THE CHILD
IN THE CURDS

One dark season, Grandible became certain that there was something living in his domain within the cheese tunnels. To judge by the scuffles, it was larger than a rat, and smaller than a horse. On nights when hard rain beat the mountainside high above, and filled Caverna's vast labyrinth of tunnels with the music of ticks and trickles and drips, the intruding creature sang to itself, perhaps thinking that nobody could hear.

Grandible immediately suspected foul play. His private tunnels were protected from the rest of the underground city by dozens of locks and bars. It should have been impossible for anything to get in. However, his cheesemaker rivals were diabolical and ingenious. No doubt one of them had managed to smuggle in some malignant animal to destroy him, or worse still his cheeses. Or perhaps this was some ploy of the notorious and mysterious Kleptomancer, who always seemed determined to steal whatever would cause the most chaos, regardless of any personal gain.

Grandible painted the cold ceiling pipes with Merring's Peril, thinking that the unseen creature must be licking the condensation off the metal to stay alive. Every day he patrolled his tunnels expecting to find some animal curled comatose beneath the pipes with froth in its whiskers.

3

Every day he was disappointed. He laid traps with sugared wire and scorpion barbs, but the creature was too cunning for them.

Grandible knew that the beast would not last long in the tunnels for nothing did, but the animal's presence gnawed at his thoughts just as its teeth gnawed at his precious cheeses. He was not accustomed to the presence of another living thing, nor did he welcome it. Most of those who lived in the sunless city of Caverna had given up on the outside world, but Grandible had even given up on the rest of Caverna. Over his fifty years of life he had grown ever more reclusive, and now he barely ventured out of his private tunnels or saw a human face. The cheeses were Grandible's only friends and family, their scents and textures taking the place of conversation. They were his children, waiting moon-faced on their shelves for him to bathe them, turn them and tend to them.

Nonetheless, there came a day when Grandible found something that made him sigh deeply, and clear away all his traps and poisons.

A broad wheel of Withercream had been left to ripen, the pockmarked skin of the cheese painted with wax to protect it. This soft wax had been broken, letting the air into the secret heart of the cheese and spoiling it. Yet it was not the ruined cheese which weighed Grandible's spirits to the ground. The mark set in the wax was a print from the foot of a human child.

A human child it was, therefore, that was trying to subsist entirely on the extraordinary cheeses produced by

Grandible's refined and peculiar arts. Even nobility risked only the most delicate slivers of such dangerous richness. Without as much as a morsel of bread or a splash of water to protect its tender stomach from the onslaught of such luxury, the unknown child might as well have been crunching on rubies and washing them down with molten gold. Grandible took to leaving out bowls of water and half-loaves of bread, but they were never touched. Clearly his traps had taught the child to be suspicious.

Weeks passed. There were periods during which Grandible could find no trace of the child, and would conclude with a ruffled brow that it must have perished. But then a few days later he would find a little heap of nibbled rinds in another under-alley, and realize that the child had just roamed to a new hiding place. Eventually the impossible fact dawned upon him. The child was not dying. The child was not sickening. The child was thriving on the perilous splendours of the cheese kingdom.

At night Grandible would sometimes wake from superstitious dreams in which a whey-coloured imp with tiny feet pranced ahead of him, leaving tiny weightless footprints in the Stiltons and sage-creams. Another month of this and Grandible would have declared himself bewitched. However, before he could do so the child proved itself quite mortal by falling into a vat of curdling Neverfell milk.

Grandible had heard nothing untoward, for the creamy 'junket' was already set enough to muffle the sound of the splash. Even when he was stooping over the vast vat, admiring the fine, slight gloss on the setting curds, and the way they split cleanly like crème caramel when he pushed his finger in to the knuckle, he noticed nothing. Only when he was leaning over with his long curd-knife, ready to start slicing the soft curds, did Grandible suddenly see a long, ragged rupture in their surface, filling with cloudy, greenish whey. It was roughly in the shape of a small, spreadeagled human figure, and a row of thick, fat bubbles was squirming to the surface and bursting with a sag.

He blinked at this strange phenomenon for several seconds before realizing what it had to mean. He cast aside his knife, snatched up a great wooden paddle and pushed it deep into the pale ooze, then scooped and slopped the curds and whey this way and that until he felt a weight on the end. Bracing his knees against the vat, he heaved back on the handle like a fisherman hauling in a baby whale. The weight strained every joint in his body, but at last a figure appeared above the surface, shapeless and clotted with curds, and clinging to the paddle with all the limbs at its disposal.

It tumbled out, sneezing, spluttering and coughing a fine milky spray, while he collapsed beside it with a huff, breathless with the unexpected exertion. Six or seven years old to judge by the height, but skinny as a whip.

'How did you get in here?' he growled, once he had recovered his breath.

It did not answer, but sat quivering like a guilty blancmange and staring from under pale soupy eyelashes.

He was an alarming enough sight for any child, he

6

supposed. Grandible had long since abandoned any attempt to make himself fair and presentable in a way of which the Court would approve. In fact, he had rebelled. He had deliberately forgotten most of the two hundred Faces he had been taught in infancy with everybody else. In his stubborn solitude he wore the same expression day in and out like a slovenly overall, and never bothered to change it. Face 41, the Badger in Hibernation, a look of gruff interest that suited most situations well enough. He had worn that one expression so long that it had carved its lines into his features. His hair was grizzled and ragged. The hands that gripped the paddle were darkened and toughened by wax and oils, as if he were growing his own rind.

Yes, there was reason enough for a child to look at him with fear, and perhaps it really was afraid. But this was probably nothing but an act. It had decided that terror was more likely to win him round. It would have chosen a suitable Face from its supply, like a card from a deck. In Caverna lies were an art and everybody was an artist, even young children.

I wonder which Face it will be, Grandible thought, reaching for a bucket of water. *No. 29 – Uncomprehending Fawn before Hound? No. 64 – Violet Trembling in Sudden Shower?*

'Let's see you, then,' he muttered, and before the curled figure could react he had thrown the water across its face to wash away the worst of the curds. Long, braided hair showed through the ooze. A girl, then? She made a panicky attempt to bite him, showing a full set of milk teeth with no gaps. Younger than he had thought at first, then. Five years old at the most, but tall for her age.

While she sneezed, spluttered and coughed, he grabbed her small chin and with a heavy rind-brush began clearing the rest of the clogging Neverfell curds from her features. Then he snatched up a trap-lantern and held it close to the small face.

However, it was Grandible, not the child, who gave a noise of fear when at last he saw the countenance of his captive. He released her chin abruptly, and recoiled until his back halted with a clunk against the vat from which he had saved her. The hand holding up his trap-lantern shook violently, causing the little glowing 'flytrap' within the lamp to snap its fine teeth fretfully. There was silence, but for the tallowy drip of curds from the child's long, clogged braids, and her muted snuffles.

He had forgotten how to look surprised. He was out of practice in changing his expression. But he could still feel that emotion, he discovered. Surprise, incredulity, a sort of horrified fascination . . . and then the heavy onslaught of pity.

'Thunder above,' he muttered under his breath. For a moment more he could only stare at the face his brush had revealed, then he cleared his throat and tried to speak gently, or at least softly. 'What is your name?'

The child sucked her fingers warily, and said nothing.

'Where are your family? Father? Mother?'

His words had as much effect as coins dropped in mud.

8

She stared and stared and shivered and stared.

'Where did you come from?'

Only when he had asked her a hundred such questions did she offer a whispered, hesitant response that was almost a sob.

'I . . . I don't know.'

And that was the only answer he could get from her. *How did you get in? Who sent you? Who do you belong to?*

I don't know.

He believed her.

She was alone, this child. This odd and terrible child. She was as alone as he was. More so than he, in fact, despite all his attempts to hide away. More so than a child that age could possibly realize.

Suddenly it came to Grandible that he would adopt her. The decision seemed to make itself without asking him. For long years he had refused to take an apprentice, knowing that any underling would only seek to betray and replace him. This child, however, was a different matter.

Tomorrow, he would organize a ceremony of apprenticeship with his strange, young captive. He would invent a parentage for her. He would explain that she had been scarred during a cheese-baking and had to keep her face bandaged. He would guide her pen to enter her name as 'Neverfell Grandible' on the documents.

But today, before anything else, he would send out for a small, velvet mask.

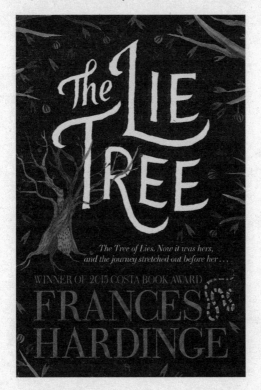

The Tree of Lies. Now it was hers, and the journey stretched out before her ...

WINNER OF 2015 COSTA BOOK AWARD

FRANCES HARDINGE

IT WAS NOT ENOUGH. ALL KNOWLEDGE – ANY KNOWLEDGE – CALLED TO FAITH, AND THERE WAS A DELICIOUS, POISONOUS PLEASURE IN STEALING IT UNSEEN.

Faith has a thirst for science and a knack for uncovering secrets that the rigid confines of her upbringing cannot suppress. When she finds her disgraced father's journals, filled with the notes and theories of a man driven close to madness, she's finally discovered a secret that might be too big even for her.

Because before her are tales of a strange tree which, when told a lie, will unveil a truth: the greater the lie, the greater the truth it reveals. Faith's search for the tree leads her into great danger – for where lies seduce, truths shatter . . .

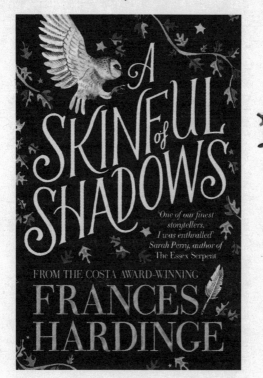

WE SEE GHOSTS. AND THEY ARE DRAWN TO US.

Sometimes, when a person dies, their spirit goes looking for somewhere to hide. Some people have space within them, perfect for hiding.

Makepeace has learned to defend herself from the ghosts that try to possess her in the night, desperate for refuge – but one day a dreadful event causes her to drop her guard.

Now she has a spirit inside her. The spirit is wild, angry and strong, and it may be her only defence when she is sent to live with her father's cruel and powerful ancestors. But as she plans her escape to a country torn apart by civil war, Makepeace must decide which is worse: possession – or death.